Stories for Amanda

A Compilation of stories in loving memory of

Amanda Todd

TELEMACHUS PRESS

This book is a work of fiction. Names, characters, places and incidents are either the product of the author's imagination or are used fictitiously. Any resemblance to actual persons, living or dead, or to actual events or locales is entirely coincidental.

Cover designed by Telemachus Press, LLC

Cover photo by Amanda Todd. Used by permission of Carol Todd.

Published by Telemachus Press, LLC
http://www.telemachuspress.com

ISBN: 978-1-939927-92-7 (eBook)
ISBN: 978-1-939927-93-4 (Paperback)

Version 2014.01.10

Printed in the United States of America

10 9 8 7 6 5 4 3 2 1

Table of Contents

~The stories in this book are cross genre~
Some may have graphic language and light adult situations.

Stories for Amanda

Out of It

By

Karen Avivi

ANGUISH, EFFORT, DETERMINATION. It was all in the shot I'd taken last night at the pickup soccer game in the park. Out of the 157 images I'd snapped, I only needed one to turn out, and this was it. I hit the upload button extra hard to send the selected picture to my online album. I was a god of memories.

Never mind that he didn't score. Never mind that it got cold. According to the image I'd framed, it was perfect. Going through the pictures and choosing which shots to show and which to delete was one of my favorite parts of photography. Without a picture, it was as if it never happened.

"Liam, we're there." My mom pulled the car up next to the school and turned to look at me. "Remember, today is the day you get involved."

Getting involved was her new crusade. Apparently she'd read some statistic that said kids who weren't in extracurricular activities were more likely to use drugs. I preferred to stay behind the scenes, but joining something would be easier than facing constant *is he on drugs?* scrutiny.

"I know. I will." I opened the door to get out. "Thanks for the ride."

My mom blew me a kiss before I closed the car door and she pulled away.

"Great picture, Liam!" My friend Andres waved his phone from where he was sitting next to the front steps of the school.

I refreshed the picture again as I walked over. Twenty-five likes already.

"I look like I should be on the cover of *Sports* magazine," Andres said.

"Good thing it doesn't show that you actually missed the goal. One of my other shots had turned out well, but it was of Jagger making a goal. He was such a jerk I didn't want him in my image collection."

"Every time he scores I'm happy for the team, but I wish someone else had made the goal. Oh, and for the record, I didn't miss. My shot got blocked."

I put my phone away. "Hopefully that picture of you is good enough to get me a sports assignment on yearbook."

"Yearbook?" Andres laughed. "I thought you hated our junior high yearbook."

I did. It was crap. "My mom is forcing me to join something. How hard can it be? I'm at school anyway. I'll pull out my camera once in a while and be done with it."

"You're not going out for football?" Andres asked.

"Yeah, right. With my build they'd put me starting defensive lineman for sure." We sniggered as we made our way into the school to our lockers.

I wasn't built like a starting defensive lineman. I was more like a cross between a distance runner and a malnourished basketball player. I ate constantly but grew up, not out. My mom had dragged me to the doctor a bunch of times probably after reading too many ridiculous stories in her *Things Parents Should Worry About* magazines. *Eating disorders aren't just for females—your son may be starving.* Each time a new issue arrived I braced myself for more odd questions. I was pretty sure the whole *get involved and stay off drugs* thing had come from a magazine article.

Our friend Dillon was sitting on the floor in front of his locker, furiously writing something in a notebook.

"Why are you so busy already?" I nudged him with my foot so I could open my locker. "School just started a week ago."

"I've got some orders lined up. Lots of customers with summer job money."

Dillon was one of those guys who could somehow get his hands on anything digital and stuck to his own code of honor about what should be accessible or not as opposed to what might be legal or not. I didn't ask too many questions about how he managed to acquire games and movies for us. It was better to not know.

~~~~

After promising Andres that I'd try to increase soccer coverage in the yearbook, I went to the classroom where the official yearbook sign-up meeting was being held. A bunch of juniors and seniors who were sitting in front looked at me, then went back to critiquing last year's book.

I sat in the back and tried to figure out who was a photographer.

Another guy sat next to me and put down his camera with a bag that said Property of LPHS.

"Is that the camera we get to use?" I asked.

"Yeah."

"Nice. Can I see it?"

He nodded and put the bag on my desk. "Are you new?"

"Liam, freshman," I answered. My parents had bought me a nice digital camera but it wasn't SLR and it didn't have the speed or the capability to change lenses like the school camera.

"Were you on yearbook last year?" I asked.

"Yeah. We had a great advisor who pretty much let us do what we wanted, but I heard we're getting someone else this year." He looked around. "I think you're the only freshman here. You're going to get the crap assignments."

My art teacher, Mr. Waymond walked in and picked up last year's yearbook from a desk. "This is an example of what we won't be doing this year." He chucked the yearbook to the side. Murmurs spread across the room.

"Forget about pages and pages of postage-size happy snaps. You can put endless dull *look at me and my best friend* shots up on whatever it is you're using to broadcast your personal lives online these days. Our yearbook will not be a collage of out-of-focus pictures that look like they were taken on a five-year-old cell phone. We have six high-quality cameras for you to use. How many photographers do I have here?"

I raised my arm with close to half the people in the room.

"I'll decide who gets these based on who I think will turn in something of quality. Everyone write down your name, what role you want to play on yearbook and when you have study hall and lunch so I can meet with you. If you have any samples of your work leave them clearly marked with your name. I'll talk to each of you individually before we meet again next week."

A senior girl in the front row raised her arm. "What about the theme?"

"Theme?" Mr. Waymond repeated. "Precious memories, special moments… that ridiculous phrase that wastes an entire page at the front of the book? It's a yearbook. The theme is class of whatever year."

The girl kept looking at him.

"Are you familiar with the term sacred cow?" he asked.

The girl nodded.

"Slaughter it. Skip the theme and make every page count."

Was he for real? This was awesome.

"We have to have a theme," the girl said.

Mr. Waymond shrugged. "It's your book so if you want to theme it up, go ahead. Anyone who wants to brainstorm themes can stay. The rest of you can go."

No way was I staying for theme brainstorming. My theme was survival. Show up, do the minimum necessary to get by, and get out. I didn't have any printed pictures with me so I left the address for my online album.

~~~~

The next day Mr. Waymond sent me a note in homeroom asking me to meet during my morning study hall.

When I went to his office, he had four of the school cameras on the end of his desk and a laptop with a picture from my portfolio showing on the screen, but he wasn't looking at the soccer shot.

"So Mr. Gavard, photography doesn't appear to be a new hobby for you. There's some promising work in here."

I sat down in the chair next to his so I could see the laptop screen better. "My parents gave me a new camera at the beginning of summer. It's not great, but I did what I could with it."

He scrolled to a picture of my aunt Katie and her new baby at a 4th of July celebration. I had taken the shot because there was tons of activity happening around her, but she looked like she was in her own cocoon of mom and baby.

"Getting the shots that others miss isn't about a zoom lens or shutter speed," Mr. Waymond said. "You've got an eye for capturing emotion."

"Emotion?" I repeated. I remembered noticing how out of place yet happy she looked. Maybe that's what he meant.

"What do you think the purpose of the yearbook is, Mr. Gavard?"

"The purpose?" I asked. "Memories."

"Memories," he repeated. "Are memories accurate? Should they be accurate? Are we photojournalists, capturing what really happened or are we artists, painting a representation of what we experienced?"

I had no idea how to answer. "That's a good question," I said. It was a cheat answer. I felt my chances of having a camera handed to me slipping away.

"Here's what I'd like you to do," he said. "You know all the clubs that get one row-by-row photo taken that looks like the pictures of all the other clubs?"

"Yes. I know what you mean." Great. The most boring photography job in the world. Lining people up. I didn't need a nice zoom lens for that. My camera would be more than enough.

"I want you to figure out what matters to them and capture them doing it." He picked up one of the school cameras. "I'm giving you a chance, Mr. Gavard. Show me three examples of what you can do by the end of the week. Do you have a printer that can print a halfway-decent color photo?"

"Yes." I kept my eyes on that camera bag.

"Good." He handed the camera to me. "Give me three printed pictures by Friday. I'm not sifting through hundreds of images online. Chess club meets today. Start there."

"Thank you, Mr. Waymond. I'll get you three shots by Friday."

"I want this yearbook to be about more than the people who are always front and center, posing for the camera. What goes unnoticed is often what's most important. Surprise me with something that others ignore."

~ ~ ~ ~

Dillon was already at our usual lunch-table spot when I got there with my tray and LPHS camera bag.

"You got the camera!" Dillon gave me a high five. "Are you the official soccer photographer?"

"Not really. Do you know anyone in the chess club?"

"I'm in the chess club," Dillon said. "And so is Rodney. I told him he could eat with us."

"Why?" I knew Rodney from elementary school and junior high, but we weren't friends.

"He was at my robotics camp over the summer and some of the guys were giving him a hard time. He's okay if you get to know him."

I wasn't sure I wanted to get to know Rodney. He never laughed at jokes or told funny stories, but he didn't bother anyone either so I guessed that it didn't really matter.

Rodney sat down across from me, nodded hello and then unlatched his black lunchbox.

"Hey." I unzipped the camera bag. "I need to shoot the chess club in action so I'll go with you after school."

"No problem." Dillon grinned. "I hope you have a fast-action lens to catch Rodney's ninja moves."

Rodney was taking rabbit bites from his sandwich, nibbling his way down each side, making a smaller and smaller rectangle.

"Yeah, I'll try to capture the energy."

Dillon made a face and put down his fork. "This needs salt, pepper, something. Does anyone need anything?"

Rodney and I both said no and Dillon left in search of flavor.

I pulled the camera out of its bag. I had to get used to it fast if I was going to turn in three surprising photos by Friday. That only gave me the rest of today and tomorrow. I took a couple of shots of the green beans at the corner of Dillon's tray when someone jostled me from behind. I clutched the camera that had been entrusted to me for only two hours. Luckily I had the neck strap on.

"Hey RodMan, I thought you were eating with us today."

Jagger. Without looking up I recognized his voice. *Please don't let him sit here, too.* It was best to stay under Jagger's radar. I kept a tight hold on the camera and focused on Rodney, acting like I was busy.

But I wasn't the target.

"Hey Rod the Bod, is that your dad over there, mopping up?" Jagger pointed to where the janitor was cleaning up a spill by the hot-food line.

"My dad's an otolaryngologist."

No Rodney, don't answer him. I tried to send silent instructions without lowering the camera. Unless you could give Jagger crap back, answering made it worse. Reacting just gave him new material to riff on.

Jagger laughed, and so did his two friends who stood behind him. "Is that an asshole doctor?" The taller of Jagger's goons shoved Rodney. "Your dad looks up people's asses?"

"That's a proctologist." Rodney straightened himself up from the shove.

Rodney couldn't see that Jagger wasn't interested in getting his facts right, he just wanted to entertain himself and his friends. It was like a small brush fire that could go either way. You needed to smother it fast, not add fuel. This was about to escalate even worse.

"Hey, Liam, Jagger, what's up?" Andres sat down and opened his lunch bag.

"These friends of yours?" Jagger asked.

"Yeah. So?" Andres took a huge bite of sandwich and gave me a funny look.

"Watch yourself." Jagger pointed at Rodney.

Rodney carefully re-latched his lunch pail and stood. "I'll see you at chess club, Liam. Bye Andres."

Andres stopped eating and watched Rodney walk away before turning to me. "I'm twenty minutes late to lunch and you've joined the chess club and become Rodney's best friend?"

~~~~

After promising the chess-club advisor, Mr. Adamson, that I wouldn't make a sound, I was allowed to stay and shoot the practice games. I watched for a while, planning to look for ways to make chess look as exciting as soccer. Surprisingly, the way Rodney played it almost was. He was kicking ass at chess. No one could beat him—not even Dillon, and Dillon was good. I'd never beat Dillon. Ever. The best I could hope for against him was to not lose in fewer than ten moves. Rodney made Dillon look like he'd just learned the game five minutes ago.

"How'd you get to be so good at chess?" I asked.

"Mr. Gavard!" Mr. Adamson held a finger to his lips, and Rodney glared at me. I put my hands up in surrender and stopped watching so I could take some pictures.

As it turned out, chess boards made cool backdrops, especially when I got shadows to fall off the pieces. It probably wasn't original, but it definitely couldn't be what Mr. Waymond called a happy snap.

I had a shot lined up with the king in focus in the foreground with Rodney in the background contemplating his move. It kind of worked, but wasn't quite where I wanted it. I played with the angle and finally found that by stacking a chair on a table next to where they were playing and then standing on the chair so I was looking down with a bird's-eye view, I had something better.

"Mr. Gavard, what do you think you're doing?" Mr. Adamson stood below me as I snapped a couple more bird's-eye pictures. "We aren't accustomed to dealing with concussions during chess practice."

"I'm fine," I said. "Just needed to get into position."

"Is he bothering you?" Mr. Adamson asked Rodney.

"A little."

"Sorry," I said. "I got some good shots that I'll put up on my album tonight." I gave them the address and told them to check after nine. People were usually less annoyed when they saw that I was actually taking flattering pictures of them.

~~~~

When I copied everything from the camera to the computer I noticed a video file. Video? I hadn't shot any video.

I hit play and saw a close-up of Rodney's face with the sound of Jagger laughing in the background. When he bumped into me I must have hit the video button. I re-watched the first minute and then clicked it off. Rodney seemed like a completely different person than the chess-club guy. At lunch he was pathetic and seemed even smaller than he really was. I think he'd skipped two grades in elementary school, so he looked like he should be starting seventh grade, not high school.

Next to a chess board, he seemed huge, even intimidating.

If he could only apply just a tiny fraction of all that chess strategy to the lunchroom he'd be so much better off.

I hit delete.

With no evidence, no one would remember. It was like it never happened. My version of Rodney would be chess master, not lunchroom wimp.

~~~~

I got my mom to drop me off early Thursday, before any buses had arrived.

The lighting looked promising for an idea I had about a school-bus shot. I set up a tripod on the steps so I had a good vantage point. I did some practice shots with the first bus, but I wanted more people in the foreground, with the bus in the background. It would be ideal if someone showed up and rode by doing something interesting like juggling while riding a unicycle.

When three buses pulled up at once I decided to play with the auto function and see what I got.

I turned the camera to the end of the first bus so I'd get the first few people filing off, but stopped when something bright green came into the frame. What was that?

It was Rodney in a fluorescent tracksuit. He could have just worn a giant target. Even my grandpa, who practically lived in tracksuits, wouldn't have worn that one.

The second bus unloaded and Jagger was on Rodney in under a minute. I could hear him all the way across the school yard.

"Nice booger suit!"

Rodney just stood there.

Give it back to him! I willed Rodney to make fun of Jagger's outfit. He didn't have the greatest wardrobe either. His pants didn't look like they fit quite right.

"What's with the big setup?" Dillon started readjusting my tripod. "This isn't leveled right."

"Can you do something?" I asked. "He's going to be harassed all day."

"Who?" Dillon looked through the camera lens.

Was he blind? How could he not have noticed?

"Rodney!" I pointed to where Rodney still stood with Jagger in his face. "Tell him not to wear a bright green tracksuit to school."

"Oh. It is kind of bright. Maybe he's being picked up by a helicopter later and he needs to be visible."

I shook my head. Only Dillon would be able to think of a cool reason why you would wear a bright green tracksuit to school. He'd have everyone talking about helicopters instead of what a dork he is.

Jagger shoved Rodney hard, sending him staggering backward three steps. Before Rodney could catch his balance, Andres was between him and Jagger, shouting and gesturing.

"Come on," Dillon said and started to run over.

I lifted my camera on its tripod and ran-walked as fast as I could but by the time I got there, Jagger had walked off, and Dillon had left with Rodney.

Andres kicked the ground, cursing in Spanish.

"What happened?" I asked. "It was nice of you to stick up for Rodney."

"Was it?" Andres clenched and unclenched his fists. "I probably just made it worse. Now Jagger will go after him when I'm not around."

"Still, not many people would help Rodney, especially in that outfit." I unscrewed the camera from the tripod and put it away.

"I know he looks stupid, but so what?" Andres clenched his fists again and faced me. "He should be able to wear whatever he wants. Why does Jagger even care?"

"I have no idea." I folded the tripod, avoiding eye contact with Andres until he cooled down more.

"Sorry." Andres kicked the grass. "It's just… Rodney used to be in my little brother's class before he skipped all those grades. I hate to think of someone my age picking on my kid brother."

Andres looked down. "If I had gotten in a fight with Jagger, I'd be kicked off the team." He turned to look at me. "Remind me not to get involved next time, okay?"

I nodded. Staying out of it was my specialty.

~~~~

Later that morning I had a cool hallway shot lined up when Rodney walked into the frame in that stupid tracksuit. He was being harassed, but not by Jagger. A lot of people were making fun of him, it was so easy. It seemed like anyone who'd ever been curious about trying bullying or just needed to vent was getting in on the action.

Go home already, burn that stupid outfit and try to regain your dignity tomorrow.

I sent my silent message, but of course, he didn't get it.

No way was I sitting at our lunch table with Rodney in that tracksuit. I went to my locker early, grabbed my sandwich and went outside to find a corner to eat by myself. If anyone asked I'd just say I was cramming for a quiz.

That afternoon one of the arms had been ripped at Rodney's shoulder seam and the top looked pretty muddy. I hoped Andres had stayed away.

~~~~

After school I ditched my plan to go back to the chess club. I needed to get out of there. I followed the skater kids to their park and got some decent shots of them riding before it was time to head home.

As I cut through the woods behind the skate park, I could see someone on the bridge. With the cloud cover, the lighting wasn't great, so I had to adjust the exposure, but before I could focus the person moved. I held up the camera and snapped as he crouched down and swung himself under the railing so he was sitting on the edge.

I checked my light levels on the image display and saw the bright green tracksuit the bridge guy was wearing.

I zoomed in and refocused as he held on with one arm and leaned way out.

Crap. If he let go... It was all rocks under there... It didn't matter if he could swim.

I let the camera dangle on the neck strap and started running toward him.

I don't know if he heard me, but he swung himself back under the railing onto the bridge and ran to the road on the other side.

~~~~

"Liam, eat!" my mom commanded.

I forced a couple of bites of dinner even though I could literally feel the gag reflex with each mouthful.

I should have gone after Rodney, but what would I have said? *Hey, you weren't going to jump off that bridge were you?*

Had he heard me? Was it enough to get him off the bridge or would he just be back tomorrow? I could tell Dillon and Andres, but what could we do, monitor that bridge every day? Become Rodney's bodyguards?

I wasn't even sure that's what he was doing. Maybe I misinterpreted what I saw. I was always projecting, trying to predict what people would do next so I could get an interesting shot. Maybe I'd just assumed he was thinking of jumping.

"Liam!" My mom was watching me too closely. I was on the verge of getting another eating disorder lecture if I didn't act fast.

"Sorry, they had a bake sale and I ate a bunch of cookies at the end of the day," I lied.

"I'm glad you're eating but please try to not ruin your dinner with cookies." My mom shook her head. "Wrap that up in case you get hungry later."

After putting my plastic-wrap-covered plate in the refrigerator, I went to my room.

Focus. I'd print my three shots and be done with it. I copied the pictures to my computer and forced myself to pick what I wanted to show Mr. Waymond. I relaxed a bit as I listened to the printer mechanically moving the paper into place and moving the ink jets back and forth. There. I was done.

Icons of the bridge pictures glowed on the screen. He'd walked away, right? End of story.

I was uninvolved. Behind the scenes.

For the sake of learning how the camera worked, I had to at least check how the lighting turned out. I zoomed in and froze. Agony, misery, hopelessness. He wasn't playing around.

If I got rid of the pictures and didn't show anyone, it didn't happen, right? What happened tomorrow wasn't my problem.

My mouse hovered over the Delete key.

It would be as if I hadn't seen him. It was up to me to decide what was noticed and what was forgotten.

I clicked the mouse and waited for the sound of the ink jets bringing Rodney to life.

About The Author

Karen Avivi

Karen Avivi is the author of *Shredded*, a contemporary young adult novel about rule-breaking, gravity-defying girls who shred riding freestyle BMX. Karen has tried surfing, skydiving, scuba diving, stunt classes, archery, winter camping, orienteering, mountaineering, mountain biking, and even attempted a bike ramp once, but it didn't end well. She's usually reading, writing, or planning a new adventure from her home in Montreal.

Visit her at http://www.karenavivi.com

~When I Met You~
(Missing scene from The Remembrance Trilogy)

By
Kahlen Aymes

Edited by Kathryn Voskuil & Sally Hopkinson

Ryan~

THE BIGGEST MOMENT of my life found me unexpectedly, crept up softly, and settled around me like a fuzzy blanket filled with rocks. It was a mere whisper that hit me like a sledgehammer. At the time, I knew it was significant, but I didn't realize just how those few seconds would change absolutely everything and leave an indelible stamp on the remainder of my life. It would become a contradiction; an unstoppable force that was out of my control, churning and shredding my emotions, yet creating the most incredible contentment I'd ever feel. One that could wrap me up in a warm, safe place or devastate me to the core and leave my heart in shambles. It would become years of want and pain, lust and love… It would hurt like the deepest hell and become the most euphoric and precious ecstasy I'd ever know.

It wrecked me. It *made me.*

I'd never forget that day, that moment, that glance. The auditorium was huge, like a massive theater, with throngs of young bodies milling around trying to find seats; bustling with activity. Only, it wasn't the premier of Harry Potter or one of those damn Twilight movies. It was Stanford University and Psychology 101.

Ugh, my brain protested. No matter what your major, whether you were pre-med or planning a future on Wall Street, you had to take some dumbass form of psychology for your liberal arts requirement. Boring as hell to me, but whatever. I had plans for med school, and this course was the most basic. Normally, I had no interest in basic anything, but because I'd just as soon skip it, it was the next best thing. I'd heard it was super easy, which explained why so many students were interested in Community Health Psychology.

Aaron had taken it the semester before and whined the whole time because he didn't get Dr. Gerrity. We'd heard that to make the course tolerable, he was the only choice for professor. I would have taken it with my brother, but the class was closed by the time I got around to the scheduling session. I didn't make the same mistake this time, but my enthusiasm was at an all-time low, despite the luck with the instructor.

I searched for a seat toward the back near the main entrance. The hell if I wanted to participate, anyway. I just wanted to show up, sign in, take the tests, and ace the fucker. *Cha'ching!* That's what I did; ace shit. School was always easy. I knew it, and was slightly arrogant about it.

I fully expected the first two years of undergrad to be fluff and loaded up on credit hours so that later, when I had clinical, my ass wouldn't be dragging. I'd even gotten special permission from the dean to take three hours beyond the max class load. My father and I discussed it and decided it was better to have more out of the way, early on, so I could take more difficult courses that would secure my future plans after I'd declared my major; Harvard Medical School. We'd shared the same goal for as long as I could remember. You didn't get there by taking the bare minimums in anything, and if Dad had done one thing, he'd drilled that into me; work your ass off and never expect success to be handed to you. So far, I hadn't had to work that hard, but I knew it was only a matter of time. He'd gone to Harvard years earlier, and while that would help, neither of us expected an easy in. Anyway, I wouldn't want one. I'd earn every piece of it, or it wouldn't mean shit.

My parents offered the same opportunities for my adopted brother, Aaron. When we were ten his parents were killed in a car accident, he moved in with us and we grew up together. He was the best friend I'd ever had.

Aaron struggled more than me; always had. I felt bad that it was more difficult for him and tried to help whenever I could; especially with math. So far, we'd only had to take Calc 101, which to me was just a repeat of my senior year in high school. This semester was Trigonometry, and I wasn't looking forward to that at all. It was the most boring part of my requirements, other than this liberal arts crap, but whatever, it was necessary.

"I hear Dr. Gerrity is hot. Let's sit more toward the front so we can get a good look," a girl with short, black hair and a red mini-skirt giggled as she moved past me.

Apparently, she had her own reasons for taking this class. I rolled my eyes. *For fuck's sake!*

Mini-skirt girl was pretty, but my eyes landed on the back of another young woman walking behind the one who was hot for the instructor. She had long, flowing dark hair that looked like a shiny, slick river of deep chocolate as she moved. It was smooth and looked very soft, dropping almost to the middle of her back. My eyes moved lower to her denim-encased ass. Her waist was small and the curve of her hips flowed deliciously out to place emphasis on the bedazzled pockets I was staring at. There was an 'M' embroidered on one side. My lips twitched in the start of a grin. 'M' was for Matthews. I took it as a sign that I needed to talk to her or I'd regret it. Regardless if it meant something or not, didn't matter. *It was a sign,* my subconscious argued. I grinned because I couldn't fucking help myself.

I picked up the backpack I'd just placed in one of the seats near the aisle and followed the two women further down. For all I knew she could be a troll, and I should rein in my eagerness until I knew for sure. A troll with a stellar ass, maybe, but I hadn't seen her face. Then she spoke, her voice soft, almost musical, but adamant. I knew I had to meet her.

"Ellie, he's old, and I don't wanna sit in the front. This class is gonna be lame as it is. We'll have to join discussion up there, and I hate this shit."

"Please?" her friend lamented.

"No! I can't put up with you and the others batting eyelashes at the professor. It's embarrassing!"

Somehow, it didn't sound like whining. The same words from someone else would have, but with this girl, it was more like a statement of fact… A verbal bitch-slap without the drama. I loved it.

She stopped and half-turned, and I got the first glimpse of her profile. My breath stuck in my lungs for a beat. She was stunning; high cheekbones and delicate features with a slight blush to her cheeks and dusky pink lips. Her skin seemed flawless; creamy perfection. If it weren't for her casual dress, I'd have placed her from some high-crotch, rich-bitch, old-money crowd. Her breasts were full, but not overly large, and suited her frame. I sucked in my breath to start breathing again. Yep. I definitely needed to find out who she was. Good thing I wasn't the shy type.

"Look, if you want to go ogle the dude, go ahead, but I'm staying up here."

I smiled, stifling a laugh. Definitely not high-crotch. I was elated. She moved into a row about six ahead of me, and I searched the surrounding seats. There was one open just behind her to her right. It would give me the prefect vantage point to observe undetected. There was something about her that intrigued me. I could almost see her intelligence as if it were written on her shirt. *"Morons to the left."* Damn. I could *not* stop smiling.

People brushed by me, and I was knocked in the shoulder as a larger guy passed. I barely noticed, my focus still on the girl as I moved into the row of seats I'd targeted.

"Sorry, dude," he mumbled.

"No problem," I said and casually waved him away as I moved toward my objective.

The red-skirt girl stopped and visibly stamped her foot. "Julia!"

Her name flew around in my brain. It suited her to a T. *Beautiful*, but without the need or desire to shorten it into something less dignified; like how Grandma Matthews had reduced my Aunt Elizabeth's name to Betty. I never understood how the hell Betty came from Elizabeth anyway.

"What?" The girl with the pretty name simply looked at her friend and stopped, flopping down her book bag and taking her seat. She patted the one next to her with a teasing smile. "You'll have plenty of time to get in the professor's pants later. Just think of all the opportunities to discuss this bullshit in his office. Of course, it might be difficult trying to convince him why you're so passionate, since psych has nothing to do with your major."

"Jeesh, Julia! Fine!" Her friend relented and threw her body down in the seat next to Julia as I moved into the one behind them and sat down. Leaving my backpack between my feet, I opened it and pulled out a notebook and a pen. Afterward, I was free to observe the girls the last few minutes before class began.

My hand went to my mouth as I leaned on my elbow to watch and listen.

"Just look around." Julia motioned with her hand. "There are plenty of hot guys who aren't geriatric." She shrugged. "Choose," she said with a small giggle, digging out her notebook and a pen. "Besides, what about Jason?"

"Nope. He's *your* boyfriend."

"Yeah. Mouthwatering, that one," she said, tongue-in-cheek. The two of them burst out laughing, and I found myself wondering about this poor bastard, Jason. Julia's laugh was infectious. I saw how the people around her noticed her, most of the men doing a double take. I didn't bother trying to hide my admiration and watched her openly.

A pretty blonde next to me was staring wide-eyed at me. I glanced at her briefly when she began speaking. "I'm really looking forward to this class. I took a college credit course online from UCLA in sociology and I just loved it."

I huffed inwardly, trying to concentrate on Julia's words. "I'm pretty sure psychology and sociology are on two different planets," I answered.

"Well, it's an *ology*." She shrugged carelessly. "So, I'm sure I'll love this, too!" the blonde said. "I'm Rita."

Okay, this chick was way too over-enthusiastic; making my brain hurt and the nasal quality to her voice was irritating. It was all I could do not to laugh out loud. Did she just fucking say what I thought she said? It's an *ology*? My eyes widened against my will. *Okay.*

"Ryan," I mumbled. I pulled the text out of my backpack and feigned interest in it as if it were Grey's Anatomy. Now, *that* was interesting. I'd spent hours as a child poring over the pictures and pages of the copy my father kept in his study, memorizing the structures and systems of the body. It was then we knew med school was in my future. Like father, like son.

I glanced at the girl named Julia as a guy on the other side of her made a move toward her. Something in my gut didn't feel right, and I shifted un- comfortably in my chair. The guy was standing there, grinning and openly gaping at her like a fool, asking her name and stammering like an idiot when she told him. *Asshole.*

Finally, after a couple more minutes of meaningless chatter and Julia's obvious indifference, he left her, defeated and minus her phone number, to go find his seat. Julia pushed her hair behind her ear, and I found myself looking for the pulse in her neck, wondering if her skin smelled sweet and if the blood rushing just beneath the surface would make it warm under my mouth. I sucked in a deep breath.

"Why are we taking this class again?" the girl named Ellie asked. She was sitting directly in front of me and leaned into Julia.

"It's required, though I'm not sure for what. It has little relevance for my marketing degree."

I couldn't help myself, I wanted her to notice me, so leaned forward and spoke.

"Or, anything else… for that matter," I interjected.

Sparkling green eyes shot to mine for the first time, and I was instantly sucked in. There was deep blue-green around the irises, lightening to jade, and then resuming the darker shade around the pupils. She paused, a small smile spreading out on her full lips. She had two barely-there dimples that showed up when she flashed her white teeth as her face lit up. She was gor- geous, though now I could see she had very little make-up on.

"Yes, well, I think we picked this class because my friend here is warm for the professor's form." Her perfectly manicured brow shot up, and she laughed softly when her friend shoved her in the shoulder.

"Thanks a lot!" Ellie protested, throwing a glance over her shoulder at me.

Julia was still looking at me, her eyes skirting over my face. She looked away, nervously glancing at her watch.

"I picked it because it was the least offensive psych class and might have a slight relevance to my pre-med program." Yeah, it was cocky, but I needed this girl to know I wasn't some brainless douche, wasting my brains and opportunities, like the loser that was just trying to pick her up. I knew I was being an asshole when I mentally dissed him, but I didn't care.

Rita continued to stare in open admiration. "Wow, med school. You must be really smart."

Julia and Ellie smirked; Julia's eyes widening in feigned innocence. "Yeah, you must be *really* smart!" she shot out in a veiled attempt to tease me about Rita's obvious attempt to divert my attention back to her. No way in hell that was going to happen. Julia was beautiful, but, also witty and smart. I found her engaging and intriguing.

Ellie burst out laughing, and Julia batted her eyelashes at me, openly mocking the other girl's comment. "I'm only teasing. I'm Julia, and this is my best friend, Ellie."

"Hi. I'm…" I began to introduce myself only to be cut off by the start of the class. *Fuck!*

The professor noisily adjusted the microphone on the podium at the front of the class before his gruff voice began rattling off the syllabus for the course. He might as well have been reciting a grocery list for all the attention I paid him. Thankfully, Rita was the type to take rigorous notes. It would be easy to get her to lend them to me if needed, or better yet, maybe I'd have to make a study partner out of the vivacious brunette who now held my rapt attention. It was stupid. I never got all giddy over women, but what I was feeling was magnified by the three times she glanced over her shoulder at me and burned me with those intense green eyes and a sly smile. My stomach did little flip-flops, my palms were sweating, and my heart sped up. I wanted to know more. Much more. I couldn't wait to speak to her, but the damn class droned on for 45 more minutes. It seemed like ten years.

When it ended, I'd already loaded my stuff in my backpack and remained seated until the two girls in front of me rose from their seats.

"So, Ryan, do you live on campus?" Rita tried to make conversation as we waited for the people to my left to shuffle out in front of us. I was essentially standing next to Julia, while she waited in her row, and I could smell her perfume wafting up like a musky dessert filled with vanilla and something that made my heart slam against my ribs.

I shoved a hand in my pocket. "Nope." I threw the answer over my shoulder with no other explanation and looked down at Julia. Her smiling eyes found mine, and she bit her lip to stifle a laugh. She knew I was blowing Rita off, and she approved.

I ignored Rita's comment and spoke instead to the object of my new fascination. "So, as I was trying to say before, I'm…"

"Ryan," Julia interrupted. As long as I lived, I didn't think I'd ever forget the first time this woman said my name. "Um… yeah, I heard. Before."

I smiled. "Yeah. Where you from?" I asked.

"Kansas City. At least, my mom lives there. My dad is closer. San Francisco."

We inched our way toward the aisle as the students filed out.

"Oh, is that why you chose Stanford?"

"No. I mean, partly. It was the reputation, and my crystal ball said I was going to meet the greatest people here."

"How's that working for ya?" I chuckled as we finally made it to the end of our row. I waited for her and Ellie to exit, allowing them to move ahead of me.

"It was rough at first, but things are looking up." She leaned in and nudged my arm with her shoulder and electricity shot through me like a lightning bolt. She was quite a bit shorter than me, I could have rested my chin on the top of her head, and I found myself wanting to do just that. I nudged back instead, and she laughed softly.

A smile slid across my face again, the damn thing seeming to settle permanently on my lips. I was giddier than I'd ever been in the presence of a girl, but I felt at ease and comfortable, too. We slowly climbed the stairs toward the exit of the lecture hall, and I realized, in literally seconds, we'd be outside, and if I didn't say something quick, I wouldn't see her until the next class two days from now. I shook my head. Just because she made me hard beneath the belt and all soft and gooey inside didn't mean I had to get stupid.

Ellie turned as we poured with the stream of other students from the auditorium into the foyer of the building. "See ya later, sweetie," she said to Julia. Her grey eyes darted from me to Julia, and she smiled devilishly like the cat that swallowed the canary. "Nice to meet you, Ryan."

I panicked slightly, even knowing there was a chance I wouldn't see them both on Wednesday, there was no assigned seating, and the hall was huge. I could easily miss her in the swarm of students. My backpack thrown over my shoulder, I rubbed the back of my neck.

"Bye, hon." Julia hesitated as Ellie left us. "Um…" she pointed in the direction of the library, but hovered, not stepping in its direction. "Do you have another class now? I was going to go read the assignment in the library."

It was the first week of classes and most of the work would be reading; except the trigonometry and chemistry class I had next hour. I nodded and pulled my sunglasses out and shoved them on. "Unfortunately, yes." I hoped she felt as disappointed as I did that we couldn't keep talking. "Chem."

"Oh, that's right. You're a science snot." Her lush lips smiled, as she squinted in the sun and lifted a hand to shade her eyes.

I chuckled at her teasing. "Guilty. My entire family is, except my mother. Tell me about the 'M' on your butt."

Her eyebrow shot up. "What?" she asked incredulously.

"The 'M'," I stammered. "On your back pocket." This was as good a way as any to make sure she knew who I was, even if it was a little awkward.

She frowned, not understanding, and then astonishment flooded her features, her eyes widening. "You were looking at my ass?"

"Well, I couldn't see your face." Shit, this was weird. I felt out of my element, nervous and ridiculous. I couldn't believe I'd just mentioned her ass. I laughed uncomfortably, hating myself for not being smoother. "'M'. My last name is Matthews. We have to be friends now. You're branded. It's a sign." I was seriously attracted to this girl, but I wanted to know her mind more than I wanted to get in her pants. The thought left me stunned as I wondered if I could be friends with someone I was this into.

"Ah." Her head nodded once as realization of what I was doing dawned on her. She raised her eyebrow and nodded to indicate someone was hovering behind me. I turned to look. It was the other girl from the lecture hall.

"So, I'll see you Wednesday?" Rita asked awkwardly, stammering slightly. I'd forgotten all about her and didn't realize she was still around.

I shoved one hand in the front pocket of my jeans and opened my mouth, then shut it again. Rita wasn't the one I wanted to sit next to during the next class. "Um… I guess?" I inwardly grimaced as my eyes locked with Julia's. I came off rude and that was unfortunate, but I wanted to speak to Julia, and I was running out of time before my next class.

"Okay." Rita answered shortly then turned away, disappointment clear on her face.

I returned my attention to Julia.

"The jeans are branded, for sure. Miss Me-s. Lots of girls have 'M's' on their butts," she challenged with a grin. "Are they all branded? Cuz, you don't look like the kind of guy who lacks female companionship. Obviously." Her eyes darted to and she nodded at Rita's retreating back.

I bit my lip and my hand swiped through the side of my hair. The last thing I needed was Julia thinking I was a user. "I think there might be a compliment in there if I dig deep enough," I teased. "Look, I wanted to meet you. So, kill me."

Our eyes met and held again, and I almost blurted that I wanted her number. I told myself to get a grip. I never acted this dumb in front of a girl.

Julia rocked on heels and glanced at her watch. "You're gonna be late."

"I'd blow it off if it wasn't the first class of the semester. I really want to talk to you some more." Suddenly, I was happier than hell that I didn't get into Gerrity's class last semester. I already liked this girl more than most people I'd met at college, and I'd only spoken to her for a few minutes. There was just something about her. Not the way she looked, though she was beautiful, but I wanted to know about her life, to invest time with her. It was a gut feeling, but this girl was going to be important to me, she was a long-term investment. "So maybe you could agree to meet me outside the lecture hall on Wednesday, and we can sit together? Then this class might be bearable."

Julia's smile widened, and she nodded. "Okay, sure. I'll make sure my ass is branded. But that other girl will be bummed."

I smiled back and wished I had more time to get her number. "Okay, good. See ya."

"Uh huh. Bye, Ryan." She waved awkwardly and started off toward the library.

I turned in the opposite direction and took three steps and stopped. "Hey, Julia," I called over the others walking between us. "If you can wait an hour for lunch, I'll be in the Student Union snack bar."

A brilliant smile flashed, and I waited, knowing I would have to run to my class now. Something wouldn't let me leave without knowing I'd see her later.

"Sounds good."

My heart sped up and the silly smile returned and didn't budge the whole time I ran across campus. Anticipation made my heart race more than the exercise. This was stupid. I met girls all the time and most of the time I couldn't give a shit. There were always more girls to meet, and a missed opportunity usually wasn't a big deal. Julia was a big deal to the point I couldn't wait for this hour to get out of the fucking way. I burst through the door to my class and breathlessly found a seat at the back, flopping down quickly amid glances from the others around me. Yeah... this girl was gonna be important.

Wow.

My face hurt from smiling, and dang if the book in front of me could hold my attention. It didn't help that this shit was boring as hell, it was made worse because my mind was full of the guy I'd just met in the class.

He was like a magnet—too gorgeous not to notice, and I'd seen him take the seat behind me right before that blonde girl started talking to him. My heart had plummeted, thinking she would mean I'd miss any chance of meeting him and would have to resort to the high school tactics of trying to sit near him for the next class. The only problem was, the auditorium was huge, and chances were, I'd never find him. Which was why it was so great when he'd taken it upon himself to butt into my conversation with Ellie.

I saw Ellie checking him out, too. Who wouldn't? Tall, easily over six feet, built, golden skin and sun-kissed hair, brilliant, dark blue eyes, and that *face*. There were no words for that face. Strong jaw, killer dimples, bright smile, straight nose, that tiny cleft in his chin. Beautiful couldn't cut it. And, to top it all off; he was really nice. Even though he'd been checking me out, for the first time in a long time, I felt like a guy was really interested in what I had to say. *Matthews*. Ryan *Matthews*. Sure, the sweet persona could be a ruse to suck unsuspecting victims in. I'd seen that crap often enough, but something inside me told me he was different. I sincerely hoped he was.

I glanced at the clock again and gave up trying to read the textbook in front of me, flipping it shut and unzipping my black backpack to slide it inside. I still had fifteen minutes until I was supposed to meet Ryan. I felt a little nervous. He was so pretty and surely had a bevy of women vying for his attention. What if he didn't show up? My stomach dropped before I could stop it, but I hoisted the heavy bag of books over my right shoulder and slowly made my way toward the Student Union. I didn't want to get there too early and look like an anxious jerk standing around waiting. I didn't want to order lunch without him. Ugh. I was overthinking this way too much. It was crazy, but something about him was unnerving and comforting at the same time. He seemed really genuine so I didn't know why I was acting so silly. Maybe it was the way every woman that came near him stared.

I found the restroom and made my way inside; weaving in and around all of the women coming out, all with book bags made for a tight fit. My eyes widened as I took stock of my reflection and quickly dug out the hairbrush and lip gloss that I kept in the front pocket of the backpack. Not one to retouch normally, I reapplied a light glaze of the gloss on my lips and smoothed my hair slightly. I didn't want to appear overly anxious to Ryan and I chastised myself that I'd made this small deviation from my usual routine. I replaced the items in my bag and smoothed the dark denim over my thighs.

When I left the bathroom, I stopped to scan the snack bar. It was nice, set up like a restaurant with wooden booths and tables. Ryan hadn't said where to meet him, and my eyes scanned the room. I didn't see him, but the Student Union was large, and there were a lot of students walking through and hovering around tables and at the end of a few of the booths. I felt self-conscious walking around like a moron, looking into booths and glancing around like I was lost. Many sets of curious eyes met mine while I wandered around seeking the striking blue gaze of the man I met two hours earlier.

I caught sight of him quickly pushing in the front entrance doors, his eyes scanning the room. He didn't see me right away, but was rapidly put upon by a group of others, a dark-haired man and two women; one with long blonde hair and one with cropped red locks. I was anxious and my feet wanted to move toward him, but I hesitated as I watched the group engage him. His gorgeous face split into a grin, and he nodded, the blonde's hand coming out to wrap around his bare forearm. He was wearing jeans and a long-sleeved white T-shirt, the cuffs shoved up to show strong muscle and golden skin, the blue and green plaid shirt he wore over it hung open. He looked hot; the layers doing nothing to disguise the hard plains of his chest and stomach underneath the fine cotton material or the broad shoulders. The two women gazed at him in adoration, and I wondered if he knew it. It was sort of ridiculous, and I made a mental note not to allow myself to act like an idiot around him. I took slow steps toward him to make sure he saw me, not wanting to interrupt the conversation with his friends.

He bent slightly to listen to something the woman touching him said, but he continued to search for me. My heart stopped when his eyes landed on mine, and his lips lifted in the start of a small smile. He was so breathtakingly handsome. This was a chance to just look at him. He put up his hand and spoke to the group around him. Excusing himself, he walked toward me with his backpack slung over his right shoulder. The two girls turned to watch him walk away, disappointment and curiosity in their eyes as they checked me out.

"Hey." His soft voice washed over me warmly as he flashed a quick smile.

He was several inches taller than me, and I had to look up into his face. I wanted to bite my lip, hardly able to contain the grin that was trying to break out across my mouth. "Hey. How was class?"

"Boring as hell. I can't wait until all of this basic shit is out of the way. Want to find a place to sit and then I can get us something to eat?"

"Yeah. Did you want to invite your friends?"

Ryan smiled again and shook his head. "Nah."

He motioned toward an empty booth in the corner, and I preceded him to it, flung my backpack in, shoving it closer to the wall as I slid in. Ryan did the same across from me. I watched him run a hand through his hair.

"Did you get the psych assignment read?" he asked.

"Ugh," I rolled my eyes, and Ryan chuckled. "It was so bad I couldn't concentrate. I think I'll have to read it out loud to get through it."

"That's what I'm afraid of. Maybe we can take turns and then just fill each other in."

I smiled, leaning back against the booth, pleased at the prospect of studying together. "Okay."

We started talking, and time flew. We talked about my parents' divorce, his life growing up in Chicago, how his family adopted his best friend when they were ten, and my father's latest criminal case, both of us leaning in toward each other intently. I ate up his words, and he was equally engaged; truly interested in all I was telling him. We fell into a rhythm that was easy, yet made my heart thud inside my chest. I'd forgotten I was hungry until my stomach rumbled loudly and Ryan chuckled.

My eyes widened. "Wow. That's embarrassing."

"It's my fault! I promised you lunch, and I've completely failed." He looked around at the clock on the wall. It was ten minutes to three. "The grill closes soon so we'd better order. What would you like?"

"I'm not picky. Grilled chicken sandwich and tea?"

"I'll be back." I watched him walk away and couldn't help but admire the easy grace with which he moved or the eyes that followed his every move. I wondered about the young woman he was speaking to before.

Surely, she wasn't his girlfriend, or she would have joined us for lunch. In no time, I had the sandwich, green tea, and a pile of fries in front of me. Ryan had a burger, onion rings, and a Coke. He shoved the rings toward me. "I wasn't sure if you wanted fries or rings, so…"

I pushed my fries in the middle of the table, too. "How 'bout we share?"

Ryan smiled and grabbed an onion ring. "I hoped you'd say that." He dipped it in the ketchup I squirted alongside and took a big bite. "How come I haven't seen you around before?"

I lifted my right shoulder in a half-shrug. "Not sure. I don't socialize much. First semester I was worried about the grades, so I kept to the books. Wasn't sure what to expect, you know?" My eyes flashed up, and he was intently studying my face. I reluctantly reached for my sandwich. "Plus, you're in arts and science, and I'm business admin. It isn't likely we'd share many classes."

Ryan nodded. "Yeah, that sucks. So, business. What are you going to declare?"

I swallowed the food in my mouth before I answered. "Well, I'm having trouble, because really, I'd like to double in marketing and art, but it crosses the schools, so they won't allow it."

"So, you're an artist, then?"

"I feel weird saying that." I shrugged a little, despite loving it and being told by teachers, friends, and family that I was talented, I still hesitated to allow myself the luxury of the label. "I've always been artistic, and I'd like to do something with it when I graduate, but my dad doesn't think there is much of a financial future in it. So, the best I can do is take as many art electives as possible. I'll also take extra classes during the summers so I can get the requirements in and at least mimic the major. Even if I can't say I have a degree, I'll have the knowledge."

"I see." The admiration on his face sent a small thrill through me. "It's sort of the same for me. Stanford doesn't offer a pre-med program per se, so I have to pick a science curriculum that I like best as a major that will still facilitate my getting into medical school." I watched him talk, how he moved his hands, and the expressions that changed his features. "At this point, I'm leaning toward chem or bio."

"What kind of doctor do you want to be?"

"Hmmph!" he let out his breath with an amused laugh. "To be honest, I have no clue, but probably some sort of specialty, though. My dad is a brain surgeon."

"Are you serious?" My eyes widened as I tried to picture Ryan's home life. Was his dad a stuffed shirt who was gone all the time and his mother a suburban princess? If so, it certainly wasn't evident in their son. He was so down to earth and genuine.

"Yes. No pressure there," he smirked. "He's sort of brilliant. He's a very giving man, but he can be tough at the same time." Ryan laughed and continued to talk about his parents. It was obvious he loved them very much and his words refuted my original mental impression of them. Ryan was so animated and enthusiastic, his mood was infectious. "Tell me about you."

"Not much more to tell, really. I mean, when my parents divorced, I moved to Kansas City with my mom. Since I was eight, I've spent every summer in California with my father. I think he felt guilty that he wasn't around more, but I liked my life with my mom. She's cool; way cooler than most of my friends' moms. We like the same music and share clothes. I can talk to her about anything."

"Is it weird for you, though? Being in the middle of your parents? I can't imagine it, since mine have always been together."

"No. They stayed friends and always parented together."

He stopped eating and leaned back, his eyes coming back to mine. "I can't imagine being in love with someone and then going back to being just friends. I don't know if I could do it."

A little shiver ran through me at his words, and I wondered if anyone had ever been lucky enough to have him in love with them. "It wasn't always easy, but I don't think they split due to lack of love. My mom resented my dad's long hours, and she didn't know many people. She got lonely and wanted to be closer to family. He was just starting out and working very hard. He wanted to be a prosecuting attorney and it required long hours in the D.A.'s office. He wasn't willing to give up that dream. Looking back, I know he was only doing it for us, but at the time, he just wasn't there. I know he was very angry when they first split." I wiped my fingers on the paper napkin in my lap. "But after we moved, she was happier, and then, so was I."

Ryan nodded in understanding.

"Do you live on campus?" I asked, wondering if he'd be heading my way and not wanting to end the afternoon, and knowing the answer since that girl, Rita, had asked him in the lecture hall.

"No. My parents argued about it. It's cheaper to rent a place for Aaron and me than to pay room and board, and anyway, the food sucks ass and Aaron would've died. Eventually my mom gave in to my dad's logic but she still worries we'll party too much." A gorgeous grin split across his face and amusement danced in his bright blue eyes.

I laughed and nodded. "And? Do you?"

Ryan joined in with a chuckle. "Nah. Sure, there are parties. Aaron's rushing Phi Kappa Nu, so some are inevitable."

"Not you, though?"

"No. I don't want someone picking my friends. At least, that's how I see it. You? Any sorority?"

I shook my head with a small laugh. "No. I'm of your way of thinking."

He smirked at me. "There are worst things."

"Agreed." I nodded, still smiling.

We got up and gathered our things and began making our way toward the door. Ryan's hand closed around the strap of the backpack hanging off my shoulder to carry it for me. His fingers brushed against my shirt, and I could feel his warmth through the material. I tried not to let him see the small tremor his touch caused. No other guy had ever offered to carry my books before. He was amazing, and I could barely stop myself from staring in rapt adoration like the girls he'd been talking to earlier.

"I'm jealous about the food. I have to be careful not to pack on the freshman fifteen. The food is awful in the cafeteria."

"Ah. So you're on campus."

I sighed. "Unfortunately. But it's all good. That's how I met Ellie. She's my roommate."

We walked across campus toward my dorm, and I started to shiver. The wind was cold, and I regretted my lack of jacket and realized Ryan didn't have one either. "Is your car this way?" I asked, indicating the direction I needed to go. "If not, you don't have to walk me. It's sort of chilly."

"Julia." My name rolled off his tongue for the first time. "I'm happy to suffer for you."

My mouth clamped shut as I tried to figure out what he was thinking. I glanced at him and then straight ahead. "Thank you for lunch. My turn next time?" I was trying to gauge the nature of our relationship. Were we going to be friends or dating?

"Um…" Ryan began hesitantly, and I wondered if maybe he didn't want to have lunch again. "Sure. I've had a good time talking to you."

"Me, too."

"That asinine class might even be tolerable now." His shoulder lightly nudged mine as we walked. I could feel myself blush as I looked down at the pavement moving underneath my feet and I smiled, returning the nudge ever so slightly.

"I'm glad I met you, Ryan."

"Yeah. Me, too. Can I get your number? We can text Wednesday and meet before class; so we can sit together. Cool?"

My heart thumped hard in my chest. "Cool."

Ryan~

I lay on the couch, my foot propped up on the back of it, rhythmically throwing a basketball against the wall over and over. Aaron was in the shower, and I was waiting for my turn. We'd just come from a two-on-two basketball game with two guys who lived next door, and despite the weather, we were both dripping sweat. My hair was damp with it. We kicked their asses, but not without a serious workout. I knew I reeked, and Aaron was worse. I thumped the ball against the wall again, catching it casually as my thoughts wandered to Julia.

It had been a month since we'd met, and I was into her in ways I'd never been into a girl before. I found myself looking forward to seeing her, and every time her name flashed on my phone, I smiled so hard my face hurt; and not because she was hot. She was, but that wasn't the reason. I huffed at the irony of it.

I wanted to take her on dates. To kiss her, and yes, I wanted her. It sucked because it didn't take long to discover she was the person I wanted to spend time with more than anyone else, and I didn't want to lose that. What if we dated and then it tanked? I'd miss her. I always missed her when she wasn't around. It didn't matter what I was doing.

We made a study date for Sunday since our first exam in psych was Monday, but it was Saturday morning, and I found myself racking my brain for a reason to see her today. I'd almost asked her to come to the basketball game just to watch us play, but that was lame and something a guy's girl-friend does. I didn't know what we were. If she did want me to ask her out or make a move, she was probably thinking I was a first class asshole for not doing so.

I was in an uncomfortable position. I didn't know what I wanted for the first time ever in reference to a woman. I liked her. More than liked her but wasn't sure what the fuck I was doing about it. My stomach tightened, and I threw the ball against the wall again, this time a little harder. I'd tried to work out why I hesitated to ask her out but the answers didn't sit well. I couldn't figure out a way to guarantee the outcome would be like I wanted.

Thump. Thump. Thump. I threw the ball over and over.

"Ryan, I'm out of the shower," Aaron called as he walked out of the bathroom into his bedroom with a towel around his waist.

Thump. Thump. Thump. I didn't move, lost in my thoughts.

Five minutes later, Aaron came out of his room, pulling a grey T-shirt over his head and sliding his arms into it. "Ryan?"

"Yeah." I clasped the ball between my hands and sat up, putting my feet on the floor. I glanced at him. When he met her two weeks earlier, he'd hammered me about why I wasn't trying to date her because she was so beautiful. How could I make him understand when I didn't understand my-self? He hadn't stopped until I'd shouted at him to shut the fuck up and that it was none of his Goddamned business.

"Okay. I'm going." I was distracted but stood and passed the ball to him. I started toward my room to gather clean clothes but stopped when he called my name.

"Ryan, there is that party tonight at the frat house. Are you coming?"

I raised a shoulder in a shrug. "I don't know. Maybe? Who's going to be there?"

"A lot of people. Can you call Julia and make sure she will be?"

"What?" I turned fully around to face him. Heat started to rush under the skin of my face. Maybe he thought if I wasn't going to date her, he would. I didn't think I could take watching it.

"David Kessling wants to meet her. He was with me the other day when I was waiting for you in the commons, and he saw her with you. He thinks she's hot and he is president of my frat. I'd like to introduce them. It will give me an in with him."

The heat in my face turned to fire, quickly licking it's way up over my face and down my chest. "Um…" I began, not sure what to say, but my chest felt tight at the thought.

"You don't have a problem with it, right? I thought you guys were just friends." He sat down and started to shove his feet into his shoes.

"Yeah, we're friends." I rubbed the back of my neck. "But," I struggled to find something to say that would dismiss the subject. "She's not really into frat guys. She thinks all that social who's who is bullshit."

Aaron looked up at me, skepticism filling his expression. "Really?"

"Sorry, dude." I began to turn away, but Aaron wasn't ready to let it go.

"Are you planning to date her? I've never known you to be indecisive about a chick before."

I stopped again. "I'm not sure what I'm planning… I'm not really planning. Just going with the flow."

"But you don't want her to see anyone else? That shit will not fly for long. Guys are into her, and eventually, someone will land her."

Exasperation welled inside my chest, and I wanted to smack him. "I don't know. She's cool. I like being with her, talking to her. I feel easy with her, and she doesn't put all that shit on me like most girls do. I mean, she's not all superficial and gooey."

"But, she's hot. I mean… spending time with her, how do you not go for it?"

"It's not easy sometimes. I'm not blind. But I like her more than I want to get her in the sack. I never end up friends with girls I have sex with and Julia isn't a girl you bang on a Saturday night for fun."

He looked at me like my head had twirled around on top of my shoulders. "So, you're not moving on her. If that's true and if you two are just friends, what's the problem if David asks her out?"

I sighed. I really couldn't argue with him. I couldn't have it both ways, and I couldn't felt at this point. I wanted her, more than I'd probably wanted any other girl before, but she was quickly becoming important in ways that were new and unfamiliar to me. I was like a fish out of water, trying to get my bearings.

"Okay, I'll see what she's doing. But, I'm going to tell her about that guy. I don't want her to feel set up." Plus, I didn't know how she saw her relationship with me. Maybe we were only friends, I didn't know. If so, that word had more to it than it ever had before. "If she doesn't want to go, she doesn't want to go. I'll expect you to drop it."

"This is weird, Ryan. If you're not into this girl like that, what's your problem?"

"Aaron, I said I'd ask her. So shut up about it, okay?"

He sat back on the couch and watched me fidget. "You *are* into her."

"I said I like her, but spending time with her is most important."

He whistled and smiled wryly. "Never thought I'd see you confused over a chick."

I huffed and went off toward my room, muttering. "That isn't a word I use to describe her. Julia is no chick."

~~~~

"Hey, you." Julia's voice was soft and a little raspy when she answered the phone. "What are you doing?"

It had become common to call each other every day, to know what and where the other was all the time. It wasn't weird for her to ask me. I might have resented it if it was anyone else, but it was how we were with each other. How I wanted it.

"Trying to get Aaron off my ass. He wants me to go to this party tonight. Some frat thing." I groaned, hoping she'd get how unenthused I was about going.

"I think Ellie is planning on something like that. Which house?"

"Kappa Nu. Aaron's frat."

"Oh. I see. Are you going?"

"No. I don't know. Look, I told Aaron I'd ask you to come."

"Aaron?"

"Yeah. Some asshole he wants to impress saw you with us and wants to meet you." My stomach felt sick when I said the words.

"Hmmph," Julia huffed. I couldn't tell if she was amused or pissed. "Well, if he's an asshole, bring him on. Sounds like my type."

The fact is, we hadn't talked about her type, or mine for that matter. I hadn't asked another girl out since I'd met her, and she hadn't dated either.

I rubbed the back of my neck with my left hand as the fingers of my right gripped tightly around the phone. "Look, I told him you probably wouldn't want to go."

"Who's the guy?"

I was taken aback that she asked, but what did I expect her to do? I had no right to be pissed or even feel upset. Not when we were only friends. "Um…" I struggled to find the name in my mind. "David something or other. Aaron said he's the president of the fraternity." I filled up my lungs and tried to let the air out without Julia hearing it over the phone.

"Should I go?"

"I didn't… I mean, I don't know." I paused.

"Are you going?" she asked again.

"I didn't make plans. Do you want me to? I can go with you. Make sure you're okay."

"I don't want to usurp your plans, Ryan."

I sat down on my bed and swiped my hand through my hair. Julia used words like usurp when so many didn't even know that the hell it meant.

"I didn't really have any plans." *Other than call you and see what you were doing*, I thought. I was pissing myself right now. Why the fuck did I even ask her about that stupid party?

"I'm not feeling the greatest. My throat is scratchy, and my nose is stuffed up. I think I'm coming down with something, so I wasn't really planning on going anywhere tonight. Anyway, I'm sure I look like crap."

I sat up a little, not happy she was sick but happy I didn't have to go to that damn party and watch some prick hit on her all night. I sighed in relief. "Want me to bring you some soup? Medicine?"

"I had one of those instant things." She cleared her throat and let out a small cough.

I hated the thought of her sick and all alone and found myself wanting to take care of her.

"Jules… why don't I come get you? Aaron will be out all night tonight. He's chasing a new girl, and with that party, I doubt he'll come home until morning. I'll stop on the way and pick up some Nyquil, Kleenex and stuff."

"That's sweet, Ryan, but you have better things to do than listen to me blow my nose. I don't want you to get it."

"I won't. I'll be over in an hour."

"Ry—" she began but I interrupted.

"Don't argue, Julia. I'll get some movies and lots of junk food, too. Lots of salty stuff to help your throat."

I hung up without waiting for an answer, and an hour later I was waiting for her in the lobby of her dorm. When the elevator opened and she came out in grey sweat pants and a dark purple parka, carrying her pillow and a box of tissues, my heart softened. Her hair was tied up in a knot on top of her head; she was pale and her nose was red. It was easy to see she felt like hell, but I couldn't help the small smile that came to my mouth as she walked toward me.

"Don't look at me," Julia muttered, wiping her nose.

I wrapped an arm around her shoulders and started walking toward the doors that would take us out to my car. "You look fine. For a sicky." I gave her a squeeze and laughed softly, happier than hell at the prospect of spending the evening with her despite the state of her health.

Her little fist came out and punched me in the ribs, but my coat provided enough padding to keep it from hurting.

"Is that all you got?"

"No. I'm gonna breathe on you and spit in your mouth," she teased miserably. "Just wait."

I laughed out loud and piled her into the waiting car to drive the short distance to the apartment Aaron and I shared. It was in an old turn of the century house that had been converted into four apartments. It was nice but not very big. I'd rushed around and picked the place up, but it still wasn't as clean as I'd wanted for the first time Julia came over. She walked in ahead of me when I pushed the door open, slowly glancing around. There was an old couch and a large TV in the living room, with two mismatched chairs and the kitchen was small, off to one side, the table cluttered with books and notebooks.

"I bought you Diet Coke, Cheetos, and one of those veggie sandwiches you like from Ike's." I murmured, setting the bag, paper cups filled with pop, and the videos on one end of the counter. I pulled off my coat and hung it over the back of one of the kitchen chairs.

"Thanks." She wrapped her arms around herself, still clad in her coat. "What'd you get?"

"Roast beef. I thought we could share, if you wanted."

"Yeah." She nodded and went to sink down on the couch, setting her pillow down.

"Do you have the chills? You look cold."

"A little."

I went to my room and pulled the comforter from my bed, and in less than a minute, I had her shoes and coat off and the covers tucked all around her as she lay on the couch. My hands shoved the covers under her legs and feet. Her green eyes locked onto mine.

"My throat hurts. Do you have ice cream?"

I rolled my eyes. "It doesn't matter. You can't have it, anyway. It'll make mucus and you're already a snotty bitch."

Her laugh followed me to the kitchen as I went to retrieve the bag of food from the sandwich shop, the sodas, and the bag of cold medicine I'd picked up at Walgreens.

"Dickhead."

My lips quirked in amusement as I unwrapped the food and set her sandwich on the coffee table in front of her alongside mine and then flipped on the TV.

Julia coughed and covered her mouth with a tissue. "Ryan," she coughed again, "this is a bad idea. I never get sick, so this must be a bad bug. I seriously don't want you to get it." She snuggled down deeper into the blanket, curling on her side and closing her eyes. I could have taken the chair at the end of the couch but I sat down next to her and lifted her legs so they rested across my lap, grabbed the remote and half of my sandwich, my arm resting across her legs. I watched her face for her reaction, to see if I was overstepping the bounds of friendship, but she just sighed.

"Not hungry right now?"

She shook her head. "Maybe in a bit." She breathed in, her eyes still closed. "This smells like you."

I flushed. Should I have gotten a clean blanket out of the closet instead? "Do you want a different one?" I started to take a bite.

"No. I like it. It's like you're wrapped all around me. It feels good."

My heart stopped. I still didn't know how the fuck to classify our relationship or what we were to each other. But one thing was for sure… to say we were friends was only scratching the surface.

"Thank you, Ryan."

"For what?"

"Getting sick with me," she said sleepily.

Yeah, I probably would get sick, and I didn't even care.

I smiled. As long as anything was with Julia, whatever it was, I was in. All in. I was done, and I knew it.

~~~~

This has been an original scene from before the beginning of
"The Remembrance Trilogy, Book #1, The Future of Our Past."
You can also read the official prologue (Ryan's Ah-Ha Moment)
free on Kahlen's blog:
http://kahlen-aymes.blogspot.com/p/prologue-future-of-our-past-
remembrance.html

Dedicated in loving memory of

Amanda Todd

Sweet dreams, Princess Snowflake

Acknowledgments

To my readers… I adore you. Thank you, for your unending devotion to my work and for your support of this very worthy cause through the purchase of *Stories for Amanda*. My daughter is close to Amanda's age and I am heartbroken for Amanda's family and for all families out there who have lost their angels to this horrific and unforgivable epidemic.

Thank you to Carol Todd for allowing us to contribute to the ongoing efforts of AmandaToddLegacy.org and for providing the cover photo. My heart is with you, always.

To my fellow authors: You bitches rock so hard!
Thank you for your dedication and hard work on this project.
I love you!

If you are being bullied, please seek help. Tell someone…
Have faith you are not alone and someone loves you.
Bullies are small people who try to dictate other's value because they have none of their own. They are not worth your tears.
They are nothing.
You are everything…
This is for you.

~Kahlen
xoxo

About the Author

Kahlen Aymes

Kahlen is an award-winning author of sizzling hot, deeply moving and angst filled contemporary romance.

Her bestselling series, ***The Remembrance Trilogy: (The Future of Our Past, Don't Forget to Remember Me & A Love Like This)*** will have you laughing, crying, yelling at your Kindle and jumping up and down screaming "Ryan is Mine!"

Kahlen and her daughter, Olivia, reside with three spoiled-rotten dogs, Gem, Riley and Sophie near Omaha, Nebraska. Creative by nature, she enjoys the arts, music and theater... But the love of her life is writing! She has a snarky sense of humor and a BSBA in Business Administration and Marketing.

Represented by Elizabeth Winick Rubinstein
of McIntosh & Otis Literary Agency.
353 Lexington Avenue • New York, NY 10016

Follow Kahlen to see what she has coming up:
Facebook: https://www.facebook.com/kahlen.aymes.author
Twitter: @kahlen_Aymes
Blog: http://kahlen-aymes.blogspot.com/

Hoping

by

E.K. Blair

(Erin, Mark's sister)

I WATCH MY big brother as he plops his duffle bag down on the floor. He's wearing the vintage Mudhoney shirt I got him for his birthday a couple years ago. I love that he still wears it, but it has grown smaller on him since he's been hitting the gym more often.

"I'm gonna miss you."

He looks over and starts walking toward me. "I'll be back in a few months for Thanksgiving break."

I love my brother, we're close; we've always been that way, but this summer we really grew tight. I was worried about him right around his high school graduation a couple months ago. He'd been really short with my twin sister, Emily, and me, and he was isolating himself from everyone. It wasn't long before I overheard him telling our parents that he was gay.

I sat at the top of the stairs and listened to him cry while he told them. I was shocked, but more than anything I was sad. He's always been my strong big brother. The one I go to with all my problems, knowing he will help me fix them. He's always been very protective over me and my sister, so to hear the pain coming out of him hurt me. I could tell he was scared. I was too. Afraid my parents would reject him and make him feel worse. I was terrified I would lose him if they did. I wanted to run down there and give him a hug, give him what little strength I felt like I had in me.

He had mentioned that a few guys at school knew and had been tormenting him toward the end of the semester. I'm glad he graduated and no longer has to deal with their bullshit. But now he's leaving me to go across the country to The University of Washington. My heart feels like it's too big for my chest as the sadness swells in me. I'm losing a big part of me, but he seems happy to be leaving, so I try and suck it up for his sake.

"Are you ready, sweetheart?" my mother asks as she walks into the living room where Mark and I are standing.

"Yeah, I think so," he tells her before reaching down to hold my hand.

I can't even keep my sadness in. I try, but my quivering chin is my tell and he sees it. He pulls me in, folding me up in his arms as I let the tears fall.

"Don't cry. I promise I'll call you as soon as my plane lands," he assures me, but it isn't enough to calm me.

"I want you to stay," I choke out around my tears.

He pulls away and looks down at me, pretending to be unaffected, and says, "I know, but I can't."

He's running. I can feel it. He would never admit to it, but I know he's scared to stay here. This summer was rough on him when nearly all his friends turned their backs on him. Word spread fast that he was gay. I try and remind myself that him leaving is probably the best thing for him, even though it hurts me.

I nod my head and sling my arms back around him.

"Where's Emily?" my mom asks.

"She went over to a friend's house," Mark tells her. "We said our goodbyes earlier."

"We should get going," she says, and Mark loosens his hold on me.

"It's gonna be weird not having you here," I mumble.

"Just don't take over my room with all of your crap. I'll be back in a few months and I want it untouched," he jokes with me.

"Promise," I say before he pecks my forehead.

~~~~

(3 weeks later)

Mark has been gone for almost a month now, but he calls and texts often. He's settled and started classes at UW last week. He seems happy, so I'm trying to be as well.

"Em! Hurry up. We're gonna be late!"

"I'm coming!" she snaps. "And we're not gonna be late."

Emily is feisty as hell. We are a lot alike in that respect, but I tend to wear my emotions on my sleeve where she has a toughness that I admire.

When Em comes down the stairs, I grab the car keys and head out. As she hops into the passenger seat, she starts, "I wonder if Gabe ever broke it off with that sophomore?"

"Why would he?" I question, and when I do, I see a huge grin spread across her face. "Oh, God. What did you do?"

"Nothing," she says in a singsong voice that tells me she has been up to no good.

"Spill it."

"You can't say a word. Promise."

Watching the road ahead, I say, "Promise."

"So that party I went to Saturday night that you were too tired to go to… well, apparently his girlfriend was tired as well and wasn't there."

"Cut to the point," I tell her, not needing all the chitchat.

"He kissed me."

"Em!"

"What?"

"He has a girlfriend!"

"Sooo?" she says as if she hasn't a clue as to how inappropriate it is. "We're in high school. It isn't like they were getting married or anything."

Shaking my head, I say, "You are unbelievable. Breaking up a relationship is not the way you want to start your junior year."

"Oh, God," she moans at me as I pull into the parking lot behind our high school.

Familiar faces are all around and everyone is happy, meeting up their friends they haven't seen all summer. I find our assigned spot and park the car.

"Well, as fun as this car ride was, I'm gonna go see if I can find Gabe before the first bell rings," she says as she grabs her backpack and opens her door.

"Em."

"Yeah?"

"That girl is gonna be hurt when she finds out. Just… don't rub it in and make it worse on her," I tell her.

She lets out a deep sigh and nods her head. "Fine," she reluctantly agrees before hopping out of the car and walking across the lot.

I reach in the back and get my bag before heading in to see all my friends. Walking through the busy halls, I find a few of my friends gathered around a locker.

"Hey guys," I announce when I walk up to them.

Turning to look at me, Jenn closes her locker and walks away. I wonder what the hell I could have possibly done to piss her off. We haven't spoke in about a month, but during the summer, that isn't too uncommon.

Adjusting my backpack higher on my shoulder, I make my way to my first class, already wanting to ditch. I pull out my phone and text Mark.

First day already sux.

Switching my cell to silent, I walk into my English Comp. class and find a desk to situate myself at. I sit there, feeling uncomfortable when I notice the whispering going on around me. I wish my phone would buzz with Mark's reply. Anything to distract me from my self-conscious thoughts.

I sit through the whole class, anxious for it to end. Fifty minutes pass and I never feel my phone vibrate, but then the time difference dawns on me. It's not even 6am in Seattle.

I shove my book into my bag and try finding Em in the hall while I make my way to second period. Instead, I see Jenn, so I call out to her. Her friends walk away when I approach.

"What's going on?" I ask.

She sighs and then says, "Come with me."

I follow her as she leads me into the girl's bathroom. She looks around to make sure we are the only ones in here before saying, "Everyone is talking about you and your sister."

"What? Why?" I ask, completely confused.

"Erin… everyone knows about your brother. It's all over school that he's a fag."

Emotions flood. A whole multitude of them. Worried. Embarrassed. Defensive. Angry. Sad.

"Don't call him that," I tell her, hating that word.

"Well, he is, isn't he?" she whispers, like the words are infectious.

"No," I snap. "He's not a fag, he's gay."

"Don't get all bitchy with me," she snaps right back. "I just thought you should know what people are saying."

"So they're calling him a fag?"

She nods her head, and then adds, "They're calling you things too."

"Are you serious? Like what?" Oh my God. I can't believe this. Panic shoots through me and I wanna run, but I stay to hear what I'm almost afraid to hear.

"That you're a dyke."

"What?!" I nearly shriek in disbelief. "Why would they say that?"

"I don't know, but they are."

"You told them I'm not, right?"

When her eyes shift down, I see it. Shaking my head at her, I plead, "Please tell me you said something."

She doesn't look at me, and my face heats as the tears begin to stain them. Jenn and I have been friends since elementary school, but I suddenly feel like I don't even know her. How could she not defend me, but instead betray me?

"Jenn?"

She meets my eyes when she looks up, and her words are drenched in annoyance when she defends, "Look, it's bad enough that they are saying that stuff about you, but I don't want them to say it about me too."

"So you'll let them make fun of me as long as your name isn't mentioned? I thought you were my friend."

"I am," she says softly. "But…"

"But what?"

She takes a moment before saying, "I don't wanna be part of the gossip."

I hear it. I hear the beating around the bush. I'm not stupid. "No. You would rather be spreading the gossip than *be* the gossip," I sneer at her and them storm out the door. Pissed that my friend would be so self-centered, worried about her own reputation, than to stand up for me.

I rush through the halls, looking for Em, and when I spot her, she's yelling at Gabe, and I know that she knows what I just found out when I hear her shouting, "What the fuck is your problem? You think you're so goddamn perfect, huh?"

"Em!" I holler, trying to get her attention, but she keeps on, not even acknowledging me.

When I get close enough, I see Gabe laughing at her, and she loses it, fisting her hand and punching him right in the junk.

"Bitch!" he squeals out and he clutches himself and falls to his knees.

"Em!" I shout but before she can answer me, the principal is there.

"Office. Now."

~~~~

"Please explain to me how you manage to get suspended on the first day of school!"

"Mom, don't yell at her," I say, trying to defend Emily.

"No, really. Ms. Childers said that you punched a boy in the crotch? I mean… what in God's name were you thinking?" she questions as I bust out laughing at the image of Emily socking that jerk in the nuts and his beet red face as he fell to the ground.

"This isn't funny," she scolds, and I immediately straighten up.

"Mom, everyone was calling Mark a faggot," Emily tells her, and my mom leans back into the chair. Sadness washes over her face.

Em and I sit together on the couch and watch her trying to hold it together. It takes her a moment when she finally speaks.

"They're calling him that?" she questions in disbelief.

"Yeah, Mom," Emily says softly, as if her words, if spoken too loudly, could hurt her.

"Jenn pulled me aside and told me that they are saying I like girls. That I'm a dyke," I add.

She sits up, and says, "Well, did you tell the principal that?"

"Yeah, but she didn't want to hear it. She was more concerned about the fight," I explain.

"Well, I want you to go talk to her tomorrow and tell her what those kids are saying."

"I'm staying home." Emily was the one who got suspended, not me, but I'm not going there without her.

"You can't just stay home. You need to go and stand up for yourself. Don't let them make you feel like you can't go to school."

"Mom, it doesn't work that way. You don't understand," I tell her and then I feel my phone buzz from inside my pocket. I pull it out to see that Mark has finally responded to my text from earlier, but honestly, it's too late. I don't even read it when I shove it back into my pocket.

"Well, I'll go up there with you."

"What? That's even worse. You can't come with me to school, Mom."

"Just let her stay home tomorrow," Emily chimes in.

Not wanting to argue, she surrenders, "Fine. One day. That's all you get," before standing up and walking out of the room.

I turn to look at Emily and say, "Thanks."

She gives me a faint smile and says, "Yeah, sure," in an almost defeated tone and then heads upstairs.

~~~~

When I finally drag myself out of bed, it's almost noon. No one has bothered me all morning. No one bothered me last night either, not even my dad. I know he has been having a difficult time accepting that Mark is gay. He loves him, there has never been any doubt about that, but he hasn't been dealing with it well. I'm sure when Mom told him about what happened at school yesterday, he went into shutdown mode. He's good at that when something is bothering him.

I go downstairs to grab a soda and when I return to my room I see the screen on my phone is lit up. When I pick it up, I see I have a missed text from Mark.

Never heard back from you yesterday. How did the rest of your day go?

Tossing the phone on the bed, I sit down and take a long drink. For the first time, I don't wanna talk to him. Honestly, I'm mad at him. Mad for creating this storm that's been slowly brewing. A storm that landed right on top of me. But he's the lucky one. He had the ability to run away, and the first chance he got, he did. Ran straight to Seattle, leaving Emily and me to deal with the backlash. He's a coward.

"Come in," I say when I hear a knock on my bedroom door.

Emily opens it slowly, saying, "Hey," as she walks in. "Mark just texted. Said he hasn't heard from you in a couple days."

"Yeah, I know," I tell her.

She cocks her head at me and asks, "What's going on?"

"Aren't you mad?"

"About yesterday?"

"About Mark. How he conveniently moved away and left us to deal with this crap," I say.

As she takes a seat on my bed next to me, she admits, "In a way... yeah. I feel bad for saying it though."

"It's not fair. He's off, having fun, while we're stuck here." I pause for a moment before adding, "Jenn didn't even defend me when she heard what people were saying about me."

"She's a twat," Emily says and I burst out laughing at her choice of words. We take a moment and fill the room with our laughter and for a moment, as brief as it is, I feel the weight being lifted.

"Yeah, she is," I agree through my now light chuckles. "But still. How shallow can you be?"

"She's pathetic and clearly not worth your time to talk to her. Let her be a bitch to someone else."

"But she's being a bitch to *me*. She was actually pissed at me when I got upset after she told me she didn't stop them from saying those things," I say.

"People are stupid. You know that."

"Yeah," I sigh.

"Call Mark so he doesn't worry, okay?" she tells me and I turn to her and nod my head. "I'm gonna go fix some Ramen for lunch. Want any?"

"Gross. No."

"Oh, I'm so sorry," she teasingly mocks. "I forgot how refined your palette is."

"Well, it's better than having it tainted by Gabe's tongue like yours is," I shoot back at her.

"Ugh. Don't remind me," she says in disgust as she leaves my room.

Picking up my phone, I scroll through and bring up Mark's cell number. I really don't want to talk to him right now, but I suck it up and call him anyway.

"Hey," he says when he answers.

"Hey, what's up?"

"Just got out of class. About to head back to the dorms. What about you? You at school?"

"No. Home," I clip out, growing more irritated that he seems so happy.

"Why are you at home?"

"Em got suspended."

"Wait. What?"

"Em. Got. Suspended." I say this slow and condescendingly.

"Why?"

"Oh, I don't know, Mark. Could it be the fact that everyone knows you're gay and you couldn't stick around here long enough to take some of the heat that's now our burden to bear?"

Silence. He doesn't respond.

"Are you gonna say anything?" I push.

"I'm sorry."

"Sorry that you ran away?"

"Erin…"

"No one will even talk to me, Mark. They're calling me a dyke. Em wound up getting into a fight and now she's suspended for the rest of the week."

"Who's saying this?"

"The whole school."

"Tell me what I can do 'cause I'll do anything," he says to me.

"Nothing. There's nothing you can do, so just have fun and enjoy your year so at least someone in this family is happy." I sling my words at him and then hang up.

My phone immediately starts ringing, and when I see it's Mark, I decline the call and switch my phone off. I'm so mad at him. I know that what the kids at school are saying isn't his fault, but I need to blame someone and he's the obvious choice, so I unload my anger onto him.

"Erin!" I hear Em shout front downstairs.

Opening my door I walk and lean over the banister. "What?"

"Jenn just posted some shit about you on Facebook."

I run back to my room and flip open my laptop. Once logged on, I type in Jenn's name and go straight to read her status update.

Jennifer Carmichael

Erin, that nasty lezbo, tried coming on to me in the bathroom yesterday. That family is nothing but disgusting homos.

"Oh my God," I whisper. There are eighteen comments and over seventy 'likes' and it was only posted ten minutes ago.

"Have you seen it?" Em asks as she walks into my room.

My heart is pounding with anxiety and humiliation for something that isn't even true.

"What do I do?" I ask as the tears rim my eyes.

Em sets her bowl down and moves to squeeze in and sit next to me on my desk chair. She wraps her arms around me, and I let the tears fall.

"Did you read the comments? People actually believe her," I say.

"People are stupid."

"It doesn't matter. They still believe her." I pull back and wipe the tears from my cheeks. "Why are you not more pissed?"

"I am. Trust me."

"So what do I do?" I ask again.

"Honestly? I wouldn't do anything. Don't even feed into it."

~~~~

I took Emily's advice, but the kids at school aren't letting up. I only have a couple of friends that talk to me at this point. I just have to wonder when this will all die down and people will lose interest.

For the past few weeks, I have been forced to walk these halls that are constantly filled with sneers and whispers. Jenn has completely turned her back on me. Tonight is our school's first football game. The one thing I refused to do was quit the cheer squad. I've been on it since freshman year.

"Hey, is it all right if I just drop you off tonight?" Em asks as she stands in the doorway to my room.

Lacing my shoe, I look up and ask, "Why?"

"'Cause I don't wanna sit around with a bunch of people I can't stand to watch a game I couldn't care less about."

Em is taking a lighter load of the bullying than I am, but I know it affects her all the same. For some reason, I'm the bigger target with people. Probably because I'm quiet where she has a loud bark. She's more intimidating.

"Yeah, that's fine. I'll just text you as soon as the game ends," I tell her as I tighten my ponytail and grab my cheer bag.

Dropping me off, I keep my head down as I make my way out to the field. I don't worry too much about anyone teasing me since the stands are loaded with parents and faculty.

The game passes slowly, and we are finally nearing the end of the forth quarter. I step out of our cheer line to quickly grab my cell out of my bag to text Emily. When I swipe the screen, I notice a text waiting on me from

Mark. I don't read it. Instead, I shoot out my text to Em and rejoin the girls.

Once the game is over, I grab all my belongings and head out to the parking lot. I stand and wait on Emily to get here, which is taking her longer than it should. I hear a few kids laughing at me when they pass, and I pull out my phone to distract me. I open up the text from Mark and read it.

I miss talking to you. I never meant to bail the way I did.

I'm surprised when I notice Ashton step up next to me. He plays cornerback and we have known each other since he moved here in the middle of our freshman year. He gives me a slight nod of his head, acknowledging me, and I turn my focus back to my brother's text.

I haven't spoken with him since I yelled at him on the phone a few weeks ago after that crappy first day of school. He calls and texts often, but I haven't ever responded. I miss him, but I'm mad at him too.

When I lean over to shove the phone back into my bag, a group of girls pass me as I am bent down and purposely bump into me, knocking me off balance. I catch myself with my hand and when I look up, I see Jenn.

"Hey, freak," she says and her friends bust out laughing at me.

"Don't be a bitch," I hear Ashton snap at her.

Standing up, I watch the girls walk away, and I turn to him and say, "Thanks," in a quiet voice. I wonder why he, let alone anyone, would stick up for the school leper.

"She's turned into such a snob this year," he says, and when I look back at him, I shyly agree.

"Sorry I'm late," Em says out the driver's side window when she pulls up.

Taking my eyes off of Ashton, I grab my bag and tell her, "It's okay," and then slide into the car.

Before she puts the car in drive, Ashton says, "See you Monday."

I don't say anything, and Emily gives me a knowing look. Turning my attention away from her, I notice he isn't standing on the sidewalk anymore. I scan and spot him walking to a white jeep with keys in his hand. I allow happiness to creep inside when I realize that he wasn't waiting for a ride like I was. He has his own car, but he stood with me anyway.

"So, Ashton, huh?" Emily teases.

"Just drive," I tell her and keep quiet as we head home.

We get home, and I go up to my room to shower and work on some of my homework. When I notice that it's almost midnight, I close my books and call it a night. Slipping into bed, I shut off the lamp and pull out my phone, to read before I fall asleep. Before opening my iBooks app, I open up the text that my brother sent earlier. No matter what, I miss him. As mad as I am about how this year is turning out, I still want him here. I type out my response, my first in weeks.

I miss you too. Goodnight.

Clicking out of my texts, I open up Facebook really quick, not really sure why since all it seems to be is another outlet for people to make my life hell. I clear my notifications and notice a Friend Request alert come through. Opening it up, I can't control the smile that creeps across my face. Maybe this could be one of the few good things this year.

Here's to hoping.

I click Accept, and immediately get a Private Message.

Ashton Yates

You're up late. :-)

About the Author

E.K. Blair

USA Today bestselling author and International Amazon bestselling author, E.K. Blair takes her readers on an emotional roller coaster with her *FADING* series. A former first grade teacher with an imagination that runs wild. Daydreaming and zoning out is how she was often found in high school. Blair tends to drift towards everything dark and moody. Give her a character and she will take pleasure in breaking them down, digging into their core to find what lies underneath.

Aside from writing, E.K. Blair finds pleasure in music, drinking her Starbucks in peace, and spending time with her friends. She's a thinker, an artist, a wife, a mom, and everything in between.

Facebook: https://m.facebook.com/EKBlairAuthor
Twitter: @EK_Blair_Author

Unforgettable
(Deleted Scene from *Rotten*)

By
Author J.L. Brooks

"YOU LIKE THAT rough, don't you? Fucking take it." My arms were growing weary from being on all fours, rocking back and forth viciously, as sweat beaded on my brow. A deep growl purred from my throat.

"Come on, you son of a bitch." It was useless. I was exhausted and ready to buckle.

Shane let out a heavy laugh before slapping my ass hard with a leather-clad glove.

"If you can show a stain on the tile that much enthusiasm, I can only imagine what you would do to my cock."

Wiping my arm across my forehead, I smirked while strutting purposefully towards the baby-faced biker that was chalking the tip of his cue.

"Let's see what you can do with that stick, big boy, and maybe you'll get to find out."

His blue eyes glistened and the corners of his sandy brown moustache turned up slightly. He was just a kid. I knew that behind his towering stature of six-six and neatly trimmed facial hair, he was a young buck of twenty-four and new to these parts. His crew was in town for a few weeks and his chopper was a little too shiny. Another indication of his newly inducted status. However, he was sweet, and despite his attempts to act like the other roughnecks, I saw right through him.

The men held their breath each time he opened his mouth, waiting for the moment I dropkicked his ass for treating me so unladylike. He had no idea who either I or my father, Stephen Knox, were; his naiveté made him more endearing.

It was when his crew would come in during the day to talk business that he opened up. More often than not, Shane would wander up to the bar after a bit to harass me and privately show a fragment of his true personality. Underneath the black ball cap worn backwards and dulled leather vest, he spoke of his ex-girlfriend's and the '69 Chevy Camaro he helped rebuild. Rooted in South Dakota via Ohio, he liked to drink beer and ride his bike. He was beautifully uncomplicated and an easy conversationalist. I was quickly developing a crush.

Picking up a stick, I sidled up to the table. "Solids or stripes?"

Taking a drink from his beer, he simply shrugged not caring. Bending over the edge of the table and bracing my wrist against the green felt, I curled my index finger around the cue. Purposely missing two shots, I watched as he set his bottle down and came up behind me. Speaking softly, he wrapped his body around my small frame and guided my fingers into a different position.

Every inch of my flesh caught fire while being pressed into the table. "Hold it like this," he said.

My eyes closed and I savored the feeling as he tried to move me into place.

Breathlessly I responded, "Yes, please."

"Yes, please what?" He sounded confused, but how the fuck he wasn't getting hard over this was beyond me.

Pushing back against his groin, I giggled. "You have no idea how hot this is, do you?"

While enjoying my impromptu pool lesson, I felt another cue slide back and forth between my legs. Shane still had both hands on me, causing me to turn in panic and yelp. I made eye contact with David just as he busted out laughing. Quickly narrowing my eyes, I waited to see if he was jealous. It was remarkable how well we could communicate without saying a word, and I could see David ready to challenge Shane, yet he looked away and headed into the office.

Shane followed him with his eyes until the door closed.

"Do you two have something going on? 'Cuz I'm not one to intrude."

I smiled and reached my hand up along his cheek to feel the coarse hair tickle my fingertips. Shaking my head back and forth, I placed my hand behind his head and drew him closer into a kiss. I had never kissed a man with a beard like this before. The whiskers brushed against my mouth aggressively, a sharp contrast to his soft lips. He tasted as sweet as I knew he really was. With a gentle tongue he began to dance against mine, unhurried and unconcerned with the spectators. Shane moved his hands languidly along my spine before trailing towards my ass and lifting me up effortlessly onto the pool table.

My ankle curled around his calf and raked up and down as the kiss intensified. Lifting off his cap and setting it beside us, his pupils dilated and his cheeks flushed.

"I really like kissing you," I whispered.

"Thank you," he responded back softly.

I wanted to giggle again—he was so adorable—but his fevered lips stopped me and continued to melt any reservations I had. I knew I was acting out because I was safe. Shane would be gone in a few days, and unless he came back into the club, our paths would never cross again.

Reaching his fingers into my hair, he started to massage my scalp as his teeth grazed my bottom lip. I moaned in delight as my legs squeezed his waist tighter. Bystanders be damned if this wasn't one of the hottest moments of my life, and I wasn't about to stop now. If it weren't for the sudden jerk of Shane's lips ripping away from mine, I possibly would have gotten naked right here on the table and let him have his way. This was a strip club after all, and naked women were the standard. He would however be the only lucky bastard that got to touch me. But I wasn't a dancer; fuck, I wasn't even available. Even though I didn't belong to David, I should have known it was only a matter of time before he became territorial over me.

The shouting sounded like a freight train as a sea of blue clothing, black leather, and flying fists surrounded me. The two men towered over the rest of the brawlers, and I feared for Shane knowing who David really was. Jumping off the table to try to stop them, it was only a matter of seconds before I heard the pop and the world went black.

~~~~

I awoke in the hospital with gauze and tape wrapped around my head and small plastic tubes shoved up my nose. I was only able to open one eye, the other swollen shut and covered with a bandage. As I moved my face, the muscles pulled against the medical tape keeping everything in place. Next to me, I could see David sitting in a chair resting, looking as bad as I felt. Blood, source unknown, was spattered across his white t-shirt. It could have been his, mine, or—heaven forbid—Shane's.

I was riddled with guilt thinking about what I caused. I knew better than this.

A soft knock at the door drew my attention away as nurse Julie moved towards the bed. Shaking her head, she turned out my wrist gently while listening to my heartbeat.

"Two generations of Knoxes underneath this roof is more than Las Vegas can handle. Especially when you come dragging the party in with you."

Looking confused, I turned to David, who was now awake. Leaning up in the chair, he nodded his head towards the door.

"Some of the crew is outside waiting for you to wake up, including your cabana boy."

Hissing a little as Julie prodded along my temples, pain began to radiate through my head. Whoever clocked me did it at close range. Although I couldn't imagine one of them gunning for me personally, I was the dumbass trying to break up two giants. Without even looking up from the computer, Julie said exactly what I was thinking.

"Sounds like someone is a little jealous. I have to admit if Toni has a cabana boy, I need to meet him. I should have known that something like that would be the root cause."

Winking back at me, she walked out of the room leaving the two of us alone.

"David, go get them and give me a little time alone, okay? I know the boys aren't supposed to be here. I don't want them catching hell for this, and the club can't afford it either."

He hesitated for a moment before slowly walking out of the room. It made me furious he would attack someone at the club over me. If I were in danger, that would be one thing, but I hadn't been. David returned with the entire crew, including Shane, a short while later. The men took off their hats and bandanas as they entered the room.

Nash, the crew's leader, came up to my side and held my hand for a moment. He wasn't sure what to say, but I could see he was upset by my condition. I squeezed back and laughed.

"So who won the pissing contest?"

Nash smiled back and looked to his men, beaming at Shane. The fight had earned him a new level of respect among the crew for taking on David Stark.

"No one won that fight, Toni. The moment you went down it was over. I will say though it was something else watching him fight off the ice."

He turned to David with a look of reverence, not the animosity I expected. It was interesting watching the men analyze the role of their primitive behaviors. Civil society was still tempered by aggression, and in this world, you kept a strong fist.

Shane was standing against the wall, stoically waiting for his moment to speak. My heart sank as I took in the cuts along his hairline and his blood-stained beard.

"Hey, can you guys give us a few minutes? I'd like to talk to him alone before you take off."

Nash nodded his head and leaned down to kiss my forehead.

"Send word when your daddy wakes up so we can head on back through, okay?"

I smiled sadly, hoping that I would be able to make that call. Biting my lip to keep from crying, I turned to David and tilted my chin towards the door. Reluctantly, he left Shane in the room with me alone, but he knew he had no choice. How many times did he have to walk away from me in a hospital room due to damage he'd caused?

Shane seemed unsure of what to do or say. I had to look like absolute shit because I could see it reflected in his expression. I raised my hand and curled my index finger to bring him closer. I didn't stop until I was able to reach my hands up to his face and rub my thumbs lightly across the battle scars. I could see the dried blood in his beard and my heart sank knowing I was responsible for this wreckage The pain in my head from the tears rushing forward was almost unbearable, yet there was no way to stop them.

"I am so sorry. I didn't mean for this to happen."

My chest rattled from trying to hold it all in, because letting it out hurt more.

"Toni, stop, this isn't your fault. You just got caught up in it. I'm okay. I got a few good swings in. I'm good. You I am worried about. I hate leaving like this."

Somehow, he managed to fit his massive frame onto the small hospital bed and cradled me in his arms. With my head curled into his blue and white flannel shirt, I could smell the desert air permanently embedded in the soft cotton. It was crisp and distinct, calming me immediately.

As he silently moved his thumb across my lips, I knew why I gravitated towards him. He was sweet, gentle, and passionate—nothing like Andrew or David. He was completely masculine, but underneath the rough exterior, he possessed infinite tenderness. Shane had all the qualities I admired in the man just a few floors away. His fingers swept over my arm and down my hands, pulling away as if burned when his palm grazed the diamond rings. Making sure he felt correctly, he picked my hand up and examined it with caution.

"I wondered about these. You're married?"

I nodded my head. "If that's what you call it. On paper, yes; by example, no. Kind of funny you're asking now."

"I normally don't ask questions. So is that why David went ape-shit on me?"

I shook my head no and laughed lightly. "I am sure David assumed if I was going to cross a line, it would be with him. He's a pretty sore loser and used to getting his way."

Shane shifted his body to angle over mine, looking down with contentment, his smile growing smug.

"Yeah, it wasn't until tonight that I found out who you really were. Your daddy is a legend. If I knew you were Knox's daughter, I would have stayed far away."

I tried to smile bravely, but he knew he touched a nerve as soon as my lips began to tremble.

"You wouldn't be the first person to stay away from me. You won't be the last. I liked that you didn't know who I was."

Shaking his head, he breathed out deeply. "Hey, let's talk about something else, 'k?"

Agreeing, I asked, "What do you want to talk about?"

With barely a whisper, he replied, "This."

Soft lips came down over mine, his beard tickling my face in the most delicious way, allowing me to revel in the feelings he evoked one last time. I knew tomorrow he would be nothing more than a ghost on my skin, reminding me why married women shouldn't stray. I wasn't sorry. I wouldn't regret this moment. Or this day. Holding the side of his face, I took him in and sighed.

"Shane, I hope you know that whatever woman captures your heart will be the luckiest one on Earth. If she doesn't respect that, I have no hesitation in shoving my boot up a bitch's ass. Besides, I have learned to recognize something extraordinary when it comes my way, because it happens so rarely. You are one of those things."

I don't think anyone could smile bigger if they tried. His face flushed slightly from embarrassment, reminding me how charming he was. Covering my mouth softly one last time, his silky tongue parted my lips, before aggressively showing me how sensual he could be too. Only I would be lying in a hospital bed, making out with a hot, young biker I met in my daddy's strip club. Before walking out the door, he picked up my hand again and looked at my ring finger.

"The moment that comes off, I better be the first one you call."

Nodding my head with a smile, it was a nice thought that would provide many more down the road.

"Hey, Shane, am I enthusiastic enough for you?"

We both chuckled as he left.

David swooped in immediately after with a sour look on his face, shifting the mood. I grabbed the remote to raise my bed up into a better sitting position.

"See what being a bully did? Nothing good came of it. Shane didn't deserve your outburst anymore than I deserve to be lying in this bed. When are you going to understand your actions are like a ripple, they go out and affect everything around them?"

David's face became even more somber than it already was. I knew what was going through his mind, and he didn't need me chastising him right now. I can't imagine what it was like for him to have put me here. He needed to know I saw that too.

"I'm sorry. It's my fault, not just yours. I got carried away. I should have stopped when you teased me with the pool cue. I was being a bitch."

He looked at me without saying a word. We were fire and gasoline arguing over who burned down the house. Scooting over, I patted the bedside next to me. If Shane could fit, David could as well, but he didn't need to know how I knew that. Before getting into the bed, he removed the bloody shirt and shivered in the already freezing room.

"Fuck it's cold. Warm me up, woman!"

I knew when he called me *woman*, it was going to be okay. Pressed against his bare skin and inhaling deeply to discover what came to mind, my brain instantly came to a very different conclusion. David was the base to which I compared all others. He did not remind me of my father. Vapors of musk penetrated my senses, the odor of sweat induced by fear. Lust pooled in my veins as my heart rate increased. I started to feel as if I was losing my mind. I craved David in an unnatural way. I ceased to function properly in his presence; rational thinking was only a theory in my textbooks. This is why I couldn't allow myself to cross the line with him—I would never come back. Yet with each breath, I feared I was already gone.

About the Author

J.L. Brooks

JL Brooks is a former columnist turned novelist. What started as a bet changed her entire course in life. With a passion for adventure, she believes everyone has a story to tell. Chances are she will try to convince you to tell yours.

Blog: http://www.authorjlbrooks.blogspot.com
Twitter: @authorjlbrooks
Facebook: http://www.facebook.com/thewenchlab

Other Novels by J.L. Brooks
Distractions
Rotten

Love is Blind

By

Claire Contreras

I DON'T HAVE a traumatizing story about being raped by a priest, stepfather or neighbor. I am who I am and I won't allow somebody to make excuse for me. No pastor can preach that I'm wrong because of who I am. No scientist can tell me that I'm chemically imbalanced because of who I choose to be with.

Aren't we all wrong?

All sinners?

Don't we all live unforgivable lives, at least in thought?

I was an outcast, ridiculed by the masses of "cool kids" for years—I was too gay looking for the "gangster kids", too normal looking for the "emo kids" and too much of a loser for the "cool kids". I went through what I considered to be hell when I was in high school. That'll happen when you're an overweight gay kid growing up in a time when bullying was shrugged off as something that was bound to happen.

"Move, fat ass," was a favorite jab of theirs. It didn't help that both of my sisters were as skinny as freaking Twiggy. And it really didn't help that one of them, the nicer one, was living with our father in Orlando, while I was stuck with the Wicked Bitch of the North, Roxana.

"Please, Rob, just act normal for once," Roxana scolded as we walked beside each other in school. I turned to face her and saw that she was speaking to me through a fake smile as she nodded and waved at the guys on the football team.

"I am acting normal, Roxy. I'm just not kissing up to every fucking girl in the school or trying to get laid by every guy who looks at me," I replied, dishing it back to her.

Roxy turned to me, her eyes feral. "Shut up. Maybe if you went on a date with Daisy or Brenda you would be happy… normal."

I scoffed. My sister damn well knew that I wasn't interested in women, she just refused to accept it. Wicked Bitch of the North, I tell you. She was worse than my mother, who just hoped she was wrong about me. Worse than my father, who mostly judged me because I chose not to play any sports growing up, preferring to stay home and cook new recipes. It's not like I had no friends or anything, but the ones I did have they didn't want to accept. The sad part about it was that instead of letting it roll off me, I let their judgmental eyes and words bother me. All I wanted was acceptance, that's what I craved, what I needed. Love was an extra perk; something that I would take if given to me freely.

"Still, you should try to make some friends," Roxy said beside me, flipping her hair over her shoulder. "And try to lose some weight! You're an embarrassment." She skipped off and giddily ran into the arms of the captain of the football team, and richest guy in school. I rolled my eyes at my sister's back and went on to my class with my head down.

Maybe I was an embarrassment to my family. My father was a hard worker, he had a window company that secured all the big accounts in Miami and was doing well for himself. My mother was a stay at home mom; she always had the house clean and food on the table when we got home. My sister Roxana had high aspirations of becoming a model, and as driven and ruthless as she was, she would probably achieve them. My other sister, the nicer one, Mireya, was in Orlando with my father for the week, trying to secure an acting gig. And there I was, gay and fat ass Rob, trying to survive another day. Trying to find myself in a sea full of lost souls. At least I had that going for me, I knew that beneath our successes, we were all lost souls.

My sister Roxana graduated that year and left me to roam the halls of high school by myself the next. She left to Europe that summer of 1982 and I felt lighter-only two judgmental eyes left in my household with me. Mireya never got a job as an actress the summer before, but she found something she loved more-dressing them. Much to my father's dismay, Mireya moved to New York City with a boyfriend and got a job dressing up Broadway actors. I'm not sure what my father was more upset about: the fact that she gave up on her acting dreams or that moved in with a guy before getting married.

"Mireya, act on Broadway!" my father would tell her. To which my sister would respond, "Please. If I'm not on the big screen, I might as well be nobody." Those were my sisters, soaring high while I was a loser trying to figure it all out.

That school year was the worst. You would think being a senior would put you at a certain level with your peers since you'd put up with their shit for three previous years. Nope, not the case for me. Brad, the head asshole was still slamming me into the lockers whenever I passed by just because I was wearing a Star Wars shirt and he clearly didn't understand the movie.

I started hanging out with the oddities. You know, losers that are too much of losers to even sit in the loser area during lunch. The people that are so invisible that you don't see them until after you run into them? Yeah, I dubbed those "the oddities". I joined Year Book Club and was glad to see how happy my father was that I was finally going to football games.

"You came around," he'd say. "Next season, baseball!"

I would smile and fist pump an excited "yeah!" Judging from the way his eyebrows pulled in, that was probably the wrong thing to do. I never bothered to tell him that the reason I went to the games was because I had to take pictures of the jocks to put in the school year book. One day, Brad cornered me in the bathroom after a game and put his fist in my face.

"I know you're a queer! Noemi told me you wouldn't even get to second base with her. She says you didn't want to touch her tits. What kind of guy are you?" he sneered. "Don't come into the bathroom when I'm using it! I don't want you looking at my wiener when I'm taking a piss," he said, his voice threateningly low.

I'm not sure what prompted me to do it, but I pushed him off of me. For the first time in four years, I finally pushed him away from me.

"Nobody wants to see your wiener, Brad! And stop calling me a queer!" I spat.

I got my ass beat that day—bad. I ended up in the hospital for broken ribs, a broken nose, and two black eyes. I had two friends at the time, real friends anyway, Mike and Carlos, and they were the only ones that came to visit. Some of my teachers sent Get Well Soon cards and balloons. Mike, who was president of the year book and always carrying around a polaroid camera, took pictures of me at the hospital and one night I got this idea that maybe I should plaster them all around school and let everyone know what a fucking bastard Brad was.

I juggled the idea for a while. On the one hand I thought I could prevent others from being treated this way, maybe we could all form a big alliance against the bullies. A pack of ants is more powerful than one cricket, after all... right? But Brad was on the football team, honor roll student, all around good kid on paper. Would teachers believe me? Would kids have my back or would they watch while he and his friends beat me down again for outing them? Bullying wasn't spoken about like it is now a days. It wasn't made a big deal of. Kids were just "roughing each other up", parents would argue. "Your son needs to learn how to defend himself," some would say. Police still went to the hospital and asked questions, but giving them information as to what happened was as good as writing it on a paper and ripping it up.

I cringed from my broken bones as I made an effort to sit up and use the bathroom. I caught a glimpse of myself in the mirror across from me, and was shocked by what I saw. I looked completely deformed to my own eyes. When had I become the guy that took the beatings? When had I become this loser, this pathetic excuse for a person? Maybe it was my fault that I was overweight, although it ran in my family and I didn't eat more food than everyone else at the table, but maybe I could work on that. Maybe it was my fault that I had acne and had to wear braces. But I was a good person, I helped others, even those that never helped back. Wasn't karma supposed to be on my side? Wasn't it supposed to reciprocate the good I did for others? Tears ran down my face, my swollen eyes throbbed painfully as I shut them.

I heard the door open, but didn't look. I was ashamed for my family and I knew it would be one of them. I couldn't bear to look at them, couldn't bear to let them see what I'd become, what I looked like for being a lesser man than I should have been. I stiffened when I felt myself cocoon in their arms.

"I'm so sorry, Rob," I heard my sister, Mireya say. I could only nod.

"Me too, Herm," my sister Roxy cooed. My body trembled in sobs at the sound of her pet name for me, one she hadn't used in so long, I thought she'd forgotten about it.

"What did I do?" I sobbed. "What did I do other than be me? Am I really that horrible?"

My sisters both began to cry, squeezing me tighter in their arms until I yelped from the pain. They both backed away and I opened my eyes as they were wiping away their tears. I looked at them, my two beautiful sisters, not one prettier than the other. They had different body types, Roxana was tall and thin and Mireya was shorter with wider hips and a bigger butt. They're faces were angelic, though, and neither of them had zits like I did. I wondered what they saw when they looked at me. Did they see the same ugly monster that everyone else seemed to see?

"You're a lovely soul, Robert," Mireya whispered hoarsely. "And whoever can't see that is a moron."

Roxana sat beside me and clasped both hands around my unbroken one. Her golden brown eyes looked straight into mine. "People are scared of different, they don't understand it. I know this now, I've seen it, lived it. There are many others like you... and they're happy." She didn't have to tell me what that meant, I knew she was referring to gays without actually saying it. I could tell she was still weirded out with the idea. "You know what? A lot of the designers I work with are... and they have..." She cleared her throat and leaned into me so that only I could hear her. "They have boyfriends and they kiss and everything! In front of everyone!" I could tell she was still shocked by this, but then she did the oddest thing, something I would've never expected her, of all people to do-she smiled. "And they're happy, Rob. They're happy being together. And their love is beautiful."

Tears filled both of our eyes as she said those words and I swallowed past the lump in my throat. "Thank you, Roxy."

She shook her head. "Don't thank me. I'm sorry for being so closed-minded. God, I'm such a bitch sometimes."

"You're always a bitch," Mireya chimed in, making us all laugh a little.

"But we love you," I said.

After my sisters and parent's left later that night, I sent Mike a beeper message, hoping he would go and see me. When he did, I asked him for all of the Polaroid photos and wrote a small message on each of them. I asked Mike to tape them to everybody's locker at school-everywhere that people would see them. Pictures of me, lying on a hospital bed all bruised up—all broken. My message was clear and I accepted the fact that maybe they would come after me again. Maybe they would beat me again and maybe the next time I wouldn't be as lucky.

Going back to school was scary. I thought for sure if one of those guys didn't kill me as I walked through the doors, I would die of a heart attack, because that's how fast my heart was beating. Nonetheless, I pushed my shoulders back, channeling a little piece of Roxy, and walked down the hall. The first pair of eyes met mine and gasped. I braced myself for a slew of hateful words, but they never came. Still, my heart clenched. Then I saw Brad. He was standing with a group of football players, some of them had aided in my beating. He stepped away from them and crossed his arms over his chest shooting daggers at me with his piercing blue eyes, but he never said a word.

Later that day, I saw him again outside of third period and this time he brushed past me, hitting me slightly with his shoulder. "You're gonna pay for that, Robbie. One day, you're gonna pay."

I tilted away from him and looked him in the eye, we were except this time I wasn't scared of him anymore. This time, if he pushed me and I pushed back, I was going to do it with no fear-nothing holding me back. I was never one to embrace violence, I'd seen enough of that at home to know that I didn't want to play with the monster that rage could turn people into, but this is one case I was willing to take a chance in. I was doing it for everybody-all of the losers being made fun of, all of the hate being thrown at undeserving people, and him. I was doing it for Brad and others like him. I was doing it because he needed to see what he was doing to me, to us. He needed to know that it wasn't right, that it wasn't fair. And I think in that moment of us looking at each other, sizing each other up in that empty hallway, he saw that.

He looked away first, then looked back at me. "You're still a pussy," he said before he walked away. I accepted his hateful words knowing that he was really calling himself that. That day I realized that Brad was fighting his own battle, his own self-hatred probably getting the best of him as he acted out on others. And that was the day I learned to let it go. I gulped down the anticipation that was lodged in my throat and walked away feeling free. Feeling light and hopeful.

I knew life would bring many more, probably much worse trials my way, and I knew that I would take the mean blows as gracefully as I could. Everybody is fighting their own demons. We all have a darkness that threatens to take over our thoughts, our feelings, and our lives. It's up to us to choose whether or not we'll let it win. It's easy to give in and succumb to it. It's easy to say, "I'm so sick of this shit. It's not worth it anymore. I'm not worth it." But you are. We all are. I've made it this far and it hasn't always been easy, in fact, it's been hard as hell. Some days I wake up not wanting to get out of bed, not wanting to see or hear anybody. But that would be easy. Locking myself up in my shell would be the easy thing to do, and over the years I've learned that easy things are usually not the best things. It's the things that take time that end up being most gratifying. Life is like fine wine, you have to take your time fermenting yourself. You have to learn the great qualities you have before you can accept others to see them. And sometimes that takes a while, learning your good qualities. Shit, it might take forever. Lord knows it's taken me forty-five years and I'm still learning. But that's the beauty of life: you live, you learn.

I thought bullying was over in high school, and a great part of it was, but I was bullied in college sometimes. Not in the same way, though. I was also bullied by my father when I decided to tell him that I was gay. He threatened to disown me, and he did. It was a rough period in my life, one where I felt alone, despite my sisters and mother being there for me. I was in my late twenties and still felt like I needed his acceptance. Unfortunately, he died before he could give it to me. I've learned to be okay with that, he didn't know any better and I can't blame him.

Now, at forty-five, I look around and see my small group of friends and family. As tears threaten, I squeeze down on the hand that holds mine and look at his handsome face. It's been a long and bumpy ride for my fiancé Victor and I. Some people give us weird looks when we hold hands in the street and others preach that our love is wrong, but when I look into the eyes of the man that accepts me and loves me, I know there's nothing about us that is wrong. When the door opens, I hear my family stand up behind us and cheer, knowing that Victor and I are about to make our union official. My heart skips a beat as Victor draws small circles over my palm and links our fingers together.

"I'm here to marry Mr. Robert Casas and Victor White," a deep voice says, drawing our attention to it.

The officiate walks and stands before us, he looks at our joined hands with a smile before his eyes lock with mine and then Victor's. He starts the ceremony by speaking about love and kindness. He tells us a personal story of his own and the way he used to bully a gay kid as a teenager. He says, as he looks at us, how sorry he is for what he'd done and how he makes it up to the bullied kid every day of his life. It turns out that the kid he used to bully is his younger brother and the only family he has left.

"Love knows no boundaries, because love is free," he says.

I've learned that life is life a fucked up merry go round. You think you know where you're going, you think you've got it all figured out until one day BOOM, it hits you that you don't know shit. Nobody does. You don't know if that kid you're making fun of is going to end up hiring you to work for his company in thirty years. Or if the one that makes fun of you is going to end up scrubbing your floors.

Things change, people change, but there will always be constants: love and hate. They've been there from the beginning of time, and they'll continue to be there long after we're all gone. One of those two will make your heart full and fulfilled, the other will tear you down with time. Choose wisely.

"You may now kiss your spouse," the officiate says to end the ceremony

Victor and I turn our bodies towards each other and hold hands. In his eyes I see the only things I need to see, the things that break the shackles I once confined myself in: truth, love, and hope. We close our eyes as our lips lock in a soft kiss as the lovely melodic cheers from our friends and family fill our ears and in that moment we're sounded by so much love that I know hate could never stand a chance against us.

My name is Robert Casas, and this is my story.

About the Author

Claire Contreras

Claire Contreras graduated with her BA in Psychology from Florida International University. She lives in Miami, Florida with her husband, two little boys, and three dogs.

Her favorite pastimes are: daydreaming, writing, and reading.

She has been described as a random, sarcastic, crazy girl with no filter.

Life is short, and it's more bitter than sweet, so she tries to smile as often as her face allows. She enjoys stories with happy endings, because life is full of way too many unhappy ones.

Facebook: http://www.facebook.com/ccontrerasbooks
Twitter: @claricon
Web: clairecontreras.com

BEAUTIFUL

By

Kelly Elliott

Editor Jovana Shirley

CHAPTER ONE
Skylar

THE MOMENT I saw him walk into my English class, I had to catch my breath. That was twice now that I'd seen him. He was breathtakingly handsome. All of the girls immediately started whispering, praying he would notice one of them.

I sat in the back right corner as far away from everyone as I could. There was no chance of him noticing me.

Then, our eyes met. I instantly felt my cheeks blush when he smiled. *Is he smiling at Jenny or at me?* Jenny was a beautiful blonde-haired, blue-eyed cheerleader, who pretty much just had to look at a guy, and he would fall for her.

Mrs. Hathaway grinned at him and then told him to pick a seat. He turned and looked directly at me again. My heart started pounding so loud that I was sure everyone could hear it.

"I heard he moved here from New Mexico. He wanted to play football for a Texas high school, so a college would notice him," Jenny said as she started to mess with her hair.

"What's his name?" Mary Beth asked.

Jenny shrugged her shoulders. "Who cares? Look at that body." Jenny jumped up and moved over a seat right before he got to her table.

For some reason, my heart was breaking. *How stupid of me to even think he would notice me. Even if he did, everyone would tell him to stay away from me.*

He passed by her table and walked right up to mine.

Oh. My. God.

"Hey, I'm Wyatt. Mind if I sit here with you?" he asked with a drop-dead gorgeous smile that melted my heart.

I smiled. "No, not at all. It's open."

He sat down, and I glanced over toward Jenny and her posse. They were all just staring at me. Trying not to look at them, I moved my gaze up toward Mrs. Hathaway, who was smiling the biggest smile I'd ever seen.

Mrs. Hathaway was also my next-door neighbor. She was one of the youngest teachers at my high school. She hated the way I got treated by other students, and she was always defending me. I was worried that one of these days, it would come back to haunt her.

Jenny stood up and walked over toward my table. "Um... hey there. Wyatt, is it?"

Wyatt turned and looked at Jenny. "Yes, ma'am, it is."

"I think you would be more comfortable sitting at my table." She leaned over and flashed her breasts as I rolled my eyes. "If you know what I mean," she said with a purr.

Wyatt smiled at her and looked at me, giving me an is-she-for-real look. He turned back around. "Thanks, but I'm rather comfortable here."

Jenny stood up and looked stunned. "What?"

"Thank you, but no, thank you. I'm fine right where I am."

"Jenny, please take your seat now," Mrs. Hathaway called out.

I sat there for forty-five minutes, trying to pay attention to what was being said about *Romeo and Juliet*, but all I could really focus on was the drop-dead gorgeous guy who kept bumping his knee into mine every five minutes and apologizing.

Don't get used to it, Skylar. The moment he finds out that hanging around you is committing social suicide, he won't be talking to you… let alone, sitting next to you tomorrow.

Right before class was over, Wyatt leaned over and bumped my shoulder. I looked at him and smiled.

"I was wondering if I might be able to borrow your notes during class tomorrow, just to get caught up. Mrs. Hathaway told me to ask someone."

"Oh, um… yeah, sure. Of course! You can take them tonight if you want. I won't need them. Our next test isn't until next week," I said as I handed him my notebook.

"Awesome! Thanks so much. By the way, I told you mine. Are you going to tell me yours?"

I shook my head, confused by what he was asking. "Tell you my what?"

The moment he smiled that crooked smile, I thought I was going to die. He had a dimple in his left cheek. *Oh dear Lord.*

He laughed as he shook his head. "Your name, angel. What's your name?"

"Oh!" I said with a small laugh. "Skylar. Skylar Woods."

He smiled bigger as he reached for my notebook. When his hand brushed against mine, I wanted to let out a gasp. My whole hand felt like small bolts of lightning had just gone through it. He looked down at our hands and then looked up and captured my eyes. His eyes clearly showed he'd felt the same thing I felt.

As the bell rang, he slowly moved his hand off of mine and smiled. "It was a pleasure meeting you, Skylar. I hope I see you around."

"Same here, Wyatt. Welcome to Marble Falls," I said with a smile.

He stood up and started to walk off. I noticed Mike Barnes and a few other football players stopped him to introduce themselves. They must all know that he was here to play football.

I glanced up toward Mrs. Hathaway as I gathered my things. She smiled and gave me a wink. I gave her a weak smile back, knowing after the football players all started telling Wyatt about my past, he would try to quickly distance himself from me.

CHAPTER TWO
Wyatt

I WASN'T ABLE to stop thinking about Skylar. I'd never seen such a beautiful girl before. That curly, long brown hair and the bluest of blue eyes were burned into my mind. The moment I saw her in the parking lot that morning, I'd known I needed to get to know her.

Then, when I saw her in my English class, something had happened. It was something that had never happened to me before. My heart had started pounding, my hands had started sweating, and I'd felt like I couldn't catch my breath.

I walked into the lunchroom with Mike and a few other guys from the football team. I was really surprised that they were accepting me so quickly. From what my father was told, the coach had watched my games from my old high school. I was probably the best high school quarterback in New Mexico, and this high school needed a good quarterback.

I glanced over and saw that girl, Jenny, waving at me like a fool. When I looked away, I saw Skylar sitting at a table with another girl and a guy. They were sitting alone at a huge table while everyone else was crowded around two tables.

"Dude, get your lunch, and then come sit with us. Just watch out for Jenny. She's already tried to get her claws into you once," Mike said with a smile.

I laughed and shook my head. "Thanks, dude, but I think I'm going to go sit with Skylar."

Mike's smile faded. "Skylar? Skylar Woods?"

"Yep."

"Ah, dude... I get that you're new and everything, so I'm gonna let that one slide. You can't hang out with Skylar."

I instantly felt anger boiling in my blood. *Holy shit. What is going on with me? Why am I getting so mad?* "Why not?"

"Um... well, Skylar is, um..." Mike looked back over toward Skylar and then back at me.

I stood there, shaking my head. *Holy shit. Does this guy even know why he's not supposed to like this girl?*

"Jacob, Wyatt wants to know why he can't hang out with Skylar."

Jacob laughed. "Dude, Skylar is... tainted if you know what I mean."

I just looked at him. "No. I don't know what you mean."

Jacob let out a sigh and looked around. "She has an older brother who's in the Marines. He was always worried about Skylar because she was so innocent yet beyond beautiful. She had no idea how many guys wanted to be with her. While her brother was gone, he asked his best friend, Charlie, to 'watch over' Skylar. Well, he watched over her all right. Charlie ended up talking her into going to a movie with him one night. Her mom and dad didn't have a problem with it since they knew Charlie, and he was their son's best friend. Well, he had sex with her. Next day, he bragged all over town about what a good piece of ass she was. Problem was that Sky said he'd raped her." Jacob stared over toward Skylar with an almost sad look in his eyes.

My heart started pounding, and I balled my fists together.

"Sky's brother came home and found out about it. He beat the shit out of Charlie before he had to leave to go to Iraq. Charlie ended up telling everyone that Skylar had lied and that she had begged him to have sex with her. Most everyone took Charlie's side, and Sky ended up with... well, with a bad reputation. Most of the girls were jealous of Sky, so they took off with the story Charlie had told, and they spread it around like wildfire."

I looked at this kid and shook my head. "Did you know her well before this happened?"

Jacob glanced down at the floor and nodded his head. "Yeah, I, um… I used to date her."

"You ever have sex with her?" I asked.

He looked up at me, shocked. "Jesus Christ, dude. I'm not going to talk to you about that. Sky's not some tramp who just fucks and moves on. We dated. It was different."

"Yet, you stand here and tell me she's 'tainted.' That's pretty fucked-up. Sounds to me like the only problem Skylar had was a bunch of asshole friends who turned on her when she needed them the most."

Jacob just stood there and stared at me.

Mike shook his head. "Dude, you don't get it. Charlie said she'd begged him to fuck her."

Jacob glared at Mike. "Shut the fuck up, Mike. If Wyatt wants to talk to Skylar, let him. We'll see you on the football field, dude."

They walked over toward the table where Jenny was. She watched me as I headed over to Skylar's table. The next thing I knew, Jenny was standing in front of me, blocking me.

"Hey, there. Why don't you come and sit with us? Get to know some of the cheerleaders and other football players," she said as she bounced around, making sure her breasts were moving all over the place.

I wanted so badly to tell her to push off, but I just smiled at her. "Thanks, but I actually think I'm going to sit and get to know Skylar."

Jenny turned and looked at Skylar who was deep in conversation with her friend. "Really? Skylar? I don't think you understand, Wyatt. Skylar is a bit of a… whore. Like, if we could, we would plaster a big red A across her chest," she said with a laugh.

What a bitch. "Wow…"

She nodded her head and smiled. "I know. Good thing I warned you, huh?" She turned and looked over at Skylar and then back at me.

"No, that's not what I was wowing," I said as I walked past Jenny and made my way over toward Skylar.

Skylar's friend noticed me first and smiled. I smiled back as I sat down on the same side of the bench where Skylar was sitting, and I started to slide over, closer to her.

The guy that was sitting at the table was good-looking. He was a big guy, so he must be athletic. I smiled, and he just looked at me. He kind of resembled Skylar.

"Hey," I said as Skylar turned and looked at me.

Her face turned ten shades of red.

"Um… hey," she said as she glanced around.

The kid sitting across from me was looking me up and down. "I take it your friends haven't talked to you about my sister yet?"

Ah, another overprotective brother. I smiled and nodded my head. "Oh yeah. I've heard all their rumors. Funny thing about me is that I actually like to get to know someone before I label them." I reached my hand across the table and introduced myself. "Wyatt Smith. I take it you're Skylar's younger brother?"

He reached out and shook my hand. "Only by five minutes," he said as he looked at Skylar and winked.

"Twins. Oh, wow," I said as I looked at Skylar and smiled.

The blonde friend reached across the table toward me and smiled again. "Hey, I'm Michelle, Sky's best friend and this idiot's girlfriend."

I laughed and turned back at Skylar.

"My brother, Mitch," Skylar said.

I looked at Mitch and then Michelle with a grin. "Nice to meet you both."

For the rest of lunch, we all sat there and talked. Mitch loosened up a lot, and I found out he played football and baseball. Michelle and Skylar had been best friends since kindergarten. I also learned that Mitch and Skylar's older brother, nicknamed Skip, was in the Marines, and he would be home on leave during Christmas.

Skylar had a beautiful laugh, but she seemed to be really uncomfortable around me. I couldn't tell if she was just a shy girl or if it was because of what had happened to her with the label everyone had placed on her.

When the bell rang, I asked her what class she had next.

She rolled her eyes. "Calculus."

My heart slammed in my chest. "I do, too."

She smiled. "Oh yeah? Cool."

"Can I walk with you?"

She stopped and looked around. "Um… sure. I mean, if you want to."

We talked all the way to class about how much she hated calculus, but she was trying her best to keep her grades up. Her parents were pretty hard on her about keeping a B-average and above in all her classes.

"I'm great at it. I love it. Let me know if you ever need any help." I gave her a wink.

She smiled and then dropped out of sight. I watched as she fell to the ground. I looked up and saw Jenny and another girl walking by.

They both laughed before Jenny said, "Oh, sorry, strumpet."

I leaned down and tried to help Skylar up. She pushed my hand away, and I could see tears building in her eyes.

"I'm fine." She stood up and started walking away at a fast pace.

"Skylar, wait."

She walked into the classroom and made her way to the very back.

Does she sit in the back of every classroom? Alone?

Jenny stood up and grabbed my arm. "Empty seat here." She wiggled her eyebrows up and down.

"No, thanks." I made my way over toward Skylar.

She was looking out the window, but she moved over a little when I sat down. I swore I thought she was crying.

For some reason, the idea of her crying broke my heart in two, and I never wanted to see her cry again.

CHAPTER THREE
Skylar

IT TOOK EVERYTHING out of me not to look at him during calculus. I glanced over toward Jenny. *I hate her. I can't even believe she was my best friend or that I was ever a part of their stupid cheerleading squad. I hate them all.*

As soon as the bell rang, I jumped up and made my way out of the classroom. I practically ran to my locker. When I opened it up, a note fell out, and I reached down and picked it up.

Really, Skylar? Do you really think someone as attractive as Wyatt would ever be interested in the school tramp? You're not even beautiful enough for Charlie to want you. Might as well give up now.

Just seeing his name made me want to throw up. I looked around, but no one was watching me. I ripped up the note and threw it back into my locker as I reached for my car keys.

I never skipped school—*ever*. But I just couldn't stand to stay here another minute.

I decided to go to the nurse. I told her I was feeling really sick. I never asked to go home, so I wasn't surprised when she let me sign out without calling my mom or dad.

I got in my car and drove out to the lake. It was my place to clear my head and get all the hate out of my heart. I reached into my shirt and pulled out my heart necklace that Skip had given to me.

"Anytime you need me, Sky… hold on to this necklace, and I'll be with you."

I felt the tears burning in my eyes. I pulled in, parked, got out, and sat on the hood of my car. *Why? Why did this happen to me?*

I'd begged my parents to let me go to another school, but my father had said that I had to face my fears and stand up for myself, or they would always brand me as something I wasn't. Only problem was that no matter how many people had tried to defend me, Charlie's parents would somehow get to them and convince them I was the one lying. They couldn't have their son branded with a bad reputation as a rapist.

Oh my god, I was so stupid for trusting him.

I felt my cell phone vibrate in my back pocket. I took it out to see a text from Mitch, asking where I was. I replied back, telling him I left school early because I needed some fresh air.

I turned my iPod on as I leaned back and slowly felt myself letting go of everything—every fear, hurtful word, painful memory. Each disappeared with every breath I took until I fell asleep, so I could forget for a while.

While I was dressed in a beautiful gown, Wyatt twirled me around. We laughed as he looked at me with such love in his eyes.

I never wanted to wake up from this dream—ever.

~~~~

"Skylar?"

I heard his sweet voice calling out for me. *This is the best dream ever.*

"Skylar. You're going to get sunburned, angel."

I just wanted to feel his lips on mine. I wanted to know what it would be like to have someone kiss me with love and passion instead of lust and greed.

Then, I felt my skin burning on my arm.

"Skylar. Please wake up."

I snapped my eyes open and sat up as I pulled my earbuds out of my ears. I was looking directly at Wyatt. *What in the hell is he doing here? Who told him where to find me?*

"Did you follow me here?" I asked as I slid down the hood of my car and backed away from him.

He looked so confused, and then he took a few steps back.

He thinks I'm scared of him. Oh shit.

"Um… no, of course not. I found this place a few days ago, and I fell in love with it. It's a good place to come and study… to just relax. I didn't even know it was you until I walked up closer to see if you were all right. Your face is sunburned. How long have you been out here, angel?"

I just stared at him. *Why does he keep calling me angel?* I shook my head to clear my thoughts. "I, um… I'm not sure. I was listening to my favorite song and I guess I fell asleep."

Wyatt smiled and asked, "What's your favorite song?"

"Um, Christina Aguilera's 'Beautiful'. What time is it?"

"It's five."

Oh no! Oh shit! I pushed past him and opened up my car door.

"Hey, where are you off to in such a rush?"

I stopped and looked at him. "Work! I work at Pizza Mia. Sorry, Wyatt. I have to go, or I'm going to be late." I jumped in my car and raced to work. *Thank God I keep an extra uniform in my car.*

Just when I thought my day couldn't get any worse, I walked into work to find Jenny, Michelle, and Rachael sitting at a booth. I passed them and ran to the back to change. I clocked in with one minute to spare.

"Do you want me to take their table? They know that's your booth."

I nodded my head and smiled at Eva. She was a sweetheart of a lady and one of the few people in this town who actually believed me about Charlie.

Once Eva walked over to take their order, I heard Jenny ask, "What section is Skylar's?"

"Her section is full. Are you going to order or what?"

I heard the front door open, and the bell rang. I looked up and saw Wyatt walking in. *What in the hell?* He looked at me and smiled. I couldn't help but smile back at him. *Shit! There's just something about him that draws me to him.* As he walked up to me, his smile grew bigger, and I noticed people were staring.

"Hey," he said as he sat down at the bar.

I smiled and walked over to one of my tables to take their order. The whole time I felt Jenny's eyes just piercing me.

Why is Wyatt doing this? Doesn't he realize how they're going to harass me for this?

For two hours, while I was running around, working, and trying to avoid Jenny, Wyatt was talking to Mr. Jones, one of our regulars, about World War II. Jenny attempted to talk to Wyatt once, but she was quickly bored with his conversation about war. When she got up and went back over with her friends, Wyatt looked at me and winked. I had to giggle because he really didn't like Jenny at all. After getting tired of waiting for Wyatt to stop talking, Jenny and her friends finally decided to leave.

When the place started to clear out and Mr. Jones couldn't keep his eyes open a second longer, Eva told me to take off.

I clocked out and walked up to Wyatt with a smile. "Hey."

He laughed and smiled that panty-melting smile of his. *Good Lord, that smile about knocked me to my knees.*

"May I take you out for coffee?" he asked as he reached out for my hand.

My heart started pounding.

"Let me take you out for a movie, Sky."

I started to shake my head, and Wyatt must have noticed how freaked out I was.

"I mean, not on a date… just as friends. I'll follow you there in your car… you don't have to drive with me or anything."

He knows everything. I wanted to crawl in a hole and die. My brain clearly wasn't thinking tonight. Before I knew it, I was agreeing to meet him at the coffee shop.

As we walked out of the pizza shop, I noticed people staring at us. I looked around and saw two girls whispering something to one another as one glared at me like I was a piece of trash.

"Maybe this isn't such a good idea," I said as we got outside.

"Skylar, you can't let what other people say about you run your life. Please come have coffee with me. Please."

I smiled as I nodded my head. "I'll meet you there in five minutes."

I got to my car and called my mom. "Hey, Mom. Um… is it okay if I meet a friend for coffee for just a bit?"

Silence.

"Mom?"

"A friend? A girl friend or a guy friend?"

I sucked in a deep breath of air and slowly let it out. "A guy, Mom, but he's new. He's offering to help me in calculus, so it's nothing. Besides, Jenny has her sights on him."

My mother laughed. "Well, it's nice of him to ask you and to offer to help."

I heard the excitement in her voice. My parents knew I was teased at school, but I never let them know how bad it really was. I'd made Mitch swear that he wouldn't tell them. My father had had a heart attack not long after he found out I was raped, and he didn't need the added stress.

As I pulled up and parked, I looked into the window. Wyatt was already there, and the waitress was flirting with him. I leaned my head on the steering wheel.

"Shit! What in the hell am I doing?"

I looked back up and just stared at him. He was breathtaking with his dark brown hair and the greenest of green eyes. He had the kind of hair that Michelle called "just fucked" hair—all messy but hot as hell. If I had to guess, I would say he was about five feet ten inches. He was built, really built—more so than Skip.

He looked out the window and saw me sitting in my car. He frowned for just a second before smiling and waving.

I reached over and grabbed my purse and took a deep breath. *Here we go. Let's see how this turns out.*

CHAPTER FOUR
Wyatt

I'D NEVER IN my life met anyone like Skylar. She was beautiful and funny, and she had the most positive outlook on life, even after everything she'd been through.

"Dreams for after high school?"

She smiled. "To leave Marble Falls... and never look back. I'd like to go to the University of Texas. Get my degree in history. I love history."

"Teacher?"

"Nah, probably law." She slowly looked away. She glanced at the time and then turned back to me with a smile. "I guess I should probably head home. My parents might be worried about me."

I jumped up and started to walk her out to her car. I wanted nothing more than to take her in my arms and hold her to let her know what it was like to have someone care about her.

"Do you work every day?" I asked right before we got to her car.

"Not every day. I've been having a hard time in calculus, so my parents are making me cut back on some hours. We have a big test coming up, so..."

I smiled as I looked into her beautiful blue eyes. She seemed so strong on the outside, but her eyes were so lost. "I'll help you study. Meet me here tomorrow. What time works for you?"

She let out a small laugh. "How about right after school? I don't work tomorrow."

"Perfect! I'll meet you here, angel." I almost reached down to kiss her on the cheek before I caught myself.

She smiled and got in her car. I watched her drive off until I couldn't see her car anymore.

I smiled as I walked back to my car. *What is it about her that makes my stomach do twists and turns?*

~~~~

Skylar and I had been meeting at the coffee shop for over a few weeks now. When she had to work, I would go and sit in Pizza Mia and wait for her to get off. It wasn't lost on me that all the people at school were whispering and talking. I even had one asshole ask me if I was fucking her.

Prick.

Mitch had told me yesterday that this was the happiest he'd seen Skylar in a long time. That made my heart swell up. I'd told my parents about her and what had happened to her. My mom, being a therapist, had wanted to know if she had talked to someone about everything.

Out of the corner of my eye, I saw Jenny and her little gang coming in to the pizza shop. They just stood at the entrance for a minute or two. My guess was that they were trying to see where Sky's section was.

Bitches. Why they couldn't just leave her alone was beyond me.

Eva was walking by with a soda. When I grabbed it off her tray, she just looked at me. "Sorry, Eva. I'll pay for it."

I got up and started making my way over toward Jenny. I knew the moment she saw me, she would bounce right on over.

When she looked up at me, sure enough, she came walking over. I looked away and didn't stop walking… and I collided straight into her, spilling the soda all over her shirt.

She let out a scream, and I apologized. "Oh shit, Jenny! I didn't even see you. I'm so sorry."

She looked pissed, but for some strange reason, she smiled at me.

What in the hell?

"It's totally okay, Wyatt. Accidents happen right? It's just a shirt, and it'll dry. You can make it up to me by sitting with us though."

Oh hell, that totally just backfired on my ass. I looked up at the clock. Skylar was about to get off work.

"Sorry, Jenny. I'd love to, but Skylar and I are heading to the coffee shop to study for calculus."

Her eyes turned to pure anger as she looked around me toward Skylar, who was so busy that she didn't even notice what had happened. "Really? Study partners with the school…" She stopped what she was about to say as she looked back at me.

"Yeah… study partners." I turned and walked away from Jenny. When I sat down and turned back around, they were gone. I let out the breath I'd been holding. *Thank God they left.*

When Skylar's shift ended, I went up to her and got that beautiful drop-me-to-my-knees smile of hers.

"Coffee?" I asked with a wink.

She let out a giggle. "Coffee."

I pulled up to the coffee shop and got out. I walked in and ordered my coffee and Sky's since she was going to be a few minutes late getting here. I sat down and took out my notes.

"Hey, handsome."

I looked up to see Jenny standing there. *Fuck me. What does it take for this girl to get a hint?* "Hey, Jenny. I'm actually waiting on someone."

She sat down anyway. I noticed she'd changed her shirt, and the shirt she put on actually caused my dick to jump a little when I looked her up and down. She had on a low-cut, V-neck shirt that practically had her breasts spilling out of it.

Damn, she has a nice body, that's for sure. But it was nothing I was interested in.

"Listen, Wyatt… some of the football players have been talking. They don't like that you're hanging around Skylar. I mean, she has a bit of a reputation." She licked her lips.

Shit. I really wish she would just leave before Sky gets here.

I looked down at her lips as she bit down on her bottom one. I noticed she quickly glanced out the window before leaning over the table as she stared down at my lips. Before I even knew what was happening, she started kissing me. Her lips were so soft, just like how I imagined Skylar's lips to feel. She let out a moan that snapped me out of it. I pulled back and glared at her.

"What the fuck, Jenny?"

She sat back, glanced out the window, and smiled. I slowly looked out and saw Skylar standing there. She quickly looked back and forth between Jenny and me. I saw tears building in her eyes before she turned and walked back to her car.

I turned back to Jenny. "You planned that, didn't you?"

She tried to appear stunned. "I don't know what you're talking about. I saw the way you were looking at me, Wyatt. You want it as much as I do." She winked.

"You're sick and twisted, you know that?" I shook my head and stood up.

I felt sick to my stomach as I made my way outside to find Skylar.

CHAPTER FIVE
Skylar

"HEY, I THOUGHT you had a study date with Wyatt," my mother called out after I walked in the door.

"Yeah, well, he had other plans."

I headed up to my bedroom and slammed my door shut. I heard a small knock on the door.

"Are you okay?" my mother asked.

"I'm fine, Mom. Really… it's okay. I have a lot of studying to do."

My phone started ringing, and I looked down to see Wyatt was calling. I hit Decline. I opened up my calculus notes and tried to start studying. When I heard my Facebook notification go off, I jumped up and checked it. I was tagged in a picture. I threw my hands up to my mouth and instantly started crying.

Someone had taken a picture of me standing outside the coffee shop, looking at Wyatt kiss Jenny. The caption said, *Looks like Wyatt is sending the whore a message!*

I closed Facebook and walked back over to my bed. I grabbed my pillow and cried into it, so my mother wouldn't hear me. I heard a knock on the door.

"Mom, I'm fine!"

"Sky… let me in," Mitch said.

I got up and opened the door. I tried my best to seem like I was okay.

He looked me up and down, walked into my room, and shut the door. "Wyatt called me, and he's really upset."

I just looked at Mitch.

"Skylar, I saw the picture on Facebook. Wyatt is pissed about it. He said that Jenny reached over and kissed him, and she set the whole thing up."

"Well, he sure looked like he was enjoying it, so—"

Mitch let out a long sigh. "Sky, don't push him away. He really cares about you, and he doesn't believe all the bullshit everyone feeds him."

I sat down on my bed and let a tear slide down my face. "I've been getting notes in my locker again."

Mitch closed his eyes and shook his head. "Sky... you've got to tell someone. This has to stop. You aren't going to be able to take much more of this. Do they say the same thing?"

I shrugged my shoulders. "Pretty much, except they keep saying Wyatt is using me to try and get sex... and I'm only good for sex... that kind of thing."

"That's bullshit, Sky. You know Wyatt is not after you for that, right? I mean, as much as I hate to say this... he's a nice guy. I like him. He's cool, and he really cares about you."

I stood up and started crying again. "I don't know anymore, Mitch. I don't know who to trust and who not to trust. I think it's best if Wyatt just leaves me alone. I just want to finish school and get the hell out of this town. I'm going to suffocate if I have to stay here any longer. I have enough credits to graduate in December, so I'm going to. I'm going to talk to Mom and Dad about taking a trip before starting college. I just need to get away."

"Sky, running away is not going to help anything. What are you going to do? Never come home again? You'll miss prom."

I started laughing as I shook my head. "Really, Mitch? Prom? Why in the hell would I ever want to go to prom? I'd be the laughingstock of the school."

There was another knock on my door, and I quickly wiped the tears away.

"Skylar? Mitch?" my mother called from the other side of the door.

Mitch looked at me with pleading eyes. "Sky... *please* tell her what's going on."

I shook my head and gave him a look. "Come in, Mom."

When she opened the door, I put on a fake smile. "Hey... what's going on in here? Skylar, you rushed up the stairs so fast."

I shrugged my shoulders. "Nothing. Mitch is trying to talk me out of wanting to graduate early."

"What? Skylar, we talked about this. Your father and I think it would be best to just finish out your year. There's no rush here. Why are you in such a hurry to leave?"

Mitch looked over at me, and I just smiled.

"I just thought it would be nice to take a trip before I started college. You know, get away for a bit. I've always wanted to go to Italy."

My mother laughed. "Honestly, sweetheart, there's no way in hell that your father and I would ever let you go to Italy alone. We told you that we'll all go as a family this summer." She smiled and leaned down to kiss Mitch and then me on the cheek. "Get some rest, Sky. You look tired." She turned and walked out the door.

I sighed as I fell back on my bed. "I'm never going to get out of this damn town—ever."

"Skylar, what about Wyatt? He really wants to talk to you."

I looked over at my brother as I felt tears stinging my eyes. "I think it's best if Wyatt just leaves me alone. I have a feeling this is not going to blow over fast."

Mitch shook his head. "I think you should call him."

"No! He kissed Jenny, and it's been posted on Facebook for the world to see. I'm done. I just want to finish up the school year. I knew I shouldn't have even talked to him. What in the hell was I thinking?"

"Sky, he didn't post the picture."

"Mitch, please. I need to study. Can I please be alone for just a bit?"

He turned to go. He looked back at me and tried to give me a weak smile. "He knows the truth, and he really does like you, Sky."

I looked away before Mitch could see another tear rolling down my face. "Yeah... well, I don't think that's enough."

~~~~

For the last few months, I'd done a pretty good job of avoiding Wyatt. Every time he tried to talk to me, I'd just walked away. I'd changed my schedule so that I wasn't in the same classes as him, and I would either eat my lunch in the library or in my car.

Wyatt had called my cell phone every day, at least twice a day. Jenny was doing everything in her power to remind me how I was not good enough for Wyatt, saying he deserved more than the town whore. The notes were slowly starting to stop. *Thank God because I was about to go insane.*

Wyatt would still come to my work every now and then, but I did my best to ignore him. My heart broke every time he would plead with me to talk to him.

Standing at my locker, I took in a deep breath of air. I opened it and saw the note fall to the floor. I wasn't even reading them anymore, but for some reason, this one caught my eye. There was a photo in it. I looked around as I bent down to pick it up. I slowly unfolded it and caught my breath as I saw a picture of Jenny leaning against a wall with Wyatt resting his hand on the wall. He was smiling at her as she laughed. My heart fell to my stomach.

"You finally pushed him away."

I looked up and saw Michelle, the only friend I had left, staring at me. "What?"

"Sky, did you think he would just sit around and wait for you? It's been months since you've even talked to him. He probably got tired of waiting around for you to come to your damn senses."

I shook my head to clear my thoughts. "Why are you saying that? You know I can't, Michelle. They are just going to start up again with all the hate notes and the threats. It's better this way. I only have a few more months, and then I'm out of here."

I glanced up and saw Wyatt walking up to me. "Hey, Skylar. Can I talk to you for a minute?"

Michelle gave me a look, and I just stared at her.

"Um... I was actually getting ready to leave. I have a dentist appointment."

Wyatt smiled that drop-dead gorgeous smile of his, and my heart dropped to my stomach.

"May I walk you out?"

I looked around to see if anyone was watching us. "Uh… sure." I slammed my locker shut. "I'll call you later, Michelle."

Michelle smiled and nodded her head. "Okay, talk to ya later. See ya around, Wyatt."

"See ya." Wyatt pushed his hand through his hair.

Oh god, I've missed seeing him do that. I felt an ache between my legs, but I pushed it aside.

As we started to walk outside, Wyatt tried his best to make me laugh, and I tried my best not to be charmed by him, but I felt myself smile.

He grabbed me by the arm and stopped walking. "Skylar, please. Please stop ignoring me. I can't take it. All I do is think about you, and it's killing me. I miss you, Sky. I miss your laugh, your smile, your touch."

I thought about the picture of him looking at Jenny, smiling. "Seems to me you and Jenny are getting along just fine." I jerked my arm from his hand.

Wyatt let out a sigh and started to walk next to me. "Jesus Christ, Skylar. Will you stop with that?" he shouted.

I stopped and turned to look at him.

I noticed someone standing at the top of the stairs, but Wyatt walked closer to me and blocked my view. He grabbed my face, bent down, and kissed me. His soft lips slammed against mine, and I found myself getting lost in the passion of his kiss. I slowly started to move my hands up. I almost wrapped my arms around him to deepen the kiss until I heard someone behind me.

I pulled back and spun around. It was him—Charlie. My heart started beating faster, and my head was spinning.

"She's a damn good kisser, isn't she?"

It felt like someone was sitting on my chest, and I couldn't breathe.

"Yeah, yeah, she is," Wyatt said.

I turned and looked at him as he looked down at me and smiled. He had no idea who this was. Then, I looked past Wyatt and saw Jenny standing there. She was pissed.

"I have to go." I pushed my way past Charlie and ran to my car. I jumped in, started it, and drove off.

By the time I got to my house, I could hardly breathe. My phone started going off like crazy.

Facebook.

I opened it up, and the moment I saw the picture, I felt my whole world stop.

"Oh. My. God. No…"

CHAPTER SIX
Wyatt

FUCK! JUST WHEN I *got her to talk to me, she freaked again.* I watched as she ran to her car and jumped in.

I looked back at the guy who was staring at her as she drove away. He turned and looked past me as he smiled and winked at someone. I turned and saw Jenny standing on the steps. *Oh great, just what I needed.*

"Take it from me, dude. She's a good fuck." The guy threw his head back and laughed.

Wait. What the hell?

"What did you just say?" I took a step closer to him.

Just then, I felt someone touch my arm. I turned to see Jenny standing there. She started to pull me away from the guy.

"Wyatt, let's go for a ride. I could really use something to eat and drink. Please?"

I looked at her and then back at the guy. "What do you mean, she's a good fuck? Who?"

He smiled a cocky-ass smile at me.

Holy shit. This is Charlie.

"Sky. She's probably the best lay I've ever had." He looked at Jenny and winked. "No offense, Jen. You were good, too, babe."

"Shut the hell up, Charlie. You're such an asshole."

My head was spinning. *What in the hell is happening?* I felt my hands balling up into fists. I was going to kill this motherfucker. I took a step toward him, only to have Mitch step in between us. He put his hand on my chest and looked at me.

"He's not worth it, Wyatt. Let's just go find Sky. I'm worried about her."

I stopped in my tracks. "She went to the dentist… didn't she?"

Mitch shook his head. "No. She got another note. She took off."

"What do you mean, another note?"

Mitch turned and glared at Jenny. "Let's just go. I'll tell you when we get to the truck."

Jenny tried to get me to stay, but I told her I needed to find Skylar. I could tell she was pissed, but I didn't really care. I couldn't really even stand to be near Jenny. I felt like all she ever did was try to trap me into situations.

After Mitch had told me all about the notes, the threats, and everything else that Skylar had been dealing with, he told me their parents had no clue as to what was going on. My heart was breaking for Skylar. Knowing that she was going through all of this alone gutted me.

"That fucker needs to be put in his place, Mitch. When he told me she was a good fuck, I wanted to kill him."

Mitch glanced at me and smiled. "Now you know why my brother wanted to kill him. Charlie was supposed to be his best friend, and he raped our sister. Every day of my life, I fight the urge to kill him."

We drove around for over an hour, looking for Skylar. I looked out the window, wondering where in the hell she would have gone. "Mitch, where do you think she is?"

"I have no clue, Wyatt. She could be anywhere."

I closed my eyes and whispered, "Angel, where are you?"

Then, it hit me. "Fuck! The lake. Mitch, she's at the lake."

"The lake?"

Mitch turned his truck around, and we headed out toward Lake Marble Falls. I was willing his truck to drive faster. I needed to get to her and get to her fast. Then, Mitch got a text message. He pulled out his phone and handed it to me.

"Dude, see if that's Sky."

I opened it up and almost threw up. "Motherfucker. Pull over, Mitch. Pull over now!"

Mitch pulled over, and I threw his phone on the seat before I jumped out of the truck and started to throw up.

The next thing I knew, I heard Mitch cursing like a sailor. Then, I heard him on the phone.

"Dad, they posted a picture of Skylar on Facebook. No, Dad. It's Skylar… naked, and it looks like someone is… someone is…" Then, Mitch started crying.

My heart was breaking for Skylar, Mitch, and their parents.

"Why, Dad? Why would anyone post that picture? I don't know where she is, Dad. Wyatt thought she might be out at the lake."

I listened to Mitch talk to his father for a few minutes longer. I waited for him to finish before I started to walk back to his truck.

I noticed another truck driving by with music blaring. When I looked at the driver, I saw it was Charlie. *Where in the hell is he going?*

Skylar. He must know where she is.

I jumped back into Mitch's truck and yelled for him to get in and drive. He just looked at me.

"Um, Dad… listen, I have to go. I'll call ya right back. Dad, I know! We'll find her, but I've got to go right now!" He hung up. "What in the hell, Wyatt?"

"Mitch, just drive. Charlie just drove by. I think he knows where Skylar is."

Mitch threw the truck into drive. "He's not supposed to be anywhere near her. She has a restraining order out against him."

"Then, punch it, dude."

Mitch drove so fast that my knuckles where white from holding on, and I swore he said every cuss word known to man and some I'd never heard before.

I told him about the area where Sky and I had first met at the lake. When he pulled in, we both saw Skylar's car… and Charlie's truck.

"Fuck!" Mitch and I said at the same time.

I jumped out of the truck before Mitch even came to a stop. I ran toward Skylar's car.

Mitch ran up behind me. "Where is she?" He looked all around.

I took out my phone and called her, but it went right to voice mail. Then, I heard her.

Mitch must have heard her, too, because he took off running before I even had a chance to move.

I grabbed his arm and pulled him to a stop. "Wait! I have an idea."

Mitch looked at me like I was crazy. "What? Are you kidding me? My sister is alone with the fucker who raped her!"

"Just trust me, will you? When we get there, turn the video from your cell phone on, and keep it facing Charlie."

Mitch looked at me confused.

I started to walk toward Sky's voice. She sounded like she was shouting. *If that fucker hurts her at all, I swear I'll kill him.*

As we came around a tree, I saw Skylar first. Her hands were balled up in fists, and she was shouting at Charlie. I saw Mitch out of the corner of my eye, and he looked ready to attack and kill Charlie.

"Why? Why would you post that photo, Charlie? What reason do you have for posting it? I'm fucking passed out in the picture!"

"Sky, I didn't post it! I think Jenny saw it on my phone one night after we fucked, and she sent it to herself. Do you really think I want that picture out there? It only proves…"

They were both so busy shouting that neither one of them noticed us walking up.

"Proves what, Charlie? That you drugged me and had sex with me?"

Charlie ran his hands through his hair and let out a sigh. "Skylar, I didn't mean to ever hurt you. I've just always wanted you so badly, and I knew you'd never give me the time of day, and—"

"So, you drugged me? You were my brother's best friend for fuck's sake! He trusted you. I trusted you! I thought you were my friend, Charlie. *You ruined my life!*" Skylar screamed, causing all of us to jump.

"Skylar, you don't know how many times I've wanted to tell everyone the truth, but my father wouldn't let me. He just kept saying I was going to be taking over the family business and that you probably wanted it anyway. I… I didn't know what to say or what to do."

I walked closer as I saw Skylar starting to cry harder. She just kept repeating how her life was ruined.

"Why don't you be a man and tell everyone the truth, asshole? Now, with this picture out, it's just going to get worse for Skylar, and you know it," I said as I walked toward her.

When she looked up at me, I noticed as she caught her breath. For one brief moment, she had life in her eyes. She seemed relieved to see me. I wanted nothing more than for her to run into my arms. I wanted to protect her, to take her away from all of this. I wanted to love her.

I do love her.

"Skylar," I barely whispered. The next thing I knew, she was jumping into my arms. My heart slammed into my chest, and I held on to her as tightly as I could. "I promise you, everything's going to be okay. I promise, angel… I promise."

She was sobbing as she tried to talk. "It… it won't, Wyatt. Everyone has seen that picture. Everyone!"

I looked at Charlie, who was now leaning against a tree with his head in his hands.

What the hell? Is he crying? Motherfucker. I'd really like to beat the hell out of him.

"You know what you need to do. You need to tell the truth, Charlie. You owe it to her."

He slowly looked up at me and shook his head. "I'll go to jail. My dad will disown me. I'll lose everything."

Suddenly, Mitch had Charlie pinned up against a tree. "You motherfucker! You ruined my sister's life. Do you think we give a shit about your life? You're going to tell everyone the truth."

Charlie pushed Mitch off of him. "Or what, Mitch? What are you going to do?"

Mitch smiled as he held up his phone. "I don't have to do anything. I already sent Michelle the video of you saying you date raped my sister, and you were too much of a coward to tell the truth."

Skylar pulled away from me and spun around.

"What?" Skylar and Charlie said at the same time.

Mitch turned and smiled at Sky. "Thanks to Wyatt for coming up with the idea for me to turn on my cell video camera... I got everything on video. Everyone is going to know the truth, baby girl. Everyone is going to know what a lying sack of shit this asshole is."

Charlie's face turned white as a ghost. "No. My father is going to murder me. Why, Mitch?"

Mitch shook his head. "I don't think you want me answering that. I suggest you leave now before I beat your ass into the ground. Go enjoy your freedom before your ass gets thrown in jail."

Charlie started to walk up to Skylar. She moved back and leaned her body into mine. When I wrapped my arms around her, I felt her shaking. Leaning down, I whispered in her ear, "He'll never hurt you again, angel. No one will ever hurt you again."

"Sky... I'm... I'm so sorry. I know you don't believe me, but... I really am sorry."

"Get out of my face. I *never* want to see or talk to you again. Ever!"

He looked at me before turning and walking away. I felt Skylar's legs giving out as she started to slip down. I grabbed her tighter and turned her toward me.

When her eyes met mine, my heart filled with so much love for this girl that I thought it was going to burst.

She barely smiled. "My hero."

"Sky..."

She shook her head and closed her eyes. "Please, Wyatt. Please kiss me again. Make me forget everything like you did earlier."

My heart started pounding as I cupped her face with my hands. I leaned down and brushed my lips against hers as she let out a whimper. I gently kissed her, and before I knew it, the kiss turned from gentle to passionate. She reached up and grabbed my hair with her hands as she let out a soft moan that traveled through my body like a bolt of lightning.

I love this girl.

"Um, really... I don't want to see this, y'all. I *really* don't want to see this," Mitch said as he walked by.

I slowly pulled away from her as she let out a small laugh. Her eyes were looking deep into my soul, burning her love into me forever. *I'd do anything for her.*

"Skylar, I… I—"

She put her finger up to my mouth and smiled. "I know. I feel it, too. Will you do me a favor?"

"Yes! Of course. Anything."

"Will you drive me home, so I can tell my parents what's been going on? Will you stay with me while I do that? I don't think I can do it alone."

My hands started sweating, and my legs felt like they were about to give out on me. *Holy hell. What is happening to me?* "I'd follow you anywhere, angel."

She smiled as she reached down and took my hands. Both of our cell phones started ringing.

Sky pulled her phone out and frowned. "Mom? I'm on my way home with Wyatt and Mitch. Can I talk to you when I get there? Yes, I'm fine. I promise, Mom, I'll tell you everything when I get home. I love you, too."

She hung up and slipped her phone in her back pocket. She reached up and gently kissed me on the lips. Pulling away, she said, "I always wondered what it was like."

I looked at her, confused. "What, what's like?"

"To be kissed and feel such… love. To feel how much you can be loved and adored with just a single kiss."

My heart started beating faster. I wanted to be with her and more than just physically. I wanted to show her every single day how much I loved and adored her. I wanted to grab her and pull her body up against mine to show her how much I wanted her, but I didn't want to scare her.

I smiled as I put my hand behind her neck and drew her in for another kiss. I pulled back and barely took my lips off hers. "It's a good thing you're with the person who happens to be head over heels in love with you."

She leaned her forehead against mine and smiled. "I love you, too, Wyatt."

I grabbed her hand and pulled her close to me as we walked back down to her car. Mitch was standing against his truck with a stupid-ass grin on his face.

"You hurt her… I'll fucking kill you," he said to me as I held her door open while she got into her car.

Skylar let out a giggle as I looked over at Mitch.

"Good to know, dude. Good to know."

CHAPTER SEVEN
Skylar

IT HAD BEEN a few months since Michelle had posted the video of Charlie talking about drugging and taking advantage of me. Things were slowly getting back to normal.

I looked across the school parking lot and saw Jenny laughing. When she looked at me, her smile faded, and she quickly glanced away. I never could get her to confess to setting up the fake Facebook account and posting the picture of me passed out. I'd decided not to pursue it.

My parents had been furious with me for lying to them all those months about the bullying. My father was ready to rip heads apart. All I wanted to do was get through the next few weeks of school and get the hell out of Marble Falls for the summer before heading to the University of Texas with Wyatt and Mitch.

Wyatt had made arrangements to take me to Italy for a month. We were set to leave the day after graduation, much to my parents' disapproval, but somehow, he'd sweet-talked them into it. It helped that Wyatt's dad worked for the FBI, and his dad had promised my parents that he'd use all resources available to keep an eye on both of us.

Wyatt and I still hadn't made love. I wanted him more than I could stand, but I could tell something was holding him back. He kept saying he wanted it to be special for me. A part of me was afraid he didn't want me because of what had happened to me, but Michelle had told me I was crazy and that any fool could tell with just one look that Wyatt was smitten with me.

"A penny for your thoughts."

I smiled as I felt his hot breath against my neck. *Shit, I want him so much.* I wasn't sure I'd be able to wait much longer before I begged him. I closed my eyes and smiled. "Italy."

He let out a laugh as he came to face me. "I was thinking about it earlier also. Have you picked up your prom dress yet?" He wiggled his eyebrows up and down as he gave me a wicked grin that caused the need between my legs to grow ten times stronger.

"Yes, I did. Michelle approves of the easy access to putting it on… and taking it off," I said with a wink.

I knew he had made arrangements for a cottage on Lake Marble Falls. We had said we'd go to a party that Jon Fallon was throwing, but we were only planning to stay for a few minutes before heading off to the cottage.

My heart was pounding so loud in my chest that I was sure he could hear it.

"Nervous?"

I smiled as I tilted my head. "Nervous about what?"

He smiled and winked. "Dancing with me."

"Terrified. Beyond terrified but excited."

His smile slowly faded. "Sky…"

"Don't, Wyatt. I want this so much. Please."

He leaned down and gently kissed me on the lips. "Your brother has threatened me at least ten times this week."

I laughed as I looked over his shoulder at Mitch talking to Michelle. "You know, he and Michelle aren't even showing up at the party, so he's one to talk."

Wyatt looked at me, and the love in his eyes caused my heart to drop as the butterflies took off in my stomach.

"I promise to make it special for you, angel."

Oh. My. God. He was beyond perfect. I was just waiting for the floor to fall out from underneath me.

"Just being with you, Wyatt, is what's going to make it so special."

He sighed and stood back up. "So, what time should I pick you up tomorrow?"

"Probably around five, so our parents can take pictures." I rolled my eyes. I didn't even want to go to the prom, but Wyatt had insisted. People still looked at me funny as they whispered behind my back. I just wanted to forget all about the last few years.

"I promise, angel, you're going to have a wonderful time."

"Yeah… we'll see."

I pushed him, and he lost his balance. He grabbed a hold of me and brought me down with him.

Yep… as long as Wyatt is with me… there isn't anything I couldn't do.

I was finally happy.

~~~~

The moment my father opened the door, Wyatt saw me in my red corset-fitted dress with my hair pulled up, just a few ringlets hanging down. I knew it was going to be a long night. Wyatt loved my hair up, and red was his favorite color. My prom dress flared out just below my waist, and my breasts fit the dress perfectly.

When my mother saw it on me, she had rolled her eyes. "God, help me now. One look at you, and that boy is going to be fighting like hell to keep his penis in his pants all night."

My father pulled Wyatt to the side and had a *chat* with him. My mother took me into the kitchen, and when she opened her mouth, I knew I was about to get a repeat of *the talk*.

"Sky, I'm not stupid. I've been in your shoes before. I know there is a strong possibility that something might… well, that something might happen between you and Wyatt… if it hasn't already."

"Oh. My. God! Mom! Really?"

My mother looked at me with that all-knowing look. "Be careful, Skylar. Be sure. That's all I ask of you. I know I'm one of the loosey-goosey mothers, but I'm just keeping it real with you. I'm not going to sugarcoat it and pretend that kids don't have sex before marriage. Hell… I didn't wait. You're eighteen, and I'm going to trust that you know what you're doing.

Now, your father, on the other hand… I'm pretty sure Wyatt might be so scared by the time he walks out that door that he won't even lay a hand on you all evening."

I let out a laugh and hugged my mother. "I know you care, Mom. I promise I'd never do anything I wasn't ready to do. I do love him, Mom. More than anything."

She smiled as she shook her head and sighed. "I know you do, and I know he loves you, too."

I knew she wanted to say more, but she didn't. My dad and Wyatt walked in just as my mom hugged me one more time. I turned and looked at Wyatt. He looked so handsome, but his face was white as a ghost.

If my father scared him into not touching me, I swear to God… I'm going to hide his fishing poles for the rest of the summer.

Wyatt held out his arm. "Shall we, angel?"

I smiled and put my arm around his. I glanced at my dad, who was giving Wyatt a dirty look, and then I turned to my mom to say good-bye.

Wyatt's parents had been sitting on the front porch, looking at all the photos they had taken. When we walked out, they jumped up and gave us a few more instructions before we could finally head to prom.

~~~~

As we walked in, Avril Lavigne's "Here's to Never Growing Up" was playing. Then, I noticed that people were starting to stare at me.

This is a mistake, such a huge mistake.

"I can't do this. They're all talking about me. Can we leave, please?" I said to Wyatt in a panicked voice.

He smiled as he pulled me closer to him. I saw him wave to the DJ and nod his head.

"Nope. You need to dance to at least one song at your prom, angel… maybe two," he said with a smile.

I looked around as he walked me out to the dance floor. I felt like I was trapped, and I couldn't get out. All I wanted to do was run away.

Then, Christina Aguilera's "Beautiful" started playing as Wyatt held me tight up against his body.

I looked up at him. "How did you know?"

He smiled as he ran the back of his hand down my face. "You told me this was your favorite song the first time we ran into each other at the lake."

I felt tears burning my eyes, and I tried to hold them back. I shook my head as I slowly smiled at him. "You'll never know how happy you've made me, Wyatt. You make me feel…" I couldn't finish my sentence.

"Tell me, Sky. Please tell me."

"You make me feel so special, so loved. With you holding me, I feel like I can do anything. I feel… beautiful."

"You are beautiful, angel. I'll always make sure to remind you every single day for the rest of our lives how beautiful, special, and loved you are."

I closed my eyes as I placed my head on his chest, letting the tears stream down my face. Once the song ended, I pulled back and smiled. "I danced. Can we leave now?"

The way Wyatt was looking at me had my stomach doing flips. "You want to leave, angel? We just got here," he barely whispered.

I reached up as he leaned down toward me. I put my lips up next to his ear. "I really, *really* want to leave, Wyatt. I'm dying here. I need to be with you… *now*. I'm aching for you."

As Wyatt pulled me closer to him, I felt his erection against me. *Oh god.* I let out a small moan as I pushed myself into him more.

"Oh Jesus, Skylar. You're killing me."

"Please, Wyatt. I want you." I knew I was begging him, but I could see the passion growing in his eyes. He wanted me just as much as I wanted him. I smiled and tilted my head as I looked at him with pleading eyes. "Wyatt."

He grabbed my hand, and before I knew what was happening, we were heading back out to his truck. I smiled as I thought about being with him. I was scared to death but excited at the same time.

He opened the door for me, and I felt my hands shaking as he took my hand and helped me up into his truck.

He stopped and looked at me. "Sky… you know we don't have to do anything you don't want to do. You know that, right?"

I smiled as I thought about all the times I knew he'd wanted to go further, but he'd always stopped himself. He truly cared about me, and that warmed my heart so much. It was me who was pushing us to finally be together. I was going to explode if I had to keep waiting.

"Wyatt… please take me to the cottage. I want to be with you."

He slowly smiled as he ran his hand through his hair. He leaned in and so softly kissed me on the lips. "I love you, angel."

"I love you, too."

CHAPTER EIGHT
Wyatt

MY HANDS WERE practically slipping off the steering wheel. I was so nervous. *Jesus H. Christ, what is wrong with me? It's not like I haven't had sex before.*

I glanced over toward Skylar. She was looking out the window, humming to a country song on the radio.

She was the reason I was so nervous.

Shit, I just want this to be special for her.

What if she thought I sucked?

I shook my head and cleared everything out—all the worry, the doubt... the threats from Skylar's dad, Mitch, and Skip. Skip's was the best. He had sent a Marine buddy to personally deliver his threat, and it was very effective to say the least.

"Wyatt? Are you nervous?" Skylar asked, pulling me out of my thoughts.

I quickly glanced at her and smiled before looking back at the road. "I just don't want to disappoint you or push you into this too fast."

She let out a giggle and reached for my hand. "Wyatt, you could never disappoint me. I want this. I want this more than anything."

"Skip's gonna kill me, Sky, if he finds out I brought you to a cottage and had my wicked ways with you." I glanced and winked at her.

She squeezed my hand and let out a laugh. My heart started beating harder as I pulled down the country road that led to the small cottage where we would be staying the night. Skylar started humming again as she rubbed her thumb along my hand. I was instantly calmed.

As I turned down the drive, I noticed her sitting up straighter.

She pulled her hand from mine and put it up to her mouth. "Oh. My. God."

I smiled when I saw all the white lights in the trees.

"I've never seen anything so beautiful," she said as I parked my truck.

I looked over at her as I ran the back of my hand down her cheek. "I have."

Skylar turned and looked me in the eyes. Her beautiful blue eyes captured mine, and my heart just about stopped. *I will never, ever love anyone like I love her.*

The next thing I knew, Sky was jumping out of the truck and running up to the porch. When she turned back around, the smile on her face dropped my heart to my stomach. I couldn't help but smile back at her.

I got out of the truck and opened the back door to grab our bags. I reached under my seat, feeling around for the small blue velvet box. The moment my hand touched it, I felt sick. *What if she says, no? What if she says, we're too young to even be thinking marriage? Shit. Maybe I should wait.* I stood there and just held the box in my hand before Sky called my name, pulling me back from my thoughts.

"Wyatt? Are you coming or not?"

I shoved the ring box in my jacket pocket and shut the door. My mind went back to the conversation I'd had with Skylar's father two weeks ago. I had asked his permission for Skylar's hand, and at first, he'd looked like he wanted to beat the shit out of me. Then, he'd sat back in his chair with his two index fingers resting on lips. After what seemed like forever, he'd finally smiled slightly. He'd shaken his head as he leaned forward, like he was going to whisper to me. I'd instinctively moved toward him to hear what he was going to say.

"I like you, Wyatt. I always have. I can read people, and I knew the moment I met you that you loved my daughter and wanted nothing but the best for her. You're both young, and I'm not so sure how I feel about this. She has to go to school first. I won't accept anything less."

"Yes! Yes, of course, sir. I was thinking we wouldn't get married until after college. I want the same things for Skylar as you do, sir."

"You know, her brothers will help me hide your body if you ever hurt her?"

"Um… yes. Yes, I'm well aware of that, sir."

"Fine… as long as you are aware of the fact that I love my daughter more than the air I breathe."

"Very much aware of that, sir."

"Then, you have my permission to ask Skylar to marry you."

I closed my eyes and smiled, thinking about how happy he had been when I showed him my grandmother's ring.

"Wyatt!" Skylar called out.

My eyes flew open, and I started to laugh. "I'm coming!"

I walked up the steps and set the bags down as I reached into my pocket for the key to open the front door.

Skylar practically pushed me out of the way to get into the cottage. I turned on the lights, and I heard her let out a gasp. I looked around and smiled. It was perfect. It was decorated like an old English cottage, and Sky was walking from side to side, going on and on about how beautiful everything was.

"Yep. It's all very beautiful. Just like you, angel."

She spun around and looked at me. The look in her eyes was nothing but pure love. She started to make her way over to me, and I dropped the bags right as she slammed her body into mine.

"It's perfect. You're perfect! Everything about this evening is perfect."

I stroked her hair as I thought about the ring in my pocket. "Skylar, I have one more thing I need to do before we… before we make love."

She pulled back and smiled. "I just want you, Wyatt. I don't care about anything else. Please. I just want to feel you. I've wanted you, I swear, since the first day I put my eyes on you."

A few times, Sky and I had come so close to making love, but we'd always stopped. I hadn't wanted our first time to be in my truck or her bedroom. We'd almost lost control on her sofa one night, and I had been so close to saying *fuck it*, but her brother had pulled up in the driveway, getting home early from a date, so he'd saved us from making a mistake.

"Oh Christ, Sky, you have no idea how much I want to be with you. But I also want to be with you forever, not just tonight. I want to wake up every morning to your beautiful face. I want to roll over in the middle of the night, reach for you, and pull you to me, just so I can smell your hair and touch your beautiful, soft skin. I want to spend every waking moment with you. Hell, I'll even change my degree to be in every one of your classes if you asked me, too."

Skylar let out a small giggle. "Wyatt, we've already talked about this. I want that, too! I thought we were going to go apartment hunting this weekend."

Holy shit, this girl is so damn cute. She thinks I'm talking about moving in with her!

I looked around the little cabin. It screamed *romance*... at least, I thought it did. Turning back to Skylar, I reached down and brushed my lips against hers. When she let out a small moan, I wanted to just rip off her dress. I pulled back slightly and smiled.

"I love you, angel."

"Oh god, Wyatt... I love you, too."

I slowly got down on one knee as I reached in my pocket and took out the ring box. I brought it up and watched her face. Her smile faded for one brief second when I opened the box and exposed the oval cut diamond ring surrounded by round cut diamonds on each side of the center stone. The band was made of white gold, and it was encrusted with diamond accent stones. It was the perfect ring for my angel.

As she brought her hands up to her mouth, I saw a smile spreading across her face.

Before she had a chance to even think, I started talking. "Skylar, I know we're young, and we haven't been together for very long. But I know in the deepest part of my soul that you're the one I want to spend the rest of my life with. The one I want to have children with. The one I want to sit on a front porch with someday when we're so old that we probably won't even remember our names, but we'll always know we were meant to be together."

When I saw a tear slowly roll down her face, my hands started shaking. *Shit! Shit! Shit!*

"I've already asked your dad for your hand in marriage, Sky. My goal in this world is to always keep you happy and safe. I'm not asking that we run right out and get married. I promised your dad we'd wait until after college, but… but… if you would do me this honor, and…"

My throat felt like it was closing up, and I couldn't talk. My hands were shaking, and I just knew I had beads of sweat rolling down my face.

I tried again to ask her, and I felt tears building in my eyes. "Um…" I had to get my heart rate under control.

Skylar dropped to her knees in front of me and put her hands on my face. The moment she touched me, I was instantly calmed.

"Sky, will you do me this honor and accept my proposal of marriage? I'd like to give you my grandmother's ring."

The tears were now falling like rain down her face. She smiled so big as she let out a giggle.

Shit… is that a good sign or a bad sign?

She started nodding her head as she moved closer to me. "Yes! Oh god, yes, Wyatt! I want nothing more than that."

I felt tears rolling down my face as I smiled at her. I got the ring out of the box and gently took her hand in mine. I placed the ring on her finger and smiled. My parents had said if it were a perfect fit, that was a good sign. It meant we would be together for all eternity.

Fits like a glove.

I pulled her closer to my body and kissed her. At first, it was a slow, sweet kiss, but it quickly became a more passionate and heated kiss. Skylar started to take off my jacket, and then she undid the buttons on my shirt. She pushed the shirt off my shoulders and began kissing my neck and down my chest. I gulped in air and held my breath as she sucked on one nipple and then the other.

She made her way back up to my lips and gently bit down on my lower lip. I wanted to move slowly, but she was driving me crazy. I pulled her up to a standing position as I moved my hands to take off her dress. As I let it fall to the floor, I took in the sight in front of me. She was dressed in a red-and-black lace bra and matching panties.

I could hardly breathe. "So damn beautiful."

She smiled and put her face down. Taking my finger, I placed it under her chin and gently pulled her face up. Her cheeks were flushed, and she was looking everywhere but at me.

I started to walk her back to the bed. The back of her legs hit the mattress, causing her to stop. I reached down, picked her up, and gently laid her on the bed. I began moving my hands all over her body as I kissed every inch of exposed skin.

I loved how her body was reacting to my touch and to my lips on her skin. I continued to kiss her until she was practically ready to jump off the bed.

"Oh god, Wyatt. Please... don't tease me like this."

"I just want to touch you, Sky... to feel how my touch affects your body."

"Please..." she begged.

I stood up and took off the rest of my clothes. We'd seen each other naked before, but this... this was like seeing her for the first time. I watched her eyes take in every square inch of my body. My dick was so hard that I thought I was going to explode.

I crawled back on the bed and slowly started to slide off her panties. "Sit up, Sky."

Skylar sat up, and I reached behind her and unclasped her bra. Moving it off of her, I had to catch my breath at the sight of her body.

She's going to be mine—only mine. No one will ever hurt her again. I'll die before I let someone hurt her.

I moved over her body and gently kissed her stomach, making my way up to each nipple.

"Jesus, Wyatt! I feel like I could come with just your kiss."

I smiled as I thought about the numerous times I'd made her come with my lips and my fingers. I loved making her come. I slowly put my hand on her stomach, causing her to jump. I slid my hand down and spread her legs open wider. I reached my fingers to her folds, and I gently put two fingers inside her.

I was overcome with passion. "Fuck, Sky. You're so wet."

She bucked her hips into my hand. "Yes!"

I wanted her to come with me inside her, so I moved up her body. I used my tip to tease her entrance. I started to move slowly and gently into her. She grabbed my hair with both hands and let out a moan that about had me coming on the spot.

"So. Tight. Baby… you're so tight."

"Move, Wyatt… oh god… please move!"

I didn't want to hurt her, so I tried my best to go inch by inch. She slammed her hips up against my body, and I entered her in one swift move.

Motherfucker… this feels like heaven. She feels like pure heaven.

I couldn't move. If I did, I was going to embarrass myself and come before we even got started.

She began moving her hips while she ran her fingers lightly up and down my back. "Please move, Wyatt."

I started to move… slowly in and out. I wanted this moment to last forever, and the last thing I wanted to do was hurt her. I leaned down and whispered how much I loved her into her ear.

"Oh, Wyatt…"

We moved together as one. Each time it felt like I was about to come, I'd stop. I wanted this to last.

Then, she started to move her hips more. "Wyatt… faster… oh god, I'm so close, please!"

I moved faster while Sky called out, "Harder! Oh god, I'm so close. Wyatt, it feels so good."

The next thing I knew we were both calling out each other's names as I poured myself into her body. I wanted nothing more than to do this every day with this woman and only this woman.

I stopped moving and stayed on top of her while we both caught our breaths. She opened her eyes and looked directly into mine. We both smiled at the same time.

"Oh god, Wyatt. That was…"

"Beautiful."

She smiled and nodded her head. "Yes. That's the perfect word to describe it."

"That's going to be our life together, Sky. Beautiful."

"I love you, Wyatt."

"I love you, Skylar. I'll always love you."

About the Author

Kelly Elliott

Kelly Elliott is married to a wonderful Texas cowboy who has a knack for making her laugh almost daily and supports her crazy ideas and dreams for some unknown reason… he claims it's because he loves her!

She's also a mom to an amazing daughter who is constantly asking for something to eat while her fingers move like mad on her cell phone sending out what is sure to be another very important text message.

In her spare time she loves to sit in her small corner overlooking the Texas hill country and write.

One of her favorite things to do is go for hikes around her property with Gus… her chocolate lab and the other man in her life, and Rose, her golden retriever. When Kelly is not outside helping the hubby haul brush, move rocks or whatever fun chore he has in store for her that day, you'll find her inside reading, writing or watching HGTV.

Follow Kelly: http://www.authorkellyelliott.blogspot.com

Saving Snowflakes

A You & Me Trilogy Story for Book 1: Saving You Saving Me

By
Kailin Gow

Aspiring psychiatrist and high school Valedictorian Samantha (Sam) Sullivan falls for a deeply troubled young man named Daggers during a crisis call on her watch, which leads to the unraveling of her perfect world.

The Call

THE GREEN LIGHT came on like the fierce emerald eyes of a dragon in the dark along with the familiar buzz of the telephone, startling me from my brief nap at Sawyer House. It was a slow night for the crisis call center I was volunteering at as a peer counselor. So slow that even Derek, the boyishly handsome Psych major at the University of California, Irvine, who usually took the same shift with me, left early to go back to his dorm to study for his mid-term exams.

I was fine with that, already feeling confident that I could handle most calls after working at Sawyer House for a couple of months. I was relatively new, but Derek said I was a quick study and after my first week at Sawyer House, was already handling calls by myself. As a graduating senior in high school, who was used to responsibility as a former class president, head cheerleader, and all that; I felt confident taking on the role of a peer counselor at the crisis center not too far from school. It was also related to what I wanted to do for a living someday. In a few months, I would graduate from high school and be on my way to college (hopefully Stanford) to begin my formal education to become a psychiatrist. As a graduating senior who took a plethora of advanced placement classes in high school and would probably graduate as the Valedictorian in school, I was coasting my way through the rest of my senior year. Senioritis had hit most of my classmates, and it was slowly hitting me too.

Except for that one thing…

I needed a scholarship to pay for college, to get to my dream of becoming a psychiatrist to help people. And… I had a good chance of getting one with my grades and most of my extracurricular activities, except it just wasn't enough. Getting into Stanford was competitive, and Dr. Karen Green, my academic adviser wanted to make sure I did everything I could to get there. Told me I needed something more to boost my chances to getting a scholarship to Stanford, then arranged for a meeting for me at Sawyer House with the director there, for me to work as a peer counselor.

I had so many things to do already… finish high school, help out at my father's church where he was a pastor, and help take care of my little sister Nydia when Mom could not to drive her home from school. Mom? She was another story altogether. She had a lot of insecurities, which one of them made her almost incapable of taking care of Nydia most times.

Yes, I had so many things to worry about… my own problems to worry about; I didn't need to be hearing about other kids' problems on top of my own.

But as soon as I started, from day one, I was sucked into a world so different from mine that I was drawn to stay at Sawyer House longer and longer.

The green light flashed again, waking me up a second time from my doze. I normally don't sleep on the job, but since Sawyer House was staffed mostly by college student volunteers as peer counselors, and they were having mid-terms, I took on more hours to help cover for them this week.

"Hello," I said, bright and cheery, overcompensating for my groggy state. I slapped my cheeks to wake myself up and cleared my throat. "Sawyer House, this is Susan speaking," I said calmly. "What can we talk about tonight?" I asked. Using my Sawyer House name Susan, the name I used instead of my real name Sam for Samantha Sullivan, help me keep my peer counselor professionalism intact. According to Gail Green, the Director of Sawyer House and the founder, it was also to help protect peer counselors from getting too close and attached to a caller. I liked using it because it helped me assume another identity outside of my eighteen-year-old student one. Suddenly, I was Sawyer House Susan—fearless, rational, and able to dispense wisdom to all.

There was silence at the other end of the phone at first, but I waited. Most people calling into Sawyer House hesitate. It was natural... expected even, because the reason they were calling us was that they had a hard time telling anyone their problems to begin with. "Hello," I said nicely. "I am still here. Anytime you want to begin, just begin." I paused, then added, "Whatever you say will remain confidential. I'm not even allowed to know your identity so you cannot be recognized outside of this call."

I heard a sigh. Then a voice as sweet as an angel said, "I did something that I regret doing."

I waited for her to continue, but there was this hesitation again. "Why do you regret it?" I asked, not pressuring her about the "what". That would come later.

"I regret it because I know I shouldn't have done it," the sweet little girl voice said. The girl sounded like she was twelve years old.

"Why? Why do you feel you shouldn't have done it?" I asked.

"Because I didn't know the boy well enough," the girl said.

"Did you do something physical with him?" I asked.

"Yes," the girl said. "But he was a man, not a boy from school."

"Mind me asking how old are you?" I asked

"I'm not as young as I sound," the girl chuckled. "I am actually eighteen years old, but the boy, um, man is in his twenties."

I froze.

This sounded too familiar. If I hadn't slapped myself to wake me up, I would have thought I was dreaming. A strange Twilight Zone kind of dream. This girl and her man could have been Collins McGregor and I, the gorgeously sexy billionaire I had gotten into a physical relationship with a few months ago right at the same time I started at Sawyer House. Despite my initial shock, my mind started working. Overtime.

"Who is this man? And why did you regret being with him?" Now I was personally intrigued. Part of it mainly because I myself was going through a lot of issues over Collins.

"I regret going over to his house, and then getting undressed for him," the girl said.

"Is he handsome, incredibly charming, sexy as hell, makes you just want to eat him up, lick him all over, and run your fingers up and down his incredibly toned abs?" I asked quickly.

There was a brief pause and then she asked, "What?"

I caught myself and said, "Sorry, I got ahead of myself. But this man, you found him irresistibly attractive... so charismatic that you just want to spend all your time with him, kiss him and even get undressed for him..."

There was an uncomfortable pause, but she answered, "Um, not exactly like that, but he was cute enough. I mean I met him over the internet, and he asked me to meet up with him, and we did, but he turned out to be not the same guy as on his profile."

"Oh," I said. "Did he hurt you?" I stopped thinking about Collins and focused on the girl. "If he did, then..."

The girl didn't say anything for a while, and I drifted into my own thoughts. Collins and I had started becoming physical, but I had pulled away from him, out of my own insecurities. He never did anything to me that I would be scared about, but... I found myself taking steps backward, rather than forward with the relationship.

Maybe by listening to this girl's story and by trying to help her through her problems with this guy, I can get over Collins. Despite how much and how hard I fell for the deeply troubled young billionaire.

"Mind if I ask what is your name?" I asked the girl.

"Trudi," the girl said. "It's not my real name, though. I'd be too embarrassed if anyone found out I called a crisis center."

"Don't worry. Whatever you say, including your name, is safe with us," I said. "And Susan isn't my real name. It's to keep our identities safe both ways because at Sawyer House, we want you to feel comfortable enough to talk to us without being afraid that someone would know who you are. Now can you tell me what happened?"

The Crush

WITH THAT, THE walls came down, and Trudi began talking…

"I met him through Twitter. I had posted a picture of myself wearing a tank top and shorts. He thought I was cute, and he asked for more photos. I posted more, and then he posted pictures of himself. Based on his photos, I thought he was cute at first, and he seemed so interested in me. So we started chatting regularly."

She paused.

"So what happened next?" I prompted.

"I developed a huge crush on him. He seemed sophisticated, smart, witty, and handsome. He was only about ten years older than me, too."

I cringed. Collins, my Collins, was handsome and sophisticated. He was also much more worldly than I, having traveled everywhere in the world in his short but daring and interesting twenty-seven years on earth. While I had spent my entire time in school. I couldn't wait to graduate from high school and get started on a life of adventure like Collins'. He was the type of man who could sweep any girl off her feet, especially a girl my age, who haven't experienced the world yet.

From Trudi's description, she could easily be describing Collins…

"Did you feel guilty about falling for a man much older than you?" I asked.

"No, oh no," Trudi said. "It wasn't so much his age. I dated other guys older than me before, but they were all right. It wasn't so much his age that made me feel like I shouldn't have gone far with him, but what he did."

"What he did?" I asked, my entire attention now riveted on what Trudi would say next. "What did he do?"

Not What He Seemed

THERE WAS A long pause as I waited for Trudi to continue. I waited for a full minute.

"Hello, Trudi?" I asked.

Silence.

Finally, I said, "It's alright. I'll be here when you're ready to talk. You don't have to tell me tonight, if you don't feel ready. Just know you have someone you can talk to when you do. You can even ask for me directly… Susan. Or someone else you feel more comfortable with."

I looked at the clock on the wall across from my cubicle. It was already 10 pm. I had to start heading home before it got really late. Nothing had ever happened at Sawyer House before, knock on wood, but it wasn't exactly located in the nicest neighborhood in the Santa Ana and Costa Mesa area of Orange County, California. There was a juvenile detention center close by if that was an indication of the kind of mixed neighborhood it was in with corporations, shopping malls, and then non-profits like Sawyer House nearby.

Whenever I stayed this late, Derek had stayed with me, closing down Sawyer House for the night and then walking me to my car to make sure I got in safely before taking off for the night. He had become a good friend; although it was clear he wanted more than just friendship. If I was any other girl, I would already be dating him. He was very cute in a scruffy college way with his just slept in brown hair and boyish smile. But he wasn't Collins… the charismatic young billionaire with the body like an Adonis, and the sexy grin like the devil. Collins brought out so many feelings I've never felt before, feelings of passion and desire that made me risk my reputation as a Pastor's kid and good girl. He was wickedly tempting, and the short amount of time I knew him, he treated me like a princess. Only… deep down inside of me, despite how strong and independent I thought I was, I wasn't sure if that was how I wanted to be treated. It scared me.

Trudi still hadn't said anything else. The phone was so silent; I thought she had hung up. I was about to, when I heard a slight muffling sound coming through the phone. A small whimper, a breath, and some sighing. Trudi was crying on the other side of the line. I could feel her body shake against the phone, and her breath jagged as she inhaled between sobs.

It was late, but I didn't go home.

I let Trudi cried her eyes out, cried as much as she could to get the hurt out.

I just sat there, listening, not moving. Breathing steadily… loud enough to let her know, I was still here.

It was midnight when Trudi finally stopped crying, and said to me. "Thank you. I needed that."

"I have a feeling you would," I said, trying to smile. I was exhausted, but I never felt more needed in the last few weeks than right now.

"I tried," Trudi said. "I tried so many times to tell people how I felt, but they've just ignored me. Didn't care. Even made a joke of it. I'm so so sick of it."

"I'm glad you kept trying, Trudi," I said.

"To tell you the truth," she said, "I wasn't going to call. I really didn't think it would do any good."

"I'm glad you gave it a chance," I said.

"How old are you?" she asked suddenly. "You sound familiar, like you could be my age, but you also sound too mature to be a teenager. You're in college?"

I laughed. "I think I have the opposite problem you have… I sound a lot older than I am. I'm graduating from high school, but I'm eighteen."

"So, you really are a peer," she said.

"I am, I'm your age," I nodded.

"Then how can you understand what I'm going through? How can you give me advice on something you don't know a thing about?"

"I can't pretend to understand what you are going through, Trudi. But if you try, I could at least hear you out. If you want advice, I'll give you my opinion. If not, then I'm here to just listen."

"He raped me," she said.

I stopped still.

"Repeatedly. Over and over again. I thought I wanted to have sex with him at first, but I changed my mind, but he forced me to go through with it. Said I was a tease and a slut." Trudi took a deep breath. "I was a virgin. I thought I knew him, but he was so different from the computer nerd he portrayed on his profile. He wasn't even in his twenties, but early thirties, and looked nothing like his photos. I made a mistake going to his place. I made a mistake trusting him."

I heard everything she said, but the words came through to me like a funnel. I processed bits and pieces of what she had said, while my body shook as though it was freezing cold.

"Hello?" Trudi asked. "Are you there?"

My jaws were clenched tight, while I gripped the edge of my desk like vices.

"Susan?" Trudi asked.

Susan… I know that name. Susan is practical. She is logical. She can outthink through all problems to overcome anything.

Snap out of it, Sam! This is Susan speaking, and you get a grip on YOURSELF, not that table. Don't even think about going into that dark hole. Don't even think of it! That girl needs you to be strong for her right now. RIGHT NOW! So, snap out of it! Breath, relax, think of Collins.

Collins? Why Collins at a time like this? I couldn't believe my rational side would suggest such a crazy idea like think about Collins. Why?

Because he's the first guy whom your body doesn't completely go catatonic over when he touch you intimately. Because, despite his intimidatingly good looks, glamorous life-style, and vast wealth; he actually seemed to care about you.

"Susan, are you still there?" Trudi's voice had gotten higher pitched, almost frantic. "You don't believe me too? Is that why you have stopped listening to me? Just because I made that mistake, I…"

"It. Is. Not. Your. Fault!" I said. "IT. IS. NOT. YOUR. FAULT!" I repeated louder and more forcefully.

"What?" Trudi asked.

"Don't ever apologize or give an excuse for someone who abused you," I recited.

"I shouldn't…" Trudi began.

"It's not your fault," I shook my head. "It's not your fault." I swung my head from side to side, like a little girl reciting a mantra to myself over and over again. I wanted to curl up into a ball and hide away in the corner as another wave of panic rolled and crested in me. I was no longer in my cubicle at Sawyer House, safe in a world of drowning… drowning myself into the lives of other people… people whose own lives probably made mine look relatively normal compared to theirs.

I was no longer in my own little safe haven, but back at my old school when I was thirteen years old… before my family moved away from the small town we lived in, in shame.

~~~~

"So, what will it be today?" his annoying singsong gravelly voice whispered into my ear, as he pushed up against me with his hips. His hands were already groping underneath my sweater, trying to reach underneath my bra to touch my breast. His breath smelled as foul as always, a mixture of tobacco and beef jerky. I had to hold in my breath to avoid breathing in his.

"Stop it, please," I cried, tears streaming down my cheeks. "I don't want to do this."

He pressed closer, his hard-on tight in his jeans, rubbing against the crotch of my jeans. "Why Sam?" he asked. "I know you like this kind of stuff."

"No, I don't," I said.

"You do," he sneer into my face, his foul breath and saliva spitting all over my face. "I know all about you, Sam, pretending to be all prim and proper… Preacher's kid. With your pretty face, long soft hair, and sexy body; you are the most tempting girl in school."

"You can have any girl, Billy," I said. "Please just leave me alone."

"I want you," Billy said, his bluish-grey eyes dark with menace and desire. He narrowed them at my hazel ones. "You know that, Sam. To me, you are the ultimate fruit. Forbidden. I want you even more because you don't want me."

"You're sick," I said, trying to push him away.

He didn't give. Already as tall as a Quarterback at age thirteen, he knew how to use his girth to his advantage. "Nice try, Sam," he chuckled, amused with how I was struggling against his weight. "But you know you can't fight against me." He grabbed my shoulders and pushed me down to my knees until I was kneeling before him on the cold hard floor behind the bleachers in the gym where he had cornered me. "Since you can't tell me, I'll decide what it will be today." With one hand holding me down, and another hand unzipping his fly, I tried to get up and bolt out of his reach as fast as I could, but he was too strong. "No, no, no, Sam," he laughed, holding my arm in a tight grip, "You aren't supposed to run from me." He pushed me down until I fell on my butt, sprawled out before him, and he leaped down on me, pinning me to the ground. "You are so pretty when you're scared," he said, lifting my sweater up and pushing aside my bra until he was clawing at my breasts. Squeezing them and pinching them until they hurt. "Today, I'll show you who's boss." He pulled me up to stand against the wall.

Next he grabbed his belt and pulled it from his pants, until they were held like a whip in his hand. With one quick movement, I felt a burning pain across my back. Billy had whipped me with his leather belt on my bare back. I cried out in pain, but my cry was short-lived. Another slap of the leather belt fell across my torso, and I doubled over, the pain was so sharp, it felt like a knife had cut me.

I looked down, and grimaced. I *was* bleeding. The metal buckle had cut through my skin. I winced, trying to stand up and run. As if Billy knew my intentions, he came up to me to grab one of my wrists. "If you tell anyone what happened, I will make good on my threat, Sam. I know where your parents live and all about your baby sister…" I saw the evil gleam in his eyes as he menacingly thought of ways to hurt her.

"No, Billy, don't even think about it," I said standing up straighter, and walking over to him. "Leave Nydia out of this and my parents. I'm the one you want to hurt."

"Yes," Billy said, grabbing my face with both hands to pull me close to his. "You are the one I want." He kissed me then, his foul mouth sloppily trying to devour my mouth. "I love how scared you look when I do this." He unzipped his fly and was about to pull out his penis when he stopped and started laughing. "See how scared you look," he laughed. "All I had to do is unzip my pants, and you look as frighten as a scared rabbit." He zipped his pants back up and said, "Don't worry for now, Sam. I won't do it to you today, but I will someday when you least expect it. I will bend you over and rape you hard. You be on the lookout all you want, but you won't even know." He looked at the clock on the wall, and smiled. "Lucky for you, we ran out of time. I need to go smoke a joint before I cut out of school." He raised his hand up in a mock wave. "Until next time, Sam," he laughed. "I will be waiting for you."

With that, he left, while I wrapped my arms around myself and sunk to the ground in a heap, sobbing. Every day at school, he would find me. What he did today was slightly different than what he did everyday, but it was always there. That fear, that anticipation of when and where he would get me. That day, the pain of the belt was too strong; I had to go to the nurse's office to get my cut patched up before returning to class. The nurse would bandage it up, taking care of the cut, which I lied about saying I had accidentally scraped myself on a fence. Although the physical wound healed up in a few days, the wounds Billy inflicted on me psychologically went far deeper.

<u>Being Here</u>

TRUDI HAD ALREADY hung up the phone when the waves of involuntary panic washed over, and I was breathing normally again.

What must she have thought when I didn't answer her back? I was going to call her, as soon as I could retrieve her phone number, but one glance at the clock again, and I decided to wait. She probably went to sleep. It was now 3 AM in the morning, and I was exhausted.

I was packing up my bag to go when the green light on the phone lit up again. Could it be Trudi calling back? I looked at the screen above the phone and was disappointed to see the phone the caller was calling from was not listed. Darn. I could not tell if it was Trudi or someone else. If it was Trudi, I owe her a call session. If it was someone else...

The green light kept going on and off until I picked up. "Hello, Sawyer House, Susan speaking. What do you feel like talking about this morning?"

"Sam?" a familiar voice asked. My heart fell down, disappointed it wasn't Trudi, but at the same time it was a voice that made me feel safe. "You're still at the Center?"

"I'm leaving to go home right now, Derek," I said, grabbing my purse. "I have to switch phones. You called on the main hotline." I hung up and dialed Derek's phone from my own, while walking down the hallways of the Center, locking up and closing up for the night.

"I know," Derek said laughing. "Habit when I call into the Center. I was going to check up on you since I was supposed to close up tonight. Thank you for taking on the shift all by yourself. How was tonight by the way?"

"Intense," I admitted.

"Well, I'm done with my all-nighter. I feel ready to grab some coffee and some bagels. I can come by with some nourishment." He sounded sweet and hopeful.

"I'm about to head home to sleep, Derek. Getting breakfast is the last thing on my mind at the moment."

"I can drive by and make sure you get to your car safely," Derek said. "I'm right around the corner."

"That was fast," I laughed. "I thought you were getting bagels and coffee…"

"I skipped that just now so I'm about a couple of minutes away. No traffic at this time of day, no wonder why I'm flying," he exclaimed.

"You leave me no choice, then," I joked. "I have to wait for you or you would think I'm very rude. Not that you should really care what I think of you."

"But I do," Derek said. "I do care what you think of me. Very much so."

"Then," I joked again, "You'd better let me think highly favorable thoughts towards you, Derek."

"I'd like that," he said softly. "Are you still seeing the guy?"

I blinked. Where did that come from? "You mean Collins…"

"Whatever his name is, that guy you seemed to get all knotted and twisted up about," Derek said bitterly.

"I don't know where we are at," I said truthfully.

"Are you two together together?" Derek asked.

"No," I said quickly. "We haven't…" I didn't want to tell him I haven't slept with Collins, but I also didn't want Derek to know that I have.

"Doesn't sound like you're sure about him… so…" Derek's voice drifted off, as his old blue mustang pulled up into Sawyer House's parking lot and parked right next to my car where I was standing.

Before I knew it, Derek was out of the car and in front of me, pulling me into him, his mouth crushing into mine. I was so stunned, as his tongue gently delved in to brush against mine. Instantly, I felt a shiver go through me. I almost froze, but his hands worked its way around my waist, and shoulders, massaging and coaxing me closer. I began to relax into the kiss and let the weight of the evening slowly fall off.

"Oh Sam," Derek groaned, turning me around so that I was leaning up against the back of his car as he deepen his kiss. "Forget about Collins, forget all those other guys," he said passionately. "Be with me. Give me a chance."

"Derek… I… just because I haven't seen Collins for a while doesn't mean…"

"Dammit, Sam," Derek pulled back. "Don't you see? You're a mass of confusion because of him. He's not from the same world as you and I. He's a frickin' playboy billionaire for goodness sakes. He probably goes through a girl a week, and you're just like any one of them."

"Derek," I warned. "Collins isn't like that at all. You can't talk about him that way when you don't even know him."

Derek look a little hurt. "I know that you've been moping around at Sawyer House for the last few months, acting like a wounded bird. I know that…"

I pulled away from Derek. "Derek, how many times do I have to tell you, I'm fine? And if I've been acting like a so-called 'wounded bird' it isn't because of some man."

"Really?" Derek asked. "Why do you recoil at first, freeze as though you're scared, when I kiss you?"

"Maybe because you caught me by surprise, and I wasn't ready for it, Derek?" I said.

"But you liked it," he said. "You wouldn't be kissing me back if you didn't. You are receptive to me. You're just not receptive to being touched." He stepped back and crossed his arms. "Sam, something happened tonight that you're not telling me."

"It's just been a long day, and turning out to be even longer by the second, Derek," I said. "If you haven't noticed, it is nearly dawn, and I haven't even gone home yet to sleep…"

"That's why I came over, Sam. I received an alert when I logged into check on the progress of calls at Sawyer House, and there was one call there that lasted over five hours. Five hours! Holy shit! What happened?"

"Do we have to talk about it now?" I asked, my eyes shooting him arrows. Can't he see I was not in the mood to talk?

"No, not now," Derek said more gently. Thank God, he was smart enough to sense that if he didn't drop the subject now, I'd probably bite off his head. Nothing gets between me and my five hours of sleep or else…

"Oh God, Sam," Derek said, apologetically. "I'm so sorry. I should have been with you to take that call. It must have been something for you to spend five hours with a caller. And now you're tired. I should drive you home. You can sleep in the car."

"You got that right," I joked. "I am about to… pass out."

I couldn't have timed my saying that any better. As soon as the words left my mouth, I collapsed into his chest and was out.

The Incident

I WOKE UP to a stream of sunlight blinding my eyes. And Derek lying across from me on a bed. His bed. In his dorm.

"Derek!" I screamed into his ear. "What happened? Why am I in your bed?"

Derek turned his body towards me and smiled a lazy smile. "You crashed this morning. Completely knocked out. So I dragged you back to my place for you to sleep. It's the closest place to Sawyer House, and I didn't want to wake up your family at your house."

"But why am I in your bed?" I asked.

"There wasn't anywhere to put you," he indicated how small his dorm room was, and scratched his head. "Besides this is the most comfortable place for you to sleep."

"But why are you sleeping next to me?" I asked.

Derek grinned. "I would say because there's nowhere else for me to sleep in here, and because it's my bed, but the honest truth was, Sam, I wanted to be next to you."

I backed away from Derek and got out of bed. "Derek... we didn't...."

"As much as I wanted to, Sam, no. I was a complete gentleman. I won't take advantage of you like that. No, my single mother taught me too well, the lesson of taking precaution and all that. Besides," he narrowed his eyes. "If you and I had done anything, I'd make sure you were fully aware of it and moaning the night away from my lovemaking skills."

"Oh Derek," I said, "This looks bad. I shouldn't have stayed over."

"Why would it look bad, Sam? We're two consenting adults over eighteen, and if we choose to be together like that…"

"No, no, no, Derek," I said, shaking my head. "That's the thing, we didn't do anything, but it looks like we have, and…"

"Look Sam," Derek got up. He was shirtless and wearing only boxers. I couldn't help looking at his well-defined abs and toned chest. It was the first time I've seen him without a shirt on, and he was pretty hot. Hi wavy brown hair was messier than usual with a just-gotten-out-of-bed look, and he had a small growth of stubble. "It's no secret I really like you." He came over to me and held me by my elbows as he looked into my eyes. "I know you're stuck on Collins, whatever hold he has on you, but I'm going to try to win you with whatever chance I got, too. I know you're special. From day one when I saw you with Gail during orientation at Sawyer House, I knew I really wanted to get to know you better. You're not only an exquisite beauty with the most gorgeous face and body, but you're smart, funny, fun, and cool." He bent down and kissed me gently on the lips, "and taste amazingly delicious."

He increased the pressure of his lips on mine and used his tongue to open mine further, to taste more of me. "Oh," he groaned, pressing tight against me, so tight, I could feel him getting more and more excited as he led me to the edge of his bed and lowered me down so I was lying on my back while he kept kissing me on my lips. His mouth devoured mine, as his tongue stroked my tongue. I felt a burning ache ignite from between my legs, as Derek kissed his way from my mouth down my neck, shoulders, top of my breasts through my shirt, and stomach when he lifted my shirt and started kissing my stomach.

I was delirious. Collins McGregor was the only man who I've felt comfortable touching me. He and I had even gone so far as to almost doing it, but Derek… Derek somehow ignited something in me, too. In another way, more familiar, more gentle and safe.

While Derek kissed me… there was a buzzing sound coming from my purse. It pierced through the air like a screaming hawk. Derek tried to ignore it, while he continued kissing my stomach, making his way up my ribs. "I want to make you more comfortable, Sam," he said. "You are always so tense when I touch you either on the shoulder or even when I pat your back. There's something about you that makes me want to break through that barrier."

"Derek… I'm not so sure if this is a good idea," I said, remembering my barrier. As much as I was enjoying his mouth on my skin, and his hands exploring me, in the back of my mind, I could only imagine Collins' hands on me and his skillful sexy mouth on me, making me writhe with desire. "Derek," I pulled myself up, surprising him as his head came up to stare into my eyes.

"What's wrong?" he asked, a little disappointed.

"I can't do this," I said, "And I need to get my phone. I bet my folks are worried that I didn't come home last night."

Derek got off me and rolled to one side of the bed to let me get up and out of bed.

He let out a big frustrated breath and got up, getting dressed. When he was fully dressed, he turned to me and said, "Whatever hang up you have, I'm going to get to the bottom of it. You may be a peer counselor, Sam, but you're the one who seem to need a bit of saving yourself."

"Really?" I asked, getting angry. How dare he tell me that? I was fine. Things were going great for me. My grades were top-notched, I was graduating head of the class, I have my pick of colleges, my classmates liked me, my father was a well-respected pastor of a large congregation, and my mother is a renowned beauty queen. Everything was perfect. How dare Derek for questioning that.

"Yes, really," Derek said angrily. "Just because you think you're Miss Perfect doesn't mean you don't need saving, too. Sometimes we all do."

Learning to Fall Freely

DEREK DROVE ME back to Sawyer House to get my car after I borrowed his toothbrush, cleaned up, and had a light breakfast. We were silent on our way there, me still angry at him, and him still angry at me.

He let me off right by my car, and said, "Why don't you take today off? You were here way late last night, you shouldn't have to come in today, too."

"When are you coming in?" I asked.

"After my exams are done by this afternoon. I'll be in tonight." He licked his lips and looked at mine. "I want to see you tonight."

"I don't know," I said. "You just said I should take the day off."

"You should, but that doesn't mean I can't see you tonight under different circumstances. How about having dinner with me? We can go see a movie."

"Don't you have to work tonight?" I asked, raising my eyebrows.

"For a few hours, then I'm free," Derek said.

"I don't want to give you the idea I'm easy," I said.

"I know you're not," Derek said. "In fact you're the opposite of that."

"Let's keep it at that then," I said.

Derek's face fell. "You're not even going to give me a chance, Sam?"

I took a deep breath and said, "Derek, I would, but I have some issues of my own I have to get through. I hate to admit this to your cocky self, but you're right. I probably do need a little saving here and there, so getting involved with you romantically and sexually is going to complicate a lot of things for me." I took his hands. "I hope you understand. You are right. Something happened last night that shook me to the core, and I realized that until I get some help with it, I will probably always have those issues."

Derek sighed. "Alright, Sam. There isn't anything I can say about that except I will do anything I can to help and support you."

"Then do me a favor?" I asked Derek.

"What?" he asked, lightly tapping my nose with his finger affectionately.

"If you get a caller who goes by the name Trudi, can you let me know that she called. I just want to make sure she followed up… that she's okay."

Derek raised his eyebrows and nodded. "Sure."

"Because," I added, "She was the reason why I was on a call for over five hours."

"Oh," he said. "Do you want me to text you if I do get her call?"

"Yes," I said. "If she calls, I want to be the one she talks to."

"Okay," Derek said. "I'll try."

With that, I reached out and hugged him briefly, startling him, before I headed into my car and drove off.

I was going to take the day off today, like Derek had suggested. It just so happened I had someone very important to see. What timing.

He was the one who called when I was in Derek's room. The irony of it all. It was as though he knew he had to remind me he was there. Collins. My dear Collins, whom I had tried so hard to resist, but ended up falling hard for. My troubled perfectly flawed billionaire bad boy.

I played back the voicemail he left me as I took the highway along the beach heading for his magnificent home by the beach.

"Sam," his velvety warm voice caressed my name affectionately. "This is Collins. I'll come out and say it. I miss you. I want you. I need you. Done. I'm done. Please see me today at my place. It hasn't been the same without you. I'm going crazy. Please help me."

<u>Saving Snowflakes</u>

I REMEMBER MY mother once told me that each child is unique like a snowflake. Every person born into this world have an unique purpose to fulfill, and while snowflakes look as delicate as can be, their formation is so strong that they are able to withstand the elements.

I couldn't believe my eyes as I drove up PCH towards Collins McGregor's beautiful home in Newport Coast's most exclusive area, higher up in the canyons. The sky had turned dark and the clouds looked like it was threatening to burst. When I reached the intricately-carved heavy iron gates leading to Collin's home, I could feel the air suddenly turn chilly.

The gates opened right when my small white car reach the front as though it knew I was coming. Then there was Collins, dressed in sweat pants that hung low on his hips, accentuating his hard abs and sexy v. He was wearing a loose long-sleeve grey shirt that hugged his biceps and out-lined his broad muscular chest. His icy blue eyes were already raw with hunger as he took me all in from head to toe in my jeans and t-shirt. I felt a little self-conscious, not having had a change of clothing since working at Sawyer House last night.

As soon as I pulled past the gates, Collins was already besides my car. He opened the driver's side, gestured for me to scoot over to the passenger side while he slipped in and took the wheels. "Hurry," he said. "It looks like we may have a storm brewing, and I don't want you caught in the middle of it." At over six foot, he seemed like a giant in my compact car, maneuvering through his long windy driveway up the canyon to his Italian-style villa of a

house. I giggled at the picture of him crouched down over my small steering wheel making his way up.

"A bit cramped?" I asked, trying to reach over him to the side of the
seat where he could adjust the length. My fingers accidentally brushed
against his crotch as I did so, and he let out a painful groan. He looked
down and then at me, his eyes piercing through mine with his intensity.
"You did not just do that to torture me, Sam?" he growled. "I'm already as
hard as a rock that just one touch from you... Heck, just one demure look
from you licking your lips can send me over the edge."

I had to suppress a smile, but the look of sheer agony on his face,
made me want to laugh in delight. I haven't seen him in days, and he was
still intrigued by me. It made me happy to see how I affected him. I needed
this... I needed this man who made me feel so wanted, it blew my mind
and pushed out all rational thoughts. I wanted this man with a fierce
passion.

"What are you almost laughing at?" Collins asked, his blue eyes
glancing over at me.

I bit my lips to try from laughing. Collins let out a deep breath and
said, "God, that almost did it. Do you realize how damn sexy that looked
just now? You biting your lips like that, your eyes looking so demure but
mischievous. I want to take you over my lap right now and sit you down..."

I couldn't stand it any longer myself. As soon as he parked my car in
his gigantic garage, I reached over to kiss him, but he beat me to it. He
pushed the seat all the way back, grabbed me and pulled me over his lap
where his hungry mouth crushed against mine, kissing me with the passion
of a starving man. His kisses weren't guarded like Derek's. They were raw
animal hunger. I thought Derek could get through my barrier of intimacy,
but no one except Collins could get me to the point of abandon that came
from raw hunger. I felt fearless when I was with him like this, fearless to
explore my own feelings, to let my pent up desires and passion come
through. Collins was such a man who made me want more, who made me
feel incredibly beautiful and sexy... not at all dirty or slutty for having desires of my own.

Tall, gorgeous, suave and a golden boy god, with icy blue eyes that
could make me heat up just from one glance, Collins made me forget all of

my inhibitions when I was with him. All of my fears, even my suppressed subconscious ones… up to a certain point.

His hands had reached behind me to unclasp my bra, and he was already kneading the sides of my breasts when I stopped him.

"Baby, what is it?" he asked, pulling back and looking at me tenderly. "Did I scare you? Did I do anything wrong?"

"No, Collins," I said gently. "I just had a very rough day yesterday, and…"

Collins took a deep breath and ran is long tapered fingers through his full head of hair… hair I wanted to run my fingers through. "It's alright, baby. I don't want to push you into anything you're not ready for. I don't want you running away scared just because I don't know how to control my need for you." His hungry eyes swept over my entire body again, making me instantly hot for him. His glance felt like a tongue sweeping across me. I shivered with desire and swallowed.

God why does he have that effect on me?

"Okay, then, let's get out of this tin can of a car and go inside," he said, opening the passenger door and getting out to open the door for me. He grabbed me from the waist, lifted me up in the air, and just when I thought he was going to set me down, he wrapped my legs around his waist and pushed me up against the garage wall until I slid down to where I could feel his hardness pressed against my crotch. Even through my jeans and his pants, I could feel the heat between us, and it made me arch my back more, pushing my breasts forward toward him.

He took both of my hands and lifted it into the air, grasping them with his hands where he held me up against the wall. I thought he would kiss me passionately then, but all he did was stared into my eyes for a while, his eyes wide with wonder, love, and tenderness. "Ah, baby, having you in my arms here like this… it's a feeling I never ever want to forget." He kissed me, first softly and gently and then hard, while I kissed him back matching his passion with mine. How long have we been kissing in the garage like this, I had no idea, but when we finally walked into the house, holding hands to a startled cook in the kitchen who immediately retired into her room as she took one look at us and realized we probably needed privacy; it had already turned dark outside. Drops of rain pelted the windows with a fierceness of a tropical storm.

"I thought we only have perfect sunny weather in California," I said staring outside the window as the thunder clouds above unleashed a fury of rain.

"Only in most people's memories," Collins said. "We tend to block out the storms and remember only the good weather."

"Selective memory," I said. "It's what keeps us happy and sane… like having sunny days, rainbows, and lollipops."

"Lollipops?" Collins asked raising his elegant eyebrows. Even his eyebrows were sexy. "I know which lollipops I want to lick," he said, his eyes narrowing deliciously as he came close to stand behind me and wrapped his arms around my waist. He pulled my butt against him, and knew he was definitely still in the mood. Rainclouds or not, the storm did not dampen the heat between us.

He was nibbling my neck and swaying his hips against mine when I heard my phone go off. Someday soon, I will remember to put my phone on vibrator mode. The thought sent shivers down my spine, as everything Collins-related or being around Collins, made my mind turn to mush, and my body in heat mode.

The phone kept going and going, until Collins lifted his head from where he was kissing my shoulders and said, "I think you should answer it. It could be your mother wondering where you are in this storm."

"Alright," I said. I gave Collins a disappointed pout, and he immediately pulled me in for a quick kiss.

"Adorable and sexy," he whispered. "No wonder I can't get enough of you. Now go get your phone call. I don't want your mom sending a search and rescue team out to find you." He gave my butt a small slap. I wanted to turn my other cheek for him to give it the same treatment, but I heard the phone go off again.

I went and grabbed my phone from my purse and started walking towards Collins' office where he indicated I could go to have some privacy while I was on the phone. I looked at the caller id, and saw it was from Derek.

"Hi Derek," I said. "How are you holding up?"

"I'm fine," he said. "I know it's storming outside so I'm at least glad I'm in here. How's your day off?"

"I, uh, am enjoying myself. Glad I'm inside, too. So, what's up?"

"You know that caller you said you wanted to know if she'd call?"

"Yes, Trudi's her name. Did she call?" I asked excitedly.

"She's on the line. She wants to talk to Susan. No one else."

"I'll try to be there in half an hour or so…"

"No, it's raining too hard. Stay where you are. I think we may be able to get you to connect up so you can talk to her from your phone."

"Can you do that?" I asked.

"I can do many things," Derek said. "Some you would be begging for me to do again and again."

"Derek…" I said, almost smiling. I bet he would be good at those things.

"Okay, back to business… patching your line with hers… in just a few minutes, you will be on the phone with Trudi… okay now…"

I heard a click and then instead of talking to Derek, I was on the line with a familiar girly voice… a voice that kept me riveted for over five hours the other night.

"Hello?" the little girl voice said. "Is Susan there?"

"Hi," I said. "I'm Susan. Who am I talking to?" I wanted to make sure I was talking to Trudi and not Derek. I had already felt a connection with Trudi, and knowing if Derek was on the line might scare Trudi off.

"Trudi," she said. "The girl you were talking to the other night…"

"I remember you," I said. "Of course I remember you." I smiled.

"Oh," she said. "I didn't think you would, but anyways, I wanted to talk to you again to let you know what happened."

"What?" I asked, as excited to find out as though she was a close girl-friend telling me her latest news.

"Fred is in jail now… the man who raped me is in jail. He tried raping another girl, but she turned him in… and with my testimony this morning, we were able to send him to jail." She drew in a deep breath. "I wanted to say, 'thank you'. Thank you for listening and for giving me the time of day. That night when I called, I was seriously thinking of ending it all. No one cared whether I lived or died. It seemed anyone who knew anything about what was going on with me, thought I deserved being raped, deserved being humiliated by Fred just because I made the mistake of being 'promiscuous' and going to his house, flirting with him online and such. No one understood what I was going through... no one until you, Susan. You listened to me, and even though you didn't say a whole lot, I got the sense you were going through the exact emotions and feelings I was going through. You were with me the entire way, holding my hand, letting me grieve through the process. When he raped me, I felt as though he took a good chunk of me with him, and left an empty shell of a person behind. I felt dirty and humiliated, shameful when all along; he was the one who did the criminal act. He was the one who should be blamed. Not the victim. Not me and countless other women. So, again, Susan, thank you from the bottom of my heart. That night when you picked up the phone and sat with me through the night, you saved my life. And this morning when I helped testify against Fred, we helped saved another." She paused. "That's all I wanted to tell you, Susan."

Tears were rolling down my cheeks as I tried to compose myself enough to talk to her. "No Susan, I want to thank you for coming to me. Your bravery in opening up to me, helped me deal with some darkness of my own. I'm still dealing with it, but in time, I know I'll overcome it. Your story has started me on the way to being saved, and I thank you from the bottom of my heart, too."

I heard tears roll down Trudi's cheeks then, and heard her wipe them off. "If I can be of help to you or anyone, just let me know."

"I will," I said, and I meant it as I hung up and walked out to see Collins... my beautiful Collins standing outside in his patio by the pool. He looked so beautiful standing out there with a white blanket around him. Angelic, yet naughty at the same time, when I caught his mischievous smile.

"What are you doing?" I asked. "It's freezing out here."

"I know," Collins said, coming to me with the thick wool blanket he had wrapped around me. He unwrapped the blanket and enveloped me inside with him, snuggled together, looking out to the ocean below. It was surreal seeing what we saw on a Spring day in California.

The beach was lined with snow, and looking up, I saw snowflakes drifting down towards us. Collins reached out a hand and caught a few before he brought them over for me to touch. "Aren't these beautiful?" he asked. "So strong and delicate at the same time. Each unique in its own way."

"Beautiful," I said.

He reached out and let a few more drift down onto his palms.

"What are you doing?" I asked again, laughing at the delight I saw in his face. He looked like a sweet angelic boy playing in the snow on a Christmas day.

"I'm trying to save each of these snowflakes," he said. "You never know what each one might grow up to be?"

Again I had tears in my eyes, but this time of happiness. "You never know, Collins, but I have a feeling, snowflakes may one day bring a lot of love and peace into this world."

He came over and wrapped the blanket around us again. "No doubt." Then he kissed me before he handed me one perfectly-formed snowflake. "I'm putting this one in the freezer. I want to keep this one as long as possible. Love is a lot like snowflakes, Sam. It never dies. It just develops into another form."

As we stared into each other's eyes, I could see snowflakes having an effect on people like that. For now, all I wanted to do was snuggle into Collin and enjoy each snowflake as it fell.

About the Author

Kailin Gow

Kailin Gow is the author of over 100 books for young adult, new adult, and adult. She started the Saving You Saving Me Project as an online crisis advice site to help provide resources for teens, young adults, and women. Kailin Gow is also the author of the international bestselling *Frost Series, Loving Summer Series,* and *You & Me Trilogy,* which contained themes related to bullying and self-esteem, along with the non-fiction book, *The Shy Girls Social Club Handbook Dealing with Bullies and Other Meanies, published* by Sparklesoup Inc.

For more information about Kailin Gow and her books, you can visit:
http://www.KailinGow.com

Defying the Dust

By

Karina Halle

Featuring characters from The Artists Trilogy

I NEVER THOUGHT much about hope.

The word never meant that much to me.

Until I met Ellie Watt.

Suddenly I knew what hope was. It was something that could save me from my classmates, save me from my parents, save me from myself.

It was a crazy hot day in August when I first met Ellie. In Palm Valley, California, most days were crazy hot and I often made it worse, dressing the way that I did. It was because of my "questionable" attire that my parents decided it was about time to haul me off to the town's quack, Dr. Edison. I knew it was a matter of time and I really didn't care anymore. When the whole town thought you were a freak, what was a trip to a psychiatrist's office?

"Now remember to be *honest* with the doctor," my stepmother, Raquel, had said from the front seat, not bothering to turn around and look at me. She rarely looked at me. She only had eyes for her daughters, Kelli and Colleen, two little ten-year-old brats from hell. Even though she'd married my dad four years earlier, she still treated me like I was a nuisance, a waste of space. It would have been nice if she didn't perpetuate the evil step-mother stereotype, but no such luck there. Not that Raquel was evil. She just didn't give a shit about me. But I suppose when you're dealing with a teenager, that can be seen as the same thing.

I grunted in response and looked down at my nails. She'd confiscated the black nail polish I bought from the drugstore, so I had to fill in my nails with black Sharpie. I know she still hated it, the fact that it looked like I'd painted my nails when I was a thirteen-year-old boy. But I liked it. It made me feel dark, dangerous—different.

"We don't want you starting the ninth grade looking like a faggot," my father sneered from behind the wheel. I looked up at the rearview mirror and saw his eyes blazing in it, full of disapproving fury. Normally, I was scared when I saw those eyes with that kind of fire behind them, but I knew he wouldn't dare hit me here in the car, not in front of Raquel and not be-fore I was about to see a shrink. Raquel damn well knew he knocked me around when she wasn't looking, and though she never did or said anything about it, I don't think she'd stand for it if she actually saw it happen.

Then again, what did I know?

"For the last time, I'm not gay," I told him, my eyes trying to hold his. But like an Old West showdown, I looked away first. It was hard to be contemptuous without pressing my luck.

"Then why do you have to dress like that?" my father whined. For being Palm Valley's sheriff, he often sounded more like a spoiled dog than a man.

"It's called self-expression," I said, sighing loudly. I pressed my fore-head against the window, feeling the heat searing through the glass, and shifted in my seat.

My pants were black and skintight, covered with patches I'd sewn on myself: Nine Inch Nails, Skinny Puppy, The Ramones, The Cramps, Korn, Deftones. I loved them but even I was starting to realize that my clothing choices weren't the smartest for the end of the summer. My balls were sweating like nobody's business.

"Well what the fuck are you trying to express?" My dad said.

"George," Raquel warned.

"Oh, shut up," he sniped at her. "Like you've never sworn in front of your kids." He looked back at me. "Well? You going to tell me or do I have to guess?"

I swallowed hard. "I'd rather tell the shrink. That is why you're sending me there, isn't it? So that you don't have to deal with whatever I'm going to say. Whatever truth there is? You can just put me on medication, hoping I'll stop listening to evil music and drawing on things."

My dad just shook his head. I was right and he knew it. He couldn't handle me; he didn't know what to do with me. I was like a vermin problem, a rat that refused to get caught in the traps. And I knew what the cheese was—what he was offering. He would treat me better if I acted normal. Maybe he wouldn't beat my ass once a week. But I knew that wasn't true. I was always Dad's little scapegoat, even when my mother was around. Hell, he hit her more than a few times too, before she died.

I hoped I'd never turn into him.

We rode in silence the rest of the way before we pulled up to the medical building at the end of the main drag. Clouds of dust blew up around us as we parked and Raquel got out. She, not my father, would take me in to see the doctor. Heavens fucking forbid someone should see the sheriff bring his son to Dr. Edison.

I got out of the van and followed her through the shimmering heat of midday. Raquel was a frail-looking woman with wicked lines by her eyes, and though I didn't remember my own mom too clearly anymore, I knew she was prettier. Raquel favored handbags that looked fancy but you could tell were cheap, and high heels that made her look like an idiot in our neck of the desert. Rancho Mirage or La Quinta, sure, but Palm Valley? She both tried way too hard and didn't try at all.

She opened the door for me to go into the building just as an elderly woman with a walker was slowly coming out. The elderly woman looked at me and nearly had a heart attack. She then looked to Raquel who gave the old lady a sympathetic smile. I know she wanted to say, "He's not my son," and she'd be right about that.

I just grinned at the old woman, hoping she'd see the real me underneath. I may have dressed like a goth but I wasn't about to knock her over and steal her handbag.

Raquel jerked her head, motioning for me to get inside. The old lady was frozen in place, unblinking, as she took me all in. For once I was grateful that I wasn't wearing black lipstick or eyeliner. Lately I'd been on a big Robert Smith kick and had been trying to emulate The Cure singer's looks.

"Excuse me," I said to her as politely as possible as I walked past. She flinched at me as I came close and then shook her head, making a disgusted noise with her toothless mouth. I should have been used to the stares and whispers I got. In fact, most of the town had seen me, or at least I'd thought they had. But it didn't stop me from feeling bouts of shame, and it didn't stop them from making their pithy observations.

Raquel walked through the open foyer and up the stairs to the second level of the building and into a small waiting room. The frosted glass door with the words Dr. Edison painted in garish font clicked behind us with a sense of finality. Thankfully, the waiting room was empty, the table strewn with a mix of *Reader's Digest* and *Psychology Today* magazines, the walls covered with dull landscape paintings. If the doctor let his patients decorate his office, he'd probably be blown away at their originality. But that's what being original got you these days—a trip to the shrink. While Raquel went to go check in with the receptionist, I sat down and picked up a copy of *Reader's Digest*. The "Drama in Real Life" stories were the best.

I only got to read one page on how someone survived a bear attack at Lake Shasta before the receptionist called me in.

"I'll come back in an hour," Raquel said, giving me a smile and wave—all for the benefit of the double-chinned receptionist—as I was hustled into a dark office.

Dr. Edison was standing in the middle of the room. He looked like I thought he would—widow's peak, thinning hair, rectangular glasses that were similar to mine. He also had a steely look of observation that I was sure most psychiatrists had. I was a specimen under the glass, waiting to be examined.

"Have a seat, my boy," he said, gesturing to a love seat in the corner. I was glad he didn't make the obvious joke about me looking like a girl, thanks to my shoulder-length hair. Oh right, and the makeshift nail polish.

I smiled uneasily and walked over to the love seat, lowering myself cautiously.

"I guess there's no room to lie down, is there?" I asked, half-joking.

His thin lips twitched up into a brief smile as he peered over his glasses and sat elegantly in his stiff-backed leather chair. "That's only in the movies."

I nodded, swallowing down my uneasiness and watched him as he briefly looked over a file in his hands.

"So you're Sheriff McQueen's boy, I see," he said. It wasn't accusatory; in fact, there was no emotion in his voice. He could have been reading the back of a cereal box for all I knew. But I bristled anyway. Anytime someone brought up my father it was usually followed by a look of "where did he go wrong?"

Being born an asshole is where he went wrong.

The doctor raised his brow as he studied me. "Camden McQueen. Perhaps we should start by talking about your father. He is the one who called me, after all. He said you needed to get your head on straight. Now, what might he be talking about?"

I sighed. I was already overwhelmed. I let my eyes drift over to the window and the dust motes dancing as the harsh light came streaming in. I felt entranced by them, willing my mind to bring me somewhere else, anywhere but here. It was a coping mechanism that worked. Anytime I was upset or angry, when I felt like the rage inside was going to consume me, I could just get away in my mind. It saved me so many times. I think it was the closest thing I had to hope at the time.

I don't know how long I sat like that, just staring out the window in my own world, but eventually I heard the doctor's voice come through, as if in midsentence.

"Self-expression is normal for kids your age—teenagers especially— but I am sure your father has a right to be apprehensive about you."

I eyed him coldly. "A right?"

He pursed his lips for a second. "Yes, at least in the way he'd figure it. Being... homosexual—"

I rolled my eyes. "Jesus Christ, I am not fucking gay. Do you think Marilyn Manson is gay when he's banging Rose McGowan's ass all day long?"

"I am not familiar with the personal life of that artist."

"Okay, let's take someone like David Bowie then," I said, leaning forward. "Ziggy Stardust wore makeup, embraced his androgynous look, all for the name of art. Self-expression."

"David Bowie was a homosexual."

"David Bowie is *bi*sexual," I corrected him. Did he really think I couldn't school him on music? "He's married to a supermodel, Iman. She's gorgeous. And black, too. Another reason he's my hero. My point is just because I dress like this and just because other artists do too, doesn't mean we're gay. It doesn't mean we're weird. It doesn't mean we're a threat to society."

He barely nods. "So you consider yourself an artist?"

I shrank back in my seat and shrugged. A piece of hair fell in front of my face. "I don't know. I want to be. I like to draw, to paint. I like to create. I like playing guitar too—hope I can buy one if I save up enough money. I know my dad won't ever buy me one."

The doctor tapped his pen three times against his file and then said, "I don't think your father is against your self-expression the way that you see it. It's just that in this town, with all the military we have here and the base so close, people aren't very... accepting toward people like you."

I raised my brow. "People like me?" For a shrink, he totally lacked tact.

He sighed. "Are you this defensive with everyone?"

I blinked.

He went on and gestured to my clothing. "You're expressing yourself. I see that. Everyone sees that. But it doesn't make life easier for you. It gives people the wrong idea."

"Being gay is the wrong idea?"

"Because you're not gay, or so you say. If you're straight and normal, then you should act it. Lose the makeup and the scary clothes and go make proper friendships with people. Start looking at girls. Camden, this is for your own good."

That little thing called rage? Yeah, it was sneaking up on me again. I had to take in a deep breath and count to ten. Zoning out wasn't going to help me this time. Ten, nine, eight…

"My own good," I repeated under my breath. Seven, six, five…

"Yes. Your father told me that you don't have any friends. That you get beat up. That people are scared of you. You know why this is and yet you choose to self-express yourself this way anyway. The only thing I can think of, if you aren't gay, is that you *want* to be hurt. You want people to look at you unfavorably."

Four, three, two…

"Can you imagine how your life would change if you just acted… normal?"

One…

I breathed out through my nose in a sharp burst and looked at him with a wry smile on my face. "If I acted normal, no one would talk about me. And everyone would be happy. Except for me."

He studied me for a long time before he said, "Do you think of yourself as a martyr, Camden? Do you feel like you're not done making your point?"

"There's always a point to be made," I said with a shake of my head. And if I didn't make a point—about life, about everything—then no one ever would. Not in this close-minded, ignorant town of dust and decay.

The rest of the session was complete nonsense as well. The more that Dr. Edison talked, the more I realized he wasn't here to help me—if I even needed help. He wanted to help my father and the town and the overall look of things. He wanted to stop looking at me. He wanted *me* to go away and come back as somebody else.

That wasn't going to happen.

When it was all over, I got up and thanked him for his time. It was the polite thing to do and made me look better. Sometimes being nice was the best ammo of all.

I was at the door when he called out to me, "One day, Camden, you'll leave this town and wish you did something nice for the people in it. Maybe even for your own family. There are other lives out there other than your own. Sometimes we need to make sacrifices in order to keep loved ones happy, even if we don't think they deserve it."

I didn't turn to look at him. I ignored his words, letting them roll off me like drops of oil, and stepped out into the receptionist's area. There was a lanky woman with blonde eighties hair sitting in the corner pretending to read a magazine. In reality, she was eyeing me with disdain. My stepmother wasn't anywhere.

I looked at the receptionist. "Um, have you seen…"

She jerked her head toward the exit. "Your stepmother called and said she's running late and for you to wait for her outside." She didn't even look at me, just called the other woman over instead.

I exhaled and headed out of the medical building and back into the inferno. The sun was high in the sky now, searing my pants to my legs in seconds. I shielded my eyes from the glare and looked around. The van wasn't in the parking lot. I guess Raquel and my father fucked off somewhere. Too bad it was too hot out to even think about walking back home by myself.

I sat down on the curb and waited. A few cars puttered past on the main road, the dust rising like sandy plumes behind them. There was something pretty about that and had I been in a better mood, or at least had my sketchbook on me, I would have tried to capture that in colored pencil. Pen was too blunt for something that ethereal.

Then I saw something even more poetic: the silhouette of a girl walking through the dust clouds along the sidewalk. I couldn't see her face, just her shape, though I could tell she was small and walked with a pronounced limp. She turned in my direction and headed toward me. As soon as the dust cleared, she stopped and looked around as if she were lost.

Wow. She was pretty. Very pretty. She looked about my age, too. She had long blonde hair pulled back in a ponytail, big dark eyes, a round face, and pouty lips. I'd never seen her before—I would know if I had. I knew every girl in town—from afar, of course. No girls ever talked to me. But I kept all their names and images in my head, using the prettiest ones when I was spanking it in the shower.

But unlike a lot of the girls in Palm Valley, this one wasn't showing a lot of skin. You get used to it in this heat, seeing your classmates walking around in cut-offs and bikini tops that only the coolest girls could fill out. This girl already stood out by wearing flared jeans, Doc Martens boots and a T-shirt. She must have been boiling hot, just as I was.

She started walking toward the building, but stopped as soon as she saw me.

My first instinct was to smile at her. It made most girls turn and run away.

But then she started walking again, slower this time and with deliberation. She was trying to control her limp, her focus now dead ahead, not letting her eyes waver to me. I couldn't tell if it was because I weirded her out or if she was self-conscious. Maybe both.

She was just a few feet away, refusing to look at me, when I said, "If you're looking for the psychiatrist, he's upstairs."

The girl stopped and looked at me, a mix of shock and fear on her face. Up close she was even prettier, with a smattering of freckles across her petite nose. She filled out her jeans and black shirt pretty well too. I adjusted myself and prayed I wouldn't get another inappropriate boner, though at least there'd be a reason for it this time.

I kept my face deadpan. Might as well give her another reason to be turned off. "I mean, I'd know, I was just at the shrink. Guess my father thinks I'm a bit nuts."

She looked me up and down, her face relaxing slightly though she still looked puzzled. Finally she said, "I'm looking for a pharmacy."

I squinted up at her. "You're not from here, are you? I mean, this town?"

She shook her head. She looked really uncomfortable.

"Aren't you hot in those jeans and boots?" I asked.

Her face immediately went red and I knew I struck a nerve. But instead of feeling proactive, like I'd shut her down before she had a chance to shut me down, I just felt bad.

"I'm sorry," I said quickly and got to my feet. "I'm not one to talk." I towered over her, awkwardly adjusting my pants and rattling my wallet chain, but to her credit she still stood there and folded her tanned arms across her chest. Her T-shirt was an aged looking Metallica *Master of Puppets*. I nodded at it. "Cool shirt. Do you like Metallica or did you pick that up at a thrift store?"

"Both," she said, raising her chin. Her eyes darted to the building. "So is there a pharmacy in there?"

"Yep," I said. "What are you looking for?"

She gave me a look that said it was none of my business.

I raised my hands in apology. "Sorry. Just trying to make conversation. Usually I have about two seconds before someone throws a lame insult in my face. You're breaking a record here."

She sucked on her bottom lip—completely adorable. I had the sudden urge to do the same thing.

"Did you really see the psychiatrist?" she asked, still appraising me.

I looked down at my clothes and back up again. "Look at me. Don't I look like I need to see a shrink?"

She smiled but shook her head. "No. I like the Deftones," she said, nodding at my patch. "I have all their albums."

No way. No way this cool pretty chick in the Metallica shirt would also like one of my favorite, more obscure bands. I was pretty sure my mouth was open so I quickly tried to fill it with words.

"Uh, oh really? Cool. Have you seen them live?"

"No... I've never been to a concert. How about you? You look like you go to a lot."

I laughed, trying to figure out if she was insulting me or not. Her face was still guarded, yet sweet, and I decided she was being genuine... which was rare around me. "No, I've never seen them live. I took the bus out to Palm Springs when I heard Queens of the Stone Age was playing at a small bar there. Course, they wouldn't let me in, I was only ten at the time, but I saw Josh Homme from far away."

I wondered if she knew who the singer/guitarist was but she just said, "Was he tall?"

"Yeah, he was tall." Even though our conversation must have sounded pretty stilted and lame to anyone listening, I felt like I was having the best talk of my life. "All the girls were throwing themselves at him," I added, trying to appeal to her even more.

She shrugged. "I don't like redheads much but he's good on guitar." Her eyes drifted to the building. "Are you busy or do you want to help me with something?"

"I'll help you," I said a little too quickly. I winced at my own over-enthusiasm but she just nodded at me with a straight face.

"Good," she said. She started walking toward the building, her movements stiff. She glanced at me over her shoulder. "Come on."

I looked back to the road, wondering if my dad was going to kill me if I wasn't waiting by the curb. Then I decided that for this girl, death was worth it.

I followed her into the building, the smell of strawberries and vanilla wafting behind her. I tried not to stare at her ass as it wiggled in her jeans, but I caught a few glances while I could. Who knew if I'd ever be this close to a girl again? To be honest, I was surprised that not only was she cool as hell, but she was actually still talking to me. There had to be a catch…

As soon as we were in the mall-like foyer and spotted the small pharmacy shop—the type filled with canes and footbaths and gauze, not fun stuff like Sharpies and Super Soakers—I tried to make conversation.

"So where did you move here from?" I asked.

She shrugged. "Out East, the South, whatever," she said and then stopped suddenly. I nearly ran into her and stopped myself just in time. I'm sure the last thing she wanted was a sweaty Camden all up against her.

She smiled like she was about to let me in on the world's biggest secret. I felt like my breath was being leached from my lungs.

"You go talk to the clerk and distract him," she said, her voice low and hushed.

"What?"

She frowned, her smile becoming wry and twisted. "Come on. Be a pal."

Now it was my turn to frown. "I just don't understand. You want me to distract Mr. Sirk, the guy behind the counter? Distract him from what?"

"Haven't you ever shoplifted before?"

I was taken aback and laughed. "No." Her mouth turned into a tight line. Oh my god, I thought she'd been joking. "You're serious."

"Man, you guys in this town are no fun," she said and quickly turned to the store.

I reached out, grabbed her elbow, and dropped it as soon as I felt awkward, which was pretty much right away. "No, no. I mean. Yeah. This town is no fun. But I'll help you. I've just never done it before." For obvious reasons, too. I mean, one was that everyone watched me like a hawk anyway. I looked like I played Troublemaking Teen Number One in a *Lifetime* movie. Two was the fact that my dad was the sheriff.

Although the fact that I'd be helping this girl steal something—commit a crime—did make me feel like I was sticking it to my dad a bit.

"What's your name?" I asked her.

She raised a thin brow. "Why?"

I pushed my glasses up the bridge of my nose. "Well I figure if I'm going to be your accomplice, I might as well know your name. Bonnie and Clyde knew each other's names."

"They knew a lot more than that," she said and I could have sworn another shade of crimson dotted the center of her cheeks. "My name's Ellie."

"Camden," I said. I stuck out my hand then thought better of it. Then I raised it again because I'd already gone too far. I stared at it dumbly, like it was stuck in greeting limbo.

Luckily, Ellie was a good sport and she shook my hand anyway. Her grip was strong, surprising. Most girls my age shook hands like everyone had some disease—or maybe that's just the way they were with me. But there was a strange sort of confidence in her handshake just as there was a strange sort of vulnerability in her eyes. She was already an enigma to me.

"Camden," she said slowly, as if my name felt good on her tongue. "Isn't that a town?"

I nodded. "I can be a lot of things."

"So can I." She looked to the store and back again, a grin making her cheeks pop. "So you'll be the fall guy? I mean, you'll distract him?"

"Sure," I said, trying to sound more nonchalant than I felt. "What are you stealing?"

"Just... nothing," she said.

"And you're sure you can't buy it?"

Her face fell briefly and a wash of sadness flashed through her dark brown eyes. "No. My family is poor. We live on my uncle's date farm. It's just temporary but…"

I patted her on the arm. "I get it. Let's do it." I could tell that whatever brought Ellie to this town, she wasn't happy about it. I didn't mean to sound like the moral police anyway. I was just curious as to whether it was something she actually needed or something she was doing for kicks. From the grave look her eyes suddenly took on, it seemed to be something she needed.

We walked into the store and she veered off to my right, walking purposefully down the aisle while I took in a deep breath and approached Mr. Sirk. The minute he looked up from his tattered paperback novel—Tom Clancy—and saw me, his eyes narrowed in suspicion.

"May I help you?" he asked. He licked his lips nervously. Sometimes I wondered just how scary I looked to people. I mean, sure I was in all black and kinda weird, but still, I was obviously just thirteen. I wasn't a threat. Then again, people had said that before the Columbine incident, too.

Of course, now I had to distract him long enough for Ellie to steal whatever she was stealing.

I leaned on the counter, noticing him inch back slightly, and said, "Got any comic books?"

He looked slightly relieved. I bet he thought I was going to ask him for hard drugs or something.

"Did you check the magazine rack?" he asked.

"No," I answered. "Thought I'd ask you first. So do you?"

"No," he said. He brought his book out and was about to resume reading when I said, "Could you order some in for me?"

Okay, it was lame, and I was seconds from being thrown out of his store, I could tell.

He sighed angrily and said, "Look, kid, this ain't a library. If you want to buy comic books, I suggest…"

I know he kept talking, but I stopped listening the minute I caught Ellie leaving the store out of the corner of my eye. I tapped the counter with my fist, making the man jump, told him "thank you", and quickly walked out of the store after Ellie.

She hadn't looked behind her or stopped until she was well clear of the building. Though she was still limping, she looked casual and carefree, like she hadn't stolen anything at all. In fact, I couldn't be sure of it until I was right beside her in the insufferable heat looking down at her jean pocket, which bulged at the front.

"Is that it?" I asked.

She kept her eyes to the road. "Yep. Thanks for that."

"No problem." I really, really wanted to ask again about what it was she stole, but from the clipped way she finished her sentences, I knew she wouldn't tell me. Maybe it was something as simple as makeup.

I chewed on my lip for a second, trying to think of what else to say. My father hadn't come by yet, but I felt like time was running out.

"You were really good," I told her.

She shot me a funny look.

I swallowed uneasily. "I mean, you looked natural. Not that I think you always steal shit, it's just… um, well it was kind of fun. More fun than what I normally do."

"And what do you normally do? Aside from go to the shrink?"

She was a smart-ass, too. I liked that.

I smiled and brushed my hair behind my ears. "You know. Play guitar, draw, paint, listen to music. Annoy my stepsisters. You?"

She shrugged. "I've been learning a lot about harvesting dates."

"I think you need to get out more," I joked. "Maybe…"

Ellie looked at me expectantly. It was ridiculous, what I was about to say, but my mouth was moving and the words were coming out before I could stop them.

My eyes dropped to the hot asphalt as a gum wrapper blew past on a stiff breeze. "Maybe… if you wanted… I could show you around town. I mean, if you wanted. Might be nice to know the area before school starts. I could tell you all the kids to avoid… though they'd all say to start with me."

She was silent for so long that I finally had to look up at her. She was staring off into the distance, at the dry, crackled mountains. Either she was ignoring me or she was lost in her own thoughts.

I opened my mouth to tell her to forget it when she said,

"I guess you get bullied a lot, huh?"

I snorted. "Well, yeah. Last year they started calling me The Dark Queen. I've been shoved into more lockers than backpacks have. My lips get most of their action from other dude's fists."

She looked at me, her gaze leveled. "You sound proud of it."

I shrugged with one shoulder. "It's life. Gotta make something of it. I'm not going to stop being me."

"Is that what you told the shrink?"

I nodded. "Pretty much."

"But what's the real answer? Who is the real Camden?"

"Wow. You're all deep and shit, for a shoplifter." I expected her to smile at that but she just looked back to the road, just in time to see my dad's van come down into the parking lot. I took in a steadying breath. "Well, that's my ride."

I must have sounded odd to her because her head whipped toward me and she studied my face. "Is that your family?"

"My dad and stepmom," I said quickly. "They'll have a heart attack when they see me talking to a girl. Think the shrink scared me straight."

Her mouth formed an "oh" and I figured she was probably assuming I was gay. I was tired of correcting people though, so I didn't add anything to that. Besides, maybe she'd think I was less threatening if I was.

The van came to a sudden stop beside me, Raquel getting mild whiplash in the front seat. I was surprised to see my father hopping out and coming around the front of it.

"Dad," I said nervously.

Only he was smiling faintly, like he was really impressed that I was talking to a member of the female species, and a cute one at that.

"Camden," he said, his eyes fixed on Ellie. "Who might your friend here be? I don't think I've seen you around, young lady."

Ellie stuck out her hand and raised her chin to look him in the eyes. There was a hint of detachment in her gaze, like she was pretending to be something she wasn't.

"Hi, I'm Ellie. I just met your son."

"Ellie?" he prodded.

She swallowed like something was stuck in her throat. "Ellie Watt. I just moved here."

My dad's brows came together like two black caterpillars. "Watt... are you with the folks who are living on Jim's date farm?"

She blinked in surprise. "Yes, sir."

He watched her for a few moments, wiggling his jaw back and forth. "I see. Well, welcome to Palm Valley. I'm Camden's father. Sheriff McQueen."

The color quickly drained out of Ellie's face and she nervously rubbed her palms along her jeans. "Oh. How cool." Her eyes flew to mine for an instant, a mix of disappointment and fear taking them for a second or two. Then her expression was detached again.

I stared back at her, smiling lightly as if to tell her that her secret was safe with me. It wasn't until my dad told her it was nice meeting her and barked at me to get in the car that I eyed the bulge in her pocket and gave her the thumbs up.

"If you want to hang out," I started.

"Camden!" my father yelled as he got in the car. "Let's go."

Whatever delight my father initially had at seeing me with Ellie was suddenly gone, like he already knew she was the shoplifting type and disapproved.

Still, I had to try. "Do you need a ride?" I asked. I heard my father groan from inside and Raquel telling him to be quiet.

She bit her lip and shook her head. "No, I'm okay. My mom can get me. No. Wait... I can walk home."

"Phhff, you can't walk home in this," I said, glancing at the sun.

"No," she said quickly, an edge to her voice. I looked at the hardness in her eyes, the trepidation in the whites of them. "Thank you. I'll walk."

I gave her an uneasy smile. I didn't want her to walk, but it was obvious the idea of getting a ride with me and my dad scared the crap out of her. I bet she thought it was a trap and we were going to lead her straight to the police station for questioning.

"Okay, well—"

"Camden!" my dad boomed.

"—I'll be seeing you. I hope."

"I'll see you at school," she said, giving me a quick wave. I expected her to march off toward the building or maybe down the street, but she just stood there, waiting, until I was in the van and we were moving away.

I watched her until she was gone; my neck craned around until it hurt. Then I sat back in my seat and let a small smile play on my face. I didn't know what had happened, but somehow my day turned around one hundred percent. For once, I was able to talk to someone without them being weird about how weird I was. For once, I was able to meet someone who seemed to have secrets and problems of her own.

For once, I met a girl who was cool as hell and totally took my breath away.

And so, naturally, for once, I wasn't going to let this girl get away that easily.

I had hope.

~~~~

I spent the next week in a mix of agony and anticipation. The agony was because I was forced to look after the twins, Kelli and Colleen, for two whole days while Raquel attended day school in Palm Springs for floral arrangements or some shit like that. Not only were KC (as I called them), totally spoiled and bitchy, never listening to a word I said, but they were best friends with Sheila Martin. Sheila's older brother, OJ, was in my grade and hated my guts. When I had to go to their house to pick the twins up and walk them home, it was like ringing the doorbell to Mordor. OJ always had a new insult for me, plus the threat that the minute school started he was going to fuck me up so badly that even glasses wouldn't help my eyesight.

The scary thing was that he wasn't kidding. Just before school ended, OJ's friend Calvin ended up breaking my nose in front of everyone; a good old beat up on the "art fag" after class type of deal. He was suspended, but because it was the end of school it didn't really matter. My father was furious at me, saying I must have provoked it and, aside from the suspension, Calvin never really got into any shit. In fact, I was sure some punks were looking up to him like he was the king, and now it was like OJ wanted that same kind of fame. Somehow, over the course of the year, I'd gone from a victim of having lunch money stolen and atomic wedgies to being a victim of actual physical violence. I may have joked about it to myself, but deep down inside, it really did scare the shit out of me. That was one thing that Dr. Edison said that struck a chord. This was a military town with military men and ideals. My punishment for straying from that would probably get worse over time.

But along with the agony, there was the anticipation. Hope. Because I'd figured out where Ellie was staying and the easiest way to get there. She'd never come and seek me out, but I could go to her. Let her know her shoplifting secret was still safe with me.

I'd decided that Friday was a good day to do it. I tucked the latest issues of *Rolling Stone* and *Parade* into my backpack, along with my mp3 player and a minispeaker. Raquel was back now—our entire house smelled like a jungle thanks to her new fondness for plant arrangements—and I'd earned some money for the horrid babysitting. Most of it went into my piggy bank for that guitar of mine, but I decided to stick a few bills in my wallet in case Ellie wanted to go out and get a Slurpee at the 7-Eleven or something like that. A boy could dream.

I chose not to look as much like a freak that day, but I still wouldn't pass for normal. I had drawn images up and down my legs with a pen the night before, pretending they were tattoos, so I showed off the dragons and skulls by wearing cargo shorts. My shirt looked like I stole it from Freddy Krueuger. I popped a fedora on my head, a spiked dog collar around my neck, and laced up my vinyl platform boots. I thought I looked one part Monkey from Korn, one part Johnny Depp in Edward Scissorhands.

To get to Ellie's uncle's date farm, I had to take the bus that trundled down Main Street then walk for a good forty-five minutes. Luckily, I had left early enough in the morning that the sun wasn't at full strength, and there was a wind blowing up the valley, making the white blades of the windmills spin hypnotically as it dried the sweat on my skin.

When I finally made it to the street flanked by rows and rows of date palms, I felt like a dying man in the desert. Any dapperness that I might have imagined myself having was definitely gone. I really should have thought this through better. Then again, it was almost funny that I was trying to impress this girl when the first impression she had of me would probably be stuck in her head forever.

I sighed, trying not to inhale the dust that whipped through the columns of trees, and went on until I came to a small house with a cracked tile driveway and a well-kept rock garden filled with every type of cactus you could imagine. I spent my whole life in the dry valley and still found myself romanticizing cacti when I saw them, like they were some strange exotic species.

I was still admiring the cacti when the front door to the house flew open and a woman poked her head out.

"What do you want?" she said in a low, suspicious voice. She was pretty hot for an older lady, a nice face with a pointy chin and sexy, dark eyes. Her hair was dark, tinged with red, auburn, and gold, nice colors to work with—autumn colors, and pulled back from her face. I had a sudden urge to paint her.

"Oh my god, mom," I heard Ellie's voice from inside. "I know that boy."

Ellie's mother squinted at me then quickly shut the door.

Okay. Well… technically I hadn't even knocked yet. I could have been a random passerby just admiring a cactus. I stood there for a few moments, trying to figure out what to do, then decided to suck it up. I marched up to the door, still hearing frantic yet hushed voices on the other side of it, and knocked quickly.

The voices stopped. Someone squealed. Then yelled, exasperated in the way only a thirteen-year-old girl who isn't getting what she wants could. It sounded like Kelli and Colleen times a billion. Then the door opened and I saw Ellie.

She was wearing her jeans again, boots, and a flowery tank top with a bunch of silver necklaces on top, some with cool-looking spikes, others with skulls. Tough jewelry with a girly-looking shirt. I liked the combination. It was very her.

Even now, here, at ten in the morning, her face was contradictory in the same way. Her mouth was indecisive, her lips unsure whether to press against each other in worry or smile, her eyes were wide and nervous, yet hard and steady.

I'd practiced my speech on the way over here, but of course it all came out in a tumble of words and noises now that she was right in front of me and I knew her mother wasn't too far out of the picture.

"Ellie. Uh. Hi. Hi, Ellie. I... I hope it's not too early. I didn't mean to drop by. I mean, I did. But I would have warned you. But I didn't have your number. So I just... came by. I'm sorry. You're busy. I'm sorry. It's... oh, I'm Camden. We met on Monday. At the... place. In town. Where stuff happened."

I clamped my mouth shut. *God you sound like an idiot*, I told myself, closing my eyes and trying to keep calm.

"I remember," Ellie said in an oddly quiet voice. "I'm glad you came by."

My eyes flew open to make sure she wasn't joking.

"Really?"

She nodded. "Really. I just had breakfast so..." she stuck her head back around the door and said something to her mother who I knew was just standing off to the left. Ellie looked back. "My mom says it's okay if I'm back before dinner."

I grinned, a smile propelled by my heart. "Sure. Great." I completely ignored the fact that I had no idea what my plan was. I was kinda hoping we could have hung out in her room and listened to tunes and talked, but I got the hint that her mother actually wanted us out of the house and gone.

It was confirmed when Ellie quickly stepped out the door and closed it behind her, without even saying good-bye to her mom.

"Well?" she asked me.

My mouth opened and shut like a fish. "You aren't going to introduce me to your mother?"

Another weird flash of anxiety came through her eyes. "No. She's... you know moms. She's got a migraine."

I nodded. "Oh, okay, that's too bad." I understood.

"No," Ellie said quickly, placing her hand on my arm. A wave of pleasure shot through me, like art growing in my veins. "No, it's not like that. She doesn't care who I hang out with. She'd like you just fine... she just doesn't feel well right now. And she's really... weird with people. All people. Strangers. She's... paranoid."

"Where's your dad?" I asked as we walked down the driveway and to the street.

"He's in town looking for work today," she said. "Not here, like Palm Valley. But Palm Springs. You know, the casinos on the side of the highway. He was a blackjack dealer back in… where I came from."

"Out East and south and whatever?" I repeated.

She smiled and fell in step beside me. She was limping but wasn't as self-conscious about it, which gave her a unique rhythm all her own. "Gulfport. Mississippi. We lived there before the… before we had to come here."

"Why this place of all places?"

"We like dates?" she suggested. She cleared her throat and then stopped, her attention on one of the date palm rows. "Hey, ever climbed one?"

"Not really on my list of things I like to do for fun. Have you?"

"I can't."

I shot her a look. "Afraid of heights?"

She kept her eyes on the palm trees, hesitant to look at me. She waited a few beats before saying, "No. I don't have… I mean… my leg… I can't…" She sighed and started walking quickly down the street, her gait stiff again.

I watched her and then trotted after her, holding onto my hat with one hand so it wouldn't blow away. Once I caught up to her, I grabbed her hand and pulled her back.

"Ellie," I told her. I let go of her hand once I was certain she wasn't taking off again. "Ellie, it's okay, whatever you're too afraid to say."

"You think I'm afraid?" she asked defensively. "Of what?"

I smiled gently. "It's the same look I see when I catch a glimpse of myself in public. I look like… I'm on guard or something. On watch. I look afraid. So do you. But I don't know what of."

"Why are you afraid?"

"Oh, you know. Because sometimes I think I'm going to get hurt, really hurt, and it will all be for nothing. That people, bullies, bad men… fathers, will get away with shit and not get punished."

"Does your father hurt you?" she whispered, taking a step toward me, her dark eyes warm and concerned.

"Why?"

I shrugged as casually as I could. "He's the sheriff. He thinks I'm asking for it. He thinks I'm gay."

She raised her brows. "And… you're not?"

"Is that a surprise?"

"No, actually. I didn't think you were. I just thought you were kind of emo or goth."

I gave her a wry look. "Well, emo is pushing it."

"What does your father do… does he hit you?" she lowered her voice over the last words, her eyes darting around as if someone could hear us.

"Usually, yeah," I said. I could tell it shocked her that I was being so open about it, so blasé, even though nothing could be further from reality.

"But that's… against the law. You could get him in trouble. Big trouble. He shouldn't be allowed to hurt you."

"I could get him in trouble. But come on, he's who he is and I look like this. Who are they going to believe?" I looked down at my nails; the black was faded away in spots. "Besides, I don't know. I hate my father sometimes, I really do. But he's still all I have. I feel like I should make the best of it. Shouldn't I?"

A dawning light came into her eyes, like she'd just realized something. "Yeah, I get it and stuff. But still. Parents shouldn't treat their kids like that."

"And bullies at school shouldn't either. But they do."

"But it's wrong. They need to pay for it."

"They do. I stand up for myself. Or I try to. I don't act afraid, even if I am."

"Do you stand up for others?"

That took me off guard for a minute. "What do you mean?"

"When you stand up for yourself, do you think you're standing up for just you or for everyone who has ever been bullied?"

"I…" I didn't know, actually. I brushed my hair behind my ears and licked my lips. They tasted like salt. "I think I'm the only one here who gets picked on."

"You're not," she said with conviction. Her eyes began to well up with tears, a sight that made my heart break a little.

I frowned. "Did... have you been bullied? You just moved here."

Ellie sighed and looked down the row of date palms again to a ladder that was leaning against one of the trees. "I don't want to climb it but do you want to go over there and sit? Better to talk there than out here."

I nodded, eager to learn more about her, yet my chest was starting to squeeze a bit, anticipating the pain she was holding back in her eyes.

We walked down the row of palms, the air immediately cooler between their spiky trunks, and took a seat on the lowest rung of the wide metal ladder. I placed my backpack on the earth and thought about all the stuff I brought with me, the stuff I was going to impress her with. But we were already opening up to each other like kindred spirits or old friends.

We sat in silence for a few moments before I had to coax her onward. "Who bullied you? What happened?"

She wiped her hands on her jeans, back and forth and back and forth, and stared up at the sky. "I walk funny. I know I do. I... have something wrong with me. Something happened to my leg. I have horrible scars and I can't, like, ever show it. Like, ever. Or people would run screaming. Believe me. It's happened. And I can't do anything about it. But people, they look at me funny, you know? They say things about me when they think I can't hear. Not just kids, but older people too. And they look at my mom like they pity her and stuff and... anyway, it sucks. It's like... I can't even just fucking walk anywhere without it being a big deal. I feel like I can barely... live. I can't even explain it."

"You don't have to," I said quietly. I didn't have the same problem, but I knew exactly what she was talking about. "So what happened?"

She sighed and picked up some dirt in her hands, letting it run through her fingers. "Some stupid bitch at your lame-ass mall called me a retard. Told her friends that there was something wrong with the new girl, that I was broken and if I was a horse I would have been shot and put down."

I winced, my heart wrenching for her. I knew how much it was hurting her and that hurt me too, more than I thought it would. Ellie was too pretty and sweet to have this done to her, to have people be this cruel. Maybe I

brought it on myself, but I didn't see how she could. Her legs and her in-
jury, whatever had happened to her, it wasn't her fault.

She eyed me sideways. "I guess word's traveled fast here that I'm
new."

"It's a fucking backwards town. Word travels fast and from idiot to
idiot," I told her, feeling frustrated with the shit we had to live with. "I'm
sorry you have to put up with this."

"Well, I'm sorry you have to put up with it too. And your father. That
really blows. My parents… they're not the greatest either. Sometimes I
don't even think my mom loves me, and I'm pretty sure my uncle Jim
wishes we'd never come here. My family isn't exactly… honorable." She
sucked on her lip, mulling something over. "You never told your father
about what I stole, did you?"

I shook my head. "No way. That's our secret."

"I wasn't trying to be bad," she began to explain, "I mean, I don't go
around and steal shit."

"I know—you had your reasons."

"I really did," she said, her eyes wide. "Honest. I stole this special
vitamin E oil."

I made a face. "Is that for girly problems?"

"No," she said, smacking my arm. "It's for scarring. I wanted to see if
it would help my leg. My mom wouldn't buy it for me. She thinks I'm
hopeless and I don't have any money, so…"

"Ellie," I said, leaning into her and trying not to smell the top of her
strawberry-scented head, "You don't have to justify yourself or explain
anything. I get it. I would have stolen it for you myself if you wanted. I'd
steal you anything you wanted."

She smiled grimly at my proposition. Too much too soon? Probably.
"That's sweet. But I don't think a life of crime is the answer anymore."

"It was an answer before?" I asked, half-joking.

She cocked her head at me. "We're friends now, aren't we?"

I couldn't help but give her a cheesy grin at the sound of that. "I don't
have many friends, so I'd be honored if that were true."

"Honored if that were true?" she repeated, smiling playfully. "You
really are a weirdo."

My expression grew serious. "I may be a weirdo, Ellie Watt, but from now on I'm your weirdo. You and I, we need to stick together. No one else understands us, I can tell you that right now. Well, except for musicians. They understand everything. Do you ever listen to Tool?"

"Not really," she said. "But I'm all ears."

I really felt like my face was going to crack in two from the way I was smiling. I leaned down to pull up my bag and my arm brushed against hers, her fine blonde hairs tickling my skin like feathers. My boner threatened to appear and my insides felt tight and fluttery. Oh boy.

Being friends might end up being harder than I thought.

I shifted against the hot ladder, thankful that my shorts were fairly loose, and propped my bag strategically on my lap while I brought out the mp3 player and the minispeaker. I decided to introduce her to the band by playing the song "Stinkfist"; its strangely metallic and electric beginning morphed into a pummeling of chords as Maynard's ethereal yet chaotic voice filled the air around us.

"It's interesting," she said after a while. "I like it. Dark. Different."

You're interesting, dark, and different, I thought. *And I like you.* I didn't tell her that though. In that moment, it was enough that I had a friend. An ally. Someone who had the potential to be as dark and different as I was.

"It's kind of pessimistic though," she said as the song went slightly haywire with noise. "Like, it's sad. No way out. That kind of feeling. I dunno."

"No," I said quickly, getting excited. "That's what you think. You feel like you're trapped and you can't see and things are going crazy and there's no control left," I said, timing my words to the song. "But then…"

And at around three and a half minutes, the song's tone changed. It became lighter. Upbeat. It rose.

"Hear that," I said, my hands waving with the beat. "It's like that part in a movie where things turn around for the main character and you know everything is going to be okay."

She was staring at me with a puzzled look on her face. All right, well maybe I could go a bit overboard with music and art and the things that really made me feel…

"It's hope," she said.

"What?"

"That change, in the song," she explained, tapping her finger on the iPod screen, timed to the new beat of the music, "it's the sound of hope. That's what I feel in here." She put a fist to her heart. "Hope."

Hope. That's exactly what it was.

It was exactly what she was.

I stared at her with a goofy, dumbfounded expression on my face. I couldn't help it. Last week I was figuring out how to best get through the school year without dying, and now I was ready to face it with a little less fear. Now I had someone other than myself to stand up for—Ellie. Now I had someone else's battles that I would gladly fight.

I had someone that let me know I wasn't alone in this town or even in this world. I had a friend, someone to talk to, to lean on, to laugh with, and listen to music with and just... live.

I had hope that in the end, no matter what lay ahead of me, everything was going to be all right.

"What else do you have to listen to?" Ellie asked, leaning into me and swiping through my iPod.

I grinned at her, and together we sat on that ladder and kept the hope coming.

About the Author

Karina Halle

The daughter of a Norwegian Viking and a Finnish Moomin, Karina Halle grew up in Vancouver, Canada with trolls and eternal darkness on the brain. This soon turned into a love of all things that go bump in the night and a rather sadistic appreciation for freaking people out. Like many of the flawed characters she writes, Karina never knew where to find herself and has dabbled in acting, make-up artistry, film production, screenwriting, photography, travel writing and music journalism. She eventually found herself in the pages of the very novels she wrote (if only she had looked there to begin with).

Karina holds a screenwriting degree from Vancouver Film School and a Bachelor of Journalism from TRU. Her travel writing, music reviews/interviews and photography have appeared in publications such as *Consequence of Sound, Mxdwn* and *GoNomad Travel Guides.* She currently splits her time between her apartment in downtown Vancouver and her sailboat, where a book and a bottle of wine are always at hand.

Facebook: https://www.facebook.com/pages/Karina-Halle/140649372629593
Twitter: @MetalBlonde
Blog: http://khalle.wordpress.com

PIE LOVE YOU

A *Spiral of Bliss* Short Story

by

Nina Lane

CHOCOLATE PIES TOPPED with mountains of whipped cream. Spicy pumpkin pies. Apple pies with gooey, cinnamon fillings. Tart lemon meringue pies. Cheese pies. Berry pies. Brownie pies. Rhubarb pies.

Josh Piper slid a key lime pie into the cold case and calculated he'd have to make five more custard pies tomorrow morning. Like the number *pi*, Josh thought that *pie* was also a mathematical constant. Always there. Unchanging. He'd lived most of his nineteen years in his father's pie shop. A life of pie.

Josh figured that if he knew the meaning of *pi*, he'd at least learned something in his first year at King's University. Not that he knew how *pi* was at all relevant to… well, anything.

Pie either, for that matter.

He pushed his overlong brown hair off his forehead, shut the cold case, and went to grate more chocolate shavings.

A melancholy sigh came from the front of the shop. Josh's two friends, Leo Myers and Penny Dove, were sitting at a table by the window. Penny was eating a piece of apple pie, and Leo was slouched in his chair with his ever-present fedora pulled over his forehead.

"The private dick is always down on his luck." Leo stared morosely out the window. "Low on dough. Nursing the last of his hooch. Smoking his last cigarette. Threatened with eviction for not paying the rent."

Josh and Penny exchanged glances. She rolled her eyes slightly, which made him grin. He and Penny had long suffered through Leo's love for old detective movies, not to mention his tendency to blur the lines between fiction and reality.

"Then in walks the dame," Leo continued, his voice heavy. "Blonde, curvy, sultry. And the dick knows he's doomed. He knows she'll drag him into a maze of treachery and betrayal, but still he follows her. Willingly. That's the power of the dame, my friends."

"The power of *some* dames," Penny corrected, digging her fork into the apple pie.

"The power of all dames," Leo said grimly.

"I have never led a man—dick or otherwise—into any sort of maze," Penny said, "let alone one of treachery and betrayal."

"Oh, you will, my shiny Penny." Leo shook his head, expelling another gusty sigh. "One day, you will."

Josh doubted that. Not because Penny wasn't pretty, but because she wasn't the betrayal-treachery type. She was the loyal girl-next-door type, always wearing jeans and T-shirts, her reddish hair pulled into a ponytail.

Josh picked up the coffeepot and went to the table. Penny had a terrible sense of how to maintain a decent pie-to-coffee ratio, always finishing her coffee before her pie was half done. She gave him a smile of thanks and extended her empty mug.

"Funny shirt," she remarked.

"Huh?"

"Your shirt." She nodded to his black T-shirt, which bore the slogan *Bacon Gives Me A Lard-On.*

"Oh. I was… uh, in a hurry this morning. Just grabbed it." He thought he'd better change before his dad saw the shirt. Not *appropriate* for The Pied Piper, his father would say. He wouldn't like Josh's torn jeans either.

"I'm telling you," Leo said, sounding annoyed that he was being ignored. "Samantha broke up with me, and her betrayal is *bacon* my heart."

Josh and Penny both laughed. After Josh refilled Penny's coffee, he went to check on the customers who sat at the tables outside the pie shop. Locals, as usual, all enjoying the summer evening. The Pied Piper was off the beaten track, not easily accessible to the tourists who populated Avalon Street and the lakefront, but the shop was still doing okay thanks to loyal customers.

The creaky, wooden sign his father had carved years ago swung in the breeze that drifted in from Mirror Lake. The blue-striped awning was faded from the sun, the gilt paint letters starting to flake.

Josh stopped in a patch of sunlight. The air outside the shop smelled sweet. Cinnamon, hot cherries, buttery pastry, lemons, melted chocolate. Smells that reminded people of happy childhoods and cozy kitchens, making them wish there was a way back into the past.

Smells that made Josh wish there was a way out.

He went into the shop to finish sprinkling the chocolate cream pies with cocoa powder and chocolate shavings. Leo and Penny were back to discussing dicks and dames. She reached across the table to pat Leo's hand.

"It'll only hurt for a little while," she assured him.

"How do you know?" Leo grumbled. "You've never been in love. You've barely dated." He pinned her with a sudden, sharp look. "Have you ever even kissed a guy, Penny?"

Josh paused to glance at Penny, noticing the blush on her cheeks. She was seventeen, though she'd graduated from high school last spring. She'd skipped fourth grade and had always been the youngest, and smartest, in her class.

Josh had been friends with Penny since his sophomore year of high school, when she'd moved into the neighborhood and started at Lakeview High as a freshman. It had been right when his mom got sick. He'd liked being able to hang out with Penny to get away from all the crap that came with having a parent who was dying, like everyone always telling the kid that everything "was going to be all right" when of course they all knew it wasn't.

Penny had never tried to tell him that. And even though she was smart, she never made Josh feel stupid despite his struggle with schoolwork and disinterest in going to college.

"Of course I've kissed a guy," Penny said, and Josh wondered if Leo noticed the slight hesitation before she spoke.

"Have you?" Leo kept staring at her. "Who?"

Josh realized he was leaning on the counter, waiting for Penny's answer. She concentrated on her apple pie with one scoop of vanilla ice cream, which he'd put on the edge of the plate so that it wouldn't break the crust or melt too fast from the hot filling. He knew it annoyed her when that happened.

"None of your business *who*," she told Leo.

"Not Dave Thurgood," Leo said. "Tell me you did not allow Dave Thurgood to touch your kissable lips."

"I did not," Penny assured him, her cheeks still red.

Josh thought he should rescue her from Leo's interrogation, but he really wanted to know the answer. And for once Leo was right. Penny did have kissable lips. Not that Josh knew that from personal experience.

"Then *who*?" Leo persisted.

"Never mind." Penny swirled the pie filling around on her plate. "It always works out in the end, right?"

"What does?"

"The dame and the private eye. They solve the mystery, send the bad guy to jail, end up falling in love…"

"You're changing the subject," Leo said.

"I'm telling you that if there's a happy ending for the sultry dame and the washed-up private eye, there will be a happy ending for you."

"Ah, Penny." Leo sighed again. "You need to be more of a downer if you want to be a great writer."

"Lots of great writers wrote books with happy endings," she replied.

"Like who?"

"Like Shakespeare," Penny retorted. "*A Midsummer Night's Dream*. He gave his characters happy endings. Sometimes, anyway."

"Hey, Josh man, you believe in happy endings?" Leo asked.

"No."

Penny swung her gaze to Josh. "You don't?"

"By definition, an ending is an end to something, right?" Josh said. "So by its very nature, it can't be *happy*."

He rubbed a spot on the glass countertop. He swore Penny was looking at him with disappointment, which bugged him more than he wanted to admit. He didn't want to talk about happy endings anymore.

"Hey." Josh snapped his fingers at Leo and pointed at the clock. "You gotta go."

Leo swore and shoved away from the table. "You realize tonight begins my own seventh circle of hell? I'm forced to wait tables alongside the woman who dumped me and has no idea she still wants me."

"There's the rub," Penny remarked.

"Where's the rub?" Leo waggled his eyebrows at her. "And what, exactly, are you rubbing?"

Penny threw a packet of sugar at him.

"Out," Josh ordered Leo.

Leo tipped his fedora and strolled out into the summer evening. Josh followed him outside to bring in the sandwich board that sat on the sidewalk. He locked the door and flipped the Closed sign in the window.

"Still looking for help?" Penny asked, nodding to the Help Wanted sign on the sandwich board.

"Yeah. Morning shifts and Tuesday afternoons. My dad wants to do the deliveries himself, so we need someone to help with prep, then run the counter when we open."

It had taken work to convince his father that Josh could take over the morning prep and baking so that Simon Piper could get some sleep after driving all over the state for deliveries and overseeing the shop's new advertising campaign.

After one of their employees quit a few weeks ago, Simon had tried to fill in himself until Josh insisted that he could do it. He'd been glad when his father finally relented. Simon had worked eighteen-hour days for years in an effort to save enough money to send Josh to college.

Josh only wished he'd actually wanted to go to college. And after finishing his first year, he still wished he wasn't going just to avoid disappointing his father.

"I'm doing all the baking," he told Penny, "but we're having trouble filling orders because I also have to work the counter until Tom comes in at noon. And I can't work in the afternoons because of class and baseball. I'm only working tonight because Mary needed to babysit her grandson."

"I can help out," Penny said. "I know how to work a cash register. And I can sell that apple pie to any customer, no matter what they come in for."

"The hours are early," Josh warned her. "I'm here by four, and we open at seven."

"Fine. All my classes are at night, and I work at the clothing store on Wednesdays and Thursdays, so I'm available on Tuesday afternoons too. I can even start tomorrow."

"Okay." Josh hesitated. "Uh, the pay's not great."

"Doesn't matter."

But he knew it did. Unlike him, Penny had wanted to go to King's, but couldn't afford the tuition. She'd missed the scholarship deadline because, in the disorganized mess of her parents' house, her mother had thrown the university paperwork away.

So Penny was taking classes at a local community college trying to get enough credits to transfer to King's in a year or two. And she was doing it on her own.

Josh sometimes thought it should annoy him that Penny was so... plucky. Like one of those Disney princesses who sings through heartache.

Except that was exactly what he liked the most about Penny. She didn't want to end up like her deadbeat mother or her sister, who had two kids by the time she was eighteen and no way to support them.

But Penny wasn't just a bookworm or some airy-fairy dreamer. She was one of those girls who *believed* what she read about brave heroines and overcoming the odds. She lived it. If anything, Josh wished he had the guts to do what she did.

"Come on." He went toward the back door of the kitchen. "I'll walk you home, then come back and finish up here."

En route to Penny's house, they passed the industrial buildings and auto-body repair shops that populated the east side of town before crossing the railroad tracks bordering the edges of downtown proper.

Penny lived with her parents and two younger brothers in a modest tract home near the tracks. There was a sad-looking tire swing in the front yard alongside a rusted tricycle and a few other kids' toys.

"My sister had to move back in with the kids," Penny explained, pushing the trike aside with her foot to clear the path. "Broke up with her boyfriend again."

"Crowded house," Josh offered.

They went inside. The noise of a video game blared from the TV where Penny's brothers were shooting space aliens. The smells of burnt pizza, cigarette smoke, and beer depressed Josh more than they usually did. He almost didn't want to leave Penny, feeling like she didn't belong here.

Nothing seemed right to Josh these days. It wasn't right that his dad had worked so hard for so many years to pay for Josh to go to a university that he didn't want to attend. And it really wasn't right that Penny—smart, ambitious Penny—wanted nothing more than to go to King's University and yet was stuck taking night classes and working two jobs.

"I'll pick you up tomorrow morning," he said, stepping back onto the porch. "Four, okay?"

"I'll be ready."

Josh put his palm against the door to stop Penny from closing it. His heartbeat kicked up a notch, and a strange feeling filled his chest. Painful, like a bunch of pinpricks.

"Who did you kiss?" he asked.

Her blue eyes met his. He noticed—not for the first time—that they were a really pretty color.

"Just a boy," she said.

"What boy?"

"A boy I've loved for a while now." She started to close the door again.

"What boy?" Josh was surprised by the edge to his voice.

"No one you know."

Josh lowered his hand. Irritation snarled through him as he went toward the street. He and Penny had been friends for almost five years. He should have known that she loved some guy. Especially *for a while now*. And he sure as hell should know who the guy was.

"Hey," Penny called after him.

He turned. She was still standing in the doorway.

"Do you really believe endings are inherently unhappy?" she asked.

Josh scratched his head. "Uh, I haven't really given it much thought."

"Because that's kind of a sad worldview," she said.

"Well, not everything is happy," he muttered. "Besides, why do you even need to think about how things end? Why don't you just think about how they are?"

"I'm a writer. Of course I have to think about how things end. The mystery is solved, the hero and heroine fall in love, the villain gets caught, the treasure is found."

"Old Yeller dies," Josh reminded her. "Scarlett O'Hara loses both of the guys she's in love with, right? The Titanic sinks. Charlie Brown never kicks the damned football."

He felt like a jerk when Penny's expression clouded over.

"Penny—"

"So Josh Piper never gets what he wants?" she interrupted. "He struggles through college only because it's what his dad wants him to do? He never fulfills his dream of becoming a chef and opening his own restaurant? He doesn't even *try* to find a way?"

"No." Josh swallowed hard. "He doesn't."

He turned and trudged down the street. He felt Penny's disappointment in him like the burn of a hot pan, sharp and blistering.

~~~~

Josh scrubbed his hands over his face and yawned. A single lamp burned in the kitchen, casting a weird yellowish light over the cracked linoleum. The table was scattered with papers, bills, and a calculator. After draining a cup of coffee in a few gulps, Josh put his cup in the sink and went to the entryway.

As he grabbed his sweatshirt from the front closet, his father emerged from the bedroom.

"Dad, go back to bed. It's not even four yet."

"Yeah. Just wanted to finish up some stuff." Simon Piper scratched his chin. He was tall and bulky, but seemed diminished because of his slouched shoulders and the dark circles under his eyes. "I should get some supplies reordered too."

"I'll do it after prep."

"You have class and practice right after work." Simon glanced at the foyer clock. "Got money for lunch?"

Josh nodded. Sometimes he wondered if there would ever be a time when his dad didn't treat him like a kid. Since his mother had died, it had just been the two of them. And Josh knew his dad only wanted the best for him... but Simon Piper's definition of *best* was different from Josh's.

"Any luck with hiring someone for morning shifts?" Simon asked.

"Yeah, Penny said she'd take the job. She can work Tuesday afternoons too."

"Penny Dove?"

Josh suppressed a rustle of irritation. How many *Pennys* did his father know?

"Of course Penny Dove."

"Okay." Wariness flashed across Simon's face. He poured a cup of coffee. "You've got a full plate, and you've got to pass this summer class. If you don't, you'll get kicked off the team, and you can't apply for a scholarship next year. Don't let Penny be a distraction."

"She's not."

The knot in Josh's chest tightened even more. He shrugged into his sweatshirt and left the house. This business of happy endings and Penny kissing some guy had turned his thoughts in a direction they'd never gone before.

Sure, he'd noticed that Penny was pretty, that she had a cute, curvy body and blue eyes. Kissable lips. But he...

He *what?*

In high school, there had always been someone or something else. Baseball, The Pied Piper, parties, other girls, trying to keep his grades up enough to get him into King's University, then trying to find another way when it became clear he'd never make it in on academics alone. He'd barely squeaked into King's because of his pitching abilities, but he wasn't even good enough at baseball to earn a sports scholarship.

Through all of that, Penny was always just around. The one person who never made him feel like he wasn't good enough.

Josh drove his beat-up truck to her house. She was sitting on the second step of the front porch. She'd waited for him on that same step after his mother had died. Josh had been working at The Pied Piper when his dad had called from the hospital with the news.

Without thinking, Josh had texted Penny and gone to her house. She was sitting on the porch step when he got there. She didn't say anything as he sat beside her. He put his head on his knees. Felt her hand on his back. He'd started to cry, horrible, gut-wrenching sobs that tore his chest apart. Penny sat beside him in silence. Even the girl who loved books knew that sometimes words were useless.

Now Josh watched as she walked toward his truck, her ponytail swinging behind her. As she climbed into the passenger seat, he caught a whiff of something sweet and kind of girly. Coconut cream. He hadn't noticed a girl's smell since his last girlfriend, and that had been over a year ago.

"Pie there," Penny greeted him.

"Pie yourself." Josh suppressed the urge to lean closer to her and inhale. "Butter put your seatbelt on."

She smiled. Josh's heart did that weird twirly thing again.

He shook his head and drove to the shop. This didn't make sense. Besides, Penny had loved another guy *for a while*. She'd *kissed* him. It would be a huge mistake for Josh to start thinking of Penny romantically now, since she obviously wasn't available.

Besides, his dad was sort of right. Not a minute passed that Josh wasn't working, studying, in class, at practice, or thinking about doing one of those three things.

He and Penny went into the pie shop's kitchen and put on aprons. Josh began getting out the stuff for the breakfast pies. Penny brought pots to the stove, made coffee, preheated the ovens. Soon the kitchen was filled with the familiar scents of dough and butter, the sound of his rolling pin hitting the wooden counter, the bubble of fillings on the stove.

"So… who's the guy?" Josh finally asked as Penny stood beside him, trying and failing to weave a lattice-work crust over a cherry pie.

"What guy?"

"The guy you're in love with. The guy you kissed."

"Why are you so interested?"

"I'm curious. I've never seen you with a guy. Didn't even know you were interested in one."

She shrugged and stretched one of the dough strips too thin, ripping it.

If it weren't for the fact that he and Penny had never kissed, Josh might have hoped *he* was the guy Penny loved. He knew girls liked him. Though Penny had never indicated that she might like him *that way*, it wouldn't have shocked him if she did.

But it couldn't be him… so who the hell was it? And why did he care? Penny was always alone. At work or in class or holed up in her room writing stories. She wasn't a girl who got around. That was just one other thing he'd always liked about her.

He watched as she mangled another strip of dough.

"Look." Josh rolled out the dough and sliced off more strips. "Lay out the strips parallel first, then fold back every other one before putting the others perpendicular. Like this."

He wove the crust, then trimmed and crimped the edges. He felt her looking at him. He glanced at her. She looked like the same Penny he'd always known—coppery red hair, freckles across her nose, blue eyes. The same, but… different.

Now she was a girl who loved a guy Josh didn't even know.

His chest tightened. "It's not Leo, is it?"

Penny blinked, then laughed. "Leo likes sultry blondes, but even if he did like ordinary redheads… no. I'd never trust an eighteen-year-old who wears a fedora."

"Then who is it?" The more Josh stewed over the question, the more he wanted the answer.

"I'll tell you the day you believe in happy endings."

"Not believing in happy endings doesn't mean I'm some kind of jerk." Josh pushed the stupid pie away and wiped sticky dough from his fingers. "It's just that there's a bunch of stuff that comes afterward, right? So the hero and heroine fall in love and find the treasure... then what? Do they sell it? If they get married, do they have kids? What about their families? What if the bad guy escapes from prison? Even if it's happy, it's not the *end*. Other stuff happens afterward."

Before Penny could respond, Josh grabbed a tray of pies and went to the front. The display cases were filled with yesterday's pies. Cream pies, fruit pies, cheese pies, chicken pies, chocolate pies.

Lotta fucking pie.

Josh wondered how many pies had paid for his tuition at King's. He felt Penny behind him.

What was up with that? *Feeling* her looking at him, *feeling* her near him? Who the hell had kissed her?

He dropped the tray onto the counter. It hit the edge and tilted, sending a pecan pie crashing to the floor in a heap of broken crust and filling.

"Shit."

"It's okay." Penny picked up a towel and dragged the trash can over. She knelt and began shoveling the mess into the can. Josh bent to help her.

"Sorry," he muttered.

Penny didn't respond until they'd cleaned up the broken pie and straightened.

"Josh, you need to do what you want," she finally said.

"What are you talking about?"

"You've been snarly and irritable ever since you started at King's. You need to tell your father you don't want to go there."

"My father worked his ass off to afford to send me to King's. I can't drop out."

"Then you need to at least tell him you're not going to be a doctor or lawyer or whatever."

Josh stared at the golden brown crust of an apple pie. The sugar crystals kind of sparkled in the light.

"What do you really want?" Penny asked.

She knew what he wanted. She was just making him say it aloud, even though it sounded stupid.

"I want to be a chef." Josh swiped a drop of cream off the counter. "Own a restaurant one day. Maybe two or three. With no pie anywhere on the menu."

"I want to be a writer," Penny said. "But that's a totally impractical profession, right? I should be an accountant or a reporter or sell insurance. So why am I taking night classes at a community college so I can go to King's and take courses in eighteenth-century French literature? Where's that going to get me in life?"

"It'll get *you* to the top of the bestseller list," Josh said.

"The universe doesn't discriminate, Josh," Penny said. "Not in success or failure. But if you don't try, you'll never get to where you want to be."

She shook her head, and again that disappointment flashed in her blue eyes. "And then you'll really never find out what happens *afterward*."

~~~~

Professor Dean West had his shit together. Even Josh could see that.

Professor West wore good suits, he was a good teacher, he had all sorts of papers and books published. He was also just a good guy. Fair to his students but no pushover. Smart as hell. Played football. He wore a wedding ring and had a picture of his pretty wife beside his computer. He never stumbled over his words. He was never awkward. Never seemed like he didn't fit.

All of that had never been more glaringly apparent to Josh than when he was sitting in the professor's office, feeling like an asshole because he hadn't turned his paper in on time.

"How much have you written?" Professor West asked.

"Uh, couple of pages." That was a lie. He didn't even have a file created yet.

"Send me what you have so far, and I'll look it over." Professor West flipped a calendar on his desk. "I can give you until next Monday to finish it. I'll have to take off points for lateness, but if you don't turn it in at all, you won't be able to take the final, and you'll fail the class."

He looked back at Josh. "Okay?"

"Okay." What else was he supposed to say?

"Good. Email me what you have. One of my grad students is working on a similar topic, so he'd be glad to talk with you too."

"Thanks." Josh hefted his backpack onto his shoulder and trudged out of the office.

He didn't get men like Professor West. As decent a guy as the professor was, Josh couldn't imagine being stuck in an office or classroom all day. Nose in a bunch of boring books. Brain clogged with useless stuff.

Josh wanted to *do* something, not just sit around thinking. And at King's, that was all anyone seemed to want him to do. For the next *three years*.

He didn't even know what he was supposed to do with his degree, whatever it would be in. They didn't give Bachelor's degrees in cooking, and that was the only thing he was really good at. The only thing he liked doing.

Well. Maybe not the *only* thing.

He looked at his watch. It was Tuesday. Penny would be at the shop now. And he had two hours before practice started.

Fifteen minutes later, he walked in the door of The Pied Piper, trying to pretend like he hadn't rushed over like a kid needing to pee.

Leo was sitting at a table eating pie and yammering about some new girl he'd set his sights on. Penny was behind the counter drizzling chocolate over a whipped-cream topping.

Her apron stretched across the front of her body. Josh thought he'd probably worn that exact same apron. Many times. He suddenly wanted to wear it again, knowing it had just been wrapped around Penny.

"Hey." He paused beside her, feeling awkward in his father's shop for the first time. "How's it going?"

"Not bad. I finally learned what a docker is. Now I just need to learn how to use it to make a perfect crust."

"Easy as pie," Josh said, and was rewarded when she laughed.

"You have class today?" she asked.

He nodded. "So… you're a good student. You ever tutor anyone?"

"Are you asking in general or are you asking if I'd tutor you?"

"Both."

Penny wiped her hands with a towel. "Why do you need a tutor?"

"I'm supposed to write a paper on some medieval legend. If I don't finish it by Monday, I can't take the final and I'll fail the class."

He hated admitting that. Penny always had all her papers written early and started studying for exams weeks in advance. She wrote outlines, took good notes, knew how to format a bibliography.

"I'll… um, I'll pay you," he said.

"I don't want you to pay me."

"What do you want in return, then?" He wasn't about to take a free handout, no matter how desperate he was.

"I want you to enter a bake-off," Penny said.

"A jerk-off?" He blinked at her in feigned disbelief.

Leo gave a shout of laughter.

Penny flicked a spray of melted chocolate at Josh. "A *bake-off*. There's one at the County Fair the weekend after next. The sign-up form is due tomorrow."

She was serious.

"Why do you want me to enter a bake-off?" Josh asked.

"Because you have a great shot at winning," she replied earnestly. "And because it could lead to some great opportunities for you."

Even if that were true, it didn't matter. Josh would be at King's for at least the next three years. If he didn't manage to flunk out first.

"I don't even like baking," he reminded her. "Why would I enter a bake-off?"

"Because two of the judges are chefs of local restaurants, and the third is the head of a culinary school over in Forest Grove," Penny said. "The prize is the winner's choice of either five hundred dollars or a semester's tuition at the school."

He could use five hundred dollars, Josh thought, though he wished the second choice was actually an option for him.

"Look, I'll get all the forms for you," Penny said. "All you have to do is bake the best pie you've ever baked. Preferably apple."

"That's all you want in exchange for helping me with the paper?"

"That's all."

"When do we start?"

After they made arrangements, Josh went to take Leo's empty plate since he knew his friend wouldn't do it himself.

"Dude," Leo said with a shake of his head. "The power of the Penny."

~~~~

Penny and Josh studied at The Pied Piper after closing. The front of the shop was dark, the cases empty, the countertops gleaming. Josh set up his laptop and books on one of the counters in the kitchen. They sat on tall stools while Penny read the assignment instructions, and Josh fidgeted with a pen.

"First you need an outline," Penny said. "It's like a map of where you're going to go."

Josh sighed. He realized this was the reason he liked cooking rather than baking. He had to follow a recipe while baking, use exact measurements and ingredients. But when he was grilling steaks or making quesadillas, he could taste, adjust seasonings, add this or that. He could improvise.

"I don't like maps," he told Penny. "I like to just hit the road and see where it takes me."

"That approach could take you in the wrong direction."

"How would you know it's the wrong direction if you don't know where you're going?"

"Exactly," Penny said.

~~~~

Once Penny helped Josh figure out the medieval legend, he admitted it was kind of cool. All about this guy Beowulf who kills a monster with his bare hands, slays a dragon and battles a lot before getting killed by a poisoned sword.

Over the next week, he rewrote the paper a few times under Penny's instruction before she finally deemed it worthy to send to Professor West.

A day later, the professor responded with an email: *Excellent work, Josh. You earned an A. I put the paper in your school mailbox with comments. Good luck on the final. —DW*

Though Josh was pleased by the grade, he knew he'd never have gotten it without Penny's help. And he'd be on his own for the final, which was just a few days away, the day before the County Fair.

As a small thanks for helping him get an A, Josh made Penny dinner one night in the pie shop's kitchen. He seasoned filets, prepped artichokes, cooked rice pilaf. He didn't want to make it seem like he was doing anything romantic, so he put out plates on the counter and kept the overhead fluorescents on.

Penny always complimented his food, which was kind of nice. So he cooked, they talked and ate, and for an hour everything was good.

Then his dad walked in.

Simon Piper took in the scene in a glance and tossed his keys on the counter. "Hello, Penny."

"Hi, Mr. Piper." Penny put down her fork, giving Josh an uneasy glance.

Josh nodded to the still-simmering pots on the stove. "You want dinner, Dad?"

"No. Just came to get today's sales reports."

"On the desk."

Simon went into the office. Penny slid off the stool. "I should go."

Josh put out his hand to stop her, his fingers brushing against her thigh. A warm feeling ran clear up his arm. His breath got a little shaky.

Penny stopped. "Josh?"

"I… I don't want you to go."

"But your dad—"

He shook his head. He didn't just not want her to go. He wanted her to stay.

"You ready for the final?" Simon asked as he came out of the office with the sales reports in hand.

"Yeah." Josh tried to ignore a stab of guilt because he wasn't really ready for Professor West's final. And worse, he didn't much care.

"Better wrap things up here, then," Simon said.

Josh's jaw clenched. "We're fine, Dad."

"You need to be up early tomorrow."

"I know what I need to do. I don't need you to tell me."

He felt Penny beside him. *Felt* her, the girl who'd set her sights on what she wanted and would get it. The girl who made it seem easy, even though it was anything but.

Maybe that was why Josh had been looking at her differently now. It was more than jealousy over the fact that Penny had kissed another guy. It was that she had figured out she was the only person who would ever live *her* life.

"I'll see you later, Dad," Josh said.

Simon looked as if he were about to protest. So Josh shocked his father and shocked Penny and shocked the hell out of himself by putting his arm around Penny and bending toward her. Unfortunately, she turned right at the second that his mouth would have met hers, so he ended up kissing the side of her chin.

But it was a kiss.

A hush descended. Penny stared at him, her face flushed.

"I'll see you at home, Josh," his father said. "Just watch the time."

The door closed behind him. Penny jumped off the stool and gave Josh a shove so hard he stumbled backward.

"What was that?" she snapped. "Don't use me to get at your father, you ass."

"I wasn't—"

"Yes, you were. Grow the fuck up, Josh."

She grabbed her bag and stalked out of the kitchen. Josh sank against the counter. His heart raced. He couldn't grab hold of a single thought, but his brain was whirring. He dumped the rest of the uneaten dinner into the trash and cleaned the pots and countertops.

Then he got out the mixing bowls, flour, sugar, butter, cinnamon, and apples. And he started to bake.

He baked through the night, testing recipes, mixing cherries and blackberries, whipping chocolate with coconut cream. As he made crusts, poured pie fillings, tasted different mixtures, he became aware that there was *something else* he should be doing.

He stopped and looked at the clock. Two a.m. Nerves tightened his stomach. He returned his attention to a cheese filling and kept baking.

Penny showed up at dawn—neither of them mentioning the misplaced kiss—to help with the morning's prep work. Though she raised an eyebrow at the mess of the kitchen, they didn't speak aside from remarks about what needed to be done.

Finally when Penny went to open the front doors, Josh took out his phone and sent her a text: *Pie'm sorry.*

Her response came in a few seconds: *It was muffin.*

The tension in Josh's shoulders eased. After getting the daily pies out, he returned to experimenting with his own recipes. He baked a boysenberry pie that turned out too sour and a peach pie that was too sweet. He baked a lemon meringue pie, a strawberry-rhubarb pie, and a brownie pie. He also baked three different versions of an apple pie, one with pecans and one with caramel.

Hours later, Josh swiped his forehead with his sleeve and looked at the clock. He was hot, sweaty, covered in flour and pie filling. His eyes burned with exhaustion.

Professor West's final was in thirty-five minutes.

Josh looked at the box of shiny, red apples sitting on the counter. Even after baking all night, he still didn't have a satisfactory pie to submit to the County Fair Bake-Off, but he'd reached one conclusion.

He wanted to win.

~~~~

The minute Josh and Penny stepped onto the fairgrounds, the smells of fried funnel cake, cotton candy, and hot asphalt hit his nose. The Ferris wheel rotated against the evening sky, the colored lights of the game booths and rides blurring in swirls. Shrieks of joy filled the air, and music thumped from a distant stage.

Penny looked at her watch and told Josh they had an hour before the pie judging. He'd dropped his entry off earlier, so they spent the time wandering around looking at the exhibits and braving a few rides.

Josh avoiding going near The Pied Piper food truck, where his father and Tom were selling slices of pie. He hadn't told his dad about the bake-off. Hadn't told him he'd even be at the fair. Hadn't told him much of anything at all, in fact.

Ignoring a stab of guilt, Josh guided Penny toward the game booths. Leo was strolling down the midway with a long-legged blonde girl. He gave Penny and Josh a thumbs-up and a tip of his fedora. They waved in return before stopping at a ring-toss game.

"He's recovered well from his broken heart," Penny remarked.

"You were right." Josh tried and failed to throw three rings over the bottles. "Everything worked out okay for the washed-up private eye."

"It will for you too," Penny said as they walked toward the exhibition center where the bake-off judging was taking place. "Are you nervous?"

Josh shook his head, as if nerves were beneath him, but his steps faltered a little as they approached the room where an easel advertised County Fair Pie Bake-Off.

The place was half-full of people sitting in folding chairs before a narrow stage. The three judges sat behind a pink-draped table on the stage, each sampling a large piece of what looked like cherry pie. They took a bite, wrote in a notebook, took another bite, looked at the ceiling, frowned, wrote again, crumbled the crust between their fingers.

Penny and Josh sat in the back row. He crossed his arms and tried to muster an air of nonchalance. Penny scooted to the edge of her chair as the judges were served a triple-berry pie in an almond crust, and then a macadamia-nut strawberry pie with a ginger crust, then a mango-coconut-pineapple pie in a praline lattice crust.

By the time they got to the blueberry-lemon-pecan pie with a double-bottom crust, Penny's shoulders had slumped.

"No chance in hell," Josh muttered.

"That is not true." Penny sat up straighter. "It's like a beauty contest where all the contestants have been spray-tanned and air-brushed. Then after they all parade around the stage in six-inch heels, a really pretty girl from… I don't know, *Kansas* comes out and wows all the judges with her natural self-confidence and charm."

"My pie doesn't have self-confidence and charm."

"But *you* do." She flushed a little.

Josh grinned. He doubted he had either quality, but he liked that Penny thought he did.

"They're not voting for me," he reminded her. "They're voting for my pie."

"Josh, have a little faith. Your father built The Pied Piper on that apple pie."

"It's not my father's apple pie."

"You didn't make your father's pie?"

"Nope."

"What pie did you make, then? Cherry?"

"No. Just a pie I made up."

Penny swiveled toward him. "You decided to forgo The Pied Piper's famous, classic apple pie and enter a pie you just *made up*?"

"Uh, yeah."

"In the County Fair *Bake-Off*?"

"Yeah." He was vaguely irritated by her shocked response. Didn't she think he could do it?

Then Penny smiled—a wide smile that made dimples pop into her cheeks and her blue eyes crinkle.

"That's awesome," she said. "Now there's really no way you can lose."

Their gazes met for a brief, oddly intense second. The perpetual knot loosened inside Josh's chest as they both turned their attention back to the stage.

The judging went on and on. Pies were eliminated based on various criteria—too sour, too sweet, poor filling-to-crust ratio. Then the coordinator stepped to the podium and consulted her notes.

"Our next entry is from Mr. Josh Piper of The Pied Piper pie shop in Mirror Lake. Josh's entry is one dozen—" she paused and peered at her notes again, as if she'd misread them "—yes, one dozen Sweet Penny Pies."

Penny swung around to stare at Josh again, only this time with a different kind of astonishment. His face grew warm.

The servers brought out two trays of his apple pies—each one made with the crust and filling served in hollowed-out apples to create little, individual pies. Both the audience and the judges reacted with gratifying "ohhs" at the sight of the apples.

Penny was still looking at him. He felt it.

His heart pounded as he watched the judges study the apples, discuss the unique presentation, scoop up some crust, then lift their forks to examine the filling.

"Sweet Penny Pies?" Penny finally whispered.

He tried to give a nonchalant shrug. "You were the one who suggested this. Seemed logical to acknowledge you."

"Josh…"

He held up his hand to indicate that they should be quiet during the judging process. When the judges rose from their seats, the crowd began to stir.

"We will announce the results after the judges have reached their verdict," the coordinator said into the microphone. "All entries will receive a participation merit ribbon, but there will be only one grand prize winner. Second and third place winners will be given a coupon for a two-for-one dinner at Gotta Getta Grub in Forest Grove."

A few people stood up to stretch as the wait dragged on. Servers roamed around with samples of the pie entries.

When the judges marched back onto the stage, a hush fell over the room. Penny curled her fingers around Josh's arm. His breath stuck in his throat at the feeling of her palm against his bare forearm.

"Ladies and gentlemen." The coordinator stepped to the podium. "Third prize goes to Myra Micalizio for her Triple-Threat Berry-Blast Almond-Crust pie!"

Applause and cheers filled the hall as Myra hurried to the stage to claim her ribbon and coupon and to shake the judges' hands.

"Our second prize winner is Gill Selling for her Cherry-Gooseberry Nutmeg-Laced Walnut-Stuffed-Crust pie!"

Gill went to the stage with a wave of thanks to the crowd as she accepted her prize and congratulations.

"And the grand prize winner of the County Fair Bake-Off…" The coordinator paused dramatically as she consulted her cards.

Penny scooted to the edge of her seat. She was clutching Josh's arm so tightly it hurt. Not that he minded at all.

"Josh Piper for his apple pie," Penny whispered under her breath. "Josh Piper for his apple pie…"

"The grand prize winner," the coordinator repeated, "is Louise Taylor for her Chocolate-Mocha Salted-Caramel Toffee-Crunch-Cream Chocolate-Chip-Crust pie!"

The crowd roared with applause and cheers. Penny gasped in disbelief and let go of Josh's arm, sinking back against the seat. Josh deflected a wave of disappointment and stood.

"Come on, Pen." He kept his voice light as he took her hand and tugged her to her feet. "Show's over."

They walked out of the exhibition room, Penny shaking her head.

"It wasn't supposed to happen like that," she said. "Your pie should have *won*. You've spent all this time working at your dad's shop, going to college just because you didn't want to disappoint him, all the while struggling and stifling your own dreams. You were supposed to win the grand prize and go off to do what you've always wanted."

Weirdly enough, her frustration made Josh feel better. And he wondered if he was disappointed that he didn't win the grand prize or because he hadn't given Penny a happy ending.

He draped his arm around her shoulders as they walked toward the doors leading back outside. He liked how she felt, all tucked against his side. Then his heart sank.

Professor West was leaning against a wall, his hands shoved in his pockets and a big, stuffed rabbit tucked under his arm. Josh grabbed Penny's hand to steer her away, but Professor West saw him and then there was no escape.

Josh stopped. Professor West approached. Even though nerves tightened his stomach, Josh had to admire a guy who didn't seem to care that he was carrying a stuffed pink rabbit.

"Hi, Professor West."

"Josh."

"Oh, hi." Penny extended a hand. "I'm Penny Dove. I helped… er, I mean, I read Josh's paper for your class."

Professor West shifted the rabbit to his other arm and shook Penny's hand.

"You win that?" Josh asked, hoping to keep the conversation to fair-related stuff.

Professor West looked at the rabbit as if he'd forgotten he was holding it. "Yeah. Balloon darts. My wife picked it out."

"Your wife's here?"

"She went to get an ice cream."

"Great day for the fair, huh?" Josh asked.

"Indeed."

Josh cowered a little under the professor's sharp look. Even at the fair holding a stuffed animal, Professor West had an intimidating authority. One that made Josh's heart sink a few more inches.

"Word alone, Josh?" Professor West tilted his head to the other side of the hall.

Feeling like a kid going to detention, Josh followed the professor out of Penny's earshot.

"So," Professor West said. "You want to tell me why you didn't take the final yesterday?"

Josh stared at his sneakers.

"Not really," he mumbled.

"You said in your email that you were sick, but you look fine now."

Josh scratched his head. "Sorry. I... well, I didn't really study enough."

"Why didn't you even show up?"

"I was... uh, I was baking a pie."

"You missed the final because you were baking a pie."

"Yeah." Josh finally worked up the courage to meet the professor's steady gaze. "I was... well, Penny wanted me to enter a pie in this bake-off, and for a while there I thought I could win, so I was testing all these recipes even though I don't really like baking, and I came up with this great idea for an apple pie..."

He took a breath and pushed forward. "Anyway, I didn't win, but it's kind of okay because it's cool how Penny... she's disappointed but not *in me*, you know? She's like disappointed because she really believed I'd win.

And I guess… I guess it was more important not to disappoint her than it was to take your final. Sorry. I did think Beowulf was pretty cool."

Professor West looked at him for such a long time that Josh shifted from one foot to the other. He braced himself for a diatribe about how education was so important, how he'd just thrown away his future, how he should pay more attention, prioritize…

The professor didn't give him a lecture. He just looked at Josh, as if waiting for *him* to say something else.

"Look, I… I don't get it, okay?" Josh finally confessed. "Classes like yours. I mean, I get that some people are good at school and stuff… Penny is… but I don't see the point. I want to be a chef, own a restaurant, maybe have a farm where I can grow my own food. I don't want to sit around reading moldy old books. No offense."

"None taken."

"I'm just going to King's because my dad wants me to," Josh went on, unable to stop now that he was getting it all out. "He worked all these years because he didn't want me to struggle like he did, because he wanted me to get a degree. But it's not really what I want. So, you know, it's… it's kind of a mess."

"You ever tell your dad that?" Professor West asked.

"Not really."

For a guy who spent so much time lecturing in classrooms, the professor sure could be silent when he wanted to be. He studied Josh as if he were some specimen under a microscope before speaking again.

"My wife loves all the pies at The Pied Piper."

"Uh, thanks."

"Liv always talks about how good they are," Professor West continued. "She tries a different pie every time she stops in. A few weeks ago we had a friend over for dinner, and Liv wanted a pie for dessert. Couldn't decide which one would go with the dinner she made. Blueberry, chocolate, whatever. Finally she decided she wanted one cherry and one lemon meringue, so she ran to The Pied Piper to pick them up, but she was too late. The store was closed. She had to get a cake instead. She wasn't very happy either."

"Um… sorry about that?"

"My point is that you have a lot of choices," Professor West said. "And it doesn't have to be one or the other. But if you wait too long to decide, it could be too late."

"Oh." Josh didn't really get it. It was true, though, that The Pied Piper had a lot of choices. For the first time, he wondered what made people choose the pie they did.

"Come to my office hours on Monday," the professor said. "I'll talk to the administration office, and we'll figure out a time when you can retake the final. One of my grad students will help you study for it."

Josh knew he didn't deserve special treatment, but he nodded.

"Sorry," he said. "I mean, for blowing off the final for apple pie."

"Well." Professor West glanced at Penny. "She does seem like that kind of girl."

"What kind of girl?"

"The kind who's worth the risk." Professor West stepped back. "And the girl you take a risk for is the one you want to keep."

He tossed Josh the stuffed rabbit. Josh caught it. Professor West gave him a small salute and turned to walk away.

"Won't your wife want this back?" Josh called.

"No," the professor replied. "She'd want you to give it to the girl who believes in your apple pie."

Josh returned to Penny. She was studying a few tables filled with 4-H cake-decorating entries. He handed her the rabbit.

"Why did he give this to you?" she asked.

"For good luck, I think."

Penny took the rabbit, her expression still downcast.

"Hey, it's really okay," Josh said. "I'm not upset about losing."

"But it wasn't supposed to happen like that," she insisted. "The underdog always wins in the end."

"Then if the underdog doesn't win, it's not the end."

That made her smile. Josh's heart thumped hard.

He took Penny's hand, feeling her fingers close around his before he remembered that she was in love with someone else. He tugged his hand away.

"Come on. Fireworks should start soon."

They went out to the grassy field where people were spreading out blankets and lawn chairs to watch the fair's firework spectacle. Josh and Penny settled into the grass, the stuffed rabbit at Penny's other side.

The fireworks started with sprays of gold, purple, and blue, the boom echoing over the surrounding hills. The sky lit up with brilliant flashes of color that made Josh want to believe in infinity.

It always works out in the end... Josh, you need to do what you want... I know what I need to do... you have a lot of choices... the girl you take a risk for is the one you want to keep...

Josh wanted to take a risk for Penny. He also wanted to take a risk for himself.

He pushed to his feet. His father was right over at The Pied Piper food truck. Josh realized that he'd always known where to find his dad when he needed him. Like both *pi* and *pie*, Simon Piper was a constant.

"Penny, I'll be right back, okay?"

Josh hurried back to the fair and headed straight for the truck. He heard his dad's voice as he neared—booming and full of cheer as he served slices of pie.

"Fresh apple right here... best pie crust in the state... peaches this year are sweet as sugar..."

Josh waited for the small crowd in front of the truck to disperse. He steeled his spine.

"Hey, Dad."

"Josh. Didn't know you'd be here." Simon bent to look at him through the truck's window.

"I'm here with Penny. She's watching the fireworks." Josh took a breath. "Look, Dad, I want to talk to you about some stuff soon. Okay?"

Simon frowned. "What stuff?"

"You know how I told you I want to be a chef? I kept thinking there was no way I could train to be a chef and go to King's at the same time, but maybe there is. If you'll agree."

"Agree with what? You're not dropping out."

"No. But maybe I could take business and administration classes. For a year or so. If I do okay, then I want to enroll part-time in culinary school."

Josh could see the protest about to break from his father. He spoke fast to prevent it. "I have some ideas, Dad. I'll make it work. And if I learn more about the business stuff, I can help out more with the shop. All these ideas you have for delivery and expansion… if I know more, I can do more."

The creases on Simon's forehead eased a little, though he was still frowning. "We'll talk at home."

"Okay." At least it was a start. Josh turned away.

"Josh."

He turned back. Simon passed a small box and a plastic fork through the window.

"Apple pie for Penny," his father said. "I know it's her favorite."

Josh took the box and hurried back to where Penny was sitting on the grass, her hands propped behind her. She smiled at the sight of the pie and ate it as the fireworks continued bursting over the sky.

"I think I can do it," Josh told her.

"Do what?"

"Keep my dad happy, but also train to be a chef. I just need to figure out how and talk to him about it."

"All it took was losing a bake-off for you to reach that conclusion?" Penny set the empty box aside.

"No. That's not all it took."

Josh shifted his gaze from the sky to Penny, her profile illuminated by the rainbow light.

"Who is he?" Josh asked. "The guy you kissed."

Penny was silent for a minute, her face tilted toward the sky. Then she turned to face him. Her eyes looked very blue. Even in the dark, he could see the sprinkle of freckles across her nose.

"Josh," she finally said. "It was *you*."

His heart gave a wild, crazy leap, even as some logical part of his brain said she was messing with him.

"It wasn't me," he said.

"It was you."

"But we… we've never kissed."

She looked at the sky again as a pinwheel of colors spun above them.

"One night… October fifth of last year… you'd spent all day working at the shop and going to classes," she said. "I'd stopped at your house to return a book I'd borrowed. Your dad was out on deliveries. You asked if I wanted to watch a movie."

Josh rummaged through his mind and found the memory. "*Aliens.*"

"We were sitting on the sofa, and you were trying to study and watch the movie at the same time," Penny said. "You fell asleep about a quarter of the way in."

She stopped talking. He waited. His pulse was racing, and beneath his heart there was a flicker of something that felt distinctly like hope. Excited hope. Hopeful hope. The kind of hope that made him realize exactly what he'd been hoping *for*.

"You'd sprawled all over the sofa," Penny continued. "Practically pushing me off. So I got up to leave and pulled a blanket over you. I was… I was just looking at you, and then I… well, I kissed you."

A firework boomed overhead. Josh barely heard it past the beating of his heart.

"You kissed me," he repeated.

"Yes."

"On the lips?"

"Well, not on the *chin*." Penny rolled her eyes.

Embarrassment flashed through him. "Why'd you do that?"

"I just wanted to. I'd wanted to for some time."

"Uh. I… I don't think that means you've been kissed… uh, officially," Josh stammered.

"I didn't say I'd *been* kissed," Penny said. "I said I'd kissed someone. You just didn't kiss me back."

"Well." Josh cleared his throat. "In my defense, I was unconscious."

"True. Even given that, it was still a pretty good kiss, though you'll have to take my word for it."

"Actually, you… you didn't say you'd kissed *someone*," Josh said, his stomach twisting with both nervousness and anticipation.

Penny blinked. "I didn't?"

"No. You said you'd kissed a guy you've loved for a while now."

Her cheeks reddened as she averted her gaze.

"And you said I didn't know him," Josh continued.

"You don't," Penny said, after a minute. "Or at least... you didn't."

"This is beginning to sound like Leo's maze of treachery," Josh remarked.

Penny glanced at him with a faint smile.

"Josh, the guy I love is amazing. He's creative, funny, ambitious, and loyal to a fault. He can do anything he wants to do, anything he sets his mind to. He can cook like a dream. He's much smarter than he thinks he is. He's strong, dependable, talented. Oh, and he is very, very hot."

Josh's breath escaped him in a rush. "Wow. But I still don't get—"

"You didn't know all that about yourself, did you?" Penny asked. "You've always seen yourself as this guy stuck working in his dad's pie shop, a student who doesn't want to be a student, a boy going in the wrong direction but not even knowing how to get himself turned around. You didn't know the real you."

Josh's heart did a flip as he finally realized what she was telling him.

"But you did," he said.

"That's the guy I've loved for a while now," Penny told him. "The real Josh Piper."

All he could do was look at her and think about how she'd been the steadiest part of his life for years now, and he hadn't even realized that all his feelings for her—warmth, affection, respect, admiration—could all be summed up by that one word.

"It wasn't the bake-off that forced me to figure out who I am," Josh said.

"What was it, then?"

"Just one Sweet Penny Pie."

He scooted over on the grass to close the distance between them. Penny gazed at him, her lips parting as she drew in a breath. He reached out to cup her chin in his hand. He felt a tremble course through her, felt its echo in the middle of his chest.

For a moment, they just looked at each other, and he saw the fireworks reflected in the dark blue irises of Penny's eyes.

Then all the colors and lights, the booming noise, distilled to the one instant when Penny touched his face. Her cool fingers slid across his jaw and down to the pulse beating at the side of his neck.

Pleasure coursed through him. His head filled with her coconut-cream scent. Her skin was soft beneath his palm. He moved closer and finally brushed his mouth across hers. She sighed. Heat flooded his chest. He slid his hand around the back of her neck and pulled her closer. Her lips parted beneath his, her mouth soft and inviting.

Josh shifted. The world around him faded. Penny tasted like apples, cinnamon, sugar, cherries, vanilla. All those sweet pie tastes he'd thought he disliked. Now he couldn't get enough of them, couldn't get enough of her. He cupped her face in his hands and deepened the kiss as her grip tightened around his arms and her body swayed toward him.

They fitted together easily, his mouth pressed seamlessly to hers with none of the fumbling awkwardness of a first kiss. Josh thought he could sit here forever kissing Penny, tasting her, his blood humming with pleasure as fireworks burst overhead. For the first time, everything was exactly right.

Penny, who always shone the brightest. Penny, whose smile always eased the tension around Josh's heart. Penny, who thought apple pie and ice cream could solve any problem. Penny, who believed that everyone deserved a happy—

Josh eased away slightly, pressing his forehead to hers. Her breath warmed his lips, her eyes even bluer than usual. And he said it, the words he hadn't known until now that he felt for her. The feeling that he'd shoved down beneath too many insecurities and fears.

"I love you," he said. "For a while now too. I'm… I just didn't know it."

"Lucky for you," Penny whispered, reaching up to rub his lower lip. "I did."

Her smile hit him right in the middle of his heart. He kissed her on the nose as they parted, still sitting so close that their thighs pressed together. They both flopped onto their backs and looked up at the fiery, colored sky.

"We're not going to have a happy ending," Josh said.

"We're… we're not?"

"No." Josh fumbled in the dark for Penny's hand and closed his fingers around hers. "But we will definitely have a happy afterward. And it starts now."

THE END

About the Author

Nina Lane

USA Today bestselling author Nina Lane writes hot, sexy romances and spicy erotica, including the acclaimed *Spiral of Bliss* trilogy (*Arouse*, *Allure*, and *Awaken*). Originally from California, Nina loves traveling, and she also spent many years in graduate school studying art history and library sciences. Although she would go back for another degree if she could because she's that much of a bookworm, she now lives the happy life of a full-time writer.

Find out about Nina's latest news and books at:
http://www.ninalane.com
or join her on Facebook at http://www.facebook.com/NinaLaneAuthor
and Twitter at @NinaLaneAuthor

I owe debt of gratitude to the following people, who helped me immeasurably with this story: Kelly Harms Wimmer, Rachel Berens-VanHeest, Melody Marshall, Natalie Marshall, and Will Lewis. Thank you so much for your valuable criticism and unflagging support. You all take the cake.

Priceless
A ROTHVALE LEGACY STORY

By
Raine Miller

National Gallery
London
29th June

CHARITY GALAS ARE bloody horrific things. This one was sure to be no different, so I imagined surviving the next couple of hours would be priority mission number one for me. Well, I did have a little entertainment to look forward to at the end of the evening and that was something. I pulled into the National Gallery, queued for valet service, and checked my mobile for the details.

There it was. I read it twice and attempted to memorize who, what, and where.

Mr. Ivan: Maria will be wearing an emerald green gown. Victorian Gallery 8:00 p.m. Terms per contract. We wish you both a very pleasant evening.

The escort service I liked best was the one that didn't have a name and you never talked to anyone by voice. Everything was transacted by text. Simple. Efficient. Anonymous. No strings attached to get all tangled into a cocked up mess, and when the date was over everyone went home satisfied.

The less time I had to think about what I was really doing, the better. I wasn't proud of myself for my behavior, but the reasons were justified in my mind. I was just doing what I needed to do to get by.

Betrayal does that to a man.

By the time I made my way inside and found the venue, I was pleasantly surprised to see I'd missed the dinner. The polite conversation required at these kind of events was sheer torture and I often wondered how on earth that I, out of all of the eligible men in England, could have ended up inheriting a directorship on the board of the National Gallery. There couldn't possibly be a worse choice *than* me. I know next to nothing about paintings and no inclination to begin learning about them either. Being 'Lord Rothvale' in the twenty-first century did not impress me either. Having patrons address me as 'my lord' and bowing upon introduction made my skin crawl.

I was left having to fake it.

I did that a lot.

The pretense grew very tiresome to me because my whole life had been turned upside down by lies. Shredded and stripped, and then stomped and burned in front of me.

False... counterfeit... sham.

Where in the bloody hell had they set the bar up in this place?

I wandered a bit, trying to appear focused on the exhibit and praying nobody recognized me for fifteen minutes. Hell, I'd be happy with five if I could grab even that.

The landscape changed when I spotted the lovely Brynne Bennett presenting a painting of a woman with a book. It looked like it could be a Mallerton in the midst of the conservation process. It was being repaired or preserved so it could last another hundred years or so without losing its colors and clarity of image. Yeah, I'd managed to absorb a few bits of knowledge about what needed to happen to old paintings by default. I'd much rather look at the stunning conservator giving the presentation though.

Brynne was very easy to look at, but she was also very taken. By my very protective cousin, no less. Ethan runs a security business so I give him credit for the *protective* part. He has excellent taste in women. I'll give him that too.

"Enjoying the show?" Ethan's voice came at my shoulder.

"Probably more like thinking about when in the hell I could *escape* the show," I answered. "I was just thinking about you, cousin."

"Really."

"Indeed. Think of the devil and he appears as if by magic."

"Glad you could make it tonight," he said sarcastically. "We've been wondering when you'd finally grace us with your presence. Brynne wants to introduce you to her friend." He looked around as if he were searching the crowd for someone.

"Brynne looks very busy right now." I glanced over at his girlfriend admiringly. "Maybe later."

"Look, Ivan, there was a pseudo threat delivered to my office today. I'm not horribly concerned but I want you frontloaded on the details." He handed me an envelope of photos.

Ethan and I had done this plenty of times before so it wasn't anything new. Eight-by-ten black and white photographs of Brynne and me chatting at Gladstone's, where I'd met the two of them for lunch a few weeks back. Me kissing her on the cheeks, as I put her in the car. Me leaning in to speak to the both of them, and waving them off. Me on the street after Ethan's car had pulled away. Me waiting on the street for my own car to come 'round.

I grunted at the photos as I flipped through them a second time. I flipped over the pictures one by one. Nothing. Until the last one: *"Never attempt to murder a man who is committing suicide"* scrawled on the back.

Marvelous. Another fan sending me love notes.

I'd seen this kind of thing throughout my career. It had to be taken seriously of course, but more often than not, it was some lunatic fringe who had an axe to grind on the back of someone notable they perceived to have caused offense to them personally, and with cruel intent. Sports figures especially suffered this kind of crap. I had offended a ton of people in my time and had the gold medals to prove it. Even though I was a retired Olympic archer, I was still hounded by the media all the time. The hounding had grown especially fierce with what had recently happened in my private life. The upcoming Olympic Games being hosted in my home country didn't help either. It put me back on the radar and the timing couldn't have been worse.

I counted my blessings that Ethan was blood family. That alone would have earned his protection regardless, but I certainly kept him busy. After a minute I handed the whole lot back to my suave cousin. "Thanks, E, for looking out. I'm sure it'll all blow over when the Olympics are but a memory." I looked at the drink in his hand, deciding that getting one for myself was a bigger priority now than earlier. And probably three G & T's was far more realistic than just the one.

"At least I can hope, true?" I acted like I didn't care about the threat.

"It's all any of us can do, mate." He nodded, clapping me on the back with one hand.

"I need to have something along the lines of what you're having." I waved off and left for the bar, in a far worse mood than I'd been a few moments ago. If that was even possible.

~~~~

I loved my dress tonight. Brynne's aunt Marie had taken us both to a fabulous shop in Knightsbridge that sold vintage gowns. My dark green silk moved so well as I walked, I couldn't help but be impressed with the superior artistry. It definitely paid to buy quality. I'd bought the gown specifically for tonight and figured it was wise to invest in something I could wear to other formal events. And the party was as beautiful as ever. The annual *Mallerton Gala for the Arts* in honor of Romanticist painter, Sir Tristan Mallerton, was something I never missed. I knew his birthday as well as I knew the birthdays of my own family. June 29th. I ought to know. His work was the basis for my masters in Art History at University of London.

I knew every catalogued painting Mallerton had ever created and had seen a good portion of them with my own eyes. The National Gallery had the largest collection of his work on display in Britain, but it was safe to bet there were plenty of unknowns in private homes and in storage that had never seen the light of day. Mallerton had been prolific during his lifetime. Most of those pieces were in the hands of people who had no idea what they owned, and sadly, no interest in finding out either. Occasionally a painting would come onto the market from a private collection and go to auction though. And it was my job to get it evaluated and into the database.

I stopped at an equestrian portrait that I counted among my top five favorites out of all of his work. It was a happy painting, and every time I saw it I wanted to smile. Mallerton had executed it perfectly, the moment preserved in time for all to enjoy.

The subject was a young bride with long dark hair seated on a magnificent white horse, who'd been adorned with garlands and ribbons and bells throughout his tack. Even though she wasn't smiling at all like a person would today when posing for a picture, the expression of joy captured so exquisitely in her expression made you a believer. There was no doubt that this girl was a happy bride. It was titled simply, *Mrs. Gravelle*, and always made me wonder what Mr. Gravelle was like. He'd won a beautiful bride that's for sure, and I dearly hoped he'd loved her as he should have.

Even the most unsophisticated observer could see the emotion in Mallerton's work. It's the thing that had attracted me to him when I began my studies. And that rare talent was what had made him famous in his lifetime and still today nearly two hundred years later.

Two hundred years, two years. They might as well be the same thing. A lot could change in just two years…

I tried not to think about what I'd lost, but my self-imposed loneliness got the better of me sometimes, and I desperately longed for what Mrs. Gravelle had in her painting.

"I found you," a smooth voice said behind me.

I turned to see who was speaking to me and got an eyeful of beautiful. The man before me was six feet plus of dark, lean and sexy with green eyes the color of my dress. He flashed me a smile that could only be described as wicked.

"Are you sure you were looking for me?" He appeared to have money because I'd bet my extravagant new gown, that the tux hanging off his fine form was most certainly bespoke. No doubt about it. Was he a patron in need of a gallery tour? A large contributor VIP?

"Oh yes, it's definitely you," he purred, "the beauty in the green dress." He leaned forward. Close but not touching, his face tilted toward my neck. I backed up. He followed... until I was pressed against the wall. "And they were so right," he said in his silky voice.

"Right about what?" I asked, mesmerized by his features and his delicious scent, totally overpowered by how close he was to me. My God, he smelled good. "Um... d-did you want the standard t-tour?" I stuttered, amazed that coherent words were even forming from my lips.

"Mmm hmm," he said, nodding slowly, drawing his gaze up my neck, "I definitely want *your* tour."

Why are you speaking like that to me? I was clearly at a disadvantage in this situation. Something weird was going on. Who was this Greek god trapping me against the wall, looking like he wanted to devour me? And was it bad that the thought of him actually doing some devouring made a long shiver roll down my back?

Mr. Gorgeous didn't appear to be in any hurry, his green eyes tracking over my body, roving over everything they could see.

I swallowed hard.

"Who—who was it that sent you to find me, ah... mister—?"

"—Ivan. Didn't you get the text from the service?" He inhaled and moved a fraction closer, just staring with a confident half-smirk on his face. "You're definitely who I'm supposed to meet tonight. Eight o'clock it said, and wearing a green dress, which by the way, is very... *very*... nice." The last three words were spoken slowly as his eyes raked up my dress until he landed somewhere around my lips.

"Eight o'clock," I repeated dumbly, overwhelmed by his maleness, and his friggin' gorgeous... everything, to the point I had apparently lost the ability to carry on a conversation.

Wait, what service?

"So you are Mr. Ivan and you want me to give you the tour?" I said, a tad too sarcastically, wanting to slap myself for the ignorance that kept spouting out of my mouth.

I was in utter and complete bewilderment of what was going on with *him* though.

I *knew* for a fact I hadn't been informed about any VIP named Mr. Ivan needing a contributor's tour tonight during the gala. But clearly that's what he was expecting, standing there looking like a man who was *very* sure of what he wanted. I couldn't just say no and blow him off. That would be incredibly rude and possibly get me into trouble with the university. And that was the thing with VIPs. They tended to be less predictable and often just showed up, expecting special treatment. Their deep pockets were what kept the charities going though, and offending a big donor was a *big* no-no.

He tilted his head and narrowed his eyes just a bit, his brow wrinkling for an instant. "Call me that if you wish, I don't mind, and yes, I want whatever you have planned for me." He brushed back his hair with a hand and held it there gripping at the back of his neck, his elbow coming up and framing me in even more. "I'm ready to begin if you are." He smiled.

Whatever I had planned for him? I had nothing planned. I had no idea why any of this conversation between us was even happening. I knew nothing. Well, I knew one thing—I couldn't take my eyes off his hair.

Mr. Ivan's hair was dark and straight, worn deliciously long in the European style, hitting just where his broad shoulders met his neck. I wanted to touch.

He'd been blessed in more ways than just his wallet. *An alien perhaps?*

"All right," I said carefully, swallowing hard again, and wondering just how the next thirty minutes were going to go with the each of us staring and speaking in some kind of mysterious code. "Where would you like to start, Mr. Ivan? What interests you the most?"

He offered his arm, which I accepted and let him lead us down the hallway.

"Beauty interests me right now." He looked down at me and smiled darkly, his lips slightly parted and my arm tucked firmly under his.

It interests me too. "Well, there is plenty of that here to show you," I said.

"I thought so." He stopped us at a door. "I can't wait to see it all and experience it for myself."

He opened the door and led me inside a darkened anteroom. Various works in progress of restoration and archival rooms were down this way. I was about to ask him if he wanted a tour of the conservationist wing when he shut the door and pressed me back against it. "Bloody perfect," he mumbled.

"What—?" was all I managed to get out before he took my face in his hands, slammed his mouth down over mine and started kissing me.

~~~~

My "date" was interesting tonight. Sexy as all get-out but mysteriously illusive with what sounded to be an American accent. And so damn beautiful my eyes were stinging.

We really needed to get this party started, and we couldn't very well just stand here in a quiet gallery hallway mentally undressing each other now could we? That would be wholly inappropriate and someone was bound to come by and see eventually.

I don't usually go in for public shags but was far too gone in attraction to my "tour guide" to care very much. I'm a man of action. Give me a problem and I will do my damndest to find a solution.

Like right now for instance: *Where can I find a place to get Maria alone and see what she's got hidden beneath her sexy gown?*

Was Maria really her name? I tried to remember the text I'd received, and thought I was right, but details like that slip my mind consistently. I *was* however, well aware that escorts didn't like for clients to use their working names anywhere where somebody might hear.

I always followed the rules with the ladies, still shocked that this beautiful creature was even an escort in the first place, and not a model for Vogue or Harper's. She could be, in a heartbeat.

A door appeared in front of me, so I opened it and brought her in with me. Dark, empty, private. "Bloody perfect," I said.

I pressed her up against the door and took her face in my hands. Her eyes were a stunning dark green, almost the same color as mine were, but I just had to get to know that luscious mouth of hers first.

I could look into her eyes once we were shagging in a few, and I planned on it.

I wanted a taste of those lips mostly, and then I'd move on to other parts. I knew what I was doing and I was totally confident she did too.

"What—?" she murmured, just as I descended. *Time for talking is over, sweetheart.*

When I covered her mouth with mine and got a good taste, something switched on inside me and I sort of lost my normally maintained control.

I just wanted to savor and kiss and touch and get lost in her for a while.

She froze at first and sucked in a breath, but then she seemed to soften and go with the program, and started to kiss me back. She tasted like a delicious wine I couldn't seem to get enough of, so I just delved deeper and held her firmly.

It took a moment, but I felt her response grow to the point where her hands got into the action and buried in my hair. Once that started happening I knew everything was good. We had chemistry together and I was sure of one thing—I'd be getting Maria's number so I could see her again.

I moved a hand down to sweep under her skirt and slid my palm up her thigh and right between her legs. I felt lace.

And a bundle of hot, sexy female.

"Ahhh…" she moaned, standing up on her toes and throwing her head back when I touched her. I moved my mouth to her throat and down the deep neckline of her dress. My fingers dove under the lace of her knickers and found my target, skimming back and forth where it counted.

That she was totally turned on and primed for action, was never in question. I had the proof of that all over my fingers.

This goddess in my arms, wearing that dress I wished I could strip her out of was about to come on me. *Fucking hot.*

I gripped her face with my free hand and brought her back to face me. "Open your eyes."

She complied instantly, her lashes flipping up and revealing those green beauties I'd admired earlier. Her breathing was coming in heavy pants now. Time to hit a bull's-eye with Miss Maria, I decided.

I moved two fingers into position and buried them inside her. In the same moment I seized her mouth and impaled myself there too. She was totally mine to conquer and I relished the control in moments like this. I was all about control when it came to sex.

I matched the stroking of my fingers, with the pace my tongue was keeping, and in no time I had her riding the wave of an orgasm as she rode my hand.

I swallowed her tensing cries with my mouth, and slowed everything down for her until she was completely melted against the door, fighting for breaths.

Mission accomplished.

"God, you're beautiful." She widened her eyes and focused on me, a look of utter satisfaction simmering in them as she breathed against the door. What I wouldn't give to have her in my bed right now. I moved my fingers slowly out, retreating carefully from her body. She gasped softly and rolled with my movements, coming down from the rush to stand on her own again. Her head was slightly tilted and resting on the back of the door. My hand still on her face, I lowered it down to her shoulder, caressing as I went.

"My turn."

Her eyes flared at me in the dim light for an instant, as if she were considering my request, but the afterglow of pleasure boiling in her eyes told me she was *very* into what we were doing. We were just getting started on where I planned for this to go.

She sighed in contentment and dropped down to her knees gracefully before me, her fine hands reaching forward to work on opening my trousers. She pulled out my shirt and found my cock, which was more than

ready to meet her pretty mouth. I couldn't hold back the groan that came
out of me and closed my eyes in anticipation.

It had been a while and I was definitely going to enjoy this.

When she touched me I thrust into her hand. She gripped around the
shaft and stroked, pulling me closer. I felt the softness of her tongue slide
over the tip of me and welcomed the hot burn of pleasure.

My fantasy lover was just getting into the groove, and doing a superb
job I might add, when our timing went to complete shit.

The emergency light above the door began to twirl a flashing red
paired with a siren wail of ear-deafening decibels. Over all of that, the loud-
speaker announcement demanded the building be exited immediately for
safety precautions.

Well, damn, this certainly sucked.

Or not.

Maria was off me and out the door, before I could get myself tucked
back into my trousers.

By the time I managed to stumble out of our little love nest, she was
nowhere to be seen, but Ethan was sprinting down the hallway.

I ran for it, coming up behind him. He turned back and saw me.

"Bomb threat. That's what this is." He gestured to the flashing lights.
"Everyone's being evacuated."

I just exploded in anger, unbelieving that someone would hate me so
much they would blow up a museum to get to me. Disgruntled fan or not,
an act of terrorism was way out of bounds. "Are you fucking kidding me?!
All this because of me?"

"I don't know details. I was out having a smoke when the alarm went
off. Neil said in-house security got a bomb threat called in and they're
closing everything down. We'll sort it later. Just get the fuck out!"

So that's what I did.

I looked for Maria but I never found her in the crush of people
swarming the front steps of the National Gallery. I thought I saw her at one
point because there was a woman wearing a similar color green dress, but
she was blonde and not the fiery goddess I'd been with in that room earlier.

Pity. I would have asked her home with me and paid double for her
services without a second thought. Maria was definitely worth it.

Some more G & T's and a session with her would've topped off my evening just perfectly. I texted Ethan to let him know I was leaving and to ring me when he had a chance. As I drove home to my solitary existence I wasn't content and I certainly wasn't satisfied.

I felt pretty much like shit and there were plenty of other reasons for that, unfortunately. The only nice thing to happen tonight had been the encounter with a beautiful creature whose sexy scent was still clinging to my hand.

I really needed to find her again.

~~~~

Donadea
County Wicklow, Ireland
5th August

"YOU'RE JUST NOT telling me anything I want to hear right now, Paul. Sorry, but no. I need this shit out of my goddamned house and I need it gone now!" The pause from him was to be expected, and I was more than used to it. In fact, this kind of reaction from others was pretty damn typical. I bark, and people move. Things get done the way they're supposed to and the way I want.

Waiting for Paul Langley to respond on the other end of the line though, made me impatient and I started tapping the top of my desk.

I studied the worn oak grain of the wood and realized something I'd never really thought about before. My ancestors must have sat here at this same desk. Even as far back as maybe two hundred years ago I suppose, but that didn't change the fact that it was *still* just a desk. A useful piece of furniture. A tool to be used rather than just on display as a formal antique appreciated only for its aesthetic value. "Hello? You still there?"

"I wouldn't call it shit, Ivan."

"Right. Let me rephrase that for you then. Paul, would you please get someone over to my house capable of archiving the very valuable shit I have an abundance of. A graduate student perhaps? There must be some-one who needs a job. The papers tell of gloom and doom for the pissing economy. A starving artist? Work with me here, Paul. I do plenty for your organization and you know it."

Paul sighed heavily into the phone. "I'll see what I can do. There may be a possible candidate, but I'm not sure. The student I've in mind has been through a rough patch lately." He hesitated before letting me have it. "And you aren't the easiest person to… ah… work for."

"Are you trying to tell me I'm an arsehole, Paul?"

Paul laughed softly. "Yes. And I couldn't pass up that chance to tell you either."

"Nothing new there. Right. Good. So offer them a big pile of my money. I pay well. Get someone over here to do the job and you'll get your usual toward the philanthropic health of the arts and all that crap, and I won't be drawn and quartered for letting priceless paintings go to rot."

Paul muttered something about expecting a bigger donation cheque this year if he managed to find someone for me. "See that you do and you just might," I told him as we ended the call.

I looked out the window. The landscape of Donadea was stunning in all its green lushness—hills and dales dotted with trees contrasting against the blue skies above. Too bad I didn't have the heart to enjoy it much. Not anymore.

I'd loved coming here as a kid even after mum died. The best times of all had been the long breaks in summer. Riding, driving, fishing, time at the lake, picnics. It had been magical. A place to forget the harsh bustle of London and all the responsibilities that came with this blasted life I'd in-herited. But Viviana had taken even the peace of this sanctuary from me. Now Donadea just reminded me of all that I didn't have, which was sym-bolic for why I wanted this placed cleared out.

The time had come to let the past go.

I left my study and walked across the west wing of the house to the portrait gallery. The walls were filled. There was too much here. It needed to be sorted and some maybe sold, donated, or stored for preservation even. I thought of the ironic twist of fate that had left me as caretaker of such goods. An art collection to rival the best in the world and I knew next to nothing about it.

My uncle, the eighth Baron Rothvale, had not been much better, and my father had certainly not cared about any of the artwork for the short time he'd been at the helm of this slow leaking vessel. No, the paintings in this house had been neglected for a great many decades and they were due some greatly needed attention. Even my ignorant arse knew that.

My thoughts were that I could get this project started and then leave the expert to finish it. I shouldn't have to stay here for long, besides I had work in London that required me there regardless.

I told myself this was the reason I'd come here. But who was I fooling? This time of year was always the same. I had to get away from everything that reminded me of her and this was the only place I had left to go where that was even possible.

~~~~

One week later

I didn't like this. The sun was starting to set and I might as well admit to myself that I was lost.

Really lost.

The perfect metaphor for just about everything in regards to my life.

I pulled to the side of the road and looked at the directions I'd printed out from my computer. Trouble was, this was a huge estate and most of the roads were unmarked, meandering peacefully in all directions over the rolling green. The GPS that came with the rental wasn't worth a damn in places like this. It was likely to have me driving over a cliff if I depended on it.

The words blurred together on the paper anyway. My reading glasses were in my suitcase, which was sitting in the trunk of the car, where they could do me absolutely no good at the moment of course. My night vision sucked, so I was screwed. I fumbled for my cell phone and dialed the number Professor Langley had given me.

After several rings voice mail picked up. "Everley. Leave a message." The voice was curt and clipped, somewhat cold. No greeting. No other information offered. Nothing to make me feel even the slightest bit comfortable about showing up for a job in a gloomy Irish manor house, filled to the brim with god knows what. I highly doubted it would work anyway.

I was only here as a favor to Paul Langley, one of my academic advisors at the University of London. He'd pulled me into his office and basically told me that if I wanted to be recommended for the M.Phil. in Art History, then it would be prudent of me to accept this appointment, and thereby, please the patron. Professor Langley was fair but tough. He was also on the boards for every art society known to man. One did not tell him no. Not if I wanted to get a job in my field someday. And apparently one did not tell Lord Ivan Everley 'no' either.

"This is Gabrielle Hargreave from the University of London. I—I'm having some trouble with the directions to find you. It's getting dark. I suppose… I'm lost. Please call me back." I left my message and sat back in the driver's seat. I figured the best thing to do was wait for someone to return my call. All of those survival shows always said so. If you are lost, stay put until someone finds you.

The sun slowly dipped below the horizon in a gorgeous display of red and purple. I watched the whole thing and waited. And waited some more. Nobody called me back. I checked for messages every few minutes but it remained silent. The idea of spending the night in this car, afield in the Irish countryside did not appeal to me either. How on earth had I ended up in such a mess?

I called the number again and left another message. I hoped my voice did not sound too pathetic on the recording. God, didn't the man have some servants? He was a baron or a viscount or something. Didn't they have staff at their beck and call to handle every little problem that arose? How much longer would I have to wait out here in the dark? And the cold. I needed the loo too. Trying to get a handle on my rising panic, I got out of the car and opened the boot and found my suitcase.

My jacket would be a good start. For August, the weather was mostly mild but it felt like rain was imminent, and of course the temperature always dropped with the sun's departure. I found my glasses too and put them in my pocket.

I scanned the landscape and looked for anything that might resemble a manor house. Nothing. It was so dark now that the only light was from the risen moon, glowing serenely above the fast moving clouds. If I didn't want to get soaked I needed to get back in the car. I might as well start driving too. Enough of this "staying put" bullshit. It was getting me literally nowhere.

~~~~

I looked at my watch and felt my jaw twitch. This was bloody irritating and then some. I looked at the text message from Paul Langley again. **Gabriel Hargreave driving in today to assess your collection.**

Well, whoever Gabriel Hargreave was, he certainly couldn't tell time. Or know how to use a telephone. *Useless artsy twit.*

I'd stayed home purposefully this evening in order to be here to greet the student Langley had found for my archival work. Gabriel was not impressing me in the slightest, so far.

I was convinced that young people today, just did not have the drive to be successful. No initiative. Little commitment. It was pathetically shameful what I had to put up with. I refilled my drink and went to the window to look for the possibility of headlights coming up the drive. Nothing. What a waste of time. The twit was probably one of those Bohemian art students who lived life on a whim with no idea whatsoever of keeping to a schedule or the job he'd agreed to. The job I was paying him to do. Christ, what did it take to get some help around here?

Seeing my mobile blinking on the sofa, I went over to retrieve it, realizing I must've set it down when I was watching television earlier. I had a bad habit of doing that.

I checked and saw three new messages. I didn't know what I expected but what I got was not it.

Shit! My grad student, who sounded very feminine, was lost and off the road in the dark apparently. I checked my watch again and grimaced. The first call had been left over three hours ago and it was pitch black outside now. I grabbed my car keys and headed for the garage, hitting redial as I went.

A tremulous voice answered on the third ring. "Hello?"

"Is this Gabriel Hargreave?" I asked. "Where are you? I can come down in the Rover and collect you or at least lead you up the proper road." I tried to keep the harshness from my voice. I didn't want him to quit, *before* I could fire him at any rate.

"Not Gabriel, I'm Gabrielle. Gabrielle Hargreave. And how the hell should I know where I am? I told you I'm lost! And it's so dark out here."

"Oh, my bad, *Miss* Hargreave. You've been driving around with no idea where you're going for three hours?" I was pretty shocked by what she'd just told me. "Why on earth would anyone continue driving while they're lost in the dark? You're supposed to stay put and wait for help. Didn't you ever watch a survival show?"

"Nobody came and I thought I could find my way!" she wailed into my ear. "It's raining and I'm on empty and I just drove through a stream across the road!" She sounded hysterical now, and I couldn't help wincing as I moved my mobile away from my ear.

I tried to adopt a patient tone. "But I cannot come and retrieve you if you keep driving around." Dead silence greeted me, and I wondered if I'd had lost connectivity for a moment, until I heard her breathing. "What landmarks can you see?"

A muffled sob came through loud and clear, and I felt a moment's guilt for not catching her calls, when she actually rang for help. I really needed to stop setting my mobile down in random places—

"I already told you before, I can't see a bloody thing!" she blasted back at me.

"Well, you need to calm down, Miss Har—"

"Wait! I can make out the profile of some low hills to my right. And there's nothing but fields to my left. I swear I can hear waves crashing below me. Please say you know where I am!"

Was she crying? Unease started to settle in my gut. Maybe this person was not cut out for the job after all. "Are you outside of your car? I think I can find you but you need to hang on and get back in your car. Turn on your headlamps and whatever the hell else you do, for the love of Christ, stop driving and wait for me."

I headed out in the Rover, glad for the four wheel drive over country roads that had turned to slopping mud. She'd sounded frantic. The part about hearing waves crashing below her did not sit well either. There were sections of the cliff side where a person could simply slip over if they were not aware of their bearings. And Miss Hargreave was certainly not going to be the poster girl for Outdoor Magazine anytime soon, I could safely wager.

The drive was slow going due to the rain and mud until I got to the main road. I traversed that for a good two kilometers before turning off again, for where I thought she might be. When headlamps came into view I breathed out a heavy sigh in relief and pulled up alongside what I assumed was her Volkswagen.

The economy did not look promising for making it up the muddy road tonight. I came up to the driver's window and looked in. Where was she? "Miss Hargreave?" I called out.

Only the sound of rain and the rumble the windshield wipers on the Rover filled the darkness.

~~~~

Oh dear God, he was here!

I'd seen the lights of the Range Rover as soon as it pulled up alongside my rental but I couldn't just pop out to greet my new boss with my jeans around my ankles now could I? I'd needed the loo hours ago and my bladder was past the point of negotiation. Far, far past. The tree I'd chosen to shield my privacy was an ancient thing, and as soon as I was restored to my former self, I called out to the tall form bent over, peering into the window of my car. "I'm over here. Mr. Everley? That is you, right?"

His head whipped around so fast it gave me a moment's pause and I stumbled.

"Of course it's me. Who else would it be? What in the hell are you doing hiding under a tree? Why aren't you waiting for me in your car where it's dry?" Mr. Everley sounded very annoyed.

"I had—I needed to—I was desperate for a loo if you must know!" Seriously, did he talk to everyone this way? It wasn't like I'd tried to get lost or that I was actually responsible for the torrential summer rain.

The stiffness of my legs combined with the mud, the cold, and the general awkwardness of this whole situation did not help me with my balance one bit.

I slipped again and went down on my ass in the sticky mud, right at Mr. Everley's feet.

A large hand reached down to help me up. "You'll get mud all over my leather seats now," he said blandly.

I took his offered hand and let him haul me up. "No, I won't. I'll follow you in my car." I was so mortified at this point, walking in the mud and the rain sounded like a damn good idea. Closed inside a vehicle with my new boss scowling and growling at me, with mud all up my backside? So out of the question.

Mr. Everley took one sneering look at my car and shook his head at me. "That little thing will die a muddy death if you try it. You don't have a choice. Get in." He certainly had no trouble ordering me around. Must be the duke or earl in him.

I stood there for a moment and hoped for a miracle. The rain kept falling and my boss kept glaring. I swallowed and gestured toward my car. "My things. My equipment. To do the work, I must have—"

"Tomorrow." He said it quietly, and in a way that brooked no argument. Christ he was intimidating, and tall, but that was about all I could make out of him in his bulky rain jacket. The dark, the rain, and my sucky night vision made it pretty difficult to see much of anything. I mostly just wanted to get warm and dry.

He shifted and folded his arms across a wide chest. "Miss Hargreave, do you enjoy standing in the cold night rain? Slithering around in the mud to piss behind a tree? Driving around aimlessly in the dark with no idea where you are headed? Because I can assure you that I do not care for any of those things. It's nearly eleven o'clock and I would like to greet my bed. Can we get you into my Rover so that I may make this a possibility before it is indeed tomorrow?"

Ouch.

I was convinced that I had no luck at all. Not one speck of it. This man was an asshole and I had somehow landed smack dab in the middle of my own personal hell; with him in the role of the devil. With horns and cracking a whip! I turned and wrenched my suitcase from the trunk of my car, hoping my equipment would be safe for the night, but really, it would be on him if anything happened to my stuff. He could deal with it. *Pompous jackass!*

I marched alongside his Rover with the precious leather seats, tossed my bag in the back atop same said leather seats, and seated myself in front. *Mud? Meet expensive leather!*

I was determined not to speak another word to 'Lord Condemnation' if I didn't have to.

~~~~

Miss Hargreave was nothing like the grad student I had anticipated. She was a "she" for one thing, a great deal younger than I'd figured on, and from her body language, was quite enraged at the moment. I looked over at her sitting stoically in my front seat. Oh yes, she was hopping mad. Her arms were folded and the earthy scent of wet mud was all over her. She rather reminded me of a cat being given a bath, all claws and hissing. She had an interesting accent too. "You're not English are you?"

She started to turn her head toward me but then she caught herself and looked away and out her window. She was punishing me for making her wait in the rain for three hours probably. There was something about her that seemed vaguely familiar but I couldn't place whatever it was.

"My accent blows my cover every single time. Damn."

Ouch.

"American?"

"Yep."

The wiper blades sweeping back and forth pretty much filled the cold silence between us. I supposed my comment about pissing behind a tree had not been well thought out, and I wondered what she really thought of me. Probably something along the lines of, "Go fuck yourself, you sodding arsehole" I imagine. Yeah, Miss Hargreave had some pluck in her it seemed, despite her harrowing evening.

"Look, I'm sorry about not getting your call when it first came through. I didn't have my mobile on me."

She kept herself turned away and facing out toward the dark wet night. "Doesn't matter. I'll be out of your hair in the morning." She gestured with an elegant hand. "This whole thing… is obviously not going to work." She snorted a laugh. "American art student cataloging nineteenth century Romanticist masterpieces for an English earl. What a joke! I'm in way over my head—"

"That's not true. I'm only a lowly baron, not even close to being an earl." I interrupted in hopes of distracting her from what was certain to be an emotional tirade.

"My bad," she sneered, mimicking me from earlier. "I've got to work on my Debrett's Peerage too. We can't have that, now can we?" The sarcasm dripping off her was pretty harsh and she still spoke to the window.

Nope. Not distracted in the least.

I tried again. "So how does an American girl end up at University of London taking a graduate degree, and more to the point, how in the hell do you know Debrett's Peerage? Surely that's knowledge fit only for the natives." If distracting her didn't work, maybe teasing would.

She laughed. Just a short breath of air and a shake of her head, but it made me feel better. What I really wanted was to get a good look at her. I wanted to check Miss Hargreave out, and see what she was made of in a lighted room—sans wet mud preferably.

"You're not going to quit before you've even seen all the paintings I've got in my house, are you? Because, that would be a travesty. Well at least I think it would. I don't know shit about art."

She didn't move her position of staring out at the rain and I felt the sudden need to convince her to stay. Nothing about this night was going to plan. She wasn't going to be an easy sell, but I really needed someone for this job. It'd been left for about five decades too long. I required a professional, and there was one sitting in the seat next to me right now. A spitfire American with lousy directional sense, but an expert all the same.

I softened my voice. "I take that back. I know enough about art to know that I need a professional's help."

She moved in her seat and sighed, just as I pulled up to the garage and parked the Rover. She held out her hand and turned her body toward me.

"Shall we begin again? Gabrielle Hargreave, University of London. I'm the professional here to have a look at your art collection." She faced me now, but I still couldn't see her very well. I liked the sound of her voice though. It sounded... sexy.

The garage light had brightened the interior by a fraction where we sat together, and I finally got a glimpse, but could still barely make out her features. I felt surprise for the second time tonight as I closed my hand around hers for a firm shake. Gabrielle Hargreave was, again, so not what I was expecting.

Her hair was soaking wet and pulled back in a tie, but the overall impression was one of beauty. I may be a waste at social pleasantries but I do know when a woman is beautiful, and Miss Hargreave was certainly that.

I was changing my opinion about my new grad student rather quickly.

"Ahh, Gabrielle Hargreave, pleasure to meet you. Ivan Everley, inheritor of all this... and of course shuttle driver for lost American art students." I smiled at her.

She dropped my hand and looked down at her lap.

"That bad?" I tilted my head down to try to get her to look at me again. She seemed miserable.

"You forgot to add 'wet and caked in mud' to your description."

"Not really. I remembered the 'wet and muddy' but figured I was pushing my luck with the 'lost American' part already. I'm not a complete idiot, Miss Hargreave."

She arched a very pointed brow at me and I felt the hit right in the groin.

I reached for the door handle and got out of the Rover as fast as I could. This whole situation was getting a little awkward. We were bantering back and forth like we'd known each other for years rather than mere minutes.

But before I could make my way over to her side to open the door for her, she'd already exited and was bent over my leather seats earnestly attempting to remove the smudges of mud left on them from the backside of her jeans.

I got a very nice look at her bum though and I wasn't complaining. Nope. Miss Hargreave had a fine looking arse attached to those mile long legs of hers. Covered in mud or not, it was a beauty.

I cleared my throat. "Shall we?"

"Sorry about your leather seats. I can come back and clean them."

"No worries. Finnegan will take care of it. He's the man to see around here if you want anything done. I'll introduce you as soon as we get up to the house. On second thought, it's late now." I checked my watch. "He's probably gone to bed." I nodded. "Of which, you're no doubt in desperate need of yourself."

"I am exhausted," she mumbled, while stifling a yawn with her delicate hand.

I led her forward, my hand pressed against her back as we made our way out of the darkened garage. Again, I was struck with the overwhelming feeling of something I couldn't quite put my finger on. Odd, but I kept thinking that we'd met before in some capacity.

"This doesn't look nice at all," I said. The rain, which had been doing steady work up to this point, decided to unleash in biblical proportions. The sound of the drops hitting every surface as they poured down in sheets to rival Noah's flood, roared in front of us.

"Well I don't think I can get much wetter," she shouted over the noise.

"That's probably a good thing, because we're both about to find out. We've got to make a run for it!" I yelled, grabbing her hand and pulling her with me as I made for the safety of the house.

~~~~

Being dragged through a deluge along a dark path in unfamiliar territory was not my favorite, but having a guide who knew where he was going was so much better than none at all. At least I wasn't spending the night in a rental car.

The house we were dashing toward was typical stone manor, Neo-Gothic design from what I could tell in the dark and streaming rain. I held onto Mr. Everley's hand and went forward. He pulled us through puddles and small lakes until we headed up some stone steps, and finally to a door that got my attention. It was a behemoth made of oak and carved with heavy designs of flora and fauna. Fascinating. I'd get a better look tomorrow.

We entered through the door and into a mudroom of sorts. Perfect place for me. I was covered in the stuff, and could think only about getting it off me via a hot bath. A soft bed would be welcome too. In the morning I could figure out what kind of art Mr. Everley had stashed away in his gloomy corner of Ireland and decide if I'd be staying here or not.

"Here, allow me," he said, taking my coat off my back and hanging it dripping on a peg.

"Thanks."

I tried to shake the water off my hands, attempting to sort out my appearance, which must be truly horrifying by now, but it was beyond hopeless. "I don't think I've ever been so soaking wet before." I brushed at my emerald green shirt, realizing that even my poor jacket had lost to the rain and soaked me through to the skin.

"Yeah, it's downright evil tonight. I'm so glad you're not out there any longer because I fear you would've floated away by now, Miss Hargreave." He was busy hanging up his own coat and pulling off the ball cap he'd been wearing, when we both turned to face one another.

"I'm so grateful you answered your pho—"

In the light.

Where he could really see me.

And where I could really see him… for the first time.

Straight dark hair spilled down his neck. Lips that I remembered, knew how to kiss, opened in total surprise. Captivating green eyes that had held onto mine, widened as Mr. *Ivan* Everley appeared to register the same shockwave I was experiencing.

Oh no, please, God, no!

I think it's safe to say we were both in shock.

And this definitely wasn't the first time we'd met.

THE END

~*~ Look for the full-length novel, *Priceless,* in 2014 ~*~

About the Author

Raine Miller

Raine Miller is a former teacher and author of the *New York Times* best-sellers in *The Blackstone Affair* series, but she's been reading romance since that first Barbara Cartland book was discovered at the tender age of thirteen. She thinks it was *The Flame is Love* from 1975. And it's a safe bet she'll never stop, because now she writes them too! Granted Raine's stories are edgy enough to turn Ms. Cartland in her grave, but to her way of thinking, a hot, sexy hero never goes out of fashion. Never ever!!

Writing books pretty much fills her days now and she is always busy. Raine has a prince of a husband, and two brilliant sons to pull her back into the real world if the writing takes her too far away. She loves to hear from readers and to chat about the characters in her books.

You can connect with her on:
Facebook at ***Raine Miller Romance***
or visit:
http://www.rainemiller.com
to find out what she's working on now.

DEDICATION

For Amanda

I saw the angel in the marble and carved until I set her free...
—Michelangelo (1475–1564)

ACKNOWLEDGMENTS

To all of my loyal fans, I just want to say thank you for supporting the Amanda Todd Legacy by purchasing the *Stories for Amanda* anthology. The issue of bullying is one that is very close to my heart, and one for which I dearly wish there was no need for awareness. Sadly, the need for people to give attention to this issue is greater than ever. Thank you to the other authors who collaborated on this project with me, as well as the cover design, formatting, editing services, publishing, and promotional efforts that were all donated anonymously because the people behind all those are committed to this cause.

Until we all understand just how tragic the effects of bullying are, we will lose more young souls like Amanda Todd to a useless end. My time as a teacher in the public schools taught me just how priceless all those child hearts are. Thank you from the bottom of mine.

xxoo R

JACOB & NOELLE
A love story

By

E.L. Montes

YEAR OF 1938

January 8th 1938

My dearest Jacob,

My heart aches without you near. I wish I could hold you, especially on cold nights like tonight. When there's nothing but the quiet sound of the winter wind knocking on the door, I imagine you're here, with your arms wrapped tightly around me as we sit by the fire. We talk about music and art and books. Just like when we first met. Do you remember, Jacob? Do you remember the day you won my heart?

We laugh until the early morning. Oh how I miss your laugh; the way you toss your head back and howl with your hand clenched to your stomach. I'm laughing just at the thought. I also miss how the words 'I love you' whisper through your lips. No one could ever say those words and ignite my stomach to flutter as you do. I just miss you. No matter how long it takes I'm going to wait for you Jacob.

Love,
Noelle

February 24th, 1938

My beautiful Noelle,

How could I ever forget the day you took my breath away? I was a simple young man, as I still am, walking along the city searching for work when my eyes spotted gold. Yes, pure gold you were. With your stunning blue eyes, autumn long locks and glorious red lips. You were lost and asked me, of all men in the City of New York, for directions. I was the luckiest man. I stumbled over my words like a fool, but you giggled… it was the most lightening, refreshing sound I'd ever heard.

I walked you all the way to your destination, never mind that it was in the opposite direction of where I was meant to go. I didn't care as long as I could hear that sound again. I formally asked you out on date. Do you remember our first date, Noelle? I remember clearly, as if it was yesterday. Nothing in this world could prepare me for you.

You are the reason I keep going each day, fighting in this war; not just for our freedom, but for you. I will have you in my arms again, Noelle. Just wait for me as you've told me you will.

I hope your studies are going well.

Love always and forever,
Jacob

March 29th 1938

Jacob my love,

I remember our first date very clearly. I made a fool of myself. We watched a film, 'The Awful Truth' and laughed the entire time. Afterwards, we walked along the park holding hands, discussing our favorite literature and learning we had more in common than we had imagined.

As much fun as we were having, it was getting late, and being the gentlemen that you are, you respectfully walked me home. I wanted so desperately for you to kiss me; I didn't want the night to end. But you turned around to walk away. I couldn't let you go so I gripped your arm, pulled you back and pressed my lips against yours. You must have thought I was a very foolish girl, but you didn't say it. Instead you kissed me back. It was the best kiss I've ever had, Jacob. It was the kiss that made me know that you were the one. It was a magical kiss.

Oh, I wish you were here so that I wouldn't have so many distractions during my studies. I worry for your safety constantly.

I count the days, the hours, the minutes and the seconds until we see each other again.

Love,
Noelle

June 3rd, 1938

My dearest Noelle,

I'm sorry it's been months since you last heard from me. We were moved elsewhere, and I just received your letter.

Please don't ever have those thoughts of yourself. You could never be a fool. That kiss was perfect. I wanted to kiss you desperately but I also wanted to remain a gentlemen. And of course I didn't want to make you feel uncomfortable after such a wonderful night. I was beyond grateful that you pulled me back for a kiss; the kiss that officially branded our love.

I mark the passing of time as well, my love. It's late here as I write you, with a lantern under a tree, the leaves sheltering me from the rain. Some men are on duty look-

ing out, while others are talking among themselves. Some are writing to their loved ones as I am, and there are a few who are sleeping soundlessly. I find it difficult to sleep here. The loud cricket noise keeps me awake, and in the far distance I can hear grenades going off or gun shots, and sometimes even the screams of men. But through it all I know that I have something to look forward to. You.

Could you do me a favor? My mother sent me a letter. She informed me that my father is ill. Can you visit my parents on my behalf? I may not be there physically, but with you there it may feel as if I am. My parents adore you and would be happy to see you again.

Don't worry about me, Noelle. You're the reason I keep fighting. Soon, my love, we'll be together.

Love always and forever,
Jacob

July 8th, 1938

Jacob,

The moment I received your letter, I stopped everything and visited your parents. Your mother was thrilled to see me. She welcomed me in with no hesitation. Her warm, gentle brown eyes remind me of yours.

Your father is getting stronger. He has his bad days though. He talks about you a lot. They both do. Your parents couldn't be more proud of their son. I'm proud of their son too.

I spent the fourth of July with them. We sat on the front porch, drinking tea, and laughing at their memories of you as a child. When the fireworks lit up the sky, we were silent; well I was silent, as I admired how beautifully the vibrant colors splashed along the stars, like a paint brush along a canvas. Then I thought of you... how could I not? With your love of art I was sure you of all people would admire the beauty of such a sight. I didn't realize my tears had fallen until your father passed me his handkerchief.

I felt connected with your parents, Jacob. Since I'm finished with my studies for the summer, I offered to help your mother nurse your father back to good health until school starts back up again in the fall. It's the only way I can feel closer to you, Jacob. I hope you don't feel as if I've intruded, but your parents make me feel a part of the family.

How are you? Tell me as much as you can.

Love,
Noelle

August 13th, 1938

Noelle, my love:

How is it possible for me to be even more in love with you right now than I was yesterday? You have no idea how much it means to me that you're helping my mother with my father. They are very fond of you because you're beautiful and kind and mean so much to me. They treat you like family, especially since I told them you're the woman I'm going to marry. Yes. I'm going to marry you, Noelle Emma Stephens, and I hope… no I pray that you say yes.

I'm sure the painting along the sky was beautiful to witness, but if I was there I would be far too distracted staring at you. Your beauty is far more captivating and compelling than any art I have ever laid eyes upon. I only speak with experience of course, my love.

How am I? Well, today is better than the past couple of weeks. We were on foot for a while, and I thought we would never stop. Finally, we settled by a campsite. I think we'll be here for a few more days until we're off to our next destination. It's scorching hot and the sun feels deadly at times, but we're drinking plenty of water.

I can't believe it's been over eight months since I've seen you, held you, kissed you. Marry me, Noelle.

Soon.

Love you always and forever,
Jacob

September 15th, 1938

Dear Jacob,

Yes! Yes, I will marry you. Nothing would make me happier than becoming your bride. And we can live in our own little world. Because the one I'm witnessing on my own is very cruel. Not to say what you have experienced out there in the war is less malicious than what I have seen.

Oh Jacob, if you only could see what I have seen. Hear what I have heard. I made a friend; she is beautiful and smart and kind. But because her skin is darker than mine, others see her as nothing. She is beyond brilliant. Smarter than any man I've ever met. She could be a doctor, Jacob, but the world we live in may never allow this for her. It breaks my heart.

I met Sally on my way home after my studies. It was a beautiful day out, and I decided that a stroll through the park would be nice. While admiring the beautiful scenery I heard a woman's cry behind a tree. I followed the sound and saw two gentlemen, dressed in Uniform, laughing and taunting her. They heard me approaching and turned. I was afraid; not sure what they would do to me. They urged me to walk away; to leave them be. I couldn't, Jacob. I couldn't turn my back on that innocent girl. Her dress was torn; her face smeared in her own blood. I said no. I wasn't leaving. At first the two men didn't like it; they made nasty comments and called me names. So I did what I could. I screamed. Loud. Forcing my lungs to burn as I used all of my energy. I would have used my last breath for that scream. It worked, Jacob. The two evil men ran off as other people walked by and took notice of my display.

Taking my jacket, I wrapped her fragile body with it, and guided her to my tiny apartment. I wasn't sure what led me to feel for this woman. After I cleaned her up and gave her food and clothing she slept for days. It was as if she had never had a good night sleep. When she was finally energized we talked, and laughed and talked some more. Oh, Jacob, you would fancy her and her ability to partake in an intellectual debate. Though, the more we spent with each other, the more others took notice. After a couple of weeks I would hear whispers among others as I walked by. Harsh things they spat at me. I kept my head high. I wouldn't let anyone bring me nor Sally down. Sally says I'm a blessing, an angel and a Godsend. I laugh and tell her I'm neither. I'm just me.

Why oh why do we live in such a cruel world, Jacob?
I wish you well, my love.

Love,
Noelle

November 16th, 1938

Oh my dear Noelle,

But you are, you are a Godsend, to me and to all that have ever had the pleasure to be in your presence. If you take a moment and thoroughly ponder, you would reason with yourself that you were meant to be there. You were at the right place at the right time.

If you wouldn't have taken a stroll through the park that day, you would have never heard the cries of Sally, and, therefore, never had the chance to stop those men from hurting her. You were there for a reason, Noelle. Of all the women in the world, you were placed there, and that is a Godsend.

And to answer your question: 'why do we live in a cruel world?' I do not have an answer for that. I wish I knew, but you see my sweet Noelle, I have experienced cruel. I have witnessed with my own two eyes evil men, who killed with their bare hands, and laughed whilst telling the tale. I was a bystander and helplessly watched as children and women were brutally hurt by these men. Things I would not even begin to tell you in fear that you would have nightmares. And when I tried to fight it or stop it, I was pushed away or my life was threatened.

In the world of this terrible war I'm living in… nothing could stop them. They are far more evil than good. The longer we stay the more I'm losing friends; they are slowly turning into them.

Thankfully, I still have Thomas. I met Thomas one night on the battlefield. A bullet punctured through his shoulder and I helped him to safety. Since that night we became close friends. We look out for each other. He has a wife and two little girls. He's eager to get home to his family as I am for you.

Noelle, I don't want to tell you all of this and lead you to believe that our world is nothing but evil. Yes, there are bad things in this world, but there are also good things, and believe it or not there are still good, genuine people. Like yourself.

I miss you dearly.

Love always and forever,
Jacob

December 24th, 1938

Jacob,

Have you ever studied your reflection and wondered who the person was staring back at you? I have. I feel lost. Every day that goes by I feel like I'm losing a bit of myself.

I'm not the naïve, little girl I once was. Pain is a true feeling. Love is a far stronger feeling than I have ever grown to know. And loving you so much as I do hurts, Jacob. Today, I was reminded with how unbearable it could be without having a love one close.

I knew almost one year ago when you left, that I would miss you dearly, but I thought I could be stronger. That it would only be a few years and it wouldn't feel like an eternity. Each day, each minute that ticks by, each letter I receive from you, continues to remind me of just how much more it hurts.

I received a telegram today. My youngest brother, Eric, was killed on the battlefield. My heart was crushed into a million pieces and I'm not sure I can heal from this. As I write you this letter, my eyes full of tears; all I can think of is you. I don't want to lose you as well.

Will I see you again, Jacob? Am I strong enough to handle the thought of never having you in my arms again? For you to hold me, kiss me and whisper those three precious words?

It hurts to love you, Jacob. I'm not sure I can do this.

Noelle

YEAR OF 1939

January 30th, 1939

My love,

I know that it's hard. Trust me. I live it every day. There are times that I close my eyes and all I see is you. I reach out to touch you, but you're not there. I dream of you constantly.

Please don't give up just yet. I love you more than anything. You're the light to my darkness. You're the air that I breathe. You're the reason my heart beats every single day.

I'm so sorry that Eric is gone. I'm sorry that I wasn't there to help heal your pain. You shouldn't have gone through that agony alone.

But please don't let us go.

Thomas once said, "Love is hard to bear. It can ruin you. Hurt you. Break you down. Yet, it is the most beautiful experience and feeling one could ever contain. If the love is strong enough, it can survive any obstacle."

We can survive this, Noelle. All I ask is for you to be a little more patient. Soon, my love, this will all feel like a dream and we can put it behind us and continue where we left off.

I love you.

Love always and forever,
Jacob

April 2nd, 1939

My dearest Noelle,

I have waited for a response, but as the months flash by, I fear that I have lost you. And pains me more than any pain I have ever endured.

There were days where I could not sleep or eat, because my mind drifted to thoughts of you; wondering if you are safe and happy. I pictured you with friends, laughing and debating on politics. You're quite feisty at times when you feel strongly about a particular subject. That was one of things that made me fall in love with you. The passion you had for things you believed in. I only pray that you still believe in us.

I pictured you with another man who has won your heart. You're a beautiful, intelligent woman, and I couldn't imagine a man not swooping you up by now. As much as that thought enrages me, your happiness is what matters most.

So, I guess, this letter is to say goodbye, my love. I wish you everything you desire in this world.

Just know that I will always be here for you.

Love you always and forever,
Jacob

June 24th, 1939

My dearest Jacob,

I'm sorry it's been over six months since you've heard from me. I've been trying to forget. I'm not sure if I was trying to be rid of you, or the love we had, or the pain of dealing with Eric's death. I just wanted it all to go away. It wasn't fair to you, and I should have written sooner. You have a right to know what the past six months have been like for me.

Each day I forced myself out of bed and continued my life as if it was any other day, but without you in it. And each day I grew a bit stronger. Granted, deep within my mind you were still there, still trying to poke through. I brushed those memories aside and continued on with my studies.

I was becoming myself again; more social with others and less depressed. I gained friends at the University and we did in fact laugh and discuss politics, but also discussed art, theatre, and literature. It was thrilling that I could live my life, Jacob, by surrounding myself with people that were like me.

But after all of the laughs, when I lay my head at night to rest, I couldn't help but cry myself to sleep for feeling so selfish and guilty, because I still thought of you.

Then one day while out in the city with a few friends, I bumped into a man. His is name was Alexander Fitzgerald. He was everything a woman could dream of: tall, handsome and a gentleman who came from a wealthy family. He asked me out for tea. At first I refused. I wasn't ready to be courted by any man. He was very insistent and followed me the entire night, using his wicked charm, until I finally agreed.

Now, I'm not telling you all of this to cause you rage, I'm telling you this because, you see Jacob, it was always you. When Alexander held my hand, I didn't have that tingling feeling as when you touched me on our first outing. When he laughed I didn't have the flutters in my stomach as I did when you laughed. When he pressed his lips against mine to kiss me, I shut my eyes for a mere few seconds as I pictured you on the other side. But there was something missing. That spark. That magical kiss. The one that only you gave me every time your lips touched mine.

But I continued to see Alexander for a few months. I realized each time I spent with him, I compared him to you. I tried to find flaws to push him away and there were none. He was wonderful in every way. Alexander's smile, charm, handsome features were all perfection. But why couldn't I feel anything more for him? Because He. Is. Not. You.

He asked me for my hand in marriage and that's when I had to let him go. Because the moment he went down on one knee, I knew he wasn't the man I was destined to spend the rest of my life with. When a man asked for your hand in marriage, you should be able to jump up and say "yes." But I couldn't. I was afraid, because I couldn't see him in my future, as I did you.

Jacob, please forgive me. I know that this letter will cause harm, but you have to believe me when I tell you that I wasn't in the right state of mind. I wasn't sure what I was doing. I wanted to live my life and I realized that life is not worth living without you in it.

I love you, Jacob.

I just hope you can find it in yourself to forgive me.

Love,
Noelle

July 26th, 1939

Dear Jacob,

I know you're angry because of what I told you in the last letter, but you had to know the truth. Since then I have waited patiently for your response. I know it's not fair to ask for one, because I made you wait so long to hear back from me.

I want to know that you're safe. I want to know if you'll forgive me and my foolish ways. I want to know if we can be like once were. I want nothing more than that. I miss you desperately.

Please write back, tell me what's on your mind, and even if you're mad… just tell me.

Love,
Noelle

August 25th 1939

Noelle,

You state you didn't say these things to cause me any rage. Though, that's exactly what I felt; full blown aching rage. You want to know why, Noelle? Well here it goes: you get to live your life. You are able to watch a movie, read a book, go out of town with friends and enjoy yourself in the City. You're able to have tea with your mother. You're able to study at the University. All of these things mean that you are living your life.

Want to know what I do? I'm stuck here. Waiting as the time ticks by me to be able to live my life. All I had was you in my letters. The love you poured into those letters made me feel alive, Noelle. Until that one letter. I keep reading it over and over again. How you wrote that he held your hand. That he kissed you. His lips were pressed against the lips that I had loved. I was furious and raged and then after that… hurt.

I don't know if I could forgive you, Noelle. I thought I knew who you were. But now it just feels you're a stranger to me.

I'm safe.

Jacob

September 29th, 1939

Jacob,

I understand that I caused you harm. You have to trust me when I say I didn't want any of this. I was in a bad place and how I handled my actions were wrong. It hurts me to know that you see me as stranger. I'm still me, just a bit older, a bit wiser. I'm still the same Noelle, you met that afternoon in the City. Looking for directions. I'm still the same Noelle, who fell in love with your laugh, your smile, and all your charming ways. I'm still the same Noelle that wants nothing more than to be your wife, because I'm still madly in love with you. This may all seem confusing but it's all true.

We can start over if you like? Almost two years apart can seem like we've lost a bit of each other. I've grown to love new things as I'm sure you as well. Let's start over, Jacob?

I'll begin.

I've recently found a knack for painting. There's something about it that makes everything around me fade away. I just hold the paint brush and then it's like magic. My mind takes over and before I know it, there's a beautiful piece before me.

I would love for you to see some of the paintings I've created when you come back, Jacob. Only if you would like too of course.

Have you found a new talent that you've kept hidden from me throughout our time apart? If so I would love to hear about it.

I miss and love you dearly.

Love,
Noelle

October 31st, 1939

My dearest, Noelle:

I've had time to think over a few things, and I would like to apologize for the last letter I sent you. My actions and words were over reacted. I was very angry and then hurt at the time, please forgive me. I love you, Noelle. I always have and I still want us to be married once I'm home.

I'm happy to hear that you found a love for painting. That brings me joy. Of course I would love to view your paintings. I'm sure they're absolutely beautiful.

I've indeed found a talent I wasn't aware of: writing. I've kept a journal (several actually) and began writing my experiences in the war, in life and love. I may be a young man and I still have lots to learn, but what I have learned throughout the years has made me a stronger man. Writing has helped me cope with being away from home and you. It has become my safe place. My passion. To place words on paper and allow it to create a story of its own, is quite remarkable.

I would love for you to one day read my journals. Who knows, maybe it could be placed in the paper or published into a book. But for now I will continue to write, as I found it is my true solace in life.

I received a letter from my mother. She says that you went over for dinner one night and it was a delight having you around again. Thank you for visiting my parents. I only wish that I had the opportunity to meet yours.

Thank you for giving me hope in us again, Noelle.

Love always and forever,
Jacob

December 1st, 1939

My dearest Jacob,

Oh how my parents would have loved you. My mother would have laughed at your wonderful charming humor. My father would have spoken warmly at how brave and smart of a man you are.

My mother would also have loved that you found a passion for writing. I'm not sure if I ever told you this before, but my mother was a writer. Romance was her passion. She loved writing about two young foolish couples, falling madly in love and their journey throughout their struggles. When I was child she'd read me bed time stories, mostly some she had written on her own; of prince charming fighting for his beloved princess. I remember dreaming as a little girl that one day I would find my prince.

I wish they were still alive and were able to have met you. After their death in the car crash, I thought my world was over. Until you walked into my life just a short year later. It was as if, from heaven, they searched for the perfect man for their daughter. They found you for me. I'm thankful for that blessing each passing day.

Your stories will be published one day. I have so much faith in you. I cannot wait to read what you have.

When I visited your parents, your mother thought it would be best if we began planning our wedding. So that when you're finally home no more time is needed, we can be married instantly. I told her that I would ask you if this was okay before the planning began.

Love,
Noelle

YEAR OF 1940

January 22nd, 1940

Noelle,

I wasn't aware that your mother was a writer. I hope you enjoy my writing as well as you did hers. I'm sure I'm not nearly talented as she was.

Most of my work is inspired by you. Your beauty, love and devotion; of how strong you are. When I'm with you, I feel free, and these letters give me a sense of pride and hope. When a man is gone for so long he loses himself a bit, especially when he's fighting in war that he slowly forgets why he is fighting in the first place.

Yesterday, Thomas received a letter from his wife. His youngest daughter passed of pneumonia. It was agonizing just witnessing his pain.

Life flashes us by within an instant. Before we know, so many of our loved ones are gone. Some too young before they even get to experience life on their own. Others after they were gifted with a full life filled with love and complete with a family. Life is not always certain or promised, but it's beautiful. To even have breathed and lived. To give someone else a memory to cherish is a blessing within itself.

Thomas smiled at the pleasant memories of his daughter. He says he will remember her as she was: a healthy, joyous, and beautiful little girl.

Life will have us together again, Noelle. I know it.

Soon my love.

Love always and forever,
Jacob

~~~~

Men grunted as they stomped tirelessly through the battlefield. The moon casting its way down gave them just enough light to navigate their way through. Some hadn't eaten in days; others were injured, and most were just plain exhausted.

Jacob marched a little further behind in line, keeping his head high, and his eyes alert. His hearing narrowed in to listen to his pal, Thomas, whistle beside him, the only soothing sound along with the crickets in the open space. It had been a few weeks of walking and as restless as he was he pushed through each step. Jacob had purpose to keep going each day.

His mind drifted to thoughts of Noelle. He wondered what she might have been doing at this very moment; probably asleep peacefully thousands of miles away. He couldn't wait to wrap his arms around her and inhale her intoxicating vanilla scent. Allow his fingers to tangle within the red locks of her hair, and simply get lost into the most beautiful blue eyes he had ever seen.

The moment he had set eyes on her he had known she would be the one he'd spend the rest of his life with. Although, fear that he might lose her to someone else momentarily crept in, he brushed aside that feeling and allowed himself to bask in the memories he had of their time spent together. Late, long walks in the park, discussing their favorite things, listening to her go on and on about her hopes, dreams, future, daring to hope that he was a part of it.

Unknowingly, Jacob ran the palm of his hand along the front right pocket of his jacket. There held the most recent letter he received from Noelle. He always waited until his group reached their next destination before reading a letter he received from her. It was his way to continue to push, fight and not give up. He looked forward to her letters. It was his one time of peace.

"Thinking of Noelle?" Thomas poked through Jacobs thoughts in mid whistle.

"Yeah. It's hard not to." Jacob confessed as he lifted his head to admire the moon.

"I understand, my friend." Thomas replied and then continued on with his whistling, this time picking up the pace and walking before Jacob.

It was a cold night and Jacob tried to keep warm by rubbing the palm of his hands together. He could be sitting by a fire at this very moment, wrapped in the warmth of Noelle. As much as he loved fighting for his country he loved her far more.

A loud gunshot in the air stopped him in his tracks. Men scattered in all different directions; some squatting and drawing their weapons. Instantly Jacob was in protective mode. He gripped his gun and scanned the perimeter searching for the enemy. So far, those among him were familiar faces. The men he had fought alongside for the past few years. He spotted Thomas a few feet away. *Good he was okay.*

Stepping back a few steps Jacob turned on the heels of his boots and continued to search his surroundings. Another gunshot went off. He turned back around and saw nothing. *Where were they coming from?* No spark or smoke in the air from what he could witness caught his attention.

A loud BOOM erupted. A few of his men screamed, and this time he knew there were bombs being tossed their way.

Jacob and a few other men began to run as fast as they could; trying to locate a safe ditch to hide in. His breathing grew rapid as he heard screams and then his name, "Jacob!" He turned to see in the far distance his friend, Thomas, waving his arms in the air while running toward him. Jacob waited for Thomas, encouraging him to hurry with a few movements of his hands. Thomas continued to yell something out, but Jacob couldn't make out what he was saying.

As Thomas ran toward him, he began to make out some of his friends' words. Another explosion roared to life, "Jacob, move!" Thomas yelled from the top of his lungs pointing over Jacobs head. Jacob turned around.

A grenade. A loud pop. A ringing noise and then…

Silence.

~~~~

March 5th, 1940

My dearest Jacob,

I'm not sure if you received my last letter, but if you receive this one I pray that you are well. It can be difficult at times when I don't hear from you, but I always feel like you're near me; protecting me somehow. It may sound foolish, but it's the best way for me to explain it.

I had a dream last night. It was dark and I kept searching for something or someone. There was no one around. I felt as if I walked for miles and miles until I couldn't take it anymore. I spotted a small tree nearby and sat down. It was nice to just sit there and allow my feet to rest. I admired the snow. Breathing it in as my fingers twirled in the air allowing the soft delicate flakes to brush my fingertips.

In my dream memories as a child with my family played as a big movie screen before me. It was my mother, father, Eric and I, and we climbed up a steep hill behind our home. Snow covered the ground but the sky was clear. My father grabbed lids from the trashcans and allowed Eric and I to slide down the hill. When we were at the bottom, Eric and I would stumble up the hill again and try to race each other back to the bottom.

I laughed. It was a pleasant memory to replay, even in my dream.

Then I heard another voice chuckling behind me. I knew whose laugh it was before even turning around. I shut my eyes and allowed the sound to trickle through my ears. It was peaceful and beautiful.

But when I turned around, no one was there. You were no longer there. I instantly felt alone. Not just at that one moment, but alone in this world.

Then I woke up.

I dreamt of my family and you last night. Although I felt alone in my dream I woke up knowing that I still have you, Jacob.

I pray that you're safe. I miss you dearly.

Write to me soon.

Love,
Noelle

April 8ᵗʰ, 1940

Dear Jacob,

I'm worried. I haven't heard from you in months. Are you okay? Are you hurt? Will you even receive this letter? I know I am asking questions that cannot possibly be answered with any prompt measure of time, but the constant worry for you is overwhelming. I sometimes feel like I cannot breathe and am suffocating as I await any news regarding you and your safety.

My dream continues to reoccur every so often. I smile at the laugh I can still hear although when I turn around you are not there. My greatest fear now is that with each month that passes and I do not hear from you, the laughter in my dream will fade away. It is becoming harder and harder to remember the sound as distinctly as it once did. Oh Jacob, I hope that my dreams are in no way a sign of something I have yet to discover in regards to you, wherever you may be.

I yearn for you, my love. Right now, I pray that you are safe and in good company. I always pray for these things.

Sally has stopped by a few times to check on me and to see if I've heard anything at all. But alas, the disappointment she sees in my face tells her everything she needs to know. I in no way intend to make you feel guilty, my love. I am sure you have much more to deal with than I could ever fathom surrounding you. I want to know what you're facing, but then again, I shudder to think of what reality must be like for you right now.

I know that I am rambling on, but know that writing to you brings me solace. I feel you should have something to smile about. In the times that Sally has stopped by, she has been teaching me how to sew. She has become such a good and loyal friend to me, Jacob. I really cannot wait for you to meet her. In my spare moments, I have been working on something very special for you. Thinking about what I am making brings a smile to my face. I only hope you love it as much as I do. I will keep to myself what it is. Knowing that you are probably guessing at this very moment, gives me hope; to see you again, to hear your laugh, to witness your smile. Please be safe and know that I love you dearly.

All my love,
Noelle

May 10th, 1940

Jacob,

I don't know what else to do. I'm always by the mailbox, searching for a response from you. Each day is like a ticking bomb waiting to go off. I try to distract my mind from the negativity, but it's difficult at times.

Your mother fears something has happened to you. I try to console her and tell her that you're safe and just in the battlefield fighting for our country. As much as I keep repeating to others that you are in fact safe, there's slight doubt in the back of my mind and maybe she is right. Then I picture you in pain, lying somewhere in a ditch, alone and scared.

But then I shake it off and keep going about my day. You were meant for me. I know you were, Jacob. And I can't accept the fact that there is the slightest chance that you may not be a part of my future.

I finished that gift I was making for you. I can't wait to see you again, so that I can see your face light up when you open it. I dream of giving it to you on my graduation day. It will be next month. I invited your mother and father. They're the only family I have. Sally is not allowed to join the Ceremony, but she'll be back at my place for cake and coffee to celebrate afterwards.

I wish you could be there to watch me receive my diploma. It was something that I didn't expect to receive, especially after my parent's death. I wish they were here to witness it as well. Don't misunderstand me, your parents have been beyond supportive of me. They are more than what I could wish for. The thought of having my mother there smiling as I'm handed my diploma, and my father clapping at how proud he is would have meant so much to me. Eric would probably make fun of how large my cap and gown are. I miss them. I do.

It's the little things in life that make each day worth living. I have hope. I have dreams. And I know I have a future with you.

Soon.

Love,
Noelle

~~~~

Every day that went by was a constant reminder; a reminder that not a word had been heard from Jacob. Noelle's heart was torn. Some had made suggestions that Jacob may have been killed on the battlefield. Noelle refused to believe it. She still felt his presence nearby. Even when her heart ached as she opened her mailbox to find it empty. Even after the countless letters she continued to send him, all unanswered. She still had hope. Through it all she knew Jacob would find her again.

She continued to send him one letter each month since the last she'd heard from him, hoping she would receive one in return. And in each letter she poured out her heart and soul. She wrote about how much she loved him and missed him. She reminisced about their time when they were together and her time while they were apart.

Throughout the wait Noelle studied furiously as a way to distract her haunted thoughts. Before she knew it, graduation was approaching. This was supposed to be a joyous event for her, and even though Jacobs's parents were going to show their support, there was something missing. Not having Jacob or her family to witness such an immense accomplishment, made her sad. Empty. Unaccomplished.

Yes, she worked harder than most women in her class to have a perfect score. Yes, she would be graduating as one of the top three in her class. And yes, she did it all on her own. But it all didn't matter anymore to Noelle. If she didn't have the ones she loved close by to celebrate with her, then why celebrate?

Noelle still clung to the possibility of a *happily ever after* ending. Why was it told for so many years throughout stories, yet in real life it seemed to be in the distance? Only heard of from afar. She wanted that more than anything. She wanted that happy ever after with Jacob.

Breathing in the warm June air, Noelle stepped out of the University building and began her walk home. She smiled at the familiar faces that passed by. She took in the beauty and warmness that the city brought to her. It was another day forward. Another day of hope. She knew she could get past it, because she was strong enough.

There were times when she thought that she couldn't, but then she was reminded of the few people that surrounded her, who showed her love and support. Although not related to her by blood, she indeed had family.

Sara, Jacob's parents and Jacob were who she had left in life. And for that she was grateful.

As she approached her door the sound of boots along the pavement behind her forced her to turn around. "I'm sorry madam. I didn't mean to scare you."

Noelle smiled at how foolish she must have looked with her hand spread along her chest and her slight gasp as she faced the gentlemen. "Oh, it's quite alright. How can I help you, sir?"

"Are you Ms. Noelle Stephens?" The man asked with a serious expression etched along his features.

Alarmed a bit, Noelle stepped forward and narrowed her eyes in confusion, "Yes. Yes I'm Ms. Stephens."

The gentlemen nodded. Revealing his arms from behind him and handed over an envelope. "You have a telegram, mam. Have a good day."

Noelle held the thin piece of paper in her hand. This was it. This was the truth. She turned around, her entire body rattling with fear, and managed a few steps toward her front door. But she couldn't open it. Her eyes remained fixated on her hand that held the envelope. Such a small item that would determine her fate.

Oh God, she thought as she brought it closer. In cursive her name was written in black ink. Her fingers traced the letters. She was stalling for time. Was she ready to face the truth after all this time? Could she possibly be able to live without another word from him?

The letters blended together and turned blurry from the tears that swelled her eyes. Knowing that she couldn't stand there any longer she flipped the envelope around and slowly tore it open.

She took a few deep breaths to give her some strength, and then removed the letter from its envelope. She blinked a few times allowing the tears to freely run down her soft pale cheeks. Her heart stopped when she saw the familiar handwriting:

My dearest Noelle,

Open the door my love. "Soon" has finally arrived.

Love always and forever,
Jacob

Shock. Pure shock ran through every fiber of her being. Could it truly be? Was Jacob finally home after all these years of yearning for each other? Was their *soon* finally *now*?

Without another thought Noelle swung open her door, and before another word could be spoken, Jacob gripped her into the tightest embrace. Their lips collided. There it was: the magical kiss; the flutters in her stomach; the pure undoubting love. It came tumbling down into that one sweet, endearing kiss.

Sniffing back tears, Noelle broke from the kiss, leaning back to get a good look at him. "Are you really here or am I dreaming?" Oh she prayed it was reality.

"No, my love. This isn't a dream. I'm truly here." Jacob swiped his thumbs across her moist cheeks, wiping away her warm tears.

"B-but, I, you, I don't even…"

Jacob lift a finger to her lips, "I was injured in the battlefield. It took months of recovery. I didn't know where I was or who I was for that matter."

Noelle kneaded her brows in confusion. She slightly pulled away to see that Jacob had a cane and when he stepped back he had a limp. "Oh, Jacob. I thought I lost you." Her arms snaked around his neck.

Pulling her in, Jacob leaned in and inhaled her scent. "I thought I lost you too. But I'm here now. I love you, Noelle."

"I love you more than anything in this world, Jacob."

Jacob pressed his lips against Noelle's again and whispered, "Always and forever, my love."

THE END

About the Author

E.L. Montes

USA Today Bestselling Author E.L. Montes lives in Philadelphia, Pennsylvania with her husband, Alex, and their English Bulldog named Butters! She has a Bachelor of Science in Legal Studies. Ms. Montes works full-time as a paralegal for a mid-size law firm. She had always loved the legal field and found it to be very interesting. She more-so "secretly" loved to write. *Disastrous* was her debut novel which was released October 2012.

The Squall

By

Alexa Nazzaro

ON A FRIDAY afternoon in July, a couple of kids decided to entertain Lillith and her twenty-two colleagues, by copulating on a roof facing the office of Avista Party Planners. This was the kind of liberating event expected to happen to people who wore bright scarves and ate raw foods— not to those who, although they organized fun for a living, did so in cubicles the colour of a laboratory, and whose biggest visual stimulant up until then was the Miss Sixty sign across the street. Having a couple of 16 year-olds practically hanging over the "y" in various states of hurried desire was therefore definitely cause to abandon one's post and crowd at a window much as people do on Much Music or the Today Show. Except for Lillith.

"Oh my God," said Susannah, who worked right beside Lillith. "You have to see this."

Susannah's cheeks were flushed and her big green glasses sat crookedly on her nose. The glasses were new, and would have made anyone else on the planet look like a shut-in who got fed oatmeal by their aging parents as they stared blankly at The Price Is Right. But Susannah could have been Lady Gaga's best friend, which is what made Lillith wonder why Susannah was friendly to her. The only thing they had in common was the "h" in their names, and even that seemed to suit Susannah more. The name Lillith, on the other hand, conjured up images of lavender and Royal Albert teacups.

Susannah pointed to the row of windows along the wall. "You have got to check this out."

"I have some stuff to do," Lillith mumbled, staring at her computer.

"Not as interesting as this."

Susannah grabbed her hand, and for a second Lillith thought it was 2006 again, when she and Susannah had gone to a bar after work to celebrate Susannah's first day at the company. Susannah's idea, both the celebration and the bar. Lillith could still remember the noise and Susannah's grip on her hand as she urged Lillith to dance. In the few hours that they had known each other, Lillith hadn't had an opportunity to tell Susannah that she didn't dance—not even to Kylie Minogue; not even at boring relatives' weddings which presented to Lillith one of two opportunities to be rather cool, the other being her occasional stints as babysitter to the five year-old daughter of her neighour Gillian in apartment 11.

She had managed to stay put on her stool while Susannah got up and danced on the spot. But this time, Susannah had Lillith out of her chair and approaching the window. A crowd had already gathered, fortuitously blocking any possible view. Lillith turned to Susannah and tried to look as disappointed as humanly possible, while Susannah, as though sensing Lillith's waning will to embrace the voyeuristic opportunity that stood before them, finally let go of Lillith's hand.

As she pushed through the crowd, getting enveloped between Joe and Chantal from accounting, Lillith consoled herself by staying put and catching the occasional glance on tip toe. She didn't stare straight ahead, but at the graveled roof, the little pipes and other things that made up its anatomy that Lillith didn't understand. She finally braved a glance at the black T-shirt and hiked up red skirt that was the girl. Lillith's eyes met hers, but only because the girl's were closed, just like they were in the movies and on television. Lillith's knees began to shake, and her gaze moved over to him. There wasn't much to see except a tattoo on his chest the size of one of those anonymous African countries one never learns the name of. Lillith was intrigued by this and, deprived of a proper view from which to see its colours, imagined them instead: green, blue and red all bleeding into one another.

"Hey Lillith," Joe suddenly called out. "Pretty uplifting, eh?"

Lillith smiled to show that she had read just enough Danielle Steel and *Cosmopolitan* to understand the sexual innuendo, and then turned away and walked back to her desk. Her legs felt wobbly, like they did when she had to contribute something to the weekly sales meeting, or when she had to go out for her ceremonial birthday lunch with colleagues, and she had to be witty.

She reached her desk and looked around. Everything was in its place: the garbage and recycling bins to the left of the chair; the basket filled with dried orange peel on the shelf above her, since, while she liked the concept of decorative orange peel, the actual smell bothered her; the calendar she got from her mother for Christmas, pinned to the corkboard with a red tack, bringing out the colour in this month's *Sailboats* by Monet; and the yellow stress ball sitting beside her keyboard. She hadn't forgotten the plastic bag standing against the wall by her chair at that perfect forty-five degree angle, but had struggled to find the right time to open it. She glanced over her shoulder. People were still at the window, she noticed. Perhaps now.

She began running her hands down her pants, a habit that always made her mother shake her head with disappointment, as though hand-rubbing was exactly the kind of thing that drastically diminished one's chances of capturing life's offerings—love, children, a home with a backyard deck.

Lillith took a deep breath and pulled the poster out of the bag. She had already found the perfect spot; to her left, beside the shelf containing the event planning dictionary, which she had never actually read, knowing perfectly well the definitions of *venue* or *food and beverage guarantees*. She unrolled the poster and moved quickly. She had rehearsed this in her mind on the train ride in this morning, down to how big the tape pieces would have to be. Her uncertainty had wavered between one inch and two, finally deciding to tape the poster with four, equal one-inch pieces. Lillith walked back a few steps to catch a look. Not bad, but her time was suddenly being cut by the voices getting closer. The show was over. Her heart quickened, she ran her hands down her pants a little harder before looking at the painting again, now completely unsure.

She heard Susannah's laugh and threw herself into the ergonomic chair that employers furnish with pride and fastened her eyes to the screen.

Susannah draped herself over Lillith's cubicle, her chin in her hand. "Where did you go?"

Lillith glanced at Susannah. She didn't know how to answer, but this seemed to matter very little all of a sudden, as Susannah's eyes widened. Lillith got nervous. She had a very good idea of what had captured her colleague's attention, but what was wrong with it? Was it crooked? This wouldn't have surprised Lillith, as she hadn't used a ruler of any kind. Had she somehow missed a price tag that was still stuck in a corner somewhere, undermining Munch's magic, reveling in being overlooked?

"What's that?"

Lillith swallowed hard. "Just a poster reproduction of *The Scream*."

She was instantly filled with disappointment. "Reproduction" hadn't rolled off the tongue half as easily as she had expected.

Susannah walked further into the cubicle, now standing in front of the poster, as though it were naked and had forgotten to shave its legs.

"Lillith, you can't put this up here," she whispered.

Lillith said nothing.

"It looks nuts," Susannah continued. Her narrowed eyes settled on Lillith's. "You aren't nuts, are you?"

Lillith looked back at the computer, mumbling something that resembled no.

"Are you depressed?" Susannah whispered.

Lillith shook her head, her fingers now typing out an e-mail comprised of haphazard letters that didn't make sense in any language.

"I'm happy," she finally said, continuing the aimless typing.

"Why don't you put up Einstein if you're happy?"

A lump formed in Lillith's throat as she watched Susannah slide a finger under each corner of the poster and peel it away from the wall, an act interspersed with grumblings of "unhealthy". Lillith felt like every drop of blood coursing through her veins had suddenly found its way to her cheeks that were ready to burst.

Susannah took a deep breath and stared down at her shoe. "You can always find another job. Like me."

Lillith could feel the blood drain her face and stopped typing. She wanted Susannah to repeat it. She wanted to catch the tone of her voice, or the speed with which the words came out. Had this announcement been filled with regret? With sadness? Lillith pulled the poster out of Susannah's hand and put it back in the plastic bag.

"When are you leaving?" she heard herself ask.

"Next Friday," Susannah replied. "They wanted me to start as soon as possible, and Louise was good about it, thank God."

So she had already made the big announcement to the boss. Lillith wondered who else had learned of the news before her.

"I haven't told anyone else," Susannah added a little too quickly, and Lillith resented herself for being so transparent and Susannah for embarrassing her. It wasn't her intent, Lillith could see that. Susannah's eyes filled with concern and her lips were being restrained from opening into a smile that this new turn in her life merited. Guilt. For a frightening moment, Lillith's resentment was replaced with hate.

"Have you ever thought of quitting?"

Lillith shook her head. This wasn't entirely true, as she had thought about it, but in the way others thought of winning the lottery. Their imaginations could sustain holding the big cheque and smiling for the camera, but lacked the experience to entertain the possibilities that could follow. This had been her only real job after graduating with a degree in art history, an illogical sequence of events Lillith found herself justifying to concerned relatives at every holiday and the monthly visits to her mother in between. The truth was, Lillith had difficulty seeing herself anywhere else. Art galleries and studios that had been idolized in her youth felt alien to her now. This was a realization that was hard for Lillith to acknowledge, and she summed it up to the poor air circulation in the office.

"How long have you been here again?"

Lillith could feel a tightening in her chest. Maybe there really was something wrong with the air. "Eight years."

Susannah let out a low whistle. "And you never thought of leaving?"

Lillith had never thought that Susannah would leave, but she knew this wasn't the kind of thing she could express out loud. It made perfect sense, of course. Susannah was a project manager, the equivalent of the glass ceiling in companies like these. Lillith was a secretary; *administrative assistant*, as Louise liked to call her, but this title made Lillith squirm. It was too long, trapping Lillith in a hell hole of underachieving verbiage.

"I'm happy for you."

Lillith wondered how convincing she sounded. Had the words bumped up against her anger and hurt? Should she have sounded more excited?

"I'll miss you," said Susannah.

Lillith sat paralyzed, her skin soaking up those words the way her mother played piano: pulling the sounds from the keys.

Finally, she turned to Susannah and said, "Me too."

"But we'll keep in touch, right?" Susannah smiled a smile that people gave to add weight to words that would otherwise take flight and settle in the clouds, forgotten.

Lillith nodded with as much vigor as she could. She understood her part and played it well. Susannah's smile grew wider in appreciation, as her eyes began to shift, seemingly searching for a proper thing to say that would push this moment into history while remaining wary of the future. Suddenly her nervousness was replaced with something Lillith couldn't quite identify. It couldn't be the suggestion of lunch, as Lillith had already guessed that their daily lunches were a thing of the past, replaced with errands and preparations for a new life. Susannah tucked her hair behind her ears.

"Want to go out tomorrow night?"

"Go out?" Lillith was scared to repeat the words in case she had gotten them wrong, but Susannah was nodding her head with an eagerness and ease that betrayed the fact that they had never stepped outside of the range of a work-related event: a sixty minute birthday lunch, an hour and a half if they went to Chinatown.

"My friends and I are going to Brutopia," Susannah said.

A late night, a Saturday. Lillith quickly painted a picture in her head of what that would entail. A nap of some kind was obvious, preferably in the late afternoon, but early enough to still have a decent supper and properly digest. Her black pants and shiny blouse would have to be cleaned and ironed. She'd have to verify the 211 bus schedule to get downtown, and make sure she had enough money for a couple of cokes, and maybe a green apple Smirnoff.

Lillith took a deep breath and forced a smile.

The next afternoon, Lillith sat at the computer, stumped. Saturday had been almost as easy as the word sounded, with the highlight of crossing paths with Him on the Friday night train still lingering. She had first run into Him smoking a joint with some teenagers in the tunnel of the Pointe Claire station a month ago. She didn't like working late, and had been nervous about walking by the gregarious group until she saw Him. He must have been in his late twenties, and Lillith felt strangely safer. How she knew it was a joint they were passing around she wasn't sure. It just was.

The first time she had run into him on the five o'clock train after that incident, she had tried making eye contact to see if he would recognize her, but looked away instantly. Last night, he was sorting things in a briefcase before slamming it shut. She imagined what he was keeping from the world in those leather interior pockets. Money, fake passports, her voice.

She transferred the weight of her head from her left hand to the right, her elbow knocking over her empty dinner plate. She bent over to pick up the crumbs and fork and on her way to the kitchen, quickly glanced at her General Electric answering machine that stood by the fridge. The red light on the machine was at its usual position: a standstill, frozen. The plans with Susannah were still on. She looked up at the clock. Only seven-thirty. Plenty of time, considering she had ironed her pants and blouse that morning.

Lillith sat at the computer again, inspiration hampered by the pit in her stomach that had been growing since yesterday. She scanned some of the other craigslist "Missed Connection" ads for ideas, but it wasn't helping. They were all short. Poorly written, really, with minimal description. Who could be the "hot girl at Fairview?" she wondered. She got up and studied herself in the mirror behind her bedroom door. Not exactly a disappointment. Her still-wet shoulder-length brown hair looked close to the promises that had been written on the shampoo bottle; the trace of lip gloss that had withstood dinner was almost shining, and her skin appeared to be doing a decent job of warding off the impending gloom of age. Lillith allowed herself to smile, confident that everything staring back at her would hold up under the forgiving light of the night. She sat back at the computer and began to type.

Saw you at the Starbucks on St. Jean's Saturday afternoon. You had a brown leather satchel and a Canadiens baseball cap on your head. You looked lonely. Give me a call.

She looked over what she had written, deciding to cut "on your head". Better. This was how it was done.

You were standing in the reference room at the Pointe-Claire Library on Sunday afternoon, with two back issues of The New Yorker under your arm. We smiled at each other as we sat on opposite sides of the same table.

Lillith wasn't prepared to equate her inspiration with what Joyce or Twain had experienced, but she hadn't posted anything in a week. She posted both ads and opened a new one.

You were on the five o'clock train on Friday. Your briefcase is black and your stop is Cedar Park. It got my attention. I'm—

Lillith's heart beat faster and she shut her computer.

Lillith wondered if the shampoo was still honoring its promises, or whether it had bailed after seeing all the shiny people teeming on Crescent Street that night. She was more unsure than ever of the mascara she had dabbed on at the last minute before leaving, even though she had checked it several times in the bathroom at Chapters before making her way over to Brutopia.

She squeezed her way through gorgeous faces and cell phones to find herself in front of the stairs leading up to the bar. Susannah was nowhere in sight and Lillith grew nervous. She glanced at her watch, worried it had failed her, and that she'd be forced to walk into the bar by herself to seek out her colleague. Or should she call her friend? Lillith decided that an evening at a bar—on a Saturday, no less—definitely pushed her and Susannah into the friend quadrant, and she got distracted by what could only be described as a strange joy that came from this realization.

She was relieved to see she was five minutes early, making waiting outside perfectly appropriate. She began pacing up and down the street, all the while searching for Susannah's large curls and green glasses in the sea of faces. She wondered who or what else might be there, brushing her shoulder, barely missing her foot. After a while she stared at the sidewalk, taking in the painted toes, silver sandals and smooth legs swarming her. For comfort, she thought of soft colours, like the pale peach bodies of Jean-Auguste Ingres. Then she thought of home. The Pointe Claire Shopping Centre and its white-haired patrons roaming the corridors like restless dandelions, the small mounds of snow that accumulated beside the parking lot in winter, the way plants blew on her balcony in summer, her living room with Chinese lanterns, the bamboo placemats on her table, the poster tucked between some books.

Lillith looked up and down the street one last time. The curls and glasses would be easier to spot in the now-thinning crowd. She was ready to check her watch again but couldn't bring herself to look down, ripping it off her arm instead with a force she hadn't known. She walked over to a garbage can standing before an all-night pizza place, and stared into the dark hole before letting the leather band escape from her fingers. She looked up and studied the street once more. Even with numb legs, Lillith could feel the earth move beneath her feet, the time pass, but she felt no comfort.

About the Author

Alexa Nazzaro

Alexa Nazzaro wrote her first novel, *Kimberly and the Seventh Grade Disaster*, when she was thirteen years old. Good thing it never saw the light of day. In the years since, she continued writing stories, earned a degree in Creative Writing from Concordia University, read a lot of books (some over and over, like *Catcher in the Rye*), watched a lot of movies, got married and became a stepmom. *The Pool Theory*, a young adult novel on teen pregnancy, is her first book that strangers are allowed to read.

http://www.thepooltheory.com
http://www.alexanazzaro.com

More Than Life Itself
A *Picking up the Pieces* Anthology

By
Jessica Prince

Gavin and Stacia's proposal takes place between
books one and two in the *Picking up the Pieces* series

Chapter 1

GAVIN

"OKAY, NOW THAT we're all here, can you please explain why you conned us into coming to Trevor's disgusting pit of an apartment?" Emmy asked as she scrubbed one of the dining chairs with a Clorox wipe before sitting in it.

"Hey, it's not a disgusting pit; it's a bachelor pad. It's supposed to look like this," Trevor threw back at Emmy with a disgruntled look.

"There's spaghetti sauce on the wall!" Savannah shouted. "Wait..." she walked over to the wall where the stain in question was and bent down to examine it further before turning back to Trevor. "Please tell me that's actually spaghetti sauce."

Trevor looked around at all of us before turning his eyes back on Savannah and giving a slight shrug. "Uh... I think so?"

Savannah threw her hands up in surrender. "That's it, I'm out," she called as she headed for the door. "The last thing I need is to get head lice by hanging around in this pig sty."

I bolted for the door to head her off. "Come on, guys. I called y'all for a reason. I seriously need your help."

I looked around the room where all of my friends were gathered and felt sweat break out on my forehead.

"Gavin, honey, you look like you're about to pass out. Why don't you sit down?" Lizzy wrapped her arm around my waist and ushered me toward a vacant dining chair.

Emmy did a quick scrub down of that chair as well before I was planted in it.

"So what's the emergency?" Luke asked from where he was standing behind Emmy's seat, his hands planted firmly on her shoulders. Ever since those two had gotten back together they couldn't be in the same room without touching. At least they weren't sucking face this time and actually seemed to be paying attention.

I reached into the pocket of my jeans and pulled out the small, black velvet box I'd been carrying around all week. I slapped it on the table in front of everyone and scanned the room to take in their wide-eyes expressions. "I'm gonna propose to Stacia tonight," I declared. I prayed my voice sounded more confident than I actually felt.

To tell you the truth, I'd felt like I was gonna hurl ever since I made the decision to propose to my long time girlfriend and love of my life.

Don't get me wrong, it's not that I didn't *want* to marry her. It was just that, even though I was pretty sure I knew what she was going to say, I was still terrified that she might say no.

A collective squeal sounded through the room from Emmy, Savannah and Lizzy while Jeremy, Brett, Luke and Trevor all gave me chin lifts and grunts of approval.

Lizzy snatched the ring box off the table and held it in front of her so that the women could all get a good look at it.

As soon as she opened it, all three of them fell completely silent and their mouths dropped open in awe… Or at least, I hoped it was awe.

Dear Jesus, please let it be awe.

After several seconds of silence, I finally found the nerve to speak up. "So… uh. What do you think?"

Three pairs of eyes shot up to meet mine, and the look in them was enough to cause my balls to shrink up into my belly.

"Is this a joke?" Lizzy asked as she put the ring box back on the table with an expression on her face similar to one you'd make it you walked into a bathroom shortly after Trevor vacated it.

I ran my hand across my forehead to brush off the perspiration that was quickly building up. "Well, no. I'm proposing tonight. That's why I called all of you here."

Brett reached across the table and turned the box so he and the guys could see it.

"Cool!" Trevor shouted. "It looks like a gold nugget. That ring kicks ass, Gavin!"

I glanced over and saw Lizzy giving Trevor the stink eye.

"It doesn't kick ass, you douche," Savannah replied before turning back to me. "Gavin, sweetie, what were you thinking when you bought that ring? Were you mad at Stacia or something?"

My chest started to feel tight and the air in the room got thicker.

"What's wrong with it?" Luke asked seriously. "I think it's kind of nice."

It was Emmy's turn to give the stink eye. "Hand to God, Luke. You ever propose to me with something that looks like that…" she said *that* like it was a cuss word, "… and you're never getting laid again, as long as you live."

Luke let out a snort and rolled his eyes. "Please, like you can resist all of this."

The smile Emmy gave him was nothing short of evil. "Oh, I can resist it, honey. And just to prove that, you're sleeping here tonight. I hope you catch crabs from Trevor's couch."

Luke's smugness completely evaporated and was replaced with fear, while Trevor fist pumped and shouted, "Guys night!"

"Can we focus please?" I asked, a little on the hysterical side. "What exactly don't you like about the ring?" I asked the ladies.

Lizzy looked at me in shock. "Um, well it's a marquise cut diamond on a gold nugget band, so… everything."

Yep, it was official. I was gonna hurl.

I dropped my head on the table and started banging it over and over.

"Who talked you into getting this?" Savannah asked as she rubbed my back.

I turned my face to the side and looked at her without raising my head off the table. "The chick at the store said it was a classic," I replied dumbly.

"Classically ugly," Emmy muttered out the side of her mouth.

I banged my head a few more times. "I freaked out, okay! I got in the store and there were rings everywhere. It was enough to give a guy a friggin' heart attack! I mean, what the hell is a princess cut anyway?"

"How much was that thing?" Jeremy asked.

"It was only five-hundred bucks. I got it for a steal," I replied.

"You got ripped off," he replied as he picked it up to take a closer look.

"Come on," Lizzy said, as she grabbed my arm and pulled me out of the chair.

"Where are we going?"

"To get you a ring that won't make Stacia cry when she sees it."

Chapter 2

WALKING THROUGH THE doors of a different jewelry store—since they deemed the place I bought the *first* ring from unworthy—with three women flanking me, brought back the anxiety that I thought I'd already dealt with. I'd progressed from feeling like I was going to hurl, to feeling like I was about to pass out.

"Okay, stay away from anything yellow gold," Lizzy stated.

"Why?" I asked.

"Oh, and no pear shaped diamonds," Savannah chimed in.

"What's a pear shape?" I got the distinct impression that no one was listening to me.

"And prong setting, not channel."

"Huh?"

They'd honed in on the engagement rings faster than a shark that smelled chum for Christ's sake. They'd abandoned me by the door, leaving me to wonder what the hell a pear setting or whatever the hell they were talking about was. I could practically see the three of them foaming at the mouth as they *oohed* and *ahhed* over the huge-ass rocks in front of them. I had a feeling if I took their advice, I'd go bankrupt.

"Oh, look at that one," Emmy said. "Two carat solitaire in a platinum setting."

What was the deal with all the fruit and vegetable references? First they brought up pears, now carrots? I was more lost than when I came by myself the first time.

"Can I help you, sir?" a polite, middle-aged woman asked from behind one of the counters to my left.

I left my friends to their drooling and walked up to the sales lady hoping she'd be able to help me. "Uh, yeah," I shot a quick glance at her name tag, "Claire. I'm trying to find an engagement ring for my girlfriend." I hitched my thumb over my shoulder in the direction of the girls. "My friends said the one I got was ugly."

Claire gave me a sympathetic smile. "I'm sure it's not that bad. Why don't we take a look?"

I pulled the ring out of my pocket and showed it to the kind-faced Claire. "Oh," was the only response I got.

"You see my situation?"

Claire screwed her face up as she bent closer to get a better look. "Yeah."

Monosyllabic responses were *not* a good sign.

I snapped the ring box shut and stuck it back in my pocket before anyone else could see it. It was bad enough I was never going to live this down with my friends, the last thing I needed was for strangers to point and laugh.

"Why don't you tell me about your girlfriend?" Claire asked.

I felt that same goofy smile I got every time someone brought up Stacia appear on my face. "Well, we've known each other since we were kids, and I guess I just always knew I was gonna end up with her, you know? Even before we started dating, I'd look at her and just know." I looked at Claire and saw she had that gooey expression women got when they thought a dude was being romantic.

"She's got this smile that, even when I'm having a really crappy day, it just... I don't know... it just makes everything better, I guess. That smile brightens up my world. She's a total goof, but it's just one of the many things I love about her."

Based on the chorus of *ahh's* coming from behind me, the girls had apparently turned their attention from the rings back to me.

"Oh, and she's got a rockin' body!" I exclaimed with enthusiasm. "Like, total 50s pin-up chick."

The gooey, romantic expression left her face and she shook her head. I could have sworn I heard her mutter "typical" under her breath at the same time Savannah smacked me in the back of the head. "Why do guys always have to ruin it?" she asked in a huff.

"Well, what about this one?" Claire asked as I rubbed the back of my head. "This is from out vintage collection. It's a one-carat center stone surrounded by pave diamonds in a white gold setting. Notice the intricate detailing along the band..."

I let her prattle on about the ring, not really listening to what she was saying because I couldn't take my eyes off it.

It was perfect. It had an antique look to it and I could see it on Stacia's hand clear as day. Looking at the ring, I got the same exact feeling every time I looked as Stacia. It was the one.

"I'll take it," I interrupted, cutting Claire off mid-sentence.

"You're sure?" she asked cautiously.

"Oh, yeah," I replied with a grin. "I'm positive."

I glanced behind me when I finally noticed the silence in the store. Emmy, Savannah and Lizzy stood behind me, all with tear streaked faces. "Oh, Gavin," Savannah croaked. "It's beautiful."

With that, all three woman busted out in full-blown sobs. I'm talking ugly crying with blotchy faces and snotty noses. I was in engagement-ring hell.

Chapter 3

"NO, YOU AREN'T helping with the proposal, Emmy. I'm not gonna tell you again."

We'd arrived Trevor's from the jewelry store and the girls instantly jumped on my proposal, throwing out ideas left and right on what *they* thought *I* should do.

"Oh, come on," she whined. "I've got a ton of awesome ideas. Ooh, ooh, how about this? You could cover her house in rose petals and have candles lit everywhere. That'd be so romantic."

"Not to mention a fire hazard," Luke replied. He was sitting on Trevor's couch—not at all concerned about what he could possibly be sitting in—with his feet kicked up on the box posing as a coffee table and his hands behind his head.

"Oh, shut up, Luke," Emmy snapped. "What are you even doing here? Don't you ever work?"

"Crime decided to take a break. What can I say? I'm such a badass, I scared all the bad guys straight, I guess."

Emmy snatched the Sports Illustrated out of Luke's hands and smacked him in the face with it. "Get lost, Deputy Dumbass. There's a speed trap with your name on it somewhere across town."

Luke stood and stretched before grabbing Emmy around her waist and pulling her to his chest. "Gimme a kiss to keep me safe first."

"Safe from what? Getting run over by Mrs. Williams because she won't listen to her doctor when he says she can't drive because of her cataracts?" Savannah asked with a roll of her eyes.

It fell on deaf ears, however, seeing as Emmy and Luke were currently locked in a heavy make-out session.

"Glad to know my tax dollars help pay for our Deputy to suck face with his girlfriend," Brett said as I threw a handful of chips at Luke's head.

He didn't even break contact with Emmy while he flipped Brett the bird.

Trevor looked as me seriously before saying, "You know, man, if you're worried about her shooting you down, you could always just knock her up. No chick wants to be single and pregnant."

Savannah rolled up Luke's disregarded magazine and proceeded to beat Trevor over the head with it. "You know, for society's sake, I hope you have weak swimmers. The last thing we need is your help populating the earth."

"Okay, I'm out," Luke called. "I don't need to be witness to Savannah beating Trevor to death."

I took that as my cue and followed him out the door. "So you don't think flowers and candles are the way to go?" I asked as we walked through the parking lot.

Luke stopped and turned to put his hand on my shoulder. "Think about it, man. You scatter flowers all over your house and who's gonna have to clean that shit up the next day, huh? She'll be too busy running around town tellin' everyone who'll listen that she's getting married to do it, so that makes it you're job."

I gave a slight nod. I had to admit, he made a valid point.

"It's not like they care that we've already done all the work anyway, just by proposing. You think they care what kind of trouble we go through to pop the question? No, of course they don't."

"Sounds like you've given this a lot of thought. You plan on askin' Emmy to marry you any time soon?"

Luke looked a little uncomfortable as he rubbed the back of his neck. "Hell, Gavin. I've asked the woman three times already. She keeps shootin' me down."

That surprised me. "She tell you why?"

"Apparently, it doesn't count if you shout it out during sex. What idiot came up with that rule?"

I threw my head back in laughter. "Probably the same person who decided tying a bow around your junk and telling your girlfriend it was her birthday present was a bad idea."

"Hey, that was a *brilliant* gift. She loves that thing almost as much as I do. She just didn't appreciate the sentiment behind it."

"Uh huh. That would explain why she punched it instead of *appreciating* it."

I saw Luke cringe a little out of the corner of my eye and I knew he was recalling how he walked around funny for days after telling Emmy to unwrap her "present".

I always knew she had a mean streak. I just never knew she could hit that hard... or that a man like Luke was capable of crying.

It was my turn to cringe at the memory.

"I think it'll be best if I just go with my gut on this one," I told him before heading for my truck. "At least by listening to you talk, I know what not to do," I called over my shoulder.

"See if I ever offer you advice again."

I pulled the car door open and turned back to Luke. "Your advice is gonna get me shot one day. Hell, I'm in shock that you're still alive and kickin' after some of the stunts you've pulled."

"What can I say, that woman worships me," he said with a chuckle.

"Is that right?" a pissed off female voice said from behind Luke. He spun around, and I caught a glimpse of a furious looking Emmy before I decided to make a break for it.

"Ah, baby. You know I didn't mean that," he pleaded. I slammed the door and put the truck in gear just as he started spouting off how much he loved her.

I swear, him saying stupid stuff and her making his life miserable for it, was almost like foreplay between those two. I was positive they each got off on it.

As much as I loved my friends and appreciated them digging me out of the hole I put myself in with that first ring, there was no way I was going to take their advice on my proposal. Trevor would have me getting Stacia pregnant on the sly, and Luke's advice would probably lead to me sleeping on the couch at Trevor's with a bag of frozen peas between my legs to keep the swelling down.

There was no one that knew Stacia better than I did. I just had to trust my instincts and hope I made it through without passing out.

Chapter 4

STACIA

"I THINK GAVIN'S cheating on me," I rushed once we were all seated around Savannah's dining room table.

I probably should have waited to drop that little bomb on my girls until *after* Emmy was finished taking a drink, but iced tea all over my ivory, cashmere sweater is a lesson in itself.

Once she finished choking, she looked at me with tears in her eyes and croaked, "What?" between coughs.

"You heard me. Gavin's having an affair. That's the only thing that can explain his behavior these past few days. That's why I called an emergency girls' meeting."

A look passed between my three best friends but I couldn't tell what it was about.

"Honey, I'm sure it's not what you think," Lizzy tried to placate me.

"Oh really? Well then, can you explain why he's been taking all his calls in the bathroom all week when he's at home? Or why, every time I ask him what's going on, he gets all sweaty and starts to stutter? Or how about why he's puking every five minutes? What do have to say about that?"

"Uhh... maybe he's sick?"

"He's guilty is what he is. I know that man better than he knows himself. He's up to something. I can feel it in my gut."

Emmy, having finally gotten control of her breathing, reached across the table and grabbed my hand. "Stacia, you know Gavin would never do anything like that to you. There has to be a logical explanation."

I reached into my purse and slapped the folded piece of paper down on the table in front of everyone. "Well, explain this then," I demanded.

Savannah picked up the paper and started looking over it. "What am I looking at exactly?"

"That's Gavin's credit card statement. When he started acting shady, I decided to do some digging. See there?" I said pointing at the charge in question. "That's a charge for five hundred bucks for some place called Angel's in Houston. I bet it's some skanky strip club where he meets his skanky stripper girlfriend for a nooner while I sit at home like a total friggin' idiot!"

The last few words came out in a choked sob right before I broke down in tears. "I bet her stripper name's Candy or Crystal Chandelier or something equally as slutty and fake as she is!" I wailed.

They all just sat there wide eyed and watched me bawl my eyes out without saying a word. "Are y'all just gonna sit there staring or are you gonna console me?" I screeched. "I just found out my soon-to-be crippled soon-to-be ex-boyfriend is screwing around with a stripper!"

They immediately snapped out of their daze and jumped up to wrap their arms around me, offering words of reassurance that it wasn't what I thought. That Gavin loved me more than life itself and would never do anything to hurt me.

I wanted to believe what they were saying but things just weren't adding up. I'd never seen Gavin act so strangely in all the years we'd known each other. He was up to something and I was going to find out what it was.

I finally got my tears under control several minutes later.

"Promise you won't do anything irrational, Stacia," Emmy said as she ran a hand down my hair. "Everything you've told us can easily be explained. For all you know, he could just be planning on surprising you with something."

"Really, like what?" I asked hopefully.

Before she could answer, Savannah hauled back and punched Emmy in the arm. "Ouch! Sonofabitch!"

I couldn't make out the look on Savannah's face, but her tight mouth and crazy eyes told me she wanted to kick Emmy's ass. "What was that for?" I asked Savannah.

"Nothing," she mumbled. "I thought I saw a spider or something."

Emmy rubbed her arm where Savannah had punched her. "Thanks," she said as she stared daggers in Savannah's direction.

I tried to pull the conversation back around to what we were discussing before the spider incident. "So you think he's planning a surprise or something?"

All three of them got nervous looks on their faces. "Uh, I don't know. Maybe. I was just saying it could be something else."

I felt my hopes that there could be some other reason for Gavin acting so strange lately dwindle.

I figured I'd just have to work on my sleuthing a little more and get to the bottom of things.

Chapter 5

GAVIN

I HAD TO hurry to get everything set up before Stacia made it home. I ran to the grocery store and picked up everything I would need to make her favorite dinner, chicken parmesan. I didn't have a damn clue how to make it, but it couldn't be that hard. All I had to do was follow the recipe and I was golden.

My phone dinged from my back pocket and I glanced at it to see a text from Brett.

Warning! Warning! Shit's about to hit the fan!

I didn't have time to try and figure out what the hell he was talking about, so I just stuffed my phone back in my pocket and went about the rest of my errands.

Once I made it back to our place, I headed to the kitchen to start dinner before I tidied up the house.

I pulled out the recipe book and sat it out in front of me before organizing everything that I needed.

"Dredge each breast in flour and tap off excess…" I read out loud, "…then dip in the egg and let excess drip off. Dredge both sides in bread crumbs. Huh… what's a dredge?"

I didn't have a clue what Bobby Flay was talking about, but I'd seen my mom and Stacia both make fried chicken once or twice, so I figured it wasn't much different. A look at the clock showed that time was of the essence, so I decided to cut a few corners to make things move a little quicker.

Instead of wasting time measuring out the oil and dividing it between pans, I just poured the bottle into each until they looked about equal and set the burners on high.

Because I didn't have time to separate the ingredients out into separate bowls and I still didn't know what the hell a dredge was, I went for the method I'd seen Mom and Stacia use and dumped the flour, a few eggs and the bread crumbs into a Ziploc storage bag, then I cut open the pack of chicken breasts and dumped them in there too.

A few good shakes later, and I was set.

Thirty minute prep time my ass, Bobby Flay. I just beat your record by twenty minutes. Suck on that!

It was obvious I could teach Mr. Flay a thing or two in the kitchen.

When I felt like the chicken was coated enough, I tossed one in each pan and decided to use the cook time to clean up.

I ran from the kitchen to the hall closet and pulled the vacuum out. I'd just plugged it in and started running it over the carpet when all hell decided to break loose.

First, I ran over the cord with the vacuum—and let me just say that Dyson wasn't lying, they really do have more suction—I know this because that little bastard sucked the cord right up and promptly started making noises that sounded like a cat drowning.

Before I even had a chance to turn the damn thing off, the smoke detectors started going haywire.

I spun around like a mad man trying to figure out what set them off when I saw bright orange flames shooting up from the stove.

Now, typically, I wasn't a total idiot, but with the pressures of trying to plan the perfect proposal all week, the added stress of finding out the first ring I bought bit the big one, and then realizing that I'd just set my kitchen on fire, it should be said that I clearly wasn't in my right mind.

That's why, instead of smothering the grease fire I'd started, I ran to the sink and filled up a cup of water.

The only saving grace in that epic fail was the fact that I wasn't able to locate the gallon pitcher in all the chaos, and therefore, had nothing but a juice glass at my disposal to dump water on the fire.

Not that that really mattered. The second that water hit the flames, they burst up to new heights, taking my eye lashes and a good portion of my eyebrows with them. With everything that was going on around me, the first thing I remembered thinking was that I was going to beat Bobby Flay to a pulp if I ever saw that asshole in person. The second thing was that I'd never get the chance to propose to Stacia, because the minute she walked in and saw the destruction I caused, she was going to kill me.

My brain kicked back into gear—somewhat—right before the flames reached the cabinets, I went for the whole bag of flour I'd just bought, and turned it over on the fire. I dumped the entire contents onto the stovetop and floor.

Plus: the fire was out.

Minus: I'd gone a little overboard at the grocery store and purchased a five pound bag of flour.

My first reaction was to grab the vacuum to try and pick up some of the white powder dusted through the kitchen, when the sound of that drowning cat reminded me that our Dyson was currently sucking in its last breath… along with the rest of its cord.

I was standing there like a dumbass with my hands in my hair, taking in the devastation around me, when the front door burst open and Stacia came stomping in like a mad woman. "Who the hell is Angel you cheating piece of…" she stopped midsentence and scanned the living room and kitchen.

"What the *hell* is going on?!"

Chapter 6

STACIA

I BUSTED INTO the house ready to unleash hell on my adulterous soon-to-be-ex when the scene before me stopped me in my tracks.

I thought I heard Gavin mumbling something about hating Bobby Flay—whatever that was about—and it looked like the kitchen had been on fire.

Before I had the chance to inspect the damage, a crazy whining, hissing sound led me into the living room. That's where I found my $400 Dyson with the swivel ball laying on the floor and its cord sucked up in the motor.

Well, that's money down the toilet.

There was a reason I never let Gavin anywhere near the kitchen or any of my expensive appliances. Mainly because I wanted to keep them!

"Gavin, what's going on? Why is the house destroyed?"

I looked at him to see him wringing his hands nervously. "Um… surprise," he whispered lamely. "I was trying to make you a special dinner and clean up the house, but…" he waved his hand to encompass the mess around us, "… things got a little out of hand."

"A little out of hand?" I hissed through clenched teeth. I felt like steam was going to start shooting out my ears at any minute. "A little out of hand?! Spilling a carton of milk is a little out of hand, Gavin! Setting the kitchen on fire and destroying a $400 vacuum cleaner is *not* a little out of hand!"

My eyes drifted to the stove top and what I saw there had me gasping for breath. "Is that... is that my Emeril Lagasse Teflon cookware?" I couldn't hear anything past the blood rushing in my ears.

Gavin didn't say anything, just stood there with a hangdog expression on his face. But he didn't need to say anything. I was on a roll.

"Who were you cooking dinner for, Gavin? Huh? Your little stripper girlfriend Crystal Chandelier from that strip club Angels? Did I mess up your romantic dinner plans?"

"Huh?" he asked stupidly. "Who the hell is Crystal Chandelier? And when did Cloverleaf get a strip club?"

"It's not in Cloverleaf you ass! But you already know that seeing as you shelled out 500 bucks on your little skank during your trip to Houston last weekend."

He shook his head like he was trying to clear it out. "Wait, what are you talking about?"

I pulled the credit card statement out of my purse and shoved it into his chest. "You tell me. The evidence is there, clear as day." I felt the tears burning the back of my eyes and Gavin's figure started to blur in front of me. "You've been cheating on me with a stripper, haven't you?" I sobbed. "That's why you've been acting so weird all week, isn't it?"

I stood there as Gavin looked over the statement and watched as his eyes grew wide. After several seconds, the paper floated to the ground and Gavin advanced on me. "Baby, you think I'm cheating on you?" he asked as he brushed my tears away gently. "Stacia, you have to know I'd never do that to you. I love you, sweetheart. Cheating on you has never even crossed my mind."

He sounded so sincere that I almost believed him. I really *wanted* to believe him.

"Then what's been going on with you? Why have you been taking phone calls in the bathroom and throwing up every five minutes? And what's Angel's?"

Gavin led me over to the couch were my beloved vacuum lay, broken and worthless on the floor, and pulled me onto his lap. "Sweetheart, I'm sorry if I've been upsetting you, but it's not what you think, okay?"

He shifted slightly to his side and reached into his pocket. He opened his hand and showed me a hideous ring. I didn't understand what he was trying to say by showing that to me. "Did you win that from one of those machines at the front of the store or something?" I asked, still totally confused.

He visibly cringed and dropped the hunk of costume jewelry onto the coffee table. "No, believe it or not, I paid for that. Angel's is a jewelry store in Houston. I went to get your engagement ring last weekend."

I eyes darted back and forth between Gavin and that god-awful ring. The first thought going through my mind was *holy shit, he's going to propose!* The second was *oh God, he was going to propose with* that!

My thoughts about the ring must have read clearly on my face because he burst out laughing and pulled me into his chest, burying his face in my neck.

God, I love his laugh.

When he pulled his face back, he looked at the ring then back at me. "It's pretty terrible, isn't it?"

That got a smile from me. "Well, what do you expect when you spend 500 bucks on an engagement ring, you cheapskate."

He chuckled again and planted a kiss on my lips. I picked up the ugly ring and studied it, trying to convince myself it was something that I could wear. "It isn't so bad, I guess." I slid the ring on my finger and smiled at Gavin brightly. "Besides, it doesn't matter what it looks like. If you bought this ring so you could propose to me, I'll happily wear it every day if it proves how much I love you."

GAVIN

I took her chin between my thumb and index finger and turned her face to mine. "You'd really do that for me?"

Stacia reached up and brushed a lock of hair from my forehead. "Of course. Gavin, I love you more than life itself. I'd do anything for you."

I shifted again and reached into my other pocket. "So, if I told you that I realized today what an eyesore that ring is and proposed to you with this one, you'd say yes?"

I opened hand and showed her the ring Lizzy, Emmy and Savannah had gone with me to buy earlier that day. Her eyes turned glassy with tears, and I was pretty sure she'd stopped breathing. "Stacia, baby, inhale."

She sucked in an audible breath and graced me with her beautiful smile. I'd never get tired of that smile. I wasn't blowing smoke when I told Claire that her smile brightened up my world. She gave a slight nod and wrapped her arms around my neck, squeezing as tightly as she could. "Yes! Yes, Gavin. Of course I'll marry you!"

I pulled away slightly and slammed my lips against hers. She'd just made me the happiest guy on Earth.

"I love my ring, baby. It's gorgeous!"

"I'm glad, sweetheart." I stood from the couch, still holding Stacia in my arms and headed for the door.

"Where are we going?" she asked.

"I'm taking my new fiancée out to dinner to celebrate starting our lives together."

She got that gooey look in her eyes at my romantic declaration. "I love you so much, Gavin," she whispered.

I kissed her again and responded, "I love you too."

"Hey! So you never told me why you've been taking all your calls in the bathroom."

I pulled the front door shut and shifted her weight around so I could lock it. "I've been playing phone tag with your folks all week so I could get their permission."

"You are so sweet, you know that?" I opened the door to my truck and deposited Stacia into the passenger seat. "What about all the puking?" she asked.

I rubbed the back of my neck, totally embarrassed that she's noticed that. "Honestly, babe, I've been freaking out all week. Ever since I bought that first ring, every time I thought about proposing to you, I'd get sick."

From the look on her face, I instantly realized that was *not* the right thing to say.

She cut her eyes at me, and I immediately started thinking of ways to get my ass out of the dog house for that one. "So the thought of asking me to be your wife made you physically ill?"

I grabbed her face and laid the most passionate kiss I could manage on her. After a few seconds, the tension left her body and she melted into me. I knew I'd gotten her back... at least for the moment.

"Love you more than life itself, baby." I declared, then took in all the brightness she gave me just from that smile.

THE END

About the Author

Jessica Prince

Jessica is a wife, mother, wino, coffee addict and avid a lover of all types of books, but romances are her main favorites. Her husband likes to say reading is her obsession but she just says it's a passion… there's a difference. She's been writing since she was a little kid and finally decided to take the leap and actually publish when *Picking up the Pieces* came to her. Now that Jessica's been bitten by the writing bug she just can't seem to stop.

Jessica currently lives in Houston Texas and when she's not spending time with her family she's reading, writing, or trying her hardest not to melt in the Gulf Coast heat and humidity.

Just Breathe

By

Madeline Sheehan

STARING OUT THE passenger side window of my father's BMW, I watched the neighborhood pass by—houses, windows, and perfectly manicured lawns all blurring together—not really noticing any of it. Nothing could penetrate the fluttering sense of unease deep within my gut.

It was my first day back to school after nearly three weeks away.

My first day back since… the incident.

I glanced around to where my brother sat in the back seat behind my father, staring out the other side of the car. His long body was cramped uncomfortably into the small space allotted him, and like me, he appeared deep in thought, paying little to no attention to his surroundings.

Joshua was a year younger than me and incredibly handsome. While he looked like our mother, blond hair and blue eyes with exceptionally strong facial features, I looked like my father, with light brown hair and brown eyes, my face heart-shaped and my features rounded.

But it wasn't Joshua's good looks I was focusing on, it was his split lip and the bruises on his cheek. They were healing quickly and had already begun fading, but they were still visible. Worse, they were all my fault, all because he'd stuck up for me.

I turned back around and glanced at my father who sat stiffly in the driver's seat, both his hands gripping tightly to the steering wheel, his eyes front and unwavering, his mouth set into a thin, hard line.

Also, all my fault.

My family was in shambles. My father wasn't speaking; my mother hardly got out of bed; they were all embarrassed and ashamed.

And it was all my fault.

Out of the corner of my eye I caught sight of my high school rapidly approaching. Redmond Academy, an elitist prep school for the offspring of only the wealthiest. Where it wasn't just an honor to attend, but a rite of passage. I'd once worn my uniform proudly, but now, looking down at my pleated blue skirt, I felt awkward and uncomfortable.

Swallowing hard, I faced front, clutched my shoulder bag a little tighter, and watched as the building that had once been my castle, but now was my personal dungeon, came completely into view.

We were right on time, fifteen minutes before the first bell would ring, signaling it was time to get to homeroom. We were also right on time to be on display for the gathered cliques milling around outside… talking, laughing, gossiping.

The car jerked slightly as my father came to a complete stop beside the curb. Without putting the vehicle in park, not even bothering to turn his head, he said curtly, "See you later."

Nausea rose from my gut, burning inside my throat as emotion began to cloud my vision. Fumbling, I unbuckled my seat belt and pushed open the car door before my father could see me crying. By the time I had the door shut behind me, my brother was already halfway down the walk and my father was quickly pulling away from the curb.

I was alone.

Shouldering my bag and trembling slightly, I turned to face my school, zeroing in on the front doors, keeping my gaze solely on those doors and ignoring the people standing around me. The people, my peers who at my

arrival had grown quiet, were now speaking in hushed whispers while staring directly at me.

One foot in front of the other, I told myself. I could do this; I just had
to place one foot in front of the other and so on and so on. And so I did, I
walked at a normal pace, staring only at my destination, the eight steps that
led to two sets of double doors that, once open, would take me directly into
the fiery pits of hell.

Loud throat clearing could be heard to the left of me. Someone else
coughed, then "Slut!" was intentionally yelled out, followed by more sarcastic cover-up coughing. And then came the laughter. It started as snickering
but quickly grew into a loud tittering that began to spread like wildfire. By
the time I'd reached the first step, my hands were clammy, my armpits
drenched in sweat, and my eyes blurry with unshed tears.

I felt much like I'd imagine Anne Boleyn or Marie Antoinette must
have felt as they were marched to their deaths, spit upon and mocked by an
unruly mob, unfairly judged by the same people who'd once adored them.

Thankfully the hallways, aside from a few quickly scattering freshmen
and sophomores, were still relatively empty. I picked up my pace, walking
faster than I'd ever walked through these halls in the entire three years I'd
attended this school, past the freshman wing, through the sophomore hall,
up two short flights of stairs, then making a quick right to—

The junior wing. A group of varsity cheerleaders in full uniform stood
in a huddle to the right of me, their cheeks painted in our school colors,
pompoms in their hands. To my left stood another group of girls, their uni-
forms pressed, their hair perfectly coiffed and makeup effortlessly done.
They were putting away designer backpacks inside lockers decorated with
magazine cutouts of celebrities and decorative mirrors and sticky-note
reminders.

And they were talking animatedly with one another, gesturing with
their hands and laughing loudly.

"I saw Josh this morning. You know what that means, right?"

"Oh my God! Do you think she's back?"

Shrug. "Her brother's back, she must be."

"Ugh, whatever. I can't believe she'd come back here after what
happened."

"I know I wouldn't. I'd never show my face in town again."

"I seriously cannot believe her parents haven't packed up and left town. Dana's mom told my mom that her dad came to the club to play golf on Saturday and no one would talk to him. No. One. And nobody's seen her mom since the whole thing started. My mom thinks she probably killed herself from the embarrassment."

"My mom won't let me out of the house! This is all her fault! Just because she's a whore doesn't mean I'm a whore! I even told my mom I wasn't friends with her anymore!"

I spun around, wanting to get as far away from my old friends before they noticed me standing there. I bolted into the stairwell and had just cleared the first flight and was swinging around for the next when I smacked right into someone and fell backward, landing hard on my backside.

"Watch where the fuck you're going!"

Startled, I glanced up into the familiar kohl-lined eyes of our high school's one and only self-proclaimed introvert, Nicholas Shelton. He was the sole heir to his father's five-star hotel billion-dollar empire, but you would never know it by looking at him. Instead of the uniform black slacks and dress shoes that were the norm, Nick wore black Dickies with black boots. And while he still wore the same collared white shirt and tie as every other male student, he wore his shirt inside out and his tie hung loose and low around his neck, decorated with safety pins and colorful buttons with band names and logos on them.

His dark hair was long, pulled back into a ponytail midskull, and looked badly in need of a wash. He had small silver hoops in each ear, a hoop in his lip, and a barbell through his tongue. And then there were his eyes, heavily ringed in black eyeliner that was always smeared, giving him the appearance of a raccoon. It was as if he purposely only put it on before bed each night.

He made fun of everyone, always directly to their faces, calling us spoiled rich bitches and brainless jocks whose only future was to breed the next generation of people just like ourselves. Needless to say, he had zero friends at our school. Not that he cared much; he had his iPod always shoved in his back pocket and his earbuds plugged his ears most of the time. I doubted he even knew what people were saying about him. Or if he did, he certainly didn't seem to care very much, or at all really.

"Walk much, Potter?" he grumbled.

"Sorry," I muttered as I got to my feet and brushed off my skirt. "I didn't see you."

"None of you see very much, do you?" he said. "Not until it's shoved up in your fucking face."

Straightening my bag, I sidestepped him and had my foot on the first stair when suddenly his hand wrapped around my forearm. Surprised, I glanced up at him.

"They're going to eat you alive, Katherine." His tone was harsh—his tone was always harsh—but the angry look in his eyes was gone. He seemed... concerned.

"I know," I whispered. "But I don't have a choice."

He stared down at me, his expression hard. "Your parents."

It wasn't a question; it was a statement. Parents like ours didn't breed disappointments and failures. Because disappointments and failures made them look like failures, and that was simply unacceptable.

I nodded and a moment later he released me. "Good luck," he said quietly and then he was gone, up the stairs and disappearing into the hallway I'd just escaped from.

I stood there for a moment longer, wondering what sort of horrors the rest of the day would bring, until a cacophony of high-pitched laughter shook me out of my thoughts. As the laughter grew closer, I bolted down the last flight of stairs and headed straight for homeroom.

Straight to where I already knew *he* was going to be. *He* being the sole reason any of this had happened, was still happening, to me.

~~~~

Luckily, I was the first student inside the classroom, and for the first time in my school career I picked out a desk in the back and slid into my seat. Untangling myself from my shoulder bag, I set it on the desk in front of me and as I went to unzip my bag, I locked eyes with my homeroom teacher. Mr. Inglefield was an older man, graying, balding, his hands and face covered in wrinkles and age spots. He was a transplant from England as a child but still retained a light British accent that, along with his deep voice, sounded lyrical and I'd always enjoyed hearing him speak. He'd always been kind to me, always had a smile on his face when we'd pass in the halls or interacted during class.

He wasn't smiling today. If fact, the moment my eyes caught his, he quickly averted his gaze to the row of windows on the opposite side of the room. I thought I'd been prepared for this, but all I'd really been prepared for was what my peers were going to do to me. I never once imagined that my teachers, adults I respected that had once treated me like a golden child, would ever react that way.

I felt my heartbeat increase and eyes prick with tears, so I began hurriedly digging through my shoulder bag, trying to busy myself by organizing the books and notebooks inside. Around me I could hear footsteps, the slap of backpacks and the thud of books hitting the desks, but still I refused to look up. I had to work up to this, to being in this small, confined space with no ready escape from the giggling and the accusatory stares and the incessant whispering.

Out of the corner of my eye, I sensed someone taking the seat beside me, but still I didn't look over. Was it someone who was purposely sitting by me in hopes of further embarrassing me? Or was it a friend? Most likely, considering what I'd heard straight from their mouths in the junior hall, I had no friends left. Not one of the girls I'd once considered my very best friends had contacted me during my weeks away from school. No phone calls or text messages, not even an e-mail or a Facebook message.

"Hey. Psst, Katie," came a hushed voice from beside me. Without thinking, I glanced over and came face to face with Malcolm Widom. He was the prettiest of the pretty boys, a rugby superstar, large and muscular with shaggy blond hair and crystal-clear blue eyes. He was also *his* best friend.

He grinned at me, all teeth and dimples, and my stomach violently lurched.

"Have you seen this?" he continued in a whisper as he pulled his arm from inside his backpack. I watched in horrified fascination as his thick forearm was slowly revealed and then his hand came into view, holding a piece of paper folded in half.

It was a knee-jerk reaction; Malcolm held out the mysterious paper and I reached out and took it from him, despite the fact that I knew inside my gut it was going to be something I didn't want to see. Beads of sweat dotted my brow as I slowly unfolded the sheet to its full length.

"Never knew you were so flexible, Katie," he whispered.

I stifled my whimper with the back of my hand but could do nothing to stifle the laughter that erupted to my right.

"Mr. Widom!"

Mr. Inglefield quickly made his way down the aisle toward us. When he arrived at my desk, he snatched the sheet of paper from my hand, glanced at it, then crumpled it up in his fist.

"Hallway," he demanded of Malcolm. "Now."

Still grinning, Malcolm slid out of his seat, grabbed his backpack, and headed for the front of the room. I watched as he passed by... *him*... and the two boys quickly bumped fists.

Feeling more than embarrassed now, I was humiliated, disappointed, and heartbroken, but most of all I was hurt. I hadn't been sure what seeing him—actually seeing him—was going to do to me, and now that I was here and he was here and I was staring at the back of his head, it was a hundred times worse than I could have ever imagined. The betrayal felt reborn, the same bitter taste flooded my mouth, my body tensed to the point of pain, and all the breath inside me suddenly evaporated, replaced by scalding-hot fire.

"Miss Potter," Mr. Inglefield said and I looked up. "I believe we should take a trip to the office."

Any other day, in another life, I would have been mortified to be escorted to the office in front of my friends and fellow students, but not today. Today I was grateful and relieved.

Trying my best to ignore the blatant stares coming from nearly everyone in the classroom, I took a deep breath and got up out of my chair. Then, with my eyes downcast, I quickly made my way into the hallway.

A brisk three-minute walk later, both Malcolm and I were seated in two of the four plush chairs directly outside the headmaster's office. Malcolm had pulled out his phone and was busy texting while I sat, legs crossed, my shoulder bag in my lap, my hands holding the side strap with a death grip.

Five more minutes went by and still Mr. Inglefield had yet to exit the headmaster's office. I could only imagine what they were doing inside with that awful sheet of paper. Were they looking at it? The very thought brought on a shudder of humiliation. The entire staff knew, everyone knew, students, parents, teachers, and probably even the janitorial staff. The thought of them all looking at me, seeing me... like that... doing those things... with *him* overwhelmed me.

I fought back the scream that had been building up inside of me for the past three weeks and gripped my bag tighter, trying hard to fight both my roiling stomach and the tears filling my eyes, threatening to spill over at any second—

The door to the reception area slammed open and in walked Nicholas Shelton. Following directly behind him was a very angry Mrs. Halverson, an English Literature teacher.

"Sit," she snapped at Nick, pointing to the empty seat between Malcolm and me.

Nick's eyes flashed with an emotion I couldn't distinguish and the next thing I knew he was barking, literally barking like a dog, alternating from his tongue hanging out while he made spittle-filled panting noises to yammering much the way an overexcited dog would.

Mrs. Halverson's beady brown eyes narrowed into fine slits. "I will give you one more warning, Mr. Shelton, or it won't be detention this time but demerits instead."

"Oh, so now I'm Mr. Shelton," Nick sneered. "A second ago, when you were treating me like a fucking dog, I was confused."

Mrs. Halverson, along with both secretaries, openly gaped at Nick. Shrugging, he turned away from them and took the seat beside me.

Shaking her head, Mrs. Halverson leaned over the desk of one of the secretaries and began speaking in hushed tones, during which the secretary's eyes again found Nick and continued widening until I could see the entire whites of her eyes.

I turned to Nick just as he was cutting his eyes in my direction.

"What did you do?" I whispered.

He shrugged. "Chelsea Nichols called me a dickless loser."

Beside Nick, Malcolm burst out laughing. "That's my girl," he drawled.

I would hardly call Chelsea Malcolm's "girl". Maybe his once-in-a-while girl and that usually only lasted a for a week, maybe two, depending on how long it took the two of them to be at each other's throats.

Grinning, Nick turned his entire body in Malcolm's direction. "Then," he said, "I told her in all likelihood I have the biggest dick she's ever seen."

Malcolm snorted. "Yeah, sure, freaktard. Whatever."

Nick shrugged again. "She seemed to agree with me after I whipped it out."

Malcolm shot up out of his chair at record speed and stood glaring down at Nick, his chest heaving with harsh, angry breaths. "You better be lying," he spat out.

Slowly, almost casually, Nick pushed himself to his feet and stood to his full height, almost an inch taller than Malcolm. He wasn't nearly as muscular as Malcolm, but no one else in school was either.

Nick cocked his head to one side and appeared to be studying Malcolm. "I never lie," he said quietly. "I'm not like you."

"No fucking shit," Malcolm hissed. "I'm not a makeup-wearing freak!"

Nick's lips split into a slow-growing grin that was nothing if not pure menace and vile intent. It was a beautiful gesture turned so blatantly, so deliberately, into something ugly. His angry scowl beginning to waver, Malcolm shifted backward a step.

Just then the headmaster's door opened and Mr. Inglefield appeared in the doorway. "Mr. Widom," he called out, crooking two fingers. "Please join us."

Malcolm shot Nick one last look before grabbing his backpack and storming across the room. Grabbing the edge of the door, he almost violently yanked it from Mr. Inglefield's grip and disappeared inside the office. Sighing and shaking his head, Mr. Inglefield followed him inside and closed the door softly behind him.

"They didn't even give you five minutes, did they?"

I glanced up at Nick. "Huh?"

"Before they started in on you. They couldn't even wait until after homeroom, huh?"

"No," I whispered. The anxiety that had evaporated during Nick and Malcolm's altercation suddenly reared its ugly head and my hands began to shake. Nick glanced down at my hands and I immediately gripped my bag as tightly as could.

"Well, Potter, I don't know about you, but I'm not spending an already shitty Monday getting ripped a new one by Headmaster Alexander. So, what do you say? You want to cut?"

I nearly laughed out loud. Cut school? Me? The idea was ludicrous. I'd never skipped school a day in my life that hadn't been absolutely necessary and accompanied by parental permission. I'd never even considered it. Not in my entire career as a student had I ever gotten a demerit, and cutting an entire day of school would undoubtedly result in an avalanche of demerits.

But who the heck cared about demerits now? I was lucky the school had allowed me back in, and even luckier if by chance a parent-approved college would actually accept me after this mess. As far as my parents were concerned, they weren't even speaking to me.

"I can't," I whispered, already second-guessing myself. "What if we got caught?"

Nick grinned deviously. "Then, Potter, I guess we'll be sharing a jail cell together."

The sound of the headmaster's office door opening caught our attention. Malcolm came out first and his angry gaze immediately sought me out. "I don't know why I'm getting demerits because she's a fucking whore!" he spat.

God, I couldn't take much more. No, I couldn't take *any* more. How could people like Malcolm, who'd slept with half the girls in school, judge someone like me, who'd only been with one person? Once.

"If you continue to be unable to control yourself, Mr. Widom, your punishment will be double," Mr. Inglefield snapped.

"Louise," he said, turning toward the still wide-eyed secretary. "Please call Mr. Widom's parents. Inform them that their presence here is required in an important disciplinary matter."

"Thirty seconds, Potter," Nick said under his breath as his gaze slid to the reception door, "before you get called in there…"

Both excitement and anticipation rose in my gut. I knew once I was called into the headmaster's office, I would be forced to relive every excruciating moment again. I would have to see that vile sheet of paper and know that not only had Mr. Inglefield taken a good look at it, but the headmaster had also seen it. My parents would be called, I would be sent home "for my own good," but home wasn't going to be any better than school. There nobody would speak to me, only judge me.

"With or without you," Nick whispered.

"Miss Potter," Mr. Inglefield called out.

Nick bolted for the door and Mrs. Halverson shot up straight. "Nicholas!" she shouted, "Don't you dare!"

My legs were shaking, my eyes were darting back and forth between Mr. Inglefield, Mrs. Halverson, and Nick as he disappeared out into the hallway.

Oh God, who even cared anymore? My life was already ruined as far as my family was concerned. High school was ruined for me, and most likely college as well. I jumped to my feet just as Mrs. Halverson fled into the hallway and grabbed the door before it closed.

"Miss Potter!" I heard bellowed from behind me as my body leapt into action. I ran as fast as I could, my heart pounding in my chest. It took me a couple of seconds to pass Mrs. Halverson. Nick was already at the end of the hallway, nearly to the exit doors, and I pushed myself harder.

"Nick!" I screamed as I slammed into the shoulder of a bewildered student passing by. "Wait for me!"

"Not a chance in hell!" he yelled back, already pushing through the double doors. "'68 Ford Torino," he called out. "Red and black!"

Duh. I knew his car. Everyone in school knew Nick's car. It was the only car in the parking lot that wasn't brand new with a luxury brand name. I pumped my arms and legs harder, running faster than I'd ever run before. Mere heartbeats later I was slamming open the exit doors, barely able to hear the screams of Mrs. Halverson over the pounding of my heart.

I heard the engine before I saw it, the rough start-up sound I'd only ever associated with muscle cars and motorcycles. Panicking, I immediately veered left toward the rumbling noise. I wove quickly through the neat rows of shiny Mercedes, BMWs, and Cadillac SUVs until I saw the Torino, heard the squealing tires as Nick threw it into reverse and hit the gas. I watched his white taillights turn red and then he was flying through the parking lot at record speed—away from me—and my heart sank. I slowed my run to a jog and then stumbled to a walk, breathing hard, tears burning in my eyes.

Now what was I going to do? This was infinitely worse than if I'd actually gotten away. The punishment for trying to get away was going to be just as severe, and yet I hadn't even been able to experience actually getting away.

"Potter!"

I whipped around and found that Nick hadn't left me at all but had instead circled through the parking lot and was idling at the end of the row I was in.

"Katherine!" came a feminine yell from the opposite end of the row. I shot out, running again, slamming into the passenger door of Nick's car and fumbling with the door handle. Once I was in, the door barely closed, Nick slammed on the gas and I shot forward, only to be restrained by a strong arm across my chest.

"Seat belt," he said, pushing me backward.

Still holding me back, Nick let go of the steering wheel, shifted into second gear one-handed, then grabbed the steering wheel and made a sharp, squealing right out of the school parking lot. Holding my breath, I frantically grabbed for my seat belt, yanking it across my body and quickly clicking it into place. Nick pulled his arm from under the seat belt and immediately shifted gears again.

"Grab my smokes," he said, pointing to the glove box. With shaking hands, I reached forward and pulled open the glove box. But instead of a pack of cigarettes, I found a plastic bag with what I knew was marijuana inside and several rolled joints.

"Potter," Nick said, holding his hand out. "Give it here."

Grabbing the bag, I pulled it out and handed it to him. Moments later he was lighting up one of his joints and reaching for his stereo. Loud, masculine yelling poured from the speakers, cursing and growling with what sounded like banging on garbage cans with a wooden spoon.

Nick held out the joint as he blew out a large cloud of potent, yet sweet-smelling, smoke.

"Um, no thanks!" I yelled, trying to be heard over the music.

The next thing I knew, Nick was yanking the steering wheel to the right and slamming on the brakes. My arms shot out as my seat belt tightened, and I braced myself against the dashboard until the car came to a jerking stop on the side of the road. Nick, with the joint in his mouth, turned off the music, unbuckled his seat belt, and faced me.

"Katherine," he said slowly, "I saw that video. The entire student body saw it. The entire town saw it. My dad saw it, hell, even my grandma saw it. How many hits did that shit get on YouTube before it was taken down? Hundreds of thousands.

"The world is a sick place," he continued as he took another drag from his joint. "People see a tagline like 'Watch a virgin get her cherry popped,' and they're going to look. Then they're going to judge. You got judged and the judgment wasn't in your favor. I know what getting judged feels like, I live it every day, but the difference between you and me is I don't give a shit."

I pressed my lips together as my chin started to tremble. Why was he doing this to me?

"You've got a month until summer break and then another year you're going to have to spend inside that hellhole, and believe me when I tell you, those assholes are not going to let you forget that your naked ass was de-virginized on the Internet by the son of a senator of this great fucking state of ours. They are going to shove that shit in your face every chance they get."

My chest constricted. Why did everyone insist I keep reliving this? Enough was enough. I was there, I knew what happened, and I was there for the fallout too. Yet it just kept coming, leaving me feeling like I would never outrun this. Leaving with Nick had been a mistake. I should have just stayed in school.

"Thanks," I whispered through trembling lips. "But I don't need to be lectured on what I already know."

"You can let it break you," he continued, ignoring me. "Or you can let it make you stronger. You can walk back inside that school tomorrow, look into the eyes of every motherfucker staring you down, trying to break you, and instead of hiding, instead of running, you can smile at them, telling them you don't give a fuck what they think."

He held out the joint again. "Cheers, Potter. To not giving a fuck."

I stared at him for a moment, at his dark, unwavering gaze, his striking cheekbones, the firm line of his lips. But most of all, I drank in the sincerity in his voice. Because of that, this time I took the offering and slowly brought it my lips.

"Small drags at first," he said, "not like a cigarette."

I let out a shaky laugh. "I've never smoked a cigarette."

The corners of his mouth lifted and he shook his head. "Why am I not surprised?"

One deep breath later, I had the tip of the joint between my lips and took a small inhale. Hot smoke filled my mouth then slid down my throat, burning softly as it exploded into my lungs.

"Hold it in," Nick said and I did as he asked.

"Blow it out," he said when I felt I might explode from lack of oxygen. As I released my breath, smoke exploded from my mouth, tickling the back of my throat and forcing me to cough the rest of the way through it.

When I was done coughing up my insides with my hand over my throbbing chest, I glanced up at Nick through watery eyes.

He grinned. "One more time, Potter."

Feeling light-headed, kind of like I'd had a beer, but different, I found myself smiling at him.

And I did it, one more time.

~~~~

"How are you feeling?"

At the sound of Nick's voice, I squinted through the glaring sun, then rolled my head to the left, felt the itchy blades of grass below me tickle against my cheek as I smiled at him.

"I feel weird," I admitted. "Relaxed and kinda stupid and sorta hungry."

Nick burst out laughing. "Sounds about right."

Maybe an hour or so ago, Nick had driven straight into an empty field with no trees, no homes, nothing but grass and wildflowers and sunshine. At first we'd sat on the hood of his car, not speaking, just smoking until we grew warm and lethargic. Then Nick had hopped off the car and yanked off his tie and his button-down shirt, revealing his surprisingly heavily tattooed chest and arms, then kicked off his boots and his socks and rolled his pants up before stretching out in the grass. I followed suit, toeing out of my loafers and knee socks, losing my tie, and untucking my blouse. Then I lay down beside him, closed my eyes, and lost myself to the sun and my thoughts for a while.

"I'm eighteen," he said, startling me. "I was held back in kindergarten."

I wrinkled up my nose. "Huh?"

Nick grinned. "You just asked me how I was able to get tattooed."

I drew my brows together. "I did? I thought I was only thinking that…"

"Beginner's mistake." He laughed and I laughed with him.

"I've kind of always wanted one," I admitted. "But my mother says tattoos are for prostitutes and criminals."

Nick snorted. "Right. And yet the same could be said about country clubs."

Smiling, I turned away and closed my eyes again. If only I could stay like this forever. Relaxed, smiling, not worrying about the thoughts running through the minds of my peers while they stared at me, whispered about me, judged me.

I didn't want to ever go back to school. Or home, for that matter. In fact, running away seemed like an infinitely better option. I could change my name, color my hair, get colored contacts, and somehow obtain a fake birth certificate and Social Security card. It had to be possible; it happened in movies all the time.

I cracked an eyelid at Nick. "So, did you really show Chelsea your… um…" I trailed off, feeling my face grow hot with embarrassment.

"My dick?" he finished, sounding the complete opposite of how I felt. "Yeah."

I stared at him. "Why? I mean, you had to know you were going to get in a lot of trouble for that."

He gave a halfhearted shrug. "It's not as if they're going to kick me out. My father paid for the new music program, not to mention the entire remodeling our freshman year. None of the shit I do ever gets put on my permanent record."

Before I could respond, Nick sat up in the grass. "Your turn."

With my palms flat against the ground, I pushed myself into an upright position. "My turn for what?"

"To answer a question." He plucked a long, thick strand of grass from the ground and popped it into his mouth.

My stomach flip-flopped. He was going to ask about the video. Other than my sudden Internet popularity, I wasn't at all interesting. My life revolved around schoolwork and hanging with friends and shopping, and that was it. I didn't have any cool stories to tell, at least nothing that Nick would be curious about.

"You can stop looking like you might puke, Potter. I was only going to ask why the hell you were with Matthews in the first place. Everyone knows what a first class douchebag the guy is."

My shoulders slumped as I released a heavy sigh. Nick might not be asking about the video but he was still asking about… *him*. Trevor Matthews—short, spiky brown hair and a pair of chocolate-brown eyes, the face of movie star and a body to match, and my former boyfriend. Or rather, the jerk who had never been my boyfriend at all but instead was following through on a bet with his friends as to how long it would take to get me in bed. Something that had ended up being videotaped, without my knowledge, for proof of his success. But even as horrible as that was, he had to take it one step further and post it to YouTube, then send the link to every e-mail in-box at school. Every. Single. One.

"He's good-looking," I admitted in a small voice. "And really popular."

Nick frowned and I dropped my gaze, realizing how shallow I sounded. Suddenly all the humiliation and pain I'd been feeling flooded back in and I hurriedly swiped at the first two tears that fell but it was a lost cause. There was too much emotion built up inside of me; I was overflowing with it, bursting at the seams, but I was finally alone. Even if Nick was here, he said he wouldn't judge me, and I didn't know when I'd get another chance like this, to just let go, to let all this pain go.

"I was stupid!" I screamed as I scrambled to my feet, glaring down at Nick through waterlogged eyes. "Okay? I admit it! I was a fucking idiot! Are you happy now?"

Nick shot to his feet. "At least you realize it now!" he yelled back. "Before you end up married to a man like Trevor or worse, like his father!"

"Married?" I yelled back as my tears turned to angry sobs. "No one of any importance will ever marry me now! No good school will accept me! I've failed my family!"

"Fuck your family!" he roared. "Fuck my family, fuck your family, fuck Trevor and his asshole friends! Fuck those stupid bitches that you thought were your friends! They don't matter, Katherine! You're going to turn eighteen next year and hopefully you're going to get the hell out of Dodge, get as far away from these people as fast as you can! I know I am! You think I want to inherit my father's money or his business? FUCK NO! My entire life I've begged him to let me take guitar lessons, to let me go to music camp, to let me do something, anything music-related but he always shot me down! But am I going to let that stop me? FUCK NO! As soon as I graduate, even though I don't have a clue where I'll go and how I'll get there, I'm out!"

Shaking from head to toe, tears streaming down my face, I clenched my hands into fists and slammed them against my thighs. "I want out!" I screamed. "I want out, too!"

And I kept screaming, yelling and screaming until I was no longer forming coherent words but instead just shrieking, sobbing, and screaming at the top of my lungs.

Strong arms wrapped around me, fighting with me to keep still, but I continued to thrash, continued to scream and cry, unable to stop what I'd begun. Nick wrestled me to the ground and into his lap, keeping both his arms around me as he dropped his face against my shoulder and squeezed me tightly.

"Breathe," he whispered. "Just breathe, Katherine."

I don't know how long we stayed that way, me thrashing and screaming in his lap, him holding me tightly, softly hushing me like a mother would their crying child. Eventually I slumped in his arms, crying softly now, my voice hoarse, my throat burning. Finally exhausted, I closed my eyes and drifted off to sleep.

~~~~

"I always knew," Nick said quietly as he reached across the small space between us and pulled a piece of grass from my hair. Lying beside me on his belly, he put the strand in his mouth and smiled at me.

"Knew what?" I asked.

"That you were different from them."

Caught off guard, I blinked several times. "But I'm not," I protested. "If I were, this never would have happened to me."

"You are," he replied. "I've known it since third grade."

My eyes went wide. "What?"

Lifting his head, Nick spit out the mangled grass. "Mr. Adholm's class," he said. "You raised your hand during one of his many longwinded speeches on the importance of the yearly Forbes employment list and said, 'But those can't be the most important jobs in the world. What about the people who make stuff? Or fix stuff? Those jobs are important too, aren't they?'"

My lips parted. I'd gotten in trouble for that statement. Nothing too severe, just a talking-to after class and a phone call to my parents, who'd given me another talking-to. Other than that, it was forgotten.

"Life isn't worth living," my father had said, "if you have nothing to show for it when you're gone."

Money. He'd meant money. All he ever talked about was money.

"My mom was a ballerina before she married my dad," Nick continued. "Everything about her was soft and beautiful. She always told me that it didn't matter if I was a plumber or a banker, that as long as I was happy, she would be happy."

I didn't say anything. I remembered, back in middle school, when Nick's mom had accidentally overdosed on prescription pain pills.

Everybody remembered. Nick disappeared for the rest of the year and when he'd returned the following fall, he wasn't the same person.

"I'm sorry," I whispered hoarsely. "I remember her, she was so beautiful."

"She was," he agreed. "But my father crushed her. Turned her into a tired and bitter woman."

He shifted slightly, lifting off the ground and pointing to his chest where he had several large sparrows tattooed. "This was my first one," he said, placing his hand overtop the sparrow on his heart. "For my mother. The ancient Egyptians believed that sparrows would catch the souls of those who had died. Later, sailors began the tradition of having a sparrow tattooed on them in hopes that if they died at sea, the sparrow would carry their spirit to heaven." His dark eyes bored into mine and even in the fading sunlight, I could see an intensity burning from within them. "A sparrow is also a symbol for finding your freedom."

He reached for me again; this time his hand landed on my cheek. "Don't let what happened to my mother happen to you," he said forcefully. "Don't let them break you down."

I swallowed hard. "I won't," I whispered.

"Promise me," he whispered back, bringing his face close to mine.

Tears welled in my eyes. After weeks of feeling so incredibly alone, shunned and hated and laughed about, this boy, this man that I'd known all my life yet had never really known at all, had somehow reversed all that damage within a matter of hours, leaving me feeling stronger than I had this morning, maybe even stronger than I'd ever felt before.

"I promise," I choked out a mere heartbeat before Nick's lips met mine.

It was such a sweet, simple kiss, only lips against lips and no pressure for more, but in shock, my brain stalled out and then as soon as it had rebooted again, I was pushing Nick off me, rolling away from him and jumping to my feet.

"Is that what this was about?" I screamed. "You think I'm easy? You thought if you took me out of there that I would sleep with you?"

Slowly, Nick pushed himself to his knees but made no move to stand. "No, Potter," he said. "I wasn't even thinking about sex. I just wanted to kiss you, is all."

"Why?" I demanded tearfully.

His brow shot up as did the corners of his mouth. "Why?" he repeated, shaking his head. "Because you're beautiful and smart and you just spent the entire day with me, talking and crying and sleeping in my arms and, fuck, I just wanted to kiss you."

"Oh," I said softly, suddenly feeling very stupid.

Sighing, Nick got to his feet and began brushing all the grass off his pants. "It's getting dark," he said. "Probably should take you home before your parents send out a search party."

Panic rose in my gut. Home? "No!" I cried out, reaching forward and grabbing his arm. "Please, not yet. I can't... Not yet."

Again he cupped my cheek, but made no move to go further. "All right," he said softly. "Then where to?"

My thoughts spun, but ultimately came up empty. "I don't know," I said, feeling defeated.

Nick looked contemplative for a minute. "How about we go get you that tattoo you always wanted?"

I stared up at him. "But I'm not eighteen."

He grinned. "Let's head into the city," he said and held out his hand to me. "I know a guy."

~~~~

"It doesn't even hurt," I said proudly, smirking sideways at Nick from the passenger seat of his car. Snorting, he glanced over at the side of my exposed thigh where my brand new pink lotus, roughly the size of my fist, could be seen in the moonlight.

Nick had told me that my name, Katherine, stood for purity, and one of the symbols for purity was a pink lotus. The artist, an absolutely terrifying man named Spider, covered head to toe in tattoos and piercings, had done an exceptional job on the flower. It was full of bright reds, pinks, and greens, and I was unquestionably in love with it. In fact, I couldn't stop staring at it.

"You were twitchy," Nick said around a mouthful of fries. "But you sat really well."

Grinning, I popped the last bite of my double bacon cheeseburger, and as my mouth flooded with the greasy goodness, I erupted in giggles. My mother absolutely forbade me from ever eating fried food. Almost everything in our house was either gluten-free or cage-free or sodium-free. Everything was free, free, free; but most of all, everything was free of taste.

"Hey," I said, leaning forward to turn up the radio. "I like this song."

"Really?" Nick teased. "No boy band love affairs for you?"

I shot him a look before leaning back in my seat. The window was down, my stomach was full, and for the very first time, I felt strangely alive, exhilarated in a way I'd never known before.

Free.

Nick started humming along to the song and soon he was singing loudly, quite beautifully, overpowering Tom Petty's voice with his own much deeper, smoother one.

I watched him drive and sing, followed with my eyes the strong lines of his features, traveling along his cheekbones, his lips, his jaw, landing on his Adam's apple as it bounced along with his voice. He really was a very good-looking guy. I'd just never really given him a second look, or thought for that matter, before. He'd always kept himself so far removed from everyone at school and in our parents' social circles.

Before I knew it, the car had stopped and Nick was staring at me.

"Where to now?" he asked, still studying me, his eyes eating up my face in a way that had my belly fluttering with anxiety, and not of the unwanted variety.

"I have seventy-eight missed phone calls," I whispered, my gaze locked with his. "And thirty-two text messages. I'm not even sure my voice mail is working anymore."

His lips twisted. "Yeah," he said, fighting a laugh. "Me too. But Halverson knows you left with me, and you know your dad isn't going to do anything stupid like call the cops and end up pissing off my dad."

I knew that. I suppose there was one perk of ditching school and running away with the son of one of the top ten wealthiest men in the world.

"I had so much fun today," I said softly. "I don't want it to end."

Nick's face grew serious and even more handsome in its intensity. "It doesn't have to," he said. "There's tomorrow and the next day and the next day and the day after that and the day after that and there's summer and—"

Leaning forward, I pressed the tips of my fingers to his lips. "I know," I whispered. "And I want that too."

How strange, I mused, what a difference a day truly makes. This morning I'd woken up feeling as it my life was over, and now…

I felt like maybe it was just beginning.

Nick's warm fingers encircled my wrist and pulled my hand away from his mouth. Threading his fingers through mine, he gently tugged on my hand until I moved as far over in my seat as I could.

"And," he prompted, "what else do you want?"

"I want you to kiss me," I said, my voice a barely audible whisper.

"It's a good thing you do," he said, leaning forward in his seat. "Because, Potter, I really fucking like you."

~~~~

I awoke to a heavy weight on top of me, to soft kisses on my lips and cheeks, on my eyelids and forehead and then back down my cheeks. As the weight shifted over top of me, making sure not to touch where I'd just been tattooed, I felt warms lips on my neck. My hands found the top of his head and my fingers wove their way through his unbound hair, grabbing fistfuls and gripping tightly.

"Are you happy, Potter?" he mumbled against my quivering belly.

"Y-y-yes," I whimpered, trembling under the feverish onslaught of his kisses and his touches and from the feel of his bare skin against mine.

I wasn't positive I hadn't made a mistake last night. After being together, I'd fallen asleep in Nick's arms, cuddled in the back seat of his car, not knowing what the morning would bring. But unlike yesterday morning, or that fateful morning three weeks ago, I wasn't terrified of the outcome.

Nick was different from the others; I could feel that truth deep within my bones. In the span of only a day, he'd made me feel more at peace than I could ever remember feeling before and I didn't want to lose that feeling. I wanted to bottle it, keep it with me at all times, safe and sound, protected from the raging storm that had become my life.

I'd never before believed in love at first sight, but this was not my first glimpse of Nick. Instead it was my first glimpse of who Nick truly was, the man behind the eyeliner and angry scowl. Was this love? I didn't know. But it felt as if maybe it could be. Someday.

I felt Nick lift his head and I glanced down my body to find him smiling at me.

"Good," he said. "Remember that, remember how you felt last night and right now… because we have to be at school in an hour."

School. Where everyone would already know what had happened. Where our parents would be waiting for us with the headmaster and all the teachers involved.

"I know," I whispered.

"Promise me," he whispered back.

I promised him. I promised him that I would remember, and then I promised him tomorrow, and the next day, and the next, and the day after that. I promised him summer, and then I promised him fall.

And as he made love to me, he promised me too.

~~~~

Nick shut off the engine, pulled his keys from the ignition, and turned to look at me. "Ready?" he asked.

As I placed my hand on the door handle, I shook my head no but then whispered, "Yes."

"We got this," he said softly, reaching for my cheek. The pad of his thumb swept over my lips. "Worse comes to worst, I'll just threaten my dad with all the dirt I have on him, then he'll threaten your dad and the headmaster and everyone will slink back into their respective corners."

I stared into his eyes believing every word he said, trusting him completely. It was such a foreign feeling to me, knowing that I could finally count on someone other than myself, knowing that not everyone was selfish, single-minded, and out to get me.

As we stared at each other a warmth began to blossom inside of me, the likes of which I'd never known before. It spread comfortably through me, giving me a strength I didn't know I had.

"Kiss me," I whispered, leaning forward, wanting him, wanting more of him than just his kisses or his touches but wanting his beautiful soul.

"I can do that," he muttered, bowing his head as his hand slid from my cheek to the back of my neck and pulled me to him.

It wasn't long before I was crawling into his lap, breathing hard as I fumbled with the buttons on his shirt.

Nick's hands encircled my wrists and gently pinned my arms to my side.

"Hold that thought," he said, grinning. "Until we find out whether we're going to be drawn and quartered or tied to the whipping post."

Several deep breaths later, once we were out of the car and winding our way through the parking lot and nearing the front lawn, Nick took my hand in his and squeezed.

"We got this," he repeated as the students mingling on the lawn in small groups came into view.

I squeezed back, straightened my body, squared my shoulders, and then, with my heart in my throat, took that first step onto the walkway. We were nearly halfway down the walk when the animated chatter started to slowly diminish. By the time we reached the bottom step, everyone on the entire lawn had frozen with anticipation, becoming utterly still.

"Slut!"

The sound of Malcolm's voice caused my already skyrocketing adrenaline to implode. My head whipped right as I zeroed in on Malcolm's sneering face and yelled back, "Dickless man-whore!" After a heartbeat, everyone in the entire yard burst into laughter.

Beside Malcolm, Trevor was staring at me, his features masked with shock. Whether he was surprised that I'd had the nerve to call Malcolm out, or because I was wearing obviously wrinkled clothing and my hair was a mess, or because I was holding the hand of the most hated boy at school, I wasn't sure. Maybe all of the above.

But it didn't matter. I locked eyes with him and smiled. It wasn't a nice smile. It was a slow-growing grin that was nothing if not pure menace and vile intent. It was a beautiful gesture turned so blatantly, so deliberately, into something ugly.

"Mr. Shelton, Miss Potter, how nice of you to join us this morning."

Mrs. Halverson stood at the top of the steps, eyeing our clasped hands curiously.

"Your parents are waiting and they have been worried sick," she continued, her gaze finally reaching our faces. "In fact, we all have."

"As you can see," Nick said, his deep voice dripping with sarcasm, "we've neither been killed nor maimed."

"Office," Mrs. Halverson snapped, pointing at the double doors behind her. "Now."

Nick and I glanced at each other and I smiled. "We got this," I said, and for the first time in my life I felt like I really did have something.

And what I had, *my something*, was grinning back at me. Together, hand in hand, we climbed the stairs and followed Mrs. Halverson inside to whatever fate awaited us.

THE END

About the Author

Madeline Sheehan

Madeline Sheehan, a "Social Distortion" enthusiast and devoted fan of body art, has been writing books since she was seven years old. She is the author of *The Holy Trinity* ebook trilogy and best-selling novel, *Undeniable*. Homegrown in Buffalo, New York, Madeline resides there with her husband and son.

Check out her website: https://www.madelinesheehan.com
Or LIKE her on Facebook:
https://www.facebook.com/MadelinesheehanBooks

Rock the Beginning
(*Black Falcon* Prequel to *Rock the Heart*)

by
Michelle A. Valentine

Chapter 1
Freshman year...
LANE

SO THIS IS it? Freshman year. I stand in the pristine hallway of Cedar Creek High School next to my best friend Cassandra Lutz as we survey the same faces we see year after year. Nothing in this town ever changes. I was hoping that I would be wowed in high school—dramatically swept off my feet on my first day by a dashing upper-classmen—living the dream of going to the prom as a freshman. Well, at least it's a big dream of mine.

But sadly, I'm disappointed yet again.

I sigh heavily and lean my back against the red locker and squeeze my books tighter against my chest. I can't wait to get out of here and run off to a big city where I can make something of myself. I've always thought a job in advertising sounded fun. Maybe I'll try that someday.

"Just once I'd love to have some fresh meat in this place," Cassandra says pulling her brown hair into a loose bun on the top of her head. "I hate knowing everything about these guys. There's no mystery. None of them do anything surprising."

I nod in total agreement. "Where are all the guys I read about in books—the ones that know exactly what to say? The first day of school is practically over and nothing remotely exciting has happened yet."

The moment the words leave my mouth, a crash against the lockers a few feet to my right draws my attention. I suddenly feel the urge to take back the last thing I said. This is not exactly the kind of excitement I was hoping for.

All the kids in the hallway stop dead in their tracks in unison and stare at the scene playing out before us like a bad teen sitcom. Roger Robertson, the guy we all know as the school bully, grips Wendell McFarland, a kid in my grade, by the collar of his shirt. Roger's large arms twist as he repositions his wrists in order to get a better grip, while he wears a sickening smile on his red, pimple-covered face. Roger isn't the kind of guy you want to mess with. His temper is about as red-hot as the flaming color of his hair and we all know he's been held back to the freshman level three times now. If Roger walks down the hallway, you get out of his way or duck for cover. His reputation of assholism precedes him.

I instantly feel sorry for Wendell. His tiny, pencil-like frame is no match for the likes of Roger. "Give it up, you fucking pussy." I flinch as Roger yanks Wendell forward and slams him back even harder. "Don't make me tell you again. I know your parents are loaded. Cough up the dough."

Wendell gasps for air as Roger shoves his knuckles into his throat. "I don't have any money."

Another slam and Wendell's glasses slip down the bridge of his nose. "Cough it up you little shit stain."

My mouth gapes open and my eyes grow wide. It's painfully hard to watch. Someone has to stop this.

I glance around. Several of my classmates stand frozen. No one is making a move to stop this outright appalling display of human behavior. This makes me sick. What's wrong with these people? A desperate need to make this stop fills me.

Before I even realize what I'm doing I take a couple quick steps and open my mouth. "Stop it! Leave him alone!"

It's like a movie when a hush falls over the crowd. I know this isn't the smartest move, but I just can't stand by and do nothing to stop this. And, okay, I know the odds of me being able to stop Roger physically are about as good as a one-legged man in an ass-kicking contest, but I can't idly sit by. I wasn't raised that way.

Cassandra grabs my arm and whispers harshly, "Are you crazy, Lanine? What are you doing?"

I pull my arm from her grip and frown as I take in the fear from her brown eyes. I straighten my stance. I have to appear brave. "Someone has to stop this, Cass."

Roger's gaze darts from me to Wendell. His eyes are so brown they almost appear black and the pure venom in them causes my legs to shake. A deep laugh bursts out of his mouth and holds me in place. "What do we have here? Is this your little girlfriend, four-eyes? Is she here to save you?"

"N—no," Wendell stutters.

No one should be able to get away with treating people like this. "Stop it, Roger!"

Roger flings his gaze at me. "Or what, Shirley Temple? You going to make me?"

I stare down at the pink sun-dress I'm wearing. While very cute for my first day of school, it doesn't exactly scream badass, but this guy doesn't know what I'm capable of, so I can't let him rattle my nerves. "I might. Now, leave him alone."

Roger sneers while opening his large hands and makes a show of letting Wendell go. As soon as Wendell is free, he takes off running without looking back to make sure I'm not the one getting pounded now.

Thanks for the back-up, Wendell.

The bully turns to me and taps his lip. "Happy now, Shirley? I let him go, but it seems we have a small problem now."

I lift my chin as Roger stalks towards me with slow steps like a tiger stalking his prey. "What's that?"

"Someone is going to have to pay me. You see, I need money for a new tire and since you chased my little buddy off who was about to pay for it, I guess that leaves you." He grins at me in a way a serial killer would right before he murders his victim.

I grip my books tighter and my hands turn clammy. If he comes at me this Geometry book is going to make one hell of a weapon. "Fat chance. I'm not giving you any money."

He shakes his head as he steps in front of me. "That's where you're wrong. Guy, girl… doesn't matter to me. I'll still beat you into submission in order to get what I need, and what I need from you is money. You're going to get that for me. A nice girl like you seems good for it."

I narrow my eyes. "No, I'm not."

Roger slaps the books from my hands and leans into me like he's about to attack, but a voice stops him. "Listen, bitch—"

"Pick those up." My neighbor and childhood friend, Noel Falcon pushes his way through the crowd. Once he's through, he narrows his eyes at Roger, daring him to cross him. "Pick those up, or I swear to God you'll pay."

The guy in front of me takes a step back and smirks as Noel steps between us, using his body to shield me from Roger. At first I'm scared for Noel's safety, but I quickly notice he's nearly an even match for the guy that's much older than him.

When did he get so tall and buff?

I guess I never noticed Noel's muscles before. The way they stretch his black t-shirt and how board his shoulders have actually gotten has somehow slipped past me all summer long. Granted, I haven't seen him as much as I normally do over the summer. Noel magically became busy every time I asked him to come over and go fishing off the dock behind my house like we always did, which was… strange considering we use to spend all of our time together.

His hair grew too. The shaggy hair he sported last school year as he got into rock music would probably touch his shoulders now if he didn't have it pulled back into a low-set ponytail. I admit, he's looking pretty good.

Roger straightens his shoulders and rocks his neck like a trained fighter before he sets his eyes on Noel. "You'll walk away if you know what's good for you. This is between me and Shirley here."

Noels fingers fold into fists at his side. "I think you got that backwards, fucker. It's you that needs to beat it. No one messes with Lane. No one."

"Brave words. You're going to wish you'd walked away when I gave you the chance after I beat your face in," Roger sneers.

"I'll never walk away from Lane. You fuck with her. You fuck with me." There's a growl in Noel's voice I've never heard before. It's low and threatening. I never knew Noel could be so scary or bad-ass or… hot.

Oh my *God*. What am I thinking? Noel isn't hot. Noel is… Noel, my friend—best friend since kindergarten.

I can't ponder on that last thought too long because Roger's laugh pulls me out of that bubble. Without warning Roger draws his arm back, launching it full force towards Noel's face. Two things happen so quick the scream building in my throat doesn't have time to come out. The first is Noel dodges the blow with ease and blasts Roger in the face first while simultaneously pushing me out of harms way.

I fall to the floor in all the commotion just as Roger tackles Noel and they crash to the ground. At first it appears that Roger has the upper-hand until Noel uses some quick *UFC* style movements and turns the tables. Noel flips Roger onto his back and straddles him before gripping a handful of Roger's shirt in his hand and blasts a right hook into the monster red-head's face.

My mouth gapes open as the boy I've known most of my life defends me like no one else ever has.

A hand grips my shoulder and pulls me up off the floor. "Jesus, Lanie. Are you all right?" Cass asks. "Thank God Noel showed up when he did."

I'm about to agree with her just as the guys roll around in the hallway again and this time Roger's in control. Hell. No.

This weird urge to protect Noel comes over me. I fling myself on Roger's back without thinking ahead any further what I would do next. I wrap my arms around his neck and hold on tight. Not getting anywhere, I get desperate and grab a handful of red hair and yank as hard as I can. "Get off him!"

I ignore the distinct sound of tennis shoes scuffling on the tiled hallway as I tighten my grip on his hair. There's no way I'm letting anyone hurt Noel.

I'm pulled back but I refuse to release my hold on Roger. "Young lady, let him go!"

My head snaps in the direction of lanky man with thinning brown hair I recognize as being my English teacher, Mr. Jones. Then it dawns on me. Oh crap! I'm in deep shit. Dad isn't going to the let the fact that I'm involved in a fight on the first day of school go without some sort of punishment. There's always the argument I was helping someone else that was getting bullied, even though that someone ran off and would probably be too scared to side with me against Roger. Surely one of these witnesses would attest to the fact this all began over Wendell and Roger isn't the innocent victim here.

I loosen my white knuckles and Roger's hair falls free from my hands. "Crazy bitch," Roger mumbles under his breath. "Umph!"

I snicker as Noel brings his knee back down from Roger's groin, shutting him up completely. Roger falls over cupping his crotch in the universal sign that a guy has been nailed in the balls.

Noel stands and kicks Roger in the stomach one time for good measure. "Don't ever talk to her that way again."

Mr. Jones sets me on my feet and turns to scolds the boys. "Knock it off and get to the principals office." I turn to head in the opposite direction, thinking I'm in the clear because I'm a girl. "Not so fast. That means you too."

I stop dead in my tracks and turn slowly on my heel.

Damn. Can't blame me for trying.

Noel smoothes his hair back, tucking the loose strands of hair behind his ear. He touches his tongue to the corner of his mouth and I notice the small cut on his bottom lip.

I tilt my head as I examine the rest of his face. "Are you okay?"

He shakes his fingers like he's trying to get rid of the pain from landing a couple punches to Roger's thick skull. "I'll be okay. What about you? I can't believe you had that in you to attack a guy like that. I haven't seen you go after someone since the third grade over a Barbie."

I shrug. "I couldn't let him hurt you."

Noel's eyes search my face and he swallows hard just as he takes a step towards me, nearly bumping his chest into mine. "I know exactly how you feel."

"Y—you do?" Where is all this nervous energy coming from? I've been in a closer proximity many times with Noel. Why does this time feel different—like all the air around us is charged?

"I said get to the office," Mr. Jones raises his voice causing me to jump and Noel wraps his arms around me. "You two need to get to the office while I finish helping Roger up. Don't make me tell you again."

Noel salutes the teacher and I giggle at his new found attitude of anti-authority. I pull away from Noel and turn towards the office. His steps fall in-line with mine and he reaches down, threading his fingers through mine.

He's held my hand before, but never like this. This moment feels like the beginning of something beautiful.

Chapter 2
One Week Later…
LANE

THE AIR IS cool for a September night in Texas, but my entire body is warm and alive with excitement. Sure, I've snuck out of the house many nights before to meet Noel on this dock for a late night swim before, but this is different. Things have certainly changed quite a bit over the last week.

Somehow over the summer we've gone from best friends to more. We've never really discussed this new territory of hand holding and hugging that we've worked our way into or what it means for us exactly. Maybe the subject will come up tonight.

People at school aren't surprised, I guess. Everyone knows Noel and I are close, so our new bouts of P.D.A don't raise too many eyebrows.

Doesn't mean we're ready to make our parents aware that our long-time friendship has blossomed into more. They'd never let us be along together again.

I tip-toe down the hill to the dock behind my house and allow my eyes to adjust in the moonlight. At the end of the dock Noel leans against the wood railing of the dock with his arms crossed against his chest, waiting for me. I'm not sure what tonight will hold for us, I just know I can't wait to see what unfolds.

A wide grin stretches across his face the moment our eyes meet. The features on his face are well defined like the new physic he acquired over the summer. His blue eyes shimmer with excitement the moment my feet hit the wood on the dock and my breath catches. Every time I see him now it's like my heart skips a beat.

I bite my lip and shove my hair behind my ear as Noel reaches his hand out to me. I slide mine into it without hesitation and my stomach flips.

He pulls me into his side. "I wasn't sure if you were coming."

I tilt my head. "Of course I was. Have I ever stood you up on this dock before?"

He swallows hard and pinches a lock of my long, brown hair before twirling it around his finger. "No, but things are a little different now, aren't they?"

I nod and notice my breathing picks up a notch. "About that… what are we doing?"

Noel's hand trembles a little as he releases my hair and touches my cheek with his fingertips. "I think it's pretty clear."

I know exactly what he's getting at, but I want to hear him say it. "You think so?"

He stands a little straighter and cups my face in his hands while staring into my eyes. "We're falling in love and finally giving into what fate has planned for us."

My heart thuds against my ribs. "Are you saying you love me?"

The grin on his face lights up my entire world. "You know I do. I think I've loved you since we were five. I'm just the idiot who didn't realize how much in love I was until this summer when I found myself getting jealous over any guy I caught looking at you. The feeling that you're meant to be mine won't leave me, and I don't know what to do about it or if you even feel the same way."

"Is that why you stayed away all summer?" I ask.

"Yeah. I was hoping it would go away and we could stay friends, but all that went to hell that first day of school when I saw you and you needed me to help you. I knew then I could never be just your friend. I'm always going to want more with you. I feel like you're my forever or something."

Emotions from within me take over and tears well-up in my eyes. "It might've taken me a little longer to come to the same conclusion, but I feel exactly the same way."

Noel's thumbs trace over my cheeks. "I love you, Lane."

I smile as a tear falls free from my eye. "I love you too."

He leans in and presses his lips to mine. My eyes drift shut and I fall into his kiss—fall into him. This is everything I never knew I always wanted. His lips part and mine move in sync with his until he finally slips his tongue in my mouth. This isn't my first kiss, but it is the first time I've ever felt something kissing a boy. It's like tasting my future and I can picture my entire life in my mind—a life with Noel.

With more skill than I knew we both possessed, we slide down to the floor of the dock without breaking our kiss. I grip hands full of his shirt and he teases the skin on my back just under the hem of my blouse. This is moving entirely too fast, but I can't find a logical reason in my brain to stop the madness. Being so close to Noel feels incredible and I don't want it to end.

Noel lies back, pulling me on top of him, allowing me to feel the bulge in his jeans against my thigh.

I'm scared as hell, but the way his lips move against the soft skin on my neck makes it a little less intimidating. "We don't have to go any further than you're ready for, Lane." He says—his breath hot and tempting on my flesh.

I press a feather-light kiss on his cheek. "I love you and I'm ready. We aren't strangers, and I can't think of one other person I would rather experience all my firsts with."

Noel tucks my hair behind my ear. "I want to be your only."

There's no fighting against that. That kind of magical romance is something all girls dream about. I'm just lucky I've found my prince so soon.

"I want you to be my forever," I tell him before he crushes his mouth to mine and we head into our forever.

Chapter 3
End of Junior Year…
NOEL

THE DRUMS POUND out the last few beats of the song and I grin as I look at my band mates. "Yeah! I think we finally nailed it!"

Sam, the drummer taps the high-hat with his drumstick. "Finally! It only took us fifteen tries. You have to stop being such a fucking perfectionist, Noel, or well never have enough of our own songs to make a demo. We can't keep spending more than a month on one song."

"We need to have our shit together because after graduation next year we need to get on the road and find paying gigs like we talked about," I answer and then run my fingers down the thread of the guitar.

"We need to play more covers," Leon says, scratching the back of his shaggy head. "That's what people want to hear."

I stare at the two other guys in the band dumfounded. Sam pushes his glasses up the bridge of his nose and glances toward Leon as they wait on me to say something. Don't they see that originality is everything in the music business? Labels want bands that are different. We have to stand out and be the best.

I shake my head and smooth my dark hair back into my pony tail. "We're going to practice our own shit until our fingers bleed. We have to be on point if we want a record deal. Don't you guys want that?"

Leon shrugs and sets his bass in its case. "We do, but we aren't obsessed with it the way you are."

I open my mouth to protest, but Sam cuts me off. "Leon and I have been talking."

I narrow my eyes. "About what?"

Sam shoves his fingers through his bright-red hair. "We aren't going with you after graduation."

I shake my head. Unbelievable. These two jackasses are supposed to be my best friends—the guys who have the same goal as me. "We've talked about this!" I throw my head back and growl. "What the fuck, guys? I thought we were taking Thunder Dome on the road as soon as schools over?"

Leon sighs and his scrawny shoulders slump a bit. "I'm a senior, dude. My mom had me fill out some college applications, and I got into a few, some offered scholarships. I'm heading to Kentucky University next fall on nearly a full ride. I can't pass that up."

"Who gives a shit about college, man? We have a great thing going here with this band. We could really be something one day. Don't you want that?" I argue. Why would anyone pass on the opportunity to become a rock star verses going to college. That's so fucking lame.

"I know you don't like it, Noel, but I'm applying to colleges as well. Music will always be there. You should think about going too, and once we get done with school, maybe we'll try then." I study the freckles on Sam's face as he speaks and try not to completely lose my shit while he's talking.

College will never be an option for me. Never. It takes me five times longer to read something than the rest of the kids in my L.D. class. Having Dyslexia hasn't been a fucking picnic in high school. Things get so jumbled in my brain and I know there's no way in hell I can make it through college courses.

I'm so glad Lane and I are on the same page about this.

"Whatever. You guys do whatever you feel like you have to do. I'm going on the road as planned as soon as we graduate next year. Lane will travel with me while I play solo shows until I find a band to hook up with." Both guys look at each other with an expression on their face that almost looks like pity and it makes my blood boil. "You know what, fuck you guys!"

"Noel…" Sam tries to stop me as I unplug my guitar and flip it around to rest against my back. "Don't be like that, man. We're just trying to be honest with you. Do you know what the odds are of us actually making it in the music industry? Slim to none. I'm just trying to be realistic. We need to go to college. It's the sensible thing to do."

I throw my hands on my hips. "You know what's sensible? Following your dream when you have the talent and the drive. I know I'm going to make it. It's okay if you guys don't believe in me. Lane does, and she's the only person I need to believe in me."

I turn to walk out of the Sam's garage just as Leon says, "You don't know Lanie as well as you think. Seems to me like you two have different ideas about the future."

I whirl around. "What's that suppose to mean? I know my girlfriend—better than she knows herself."

Leon shrugs indifferently. "Maybe you do, but that doesn't explain why she was in the guidance counselor's office getting college applications today if she isn't planning on going."

I shake my head and storm out the door. "Whatever."

I rub the back of my neck as I walk towards my black Chevelle and pull the strap from around my neck and lay the guitar along the backseat. Surely Lane would tell me if she had doubts about the plan we've had in place since we became official our freshman year. She wouldn't just leave me hanging. We're forever and there's no way I can spend years without her on the road.

I slam the door once I'm inside and fire up the engine. It roars to life and the only thing on my mind is finding out if Leon's claim has legs.

A few minutes later I park in Lane's driveway. This place has been like a second home to me since I was a little kid. I love her parents as if they are my own—another reason why we are perfect for each other.

The white cape code with a red roof, shutters and door fits perfectly into the scenery next to Cedar Creek Lake. It looks happy, like Lane. I love living on the water, and someday when I'm a famous rock star I'm going to buy a place on a lake for Lane and I to live in and start a family. She'll love that.

I knock on the door and step back as Lane's dad opens the door. He grins the moment he see's me. "Hi, Noel. How are you, son?"

I shove my hands in the pockets of my jeans. "I'm fine, Jim. Is Lane here?"

Jim scratches his dark bearded jaw-line and nods. "She's down at the dock, fishing, I think. You're welcome to grab a pole from the garage if you like."

"Thanks. I think I'll do that."

Jim steps out of the house, closing the door behind him, and pulls out a set of keys from his pocket. "Let me unlock the man-door for you."

I follow Jim inside the garage. It's funny as a kid I thought he was a huge man, but now at seventeen my height nearly matches his six foot frame. Time really does change everything.

He hands me a black rod. "She should have bait down there."

After I thank Lane's dad, I make my way down the hill to the dock. There's always a certain level of comfort that falls over me when I come out here. Most of the major events in my life have taken place on this very dock—bonding with Lane, telling her I loved her, and even our first time together has all happened out here. This is most definitely our spot.

I lay my pole down and sneak down to where Lane sits on the edge, dangling her feet over the end. I place my hands over her eyes. "Guess who?"

She grins. "Um, Ryan Reynolds."

I laugh and kiss her cheek. "Fuck Ryan Reynolds. You've got Noel Falcon, and I'm much better."

"I don't know..." she trails off in a sing-song voice.

"That's it," I growl and tackle her down to the dock and straddle her.

Lane squeals as I tickle her ribs and kiss her neck. "Stop! You're going to make me pee."

I laugh. "Never. Not until you tell me I'm the best."

She tries to catch her breath. "A little conceited, aren't we?"

"Only when it comes to you—I know I'm the best man for you."

She adjusts her back against the wood and I smooth her hair back from her face. "You'll get no argument from me."

I grin and lean in and kiss her lips. "That's good to know."

As much as I want to take this to the next level I know I can't. Her parents could be watching us out their back window and wouldn't that be awkward for all of us. I pull back and push myself up so I can sit next to her.

After helping her back up to a sitting position, I grab my pole and begin to poke around in the tackle box to find some plastic bait.

"How was band practice?" Lane asks.

I stiffen a bit, knowing the fact that this conversation will probably lead to an argument, and I hate when we fight. "Not good. The guys are both punking-out on going on the road after graduation. Looks like it'll just be me and you." I cast my line into the water and I notice Lane fidgets a bit. The best thing to do is get things in the open. "Leon has this crazy idea that you don't want to go either. He's not right, is he?"

She doesn't look at me as she cranks her reel. "I want to go with you. You know that. But, I think maybe going to college first is a pretty good idea."

I roll my eyes. "Not you too. Come on, Lane. We've talked about this a million times. Don't you want freedom? The chance to go on the open road together before we have to face all that grown-up shit, like bills that people always bitch about."

Lane sighs. "It's not that easy, Noel."

"Yes it is, Lane. Do you want to be with me or not?"

Her head snaps in my direction. "Of course I do. Why would you even say something like that?"

"Because if you want to be with me, then we have to be together."

"Then why don't you enroll in a college with me."

I shake my head. "You of all people know I can't do that."

"I'll help you." She places her hand on my thigh. "We can get through school together just like we do everything else."

"Not college. I'm not cut out for it and I can't go. Not even for you." The moment the words leave my mouth I instantly regret them.

Lane's face twists. "You're an asshole."

She shoves herself up from the dock and takes off, sprinting towards her house.

"Fuck," I curse myself as I break into a full run to chase her down. She makes it half-way up the hill before I grab her from behind and spin her around in my arms. Her breaths are ragged and her olive skin flushes. "I'm an idiot. I'm sorry. You know I didn't mean it the way it sounded."

A tear streams down her cheek. "I don't get you, Noel. Is music so important to you that'd you'd throw everything we have away to get it?"

I shake my head, but I know it would be a difficult choice. "No. You're all that matters to me."

"Then show me," she whispers.

I wipe away her tears with my thumbs before I press my lips to hers. "I will."

Chapter 4
One Year Later—Graduation Night…
NOEL

THERE ARE AT least ten parties going on tonight, and we're going to make our rounds, but first, Lane wants me to meet her on the dock for a private celebration. I grin to myself knowing this will be the last night we have to hide in order to have sex. This time tomorrow Lane and I will be out on the open road, making our way with no solid plan, going in whatever direction the music takes us.

I know she has her doubts. She expresses them nearly everyday, but I know she doesn't really mean them. Once I get her out on the road everything will be fine. I just have to prove it to her that I can make it as a musician. I want her to be proud of me.

She's already waiting for me at the end of the dock. Her long brown hair falls in waves around her shoulders. The loose strands blow idly in the light breeze coming in off the lake. A tight jean skirt and cream color shirt accentuates the deep tan she's already gotten even though it's only the beginning of summer. My girl is so damn beautiful. I'm a very lucky guy.

Excitement overtakes me and I rush down and scoop her up in my arms, lifting her off the ground. "We did it, babe. Can you believe it?"

She laughs in my arms. "I'm so proud of you, Noel."

I nuzzle my nose into her hair. "Not as proud as I am of you. You aced every single test they threw at you. You're a fucking geniuses. When I become a famous rock star, I'll pay for your tuition—anywhere you want to go."

"Noel—"

I cut her off, not allowing her a chance to argue with me. "Anywhere. I won't take no for an answer."

Lane frowns. "I can't let you do that."

I furrow my brow. "Of course you can. You'll deserve it. It'll make the little bit of struggle we have to go through at first totally worth it."

"Noel—" I cut her off again while I go on about the fancy house and cars I'm going to buy her, and she pushes on my chest.

I frown and set her on her feet. "What's wrong?"

Her delicate fingers rub her forehead before running through her hair. "I don't know how to tell you this."

I trail my hand up the bare skin on her arm and then stop when it reaches a strand of her hair. I wrap it around of my finger suddenly nervous about what she has to say. There's a slight quiver in her voice, and that's never a good sign. That only happens to her when she's nervous, and there's not one thing she should be nervous to tell me.

I lick my lips. "Whatever it is, just tell me. We'll get through it together."

Lane shakes her head. "This time we won't."

I take her face in my hands and force her to look into my eyes. "Lane, you're not making any sense."

She closes her eyes. "This is so hard."

I feel her tense under my touch as a tear falls down her face and my heart falls to the pit of my stomach. Lane never cries and it's something I can't stand to see. "Please don't cry. Baby, I'll fix it. Whatever it is, I'll fix it."

She opens her green eyes and stares at me, her eyes searching my face for answers. "Don't leave tomorrow."

I flinch. "The way you just said that makes it sound like I'll be leaving by my self."

"You will be if you go," she whispers.

I shake my head. "No. You promised you were going with me."

"I can't go with you, Noel."

I drop my hands from her face. "What do you mean, you can't? We talked about this since freshman year."

"Exactly," she cries. "We had no clue what we were talking about back then. Things change, Noel. I don't know why this is such a huge shock to you. I've been telling you for the last year that I want to go to college."

"I didn't think you were serious. Damn, Lane. Why are you waiting until just now to tell me this? We had a plan."

"*You* had a plan. Not me. Not one time have you asked me what I wanted!"

I close my eyes and pinch the bridge of my nose. "Yes I have."

"No. No you haven't. Have you heard anything I said about going to college and living in a dorm?"

"I heard you. I just didn't think you were serious." I sigh. "I can't believe you'd pick going to college over being with me."

"That's the same way I feel every time you pick music over me."

"I never pick music over you!"

"No? If I won't go with you, are you going to go anyway?" she challenges.

"Yes! Because that's been our plan," I raise my voice, completely frustrated by this blindside. "Music is my fucking life. You know that. It's all I have."

"You had me." Lane bites her plump, bottom lip as forces a cry back. "Then this is the end for us."

My heart squeezes so hard in my chest that panic starts setting in. "Please, Lane. Don't do this."

She kisses my cheek. "Goodbye, Noel."

My body turns completely numb as she turns and runs away from me. I should pull it together and go after her and force her to understand and try harder at convincing her to come with me, but I can't move. The idea that Lanie Vance is no longer mine hits me hard and I drop to my knees, shaking uncontrollably. I grab my hair in my hands and allow myself to cry for the loss of the only girl I'll ever really love.

About the Author

Michelle A. Valentine

Michelle A. Valentine is a Central Ohio nurse turned *New York Times* & *USA Today* bestselling author of erotic and New Adult romance. Her love of hard-rock music, tattoos, and sexy musicians inspired her erotic *BLACK FALCON* series.

Represented by Jill Marsal of Marsal Lyon Literary Agency
Facebook: https://www.facebook.com/michelle.valentine.7923?fref=ts
Twitter: @M_A_Valentine
Blog: http://michelleavalentine.blogspot.com/p/about-me.html

The Marriage Clause

By
Nikki Worrell

Chapter One

CARRIE MCDERMOTT'S GREAT Uncle Smitty was a cranky old man. He was what you might call the black sheep of the family. Smitty didn't have much to do with any of them, but for some reason, he tolerated Carrie, and she in turn loved the old coot.

No one understood what it was, exactly, that he liked about her. It wasn't that she wasn't a perfectly nice child, but what was it about her that made her more tolerable to him than anyone else in the family? In the beginning, the family had tried inviting him to visit during the holidays, but he always said he had too much work to do to be able to get away. Carrie had only met him a handful of times, but at the age of ten, she asked to go visit him. Shocking everyone, he said "fine".

Carrie and her family lived in hot, humid Tampa Bay, Florida while Smitty lived in Lincoln, Montana where the population was just over one thousand. His one hundred and sixty acre property was beautifully located with a backdrop of snow capped mountains. Smitty was a rancher who bred Morgan horses. They were beautiful creatures. He would prefer to be with them over humans seven days a week and twice on Sunday. Except for Carrie.

Carrie's visits to Uncle Smitty became a yearly event until it was time for her to go off to college. Even then, she kept in touch with him via e-mail and occasional phone calls (which really weren't very productive). When she finished her degree in interior design, the first thing she did was take some time off to visit him.

They spent the better part of that summer together, Smitty just as cranky as ever.

"Why do you always come back here, girl? Ain't you got someone else to bother?" Smitty was always saying things like that. It didn't bother Carrie though. She knew he was a softy underneath his gruff exterior.

"Aw, Uncle Smitty, now don't go gettin' all sentimental on me." With a wink in his direction, Carrie turned to take the apple pie out of the oven she had baked with apples harvested from the tree behind the house. "Dinner will be ready in about an hour. Why don't you go make sure the horses were put to rest for the night and then grab a whiskey while you wait? I hear your favorite rocker out there on the porch callin' to ya." Smitty liked to hear Carrie sounding like the locals. Her normal speech was too stuffy. It only took a couple of days back on the ranch for Carrie to sound like a local. He knew she only did it for him though.

"Well, I'll say one thing for ya, girl. You know what an old man needs at the end of a long day." That was about as close to an "I love you" as she was likely to ever get.

Smitty showed his love for her in other ways. When he came back from town, she would notice a bouquet of daisies on the table in a mason jar. He knew they were her favorite flowers, and she knew better than to thank him for them. Little gifts like that would show up from time to time. When she did dare mention them, he'd just humph and walk away.

Carrie noticed on her last trip out there that he was a bit slower than he'd been. Admittedly, he was getting up there in age although no one knew exactly how old he was. She guessed he was somewhere between seventy-five and eighty-five years old. His ranch hands had been taking on more of the day to day operations giving Smitty more time to rest, and they did a fine job at it. Most of them had been there for ten plus years. His foreman, George, had been there almost twenty years.

After a dinner of pot roast, potatoes and corn bread, Carrie took their dessert out to the porch. It was a beautiful Montana night. Stars didn't look the same in Florida as they did there. It just seemed like there were a million more in the Montana skies. It was getting cooler, so Carrie covered Smitty up with a blanket.

"I don't need no blanket. Why you treatin' me like an old man all the sudden like?" She really wasn't. She'd brought a blanket out for herself too.

"Fine. Give it here Uncle. I'll use both of them." She knew he wouldn't really let her take it, and she was right. He tugged it back with a grumble, almost dropping his pie.

"I'll keep the dang blanket, girl. Sit down and eat your pie. It's good."

"Such glowing praise, Uncle Smitty! Thank you!" She earned a lip curl for her sass. As far as she knew, she was the only one who could make him 'smile'.

"So what are you gonna do with that fancy degree you got? You gonna move to the big city or somethin'? Hang around all those well to do artsy fartsy folks?" Smitty was real proud of Carrie. He knew she'd be successful no matter where she went; he just wished she appreciated the beauty of Montana and his ranch a bit more. He knew she loved it there, just not enough for his liking.

Carrie shrugged her shoulders in answer to his questions. The truth was she wasn't exactly sure where she was going to go. She knew she wouldn't be returning to Florida. If she wanted to rub elbows with the rich and famous, New York or Los Angeles were the obvious choices, but she really couldn't see herself either of those places. She hoped that she would know where she wanted to go by the time she went home to visit her parents at the end of the summer.

It was nearing the end of August when she left Uncle Smitty's, and it was a little harder leaving than the last time she left after a visit. Carrie wasn't comfortable leaving with him looking less than his usual hale and hearty self. He insisted he was "just fine", of course. That was the last time she ever spoke to him. He died peacefully in his sleep that very night.

Chapter Two

A WEEK AFTER Uncle Smitty's passing, Carrie was back in Lincoln to take care of his burial arrangements. It was then that she learned he had left her everything. Not one other family member received a thing. His entire estate was hers. He had also left her a letter.

Carrie,

I know I was a miserable old coot. And I know you loved me. Even though I never said it, I think you knowed that I loved you back. None of those other people you're related to are worth nuthin', but you're worth everythin'. Don't you ever forget it, girl.

I know you got that fancy degree in decoratin' or some such thing, but I want you to think about keepin' the ranch. The hands know what to do for now, and you can learn it with some time. I know you love Montana; it's in your blood now.

I also sent a letter to a friend of mine a ways back. I ain't been feelin' quite right for a while now and wanted to prepare. He's got a right nice son who needs a ranch to run. His Papa about run his own ranch into the ground cause he wouldn't never listen to Colt. What the hell kinda man names his son after a horse anyway?

Colt's gonna come teach you the ropes. Trust him. He knows what he's about, girl. That attorney there is gonna give you all my money too. You'll never have to work if you don't want to. If you really want to sell the ranch, I'll understand. Aw hell, no I won't, but I'm dead so who cares?

Well, I said all I'm gonna say. Take care of yourself, girl.
Uncle Smitty

Carrie sat there for a moment with the letter in her hand trying to hold her tears back. Uncle Smitty never had time for sorrow, and she wouldn't dishonor his memory by giving in to it now. Taking a deep breath, she turned to address Mr. Bolton, Smitty's attorney.

"Well, I can honestly say that I'm quite shocked. He left me everything? I know he wasn't close to the family, but this, this just takes some getting used to." Carrie didn't go to school to be a rancher! She went to Pratt Institute, the number one ranked school for interior design in the country. But how could she sell Smitty's beloved ranch?

"I'd suggest taking some time to think about it Ms. McDermott. You're going through a difficult time. Snap decisions should never be made so closely following a dramatic event." Mr. Bolton had only seen Smitty a couple of times in person, and even though he could tell that Smitty was a cantankerous old man, he knew he had true affection for his great-niece.

Showing her Smitty's financial statements was yet another shock to her system. He, well now she, was worth millions. Millions, wow, she never knew he had that kind of money. Mr. Bolton told her the ranch was self sufficient. Smitty never touched the money in his investment accounts. The income from breeding the Morgans was kept in a separate operating account and was all she needed to run the ranch. She couldn't help but wonder what he was saving the millions for. He never took vacations or bought new cars or anything that she knew of.

"Thank you Mr. Bolton. I think for now I'll just go back to the ranch and let this all soak in. My parents are leaving tomorrow morning, but I'm going to stay until I figure out what to do." She shook his hand as she made her way to the door. "I hope I can call you with any questions that might arise?"

"Of course you can. I'd be happy to assist you in any way I can. I handled your uncle's affairs for years. He didn't have much use for me, but when he did we worked along just fine." He was glad she wasn't immediately going home. Hopefully spending time thinking about the ranch would make her want to stay and keep Smitty's ranch intact. Lord knew there were plenty of developers who would love to get a hold of that land. He needed to warn her about that. "One more thing, Ms. McDermott. I just wanted you to be aware that the vultures will start ringing the doorbell as soon as they hear of your uncle's passing. Developers have been trying to get that land forever."

Hearing that, she stood up ram rod straight and informed him that would never happen. "I'll keep it myself before I allow some developer to go in there and put up a strip mall!"

Well, Mr. Bolton thought, *maybe the ranch isn't lost after all.*

Chapter Three

WHEN CARRIE GOT back to the ranch, all hell broke loose.

"What do you mean you're going to stay out here for a while? You can sell this place for millions, Carrie. Millions! Let's sell it and split the money amongst the family." Carrie couldn't say she was ever particularly close with her parents. That was one of the reasons she picked a New York college to go to.

"I'm not just going to sell Uncle Smitty's ranch without thinking it through, Mother. That wouldn't be fair to him."

"What's fair got to do with it? He's gone; you can do what you want. I never could understand how you could stand to be around that man. He was my father's brother, and I can't think of one time he was ever nice to me." Granted, she wasn't nice to him either, but still. "Just sell it, write us all checks and be done with it."

Her father, thus far, was staying out of the discussion. At the sound of getting his hands on some money however, he spoke up. "I think your mother's right about this one, Carrie. What do you know about running a ranch? Sure you learned how to ride and clean out stalls, but what do you know about the business side? What are you going to do here, just redecorate the place or something? That's what you know how to do. You can't run a big business like this. You should just stick with what you know."

Did her parents really have such little faith in her? "First of all, Uncle Smitty left the ranch to me. In its entirety. You don't get a say in what I do with it. And it's not your money, it's mine. If you'll recall, he left specific instructions that no one else was to receive any money except for me. I couldn't give you his money if I wanted to. And secondly, I think I might like the chance to run this ranch. I really do love it out here. I think Montana has a piece of my heart after all of these years. Uncle Smitty and I had some nice times here."

Her mother threw up her hands in frustration. "Fine. Your father and I will leave you here. When you come home for Christmas, you can tell us how much you're going to sell it for. You'll never make it through a winter here, Carrie. You're used to the warm weather. You've only been here when it's nice. Call us when you come to your senses, and maybe we'll come back out to help you sell everything." That said, she grabbed Carrie's father and walked out the door.

Carrie went to bed that night fired up. After the discussion with her parents, she was determined to hold on to the ranch. Her degree in interior design wasn't going anywhere, and when she learned what she needed to, she could entrust the running of the ranch to the others. She could hire a bookkeeper to run the office end too. That would leave her with free time to do her interior decorating if she decided to. She would have to go to bigger towns, but she could do that with ease.

~~~~

The next morning brought a chill with it. It was nearing September, and it was hovering right around forty degrees Fahrenheit. Luckily for Carrie, Uncle Smitty had updated the old wood burning fireplace to gas years ago. Since it still reached the seventies and sometimes eighties during the day, it was too early to flip the house thermostat to heat.

She padded into the sun room off the kitchen and flipped on the switch to the fireplace. Just as she was starting the coffee pot, she heard barking coming from outside. Clad in only her white terry bathrobe and puppy dog slippers, Carrie looked out the front door.

There was a beautiful border collie running up the long driveway. She was a joy to watch, frolicking to and fro. Carrie went out onto the porch shivering as she called to the playful dog. "Come here, Sweetie." She crouched down to doggie level and braced herself for impact. Carrie had always loved animals.

A little way off in the distance, she heard a shrill whistle. The dog immediate stopped in her tracks, about fifty feet from Carrie and sat down. Looking behind her, it seemed as if the dog was waiting for another command.

As Carrie looked in the same direction, she finally saw a huge truck rambling up the driveway. It was obviously a working man's truck, complete with a shiny silver plated tool box in the bed. The driver stuck his head out the window and gave another whistle accompanied by a scathing reprimand. "You get your tail back to this truck this instant, Mollie!"

Mollie gave Carrie a friendly yip and ran back to her owner. The man stopped the truck and opened his door. Mollie jumped right in and started licking her owner's face, apparently not intimidated by his reprimand. The man laughed and ruffled the fur on her head. He gently pushed her onto the passenger side of the seat and continued up the drive.

When he reached the parking pad on the side of the house, he stepped out of the truck, with Mollie in tow. "Howdy, Ma'am, I'm Colt Remington, and no, that's not a joke. Colt for the horse, not the gun. My father likes to think he's clever." Taking his hat off, he slowly approached the front porch. When he was two stairs away from reaching the top, he stuck his hand out to Carrie, admiring her puppy slippers. "You must be Carrie. I'm real sorry for you loss, ma'am. I got word of old Smitty's death more than a week after he died. I was out on a cattle drive or I would have been here to pay my respects at the funeral. We don't get much cell phone reception when we're out on the range."

Carrie took the hand he offered in hers and was a bit startled at the jolt she felt. She wondered if he felt it too. He wasn't really all that much to look at when she first saw him. He had sandy brown hair, brown eyes and a nose that might be just a tad too big. He was tall though, which she had always found attractive in a man. He had to be close to six and a half feet tall. Even two stairs above him she was eye level with him. It was his smile, she decided. He had dimples on both sides of his face. That was good for him, because he had a pretty decent scar running from his left jaw bone up to the very corner of his left eye.

"Thank you, Colt. I'll miss the old coot. I was really the only one in the family that got along with him. I think we understood each other. There was a lot more to that man than he let people see." Carrie suddenly felt the burn of tears behind her eyes. "I have to say, he never mentioned you, but told me you were a 'right nice son' in his letter that he left for me. In Smitty speak, that pretty much means he thinks you could hang the moon." As if Carrie suddenly realized they were still standing outside in the cold air, she gasped. "Oh my goodness, I'm so sorry. Please, let's go inside. I just made some coffee and was about to make something for breakfast."

Colt followed her in and told Mollie to stay on the porch. "Oh no, Colt. Mollie is more than welcome to come in. I love dogs. She's beautiful by the way."

"She's not the only one," Colt mumbled as he let Mollie in.

"Excuse me?"

"Huh? Oh, nothing ma'am. Just admiring the scenery around here. It's beautiful."

"Please, drop the ma'am. I appreciate the show of respect, but if we're going run this ranch together and make a go of this, we should be a bit more casual, don't you think?" Carrie hoped she didn't offend him. She knew he was just using his country manners.

"I'm glad to hear you say that. I was told that you didn't know about that part of Smitty's deal. I'm glad he told you. I told my Pa that it was mighty underhanded to trick you into marriage just to keep the property."

Carrie dropped the cup she was getting ready to pour coffee into. "Excuse me? Marriage? I think you're mistaken, Colt. Smitty's will simply stated that you would help me learn how to look after the ranch and that I could trust you."

"No, I have a copy of his will right here. It clearly states that I get half ownership if I agree to marry his great-niece, one Carrie McDermott, within one year of his death. If we don't marry, I get the ranch and you get his money." Colt didn't get this lady. Was she purposefully being obtuse? He thought it was a great deal either way, but seeing her, he was thinking he wanted the girl *and* the ranch.

"We must have different copies, because mine said nothing about that."

"Did you actually read the will?" Colt challenged.

"No, but Mr. Bolton explained everything to me. At least I believe he did." She couldn't imagine he would have purposefully left that out. He seemed like a very competent attorney.

Colt busted out laughing. "He did it. The old man did it! Oh, you have to see this." Colt took out his copy of the will and handed it to her.

Carrie quickly glanced at it. "It looks the same as the copy I have." As she kept flipping through the pages, she came to an addendum.

> *Mr. Bolton—You have strict instructions to NOT read this part to my niece unless she happens to see it and questions you . I'm bankin' on the girl just skimmin' through this legal mumbo jumbo like most sane folks would do. There are some further rules for owning this property and they are as follows:*
>
> *In order to keep ownership of the ranch, Carrie has to marry Colt Remington within one year of my death. If she don't, the ranch goes to him, but she keeps the money I have in my investment accounts. They gotta stay married for at least two years to keep these arrangements. The only exceptions to this are if he physically hurts her, cheats on her or abuses her in any other manner. These stipulations (that the right word?) are non-negotiable.*

"Holy shit! Oh Geez, excuse my language. I'm sorry, Colt. I did not see that part." *Oh my goodness, what am I going to do?* "I, ah, don't really know what to say to that."

"Okay. Well, this is a bit awkward. Okay ma'am—err, sorry, Carrie; how about we just take it one day at a time. Is it okay with you if I move into the barn? Me and Mollie, we'd be fine in there. I can teach you the ropes and we can just let nature takes its course, or not. No pressure, no rules. How about it?" Colt would love to settle down and have a family. And he absolutely wanted the ranch, but he wouldn't want it without the right woman. Carrie seemed nice, and attraction certainly wasn't an issue. He'd like the chance to see if she could be the one he could build that family with.

Carrie McDermott was an Irish beauty. Reddish blonde hair that curled at the edges around her shoulders, green eyes that radiated kindness and an ass—well, he wouldn't go there. She carried a bit of extra flesh on her, which he happened to adore. She was plump enough to be nice and curvy but thin enough to be health conscious. He knew a lot of men liked the skinny model types, but he wasn't one of them. He wanted a girl he could grip that wouldn't break. He wanted a girl who'd eat steak and potatoes with him.

"This *is* a bit awkward, but I'm willing to test it out. You seem nice, we're both single, who knows? For now, let's just think of it as a business arrangement, okay? I have to say I'm a bit put off about how this all came about, but I'm not saying no. We have a year to see how things work out, right? You and Mollie don't have to sleep in the barn though. This isn't the 1800s. There are three other guest rooms in here besides the master that I've taken over. There's no reason we can't stay in the same house. I would like to keep the marriage stipulation private if you don't mind."

"Okay, no problem. If you're sure about this, then I'll just go get my stuff. Are you certain you don't mind a dog in the house?"

"Oh, I'm absolutely certain. As I said before, I love dogs. We could never have one because my mother is allergic. I never understood why Uncle Smitty didn't have one though. He loved animals, and a dog would have been great company." She'd asked him once about it, but he just grumbled and said she needed to fix his dinner. She never asked again.

"Actually, Smitty had a bloodhound that used to go everywhere with him. I swear that dog went to the bathroom with him. One year, when Sue, he named her after his late wife, was only about eight years old, she got trampled by his own horses. There was a snake in the field where the horses were grazing and they just went crazy. Sue was with Smitty bringing some of the horses into the center corral when she got trampled. She lasted about two painful days after that and finally gave up. First and last time I ever saw Smitty cry. I worked around here to help him out back then. My dad's ranch was running on its own about that time so I helped out here. Smitty swore on the day he buried his second Sue that he'd never get another dog or another wife. He never did get another of either."

Carrie had tears in her eyes over that story. She couldn't imagine her grumpy old uncle ever loving something so much.

"I think he loved you that much too. There's no way he would have left anything to his family. We all knew how much he disliked his family. You were really special to him."

"Thank you for telling me that. You know, I always saw that man in him. He was grumpy, but he was honest and true. My mother always acts happy, but she'll talk about you as soon as your back is turned. I'll take Uncle Smitty's brutal honesty over my mother's flowery speech anytime."

Chapter Four

COLT AND MOLLIE were all moved in as dawn broke the following morning. Obviously Colt was used to rancher's hours, because Carrie was woken by the smell of coffee at six am! Since that morning marked the first day of her ranch training, she climbed out of bed, threw on a sweat suit and headed downstairs. Remembering at the last second that she hadn't even brushed her hair, she jammed a Tampa Bay Lightning's cap on her head.

"Good morning, I guess," Carrie mumbled as she led herself over to the coffee.

Colt gave a chuckle as Mollie got up to give Carrie a morning lick in greeting. "Not a morning gal, huh? Don't worry, we'll change that."

"Do we always have to get up this early? Like, every morning?" Carrie was most certainly not a morning person.

"Nah, *you* won't have to, but some of the hands are already outside feeding the horses. There's not a lot of down time on a ranch. Count your blessings that you only raise horses here. If we ever add cattle to the mix, they'll be even more work." Colt had always wanted to branch out into breeding cattle. Most of the ranches around Lincoln were strictly horse ranches. He already knew how to care for heifers and bulls. Adding cattle to the ranch would make it that much more rounded and profitable.

"If we add cattle, won't we have to get up even *earlier?*" She was horrified at the thought.

Colt laughed at her facial expression. "Calm down, darlin'. If we ever decided to go that route, we would do plenty of research and hire enough cowhands to handle the cattle. They would be the ones to get up early." She sure was a cute little filly when she was riled up.

"Oh, sure, of course. So then, *why* am I up at such an ungodly hour?" If the ranch hands were the ones doing all the work, couldn't she have stayed in bed for a few more minutes?

"I thought you wanted to learn all about ranching. Well, darlin', this is part of it. After you understand how everything works and who does what, well then you can do whatever you want. What is it that you want to do with this ranch anyway?"

"Well, I don't mind mucking out a stall or two now and then, but to be honest, I much prefer riding the horses than cleaning up after them. I thought I'd like to learn the business side of the operation. My degree is in interior design, but that came with a lot of business classes too. It was my understanding that Uncle Smitty kept the books and tracked grain orders and such." George, the foreman told her he'd keep up with that until she figured out what she wanted to do. He told her that Smitty had been letting him handle the business end for the last couple of months.

"That sounds like a fine idea. How about after we get some breakfast, we find George and see how his schedule is?" Colt loved that she was interested in the business end. He hated that part of the business. He didn't mind negotiating for animal flesh or the food to feed them, but writing everything down and remembering when to order what? No thank you.

"So what is it that you would like to do on the ranch? Is there anything specific?" Carrie was curious about his experience. Did he mend fences and corrals? Did he oversee the medical care of the horses? Did he scout out new studs and see to their purchase?

"I would say my best skill is breaking horses. I'm the guy who gets them to trust people. Morgans are pretty easy to break. They seem to like people, but you always have to treat each horse like it'll trample you in the beginning. It's all about trust. They learn to trust that I won't hurt them and I learn to trust that they won't hurt me. It's a pretty special bond I feel with each horse that finally lets me sit on its back." There was nowhere he'd rather be than on the back of a horse. Although looking at Carrie in her sweats that were pulled taught across her bottom made him think of somewhere else he'd like to be.

"Okay, so it seems like we have a plan. Let's get everyone together and tell them what we are going to do. When should we do that? What would the best time be?" Carrie knew there were currently fifteen ranch hands, along with the foreman and twin stable boys that belonged to one of the ranch hands.

"Well, it might be a good idea to host an informal dinner. Do you think it's possible to get something like that together by, say seven o'clock tonight?" Colt knew that was a lot to ask. That was a lot of people to provide dinner for. Could Carrie even cook? Would she want to? Including him and her, the total would be twenty people plus one dog.

"Feed twenty people by seven o'clock? I can definitely do that. Uncle Smitty has those two huge barbeque grills in the backyard and the double ovens in the kitchen. I may have to cheat and buy some of the side dishes though. If I am preparing all of this, we're going to have to wait until tomorrow for me to start learning about the ranch. Would you have a problem with that?"

"A problem with you cooking for the lot of us? No, darlin', I sure wouldn't. I think it's admirable that you're willing to do it. I thought we could just call a caterer or something." Colt didn't *really* expect her to cook for twenty people. He hoped she was being truthful and didn't mind.

"I know this is not the politically correct way to be in this day and age, but I'm not much of a feminist. I like to cook. I like to take care of people. I'm not saying that I'll never want to have my own career, but for now, I'm content to take care of anything I can here. If that means cooking for twenty people now and then for ranch meetings, I'll be happy to do it." Carrie was already running through recipes in her head. She'd just make simple dishes, like pasta salad and baked beans.

"All right then. Thanks, Carrie. The boys will be over the moon for a home-cooked meal. A lot of them are single I believe, but it's been a while since I've been over here. I'm going to go talk to George and make sure we can round everyone up to let them know what time to meet here at the house. If you need anything, try my cell. I shouldn't be too far out today." Before he could think twice about what he was doing, he grabbed Carrie's arms and pulled her into a quick hug. "We're gonna make this work darlin'. I can feel it, you just wait and see."

Chapter 5

CARRIE HAD TO go shopping, but first she needed to take stock of what was actually in the house. When she opened the pantry, she couldn't help the smile that broke out on her face. Sitting right in the front was a value size box of double stuffed Oreos. They were Smitty's favorite. Next to them were half a dozen cans of his other favorite. Spam. That she would not be keeping.

Making a menu for the night was fun. It wasn't interior design, but she loved coming up with colorful dishes that would look as good as they tasted. She was making two dozen hamburgers, barbequed spare ribs that she could bake in the oven and then finish on the grill to get that yummy charred taste, and she'd buy a dozen hot dogs too. For her side dishes, she was making a vat of baked beans in two crock pots, multi colored pasta salad and a tomato, mozzarella and fresh basil salad drizzled with balsamic vinegar.

Along with the food she bought to make everything on her menu, she picked up some pies from the bakery for dessert. On her way home, she also stopped and bought beer and soda for drinks. All in all, she thought it was going to be a great first meal for all of them. They could make a toast to her Uncle Smitty. It would be a celebration of his life for everyone on the ranch.

As the ranch hands started drifting in, a little before seven o'clock, the ones she hadn't met before introduced themselves. They seemed to be a friendly lot for the most part. There were one or two that made her slightly uncomfortable, but she figured that was to be expected. Apparently Colt didn't care for the looks some of them gave her either.

"Tony, she's off limits, you hear? That goes for all of you. You treat Ms. McDermott with the same respect you showed her when Smitty was still alive. If you can't do that, there's the door." Colt pointed to the door and stared down the crowd around him. There were only two men who stared back. Tony Costa and Pete Barrons. That gave Colt the information he needed. Tony and Pete needed to be on his radar. He'd make sure they steered clear of Carrie.

In order to break the tension, Carrie announced that everyone should help themselves to the beer and sodas in the coolers that she'd filled on the porch. She then ducked inside the house with Colt hard on her heels.

"Colt, I appreciate your protectiveness, but maybe threatening them on the first day we take control of the ranch isn't the way to go. I can handle those cowboys. You might be surprised. Just because I went to school for interior design and I can cook a meal for twenty, doesn't mean I can't also shoot a dime out of the air." Uncle Smitty had taught her how to shoot at a very young age. She was a natural and had always kept up with it. Shooting skeet was a favorite pastime of hers.

Carrie took the burgers and hot dogs out of the refrigerator and handed them to Colt. "I already lit the grills. Go put these on and in a little bit, I'll take the ribs out of the oven and you can char them up a bit. While you're doing that, I'll get all the fixings ready and bring the salads out, okay?"

"Yes ma'am. Sorry if I stepped on your toes out there, I just don't like the way those two looked at you." He took the tray out of her hands and surprised her yet again. "Until you say otherwise, I consider you mine. No one covets what's mine, okay darlin'?" He quickly kissed her as he walk out the door.

Carrie must have stood there for a good minute feeling her lips tingle. He sure was moving fast on the whole making her his thing. There was definitely a spark there, and she had already told him she was open to the idea of marriage to keep the ranch *if* she thought it would be a good marriage, but he seemed so sure. It almost seemed as if it was a done deal for him already. They needed to have a chat.

After ten minutes had gone by, Carrie took the ribs out to Colt. "Here you go. They're fully cooked so they just need to be heated up a bit, okay?"

"Sure thing, darlin'. I had some of the boys set up those tables from the shed and wipe them down." Pointing to another table on the porch by the coolers he said, "I thought you could use that one to put the food on."

"Yes, that's fine, thanks. I'll start bringing it out now." She went back inside the house, Mollie following her every move hoping to get a morsel of something. She gave Mollie a piece of cheese and started carrying condiments, plates, napkins and other fixings out to the table.

"Ms. McDermott!" One of the twins was running up to her. "Ms. McDermott! I can help you."

"That would be great. I'm sorry, which one are you again?"

He gave her a big smile and pointed to the dimple on his left cheek. "I'm Terry. You can tell cause I have this dimple. Sam ain't got one."

Smiling at the ten year old, she gently corrected him. "Doesn't have one, not 'ain't got one'. Okay, you go on in and wash up. You can help me carry out the salads." Carrie watched him wash his hands and went to the refrigerator to take the food out. She handed Terry bowl after bowl, and he put them on the table outside.

After all the food was on the table, Carrie clapped her hands to get everyone's attention. She waited until Colt had come up to stand next to her. "Thank you all for coming. I'd just like to say that Smitty loved this ranch. He left it to Colt and I and we want you to know that we don't intend on changing anything right now. Uncle Smitty always knew you all could run this ranch. He had every confidence in you, so I do too."

Colt spoke up too. "In the coming days and weeks, we'll both be learning exactly how everything is done here so that we can help where we're needed. We both want to be hands on owners like Smitty was. I hope that you all continue on here, but if any of you have any issues, please come talk to us. Now, let's eat!"

There was a light smattering of applause as the ranch hands came up to grab plates of food. "This sure does look good ma'am. It's been a while since me and my boys have had this kinda meal. Thank you." He nudged both of the twins. "What do you say boys?"

"Thank you kindly, ma'am."

"You're welcome. Now go on and enjoy that food. There's plenty for everyone. And after you're done with dinner, I have some pie too."

After everyone had left, Carrie was alone in the kitchen when she heard the back door shut. She continued washing the larger pots that didn't fit in the dishwasher when she felt hands on her waist. She gave a little shiver of delight, but when she turned around she said, "Colt, we need to talk."

"Well, that's not really what I had in mind."

Carrie smiled but held her ground. Drying her hands off, she pushed him away. "This is all just going way too fast for me. We just met yesterday! I know I said I'm on board with the possibility of marriage to keep the ranch, but I need some time. You seem like you're ready to say 'I do' already."

"Well, I am. You're a nice lady, Carrie. I'm most definitely attracted to you, and we already have this great ranch to run. Think of all the things we could do together. We could branch out with the cattle, have a family or just enjoy each other's company. I think we suit. I trust my gut, and my gut says we're a good fit."

"But you can't just know that, Colt. Marriage is a big step. What happens if we find out we don't suit as well as you think we will? What happens to the ranch then? We split it fifty-fifty? I don't want that to happen. It's just too much, too soon." Carrie felt tears sting her eyes again. What on Earth was wrong with her? She wasn't one of those women who cried.

"Why the tears, darlin'? Don't over think this. We'll figure it out together. I didn't mean to push so quickly. I'll back off. Let's just get to know each other like we said before, okay?"

Carrie nodded her head in agreement, but to her horrible dismay a sob broke out of her. Colt gathered her up in his arms, stroking her hair and whispering soft words in her ear.

She allowed herself a couple of minutes of sorrow and then pushed away from him. "Wow, I'm sorry about that. I'm just a little overwhelmed. I'm missing Uncle Smitty too. It's just so different being here without him. I'm glad you're here. Mollie too. It's so nice to have a dog around. She's very comforting." As a matter of fact, as soon as Carrie broke down, Mollie came over and lay at her feet.

"Aw, Carrie, you're going to have to forgive me. I can't seem to help myself."

"Forgive you for what?"

Colt pulled her close again and bent his head down to hers. Placing his forehead against hers, he whispered, "for this". Before she had a chance to register what he was going to do, his lips were on hers. She resisted for all of two seconds before wrapping her arms around his neck. Colt took that as a good sign and deepened the kiss, rubbing her back and then tangling his hands in her hair.

He looked into her eyes to judge her reaction as he slowly pulled away.

"Well, yes, we do have the sparks." She smiled up at him. "I'm not sure that constitutes as taking it slow though."

"How about if I promise not to kiss you again until you're ready? Okay, darlin'?"

She agreed and then ran her finger lightly over his scar. "How did you get this?"

"I was thrown from my horse. Ironic, isn't it? The trainer getting thrown? Well, it wasn't the first time, but it was the most painful. On my way down, my face scraped along the side of an axe that was sticking out of a chopping block. It could have been much worse."

"Oh, wow. That must have hurt like the devil!"

He chuckled at that. "It wasn't pleasant for sure." He leaned in and gave her one more, quick kiss. "Sorry, that's the last one. Scout's honor. You know, you have the sweetest lips in Montana, Carrie." He reluctantly took another step away from her. "Now, I'm going to go make sure the horses are taken care of for the night. If you'll finish up those pots, I'll give you a foot rub when I get back. I know you've been in this kitchen the better part of the day. Dinner was delicious by the way. A man could get used to eating like that pretty quickly."

Chapter 6

AS TIME WENT by, Colt and Carrie got to know more about each other. They spent hours at night talking about their childhoods and their friends and families. They held hands as they took walks in the moonlight, and enjoyed the occasional picnic by the watering hole. Colt had kept his promise. Since that night in the kitchen, he hadn't made another move on her other than a quick caress here and there. The more Carrie got to know him, the more agreeable she became to the idea of marrying him. It was nearing November then, and Carrie was beginning to wish she hadn't asked him to take it so slow.

One cool night in mid November, Carrie had had enough. She wanted another taste of Colt. She wasn't sure if she wanted all of him, but she sure could use some more of his kisses.

Gathering up some blankets, she asked him if he wanted to go snuggle up with her on the porch and look at the stars. "Hell yes. I'd love to share a blanket with you, darlin'."

When they were seated together on the porch swing, Colt placed her hand on his leg and covered it with his. He loved their time together.

Carrie was fidgety and seemed slightly nervous. Looking over at him with her eyes slightly cast down, she whispered, "Colt?"

"Yeah?" She didn't say anything so answered her again. "What is it, darlin'?"

"Well, I'm not really sure how to do this. I mean I *know* how to do this, I just, well…" What the devil was she trying to say? She just wanted to kiss him. Should she just do it? He still found excuses to touch her; he was still nice to her, and they laughed together all the time, but was he still attracted to her? She thought she had seen him checking her out a time or two when he thought she wasn't looking, but maybe she was wrong.

Colt laughed. "How about if I help you out, okay?"

"Uh huh"

Colt leaned into her and she brought her lips to his. *Ah, yes. Heaven.* There might not be anything better than kissing Colt. No, she was wrong. There was something better. Colt ran his hands over her as he parted her lips so that he could taste her. His hands were gentle but insistent at the same time. She couldn't get close enough to him.

She sighed and mumbled his name. "Colt."

He pulled back from her. "Too much, darlin'?"

"No, not enough. I'm ready for the next level."

"I won't make you say it twice." He gathered her up in his arms and walked her into the house. He went straight up the stairs to her room and laid her in the middle of her bed. They made love all night long, and that's when she knew that she would marry that man.

They woke up in each other's arms with satisfied smiles on their faces. She was deliciously sore in places she didn't know existed. He was sated like he couldn't ever remember being before. He knew they'd be good together. What did surprise him though was her choice not to use birth control.

When Carrie made a decision, she went into it all the way. She was ready for the whole deal, and she wanted it all. Marriage and a house full of kids. She was already designing nurseries in her head.

"Good morning, Colt."

"Good morning, darlin'. How are you feeling?"

"Sore," she informed him with a giggle. "But I think I'll be feeling better later. Maybe around lunch time? I could make you a sandwich after."

"Carrie, that's the best deal I've been offered in a long time. It's a date, but now I have to get up. Why don't you sleep in today? I'm going to be gone until lunch time. There's some broken fencing that I'm going out to mend. It's pretty far out and it'll take me a while."

"Okay, I will. Thank you."

"What are you thanking me for now?"

"For taking this chance. For caring for my Uncle Smitty, and agreeing to marry me and help run this ranch. It means a lot to me."

"It's not a hardship, Carrie. Don't you know? I'm already in love with you, girl. I think I might have fallen for you when you invited my dog into the house. Anyone who loves animals like you do is good people." Running his hands over her ample curves he said, "This gorgeous package you're in doesn't hurt either."

"I'm glad you like my package. I've always been very aware that I'm not like those models. I'll never be thin. Just wait until I get pregnant, I'll be as big as a house."

"You will never be anything but gorgeous, Carrie. I thank god you don't look like those models." He gave her rump a gentle slap and got up out of bed. "I'm going to take a quick shower and I'm off. Go back to sleep, darlin'"

Carrie woke a bit later to a noise coming from downstairs. She looked at the clock and was surprised to see that it was almost ten am. Colt must have really worn her out the previous night.

"Colt? Is everything okay? I didn't expect you back so soon." When she didn't get an answer, she thought she must have been hearing things. She got up and put her robe on.

Making her way down the stairs, she saw a shadow in the kitchen. "Colt?" She turned into the kitchen to see Tony standing there.

"Hey, gorgeous. Looks like you got a nice tumble in bed, huh? I was waiting to see what kind of gal you were. Now it's my turn." As he walked towards her, Carrie held up her hand.

"Whoa, I'm not any kind of gal. You need to leave now, Tony."

"Aw, come on now, Sweets. You can't save all those curves for just one man. I won't tell the others."

Carrie wasn't sure how seriously to take him. She didn't really feel threatened, but she still wanted him out of her house. "I really think you've got the wrong idea here, Tony. Colt and I are getting married."

"But ya ain't married yet, are ya, honey?" He took another step towards her and she ran out the front door, straight into Colt.

"Hey there. What's wrong, darlin'?" When Colt saw Tony standing behind her, his face showed his confusion. "Tony, what are you doing in here?" Looking from Tony to Carrie, he asked her, "Is everything okay here?"

"Yeah boss, I was just chatting with Ms. McDermott."

"No, Colt. It's not okay. He was trying to push his way into my bed. Even after I told him we're to be married."

"Is that a fact?" Colt grabbed Tony by his coat and shoved him out the door. "We'll mail you your last paycheck."

George was standing outside of the barn when Colt stepped out of the house with Tony. He was on his way to the main house to check on Carrie after he saw Tony heading that way. He never did trust that man. "Everything okay here, Colt?"

"Escort Tony off the property, please. He no longer works here."

"Yes sir, happy to do it."

After George had a grip on Tony, Colt turned back to Carrie and wrapped his arms around her. "Are you okay, darlin'? He didn't hurt you, did he?" She struggled against him as he pulled her tighter. He felt something hard in her pocket. Loosening his grip as she pushed harder at him he said, "What's that?"

Carrie chuckled at him. "That's what I was trying to tell you, but you kept pulling me in tighter. I'm fine. I wasn't afraid of him. Remember me telling you that Uncle Smitty taught me how to defend myself?"

"You have a gun in your pocket?"

"No, silly. I enjoy target shooting, but I could never shoot a person." She pulled a stapler out of her robe. "I grabbed it on my way downstairs when I heard the noise and you didn't answer me. I figured if I had to, I could throw this and run for the door. There are always ranch hands around. I'm sure one of them would've helped me."

Chapter 7

THEY PLANNED A Christmas wedding held right there at the ranch. The house was decorated inside and out. White lights shown all across the porch and along the roof line. Pine boughs were wrapped around the railings with big red bows every couple of feet. It had started to snow earlier in the day, and the house couldn't look any lovelier.

Inside the house was just as festive. It was packed with the ranch hands who hadn't any other place to be for the holidays. Carrie reluctantly invited her parents who were surprisingly supportive. Colt's father and brothers were there as well. His mother had passed away years before.

It was a low key event and exactly what they both wanted. They were married by their foreman, George, who got ordained over the Internet.

Ham and turkey with all the fixings lined the table. The counter tops were filled with hot and cold finger foods ranging from cheese platters to home-made mini crab cakes. There was a full bar, and Mr. Bolton was playing bartender. It was a night filled with laughter and good cheer, just as Christmastime should be.

Epilogue
Three years later

LOOKING OUT OVER the cattle Colt had added over the last year, Carrie felt the peace that the ranch offered. That lasted a few seconds until she saw her children messing around yet again. "Colton Smitty Remington, you let go of your sister's hair right this second!" Carrie had agreed to *somewhat* name their first son after his father. They still called him Colt, but at least he wasn't named after a horse—or a gun.

They had two children at the moment. Colton was three, Maddie was two, and Carrie had just found out she was pregnant again. She couldn't be happier. Her parents were happy having grandchildren, but were, of course, still disappointed in her for not utilizing her education. She didn't even bother telling them that she had begun taking consulting jobs for an interior design company in town. She only took small jobs, as her focus was her family, but for now, it was a perfect mix for her.

Colt was the happiest man alive. He told that to anyone who would listen and constantly annoyed people with pictures of his growing family. Carrie thought was very charming.

Every once in a while, when Colt and Carrie were snuggling on the porch, she could swear that she could smell the scent of her Uncle Smitty's favorite cigar.

The End

About the Author

Nikki Worrell

Nikki Worrell lives in southern New Jersey with her husband and their furry, four-legged little girl, Mollie. She has a B.S.B.A in Human Resources and works for a law firm in Philadelphia. She started writing as a way to challenge herself and get the stories that were in her head down on paper. Her debut novel, *The Enforcer*, was published in May 2013.